THE CAT'S PAW

James Heron

The Cat's Paw

Futura Publications Limited
A Futura Book

A Futura Book

First published by Futura Publications Limited in 1977

Copyright © Gilat Limited 1977

ISBN 0 8600 7568 0
Printed in Great Britain by
Hazell Watson & Viney Ltd
Aylesbury, Bucks

Futura Publications Limited
110 Warner Road
Camberwell, London SE5

CHAPTER ONE

'Excuse me,' the man said. 'May I buy you a drink?'

Charles Hutchinson emerged from his reverie with a start, and spun round on his bar-stool to look at the intruder. He got the shock of his life: the eyes he was looking into were his own.

The stranger laughed at his astonishment. 'I suppose I should have introduced myself more gently,' he said. 'The doorman told me that someone who looked like my double had asked the way to the bar, and I felt I had to meet you. My name's James Fitzpatrick, by the way – and the man's right, the resemblance is remarkable.'

In some confusion, Charles found himself grasping the hand extended to him.

'Charles Hutchinson,' he said. 'What was that you said about a drink? I think I need one.'

Fitzpatrick laughed again, and turned to the barman. 'A double vodka for me, lots of ice and a little tonic. For you?' He glanced at Charles' empty glass.

'The same, please.'

'Another point in common,' said Fitzpatrick, watching the barman fossicking in the ice-bucket.

Charles looked at his companion. The likeness really was extraordinary: the same fair hair, fresh complexion, small blue eyes in a network of wrinkles, heavy build, broad hands with short stubby fingers. Even the deep, slightly rasping, voice was the same. As Fitzpatrick turned to face him, Charles caught his breath. His nose was slightly twisted and flattened towards the left, and there was a trace of a scar on his upper lip. Charles found himself rubbing his own nose, identically flattened and twisted by an old rugger injury.

'What size of shoes do you take?' he asked impulsively.

'Size ten. Why?'

'Same here,' said Charles. 'You know, this really is fantastic.

If we were dressed alike, I don't think our mothers could tell us apart. I'm a shade over six feet, chest forty-six, seventeen and a half neck. You?'

'Seems you could literally step into my shoes,' said Fitzpatrick with a smile. 'My measurements to an inch. Look here, this is too interesting to pass up. Tell me about yourself. What are you doing in the Carlton Tower? Forgive me if I say it seems a shade above your touch.'

Charles nodded ruefully. 'Too true,' he said. 'I came back from Nigeria nine months ago to look for a job, and here I am, the money running out, and no nearer what I want than I was at the start. The thirtieth possibility has just told me how sorry he is that I've wasted ten years in Africa, and I'm in here because it was the nearest bar. There are moments when a drink is more important than its price.' He swallowed half his drink at a gulp, and smiled a little wryly as he caught sight of the worn leather on the cuff of his aged tweed jacket.

'I can imagine,' Fitzpatrick said sympathetically. 'It's not easy anywhere nowadays. Tell me, what do you do? And why Africa in the first place? And if there, why come back here on spec?'

With sudden relief, Charles found himself telling his double more about his background and ambitions than he would have dreamt of telling anyone under different circumstances. As time went by, and the vodkas rolled up and went down, he talked of Lagos and Ibadan, of the hundred and fifty mission schools whose chaotic finances he had controlled, of the hard work and the satisfaction of seeing that the missions got value for money, that the children were adequately looked after on the shoe-string finances available, that the African headmasters were allowed to fulfill their potential, and were prevented from reaping the consequences of financial inexperience, or outright peculation. He talked of the relief of escaping from the crippling humidity and the primitive living conditions on his leaves, which came every two years in periods of six months and which had allowed him to travel widely in Europe and the Middle East. He talked of racial problems, and of his affection for the Yorubas who had surrounded him in Ibadan, vigorous,

6

outgoing people with a strong sense of humour, great party-givers, drinkers and womanisers. To his astonishment, he even found himself describing the Paradise Club, focus and safety valve of his lonely bachelor existence: the Paradise, with its fervent high-life music, its drink and companionship, above all its girls, beautiful, available and black. Charles had liked Africa and the Africans, and was not ashamed of it, but the Paradise Club was very much a Yoruba affair, not a place which a white man, careful of his reputation, would normally frequent, much less boast about. They had thrown a party at the Paradise on his departure, and a lot of the girls had cried. Many of his happiest memories were bound up with its ramshackle tin bandstand, its dark crowded courtyard, its lively clientele.

Fitzpatrick was a good listener, sympathetic and intelligent. As well as vodkas, he was adept at providing the key question, the apt comment, which would unlock a new Pandora-like box of reminiscences. Charles found himself warming to the man, even as he talked on and on. Whatever else his double might be, he thought, he was certainly a man of great charm.

At last the spate of nostalgia slowed to a trickle. Charles recollected himself, and found himself apologizing.

'Sorry to unload all this on you,' he said, a little stiffly. 'I suppose I haven't had a chance to talk to anyone like this for years, and I'm afraid I got a bit out of hand.'

'My dear fellow, not at all. Fascinating, really fascinating. I envy you. It all sounds fun.' Fitzpatrick sounded a trifle absent and preoccupied. 'But what now? What's the next step? Can you ask your family for help? Your old school?'

'My parents died during the war, and as far as I know, I haven't a relation in the world.' Charles smiled. 'As for the Old School Tie bit, I don't think night school qualifies. They've pulled down my old secondary – not before time. My only chance is to go abroad again, I suppose. I'd have liked to stay here, but,' he shrugged, 'beggars can't be choosers.'

Fitzpatrick didn't reply immediately. He sat staring at the back of the bar apparently deep in thought. After a moment he

7

said, 'Yes, well, I do understand.' He paused, and went on with a new briskness, 'Don't do anything hasty, at least not in the next few days. It occurs to me that I may be able to help. Where can I get in touch with you?'

'You can't,' said Charles, slightly embarrassed. 'I'm afraid I'm moving about a good bit at the moment.'

Fitzpatrick looked at him shrewdly. 'I see,' he said. 'Well, look,' he consulted a leather-bound, gold-trimmed diary, 'call me next Wednesday, before noon. Here's my card. Sorry I can't offer you dinner. I have an appointment I mustn't miss. Barman, put the bill on the Fitzpatrick Company account. Goodbye, Hutchinson, I must rush. Be sure to call next Wednesday. I'll be waiting.' He rose and began to walk away.

Charles caught at his arm. 'But—' he began.

'Don't worry,' Fitzpatrick said impatiently. 'Till Wednesday. I think I just may have a job for you.' He strode off.

'As an accountant?' Charles called to his retreating back.

Fitzpatrick paused and turned. 'As an accountant? Good Lord, no. I've plenty of those. No, no, my dear fellow. As me!' He waved and strode out of Charles' sight before the latter could recover his breath.

CHAPTER TWO

Charles looked after Fitzpatrick's departing figure in stunned bewilderment. What on earth could he have meant? 'As me'? Was this all some elaborate practical joke? He glanced round the bar to reassure himself that he wasn't dreaming. The well-dressed figures of fellow drinkers, the low hum of conversation, the tinkle of glasses – all was comfortingly as it should be. The slight squeak of his bar-stool as he swung back barwards was familiar. His surroundings were lightly blurred by a slight excess of vodka working on an empty stomach, but the stooped figure of the white-jacketed barman idly polishing a glass was real enough. And the rectangle of white pasteboard Fitzpatrick had left behind was concrete evidence that the last brief burst

8

of conversation had been more than a mildly drunken fantasy.
Charles picked up the card and examined it.

James Fitzpatrick, Esq.,
Chairman
The Fitzpatrick Company
London and New York

That was reassuring enough. After a moment's thought, Charles
pushed his empty glass across the counter and caught the barman's eye.

'Another, please.'

'Certainly, sir. Will that be on the account, sir?'

'Of course,' Charles said recklessly, and reached, a trifle
clumsily, for a bowl of nuts. As he crunched thoughtfully on a
handful, it occurred to him that the barman seemed familiar
with Fitzpatrick, and might be a source of information.

'Tell me,' he said, as the man pushed a new drink across to
him, 'does Mr Fitzpatrick come in here often?'

'Oh, yes, sir. At least twice a week. Stays here quite often
when he has to spend a night in town. Very generous gentleman, Mr Fitzpatrick,' the barman added, looking at Charles
significantly. Charles thought ruefully of his depleted reserves,
and made a great show of reaching for his wallet, hoping that
that barman would not take too much note of its flatness and
general air of over-worn shabbiness.

'You a relative of his, sir?' the barman was confidential. A
pound note, however crumpled, was still a pound note.

'Cousin,' Charles improvised hastily, 'just back from abroad.
Bit out of touch, actually. How is the company doing, do you
know?'

'Thought you must be a relative. Might be a twin, if you
take me, sir, most remarkable. The Fitzpatrick Company, sir?
Couldn't say, sir. But they held a three-day sales conference
here a month or so back, and that wouldn't be cheap. Not many
publishers can afford our prices, sir. I'd say they must be doing
pretty well.' The barman bustled off to serve another customer,
and Charles looked again at the card. A publisher, eh? Charles

knew nothing of publishing, but he had a vision of tweedy myopic vagueness which was the very antithesis of the smooth, polished Fitzpatrick. Fitzpatrick, he thought, looked more like a highly successful international tycoon than anything so intellectual as a publisher. It was a warming, if irrelevant, thought that Charles himself would look just like that, given the right clothes.

Charles sipped his drink, and then sat, elbows on the bar, gazing thoughtfully down into his glass. What did he know of Fitzpatrick, when all was said and done? Well-dressed, generous, obviously accustomed to the good things of life, with business addresses in London and New York, and an account at the Carlton Tower – that was on the plus side. Impulsive, mysterious, something of a joker? Perhaps. Better then to forget the whole thing?

Charles considered his immediate future gloomily. There wasn't a lot left of his Nigerian savings. Already he was having to find lodgings in places and districts little short of squalid. The Welfare State had little interest in his well-being – on the National Insurance contributions he'd been so careful to keep up while he was abroad he could fill his teeth but not his stomach. So what was there to lose? Absently Charles reached out towards the nuts and filled his hand without thinking. They weren't nuts now, they were anchovy-stuffed olives, for which Charles had a particular passion – he caught himself wondering if this too was a taste he shared with Fitzpatrick. Suddenly it seemed like a good omen.

Charles finished his drink and got carefully to his feet, his mind made up in a wave of vodka-inspired euphoria. The least he could do, he decided, was to check Fitzpatrick out. This was Thursday. He had the better part of a week to look up balance sheets and things. What was the point of being an accountant if that couldn't tell him a thing or two? There was no need to call Fitzpatrick if there seemed to be anything fishy. He waved an airy goodnight to the barman, and walked slightly too steadily to the door on his way to the underground station at Sloane Square and his dingy lodgings.

Over the next few days, the effect of the vodka wore off, but the feeling of lightheaded euphoria remained. Charles put all his accountant's expertise into investigating the Fitzpatrick Company as far as *Who Owns Whom*, the *Stock Exchange Year Book*, and the records at Companies House would take him.

Fitzpatrick, he discovered, had come down from Cambridge with a degree in Oriental languages, a fanatical determination to make money, and an idea. The idea was one of those simple affairs that leave those unfortunate enough not to have thought of it wondering why not. Basically, Fitzpatrick had in the early days acquired a near monopoly in the translation and marketing of Chinese research documents, particularly in the fields of agriculture and forestry. The market was small, but international and quite uninterested in price. Research organizations, government departments, intelligence agencies, had an absolute requirement for Fitzpatrick's product, and no shortage of funds. Fitzpatrick's cyclostyled translations were cheap to produce and were sold at a staggering mark-up. Fitzpatrick was on the way to a fortune. In due course the business had branched out. Using his uniquely good Peking contacts, Fitzpatrick was able to build up an impressive and growing two-way traffic in scientific information of all the unclassified varieties. In time, the company had involved itself more and more seriously in other ventures – books on cooking, gardening, needlecraft, self-improvement and self-help of all kinds, both in hard cover and paperback. Its turnover was now extremely impressive and amazingly profitable. Recently it had taken a new and crucial step in the financing of an American subsidiary, the Fitzpatrick Corporation, to merchandise multi-volume encyclopedias through supermarkets nationwide in the U.S. A glance at the early returns showed Charles that although the competition seemed strong, profitability was high, and capital investment, though running at a sizeable figure, was still under control. All in all, it was clear that Fitzpatrick controlled a sizeable, expanding, and financially healthy company that seemed to be making nonsense of the truism that publishing was a series of unsecured gambles.

There was no question that Fitzpatrick personally, and the

Fitzpatrick business interests, were solidly prosperous, and offered considerable scope from an employment point of view. The remaining doubts in Charles' mind arose from two associated worries: first, Charles could see no obvious niche for himself in the Fitzpatrick enterprises, and second, he couldn't quite rid his mind of the feeling that there had to be a snag somewhere, although he had now dismissed his memory of Fitzpatrick's closing remark as the product of an imagination stimulated by too much vodka and too little food.

All the same, it was a Charles transformed who strolled up Jermyn Street on the Tuesday morning, pausing to peer in at the window of Turnbull and Asser, to window-shop in Floris, to sniff appreciatively at Paxton and Whitfield. A mild, sunny spring day and a feeling of constructive accomplishment had combined to lighten Charles's mood to the point where he felt that the whole of luxurious, pleasantly decadent Mayfair was his oyster. It had crossed his mind that a spot of over-priced lunch at the Ecu de France was the least he owed himself, when an approaching figure diverted his attention.

And what a figure, he thought, watching in deep appreciation as the pert breasts bounced alluringly bra-less under the thin silk sweater. It took him a moment to drag his eyes away to take in the smoothly shapely legs, the wide dark eyes, the shoulder-length auburn hair, the whole sexy five foot seven or so of expensively groomed female walking hippily towards him, a vision in dark-blue and cream. That's what I need, he thought. An expensive lunch is all very well, but with something like that across the table ...

His attention was back on those provocative breasts again when he was startled out of his lecherous haze.

'James, you bastard,' said the vision, 'what the hell do you mean by walking straight past me as if I didn't exist?'

For a moment Charles was seized with a ludicrous urge to look over his shoulder to see who she was talking to. It couldn't possibly be him? But it was.

'Where were you last Tuesday? And what is all this? And where on earth did you get these awful clothes? Is this some kind of crazy gag?' The lady was making no effort to keep her voice down, and Charles was sure that the whole of Jermyn Street was listening. He reddened.

'I'm sorry . . .' he started, searching desperately for something sensible to say.

'James, are you drunk? You are! You must be!' The girl was very close to Charles now, and obviously lashing herself into a rage.

'I'm sorry . . .' he began, helplessly.

'You aren't, but you bloody soon will be.' With a full swing she slapped him right-handed. 'That's for last Tuesday,' she said harshly. 'And that' – she hit him again, left-handed – 'is for today. And don't bother to call and apologise. We're obviously through. You can put my key in the post.'

Charles was still reeling, a hand to his face, when she swept off down the street, head high and high heels clicking angrily. He stared after her, the marks of her slaps reddening on his cheeks, as she disappeared up Piccadilly Arcade. The whole incident couldn't have lasted more than thirty seconds, and he still couldn't think of anything to say. Obviously she had mistaken him for somebody else. But who?

Then he cursed himself for a fool. Of course. Fitzpatrick. They were as alike as two peas. I wonder what Fitzpatrick had done to enrage her, he thought. He certainly picks them fiery. For a moment he thought of hurrying after her to explain, but it was too late, and in any case he had no particular desire to risk another scene. He had a low opinion of the lady's self-control. She'd already proved that she was the kind who hit first and asked questions afterwards. Feeling remarkably conspicuous, Charles hurried up towards Lower Regent Street in search of a pub. Gone were thoughts of an expensive lunch. A stiff drink, and immediately, seemed indicated.

Over a large vodka in the decent obscurity of The Captain's Cabin, Charles was able to recover his sense of humour. After the second drink in quick succession he began to laugh, to the surprise and suspicion of the barmaid. Looking back, it really had been rather comic. I must have looked perfectly idiotic, he thought. The lady came off with all the honours. And she packed a powerful punch. All the same, this sort of thing could get a bit much. I don't think I'll wait until tomorrow. I'll call Fitzpatrick right away. At the very least, he'll be amused.

Pausing only to order another drink and to beg the reluctant barmaid for some change for the telephone, Charles dialled the Fitzpatrick Company.

'The Fitzpatrick Company. May I help you?'

'Mr Fitzpatrick, please.'

'I'm afraid Mr Fitzpatrick is out to lunch. Can his secretary help?'

'I don't know. Perhaps. Could you put me through to her?'

'One moment, sir. Trying to connect you.'

Charles stood at the phone, sipping the drink he had thoughtfully brought with him, and trying to put his mind into some kind of order. Now he'd actually made the call, he couldn't help feeling that he'd been a trifle hasty. After all, why should Fitzpatrick even have mentioned to his secretary a casual meeting with a remarkable likeness in the Carlton Tower bar? Still, it seemed too late to back out now. He waited, resigned, while the Fitzpatrick switchboard clicked and gurgled to itself.

'Can I help you? I'm Jenny Barnes, Mr Fitzpatrick's confidential secretary,' a crisp voice came to him over the wire.

'Miss Barnes? My name is Hutchinson. I don't know whether Mr Fitzpatrick mentioned me?'

'Oh yes, Mr Hutchinson. Mr Fitzpatrick is expecting you to telephone him tomorrow morning.' The voice was coldly impersonal. Clearly an appointment with Fitzpatrick was a sacred thing, not lightly anticipated.

'I know,' said Charles apologetically. 'I wouldn't have called, but the most extraordinary things has just happened. A perfectly strange woman walked up to me in the middle of Jermyn Street, and slapped my face. To the best of my knowledge, I've never seen her in my life before. It occurred to me that she was confusing me with Mr Fitzpatrick, and perhaps he ought to know about it.' Even to himself, the story sounded a little lame. Charles found, to his annoyance, that he was flushing.

His embarrassment was not relieved by the note of amusement in the cool voice at the other end of the phone. 'Have you any reason to believe that you could be mistaken for Mr Fitzpatrick?' it said.

'Well, yes, as a matter of fact. He can't have told you that we are quite ridiculously alike. And she called me James.'

To Charles' surprise, this brought an immediate response.

'That's certainly most unfortunate, Mr Hutchinson. I will tell Mr Fitzpatrick the moment he gets in. Could you describe the lady to me?' The voice was warmer now, even concerned.

'About five feet seven, auburn hair, dark eyes, smashing figure, very well dressed. A good right cross, and a better left hook.' Charles grimaced, and rubbed his slightly swollen cheek at the memory.

'Thank you, Mr Hutchinson. I'm sure that Mr Fitzpatrick will recognize the description. You say you spoke to the lady?' There was the faintest trace of emphasis on the last sentence.

'Well, no, actually, I couldn't think of anything to say except sorry, though I don't know for what.'

'And the lady? I'm sure Mr Fitzpatrick would like to know what she said. It may give him a clue to her identity.'

Slightly puzzled, Charles repeated what he could remember of the girl's remarks. 'And she said he was to be sure to return his key,' he finished.

'That was all? And you are sure you said nothing to her?' This time the emphasis was unmistakable. Charles began to get the surprising impression that what was said or not said was more important than there seemed any obvious reason.

'Not a thing, except sorry. To be honest, I felt rather a fool.' Charles found he felt even more foolish in retrospect.

'Thank you, Mr Hutchinson. That's very clear. I will tell Mr Fitzpatrick the moment he returns. In the meantime, he is of course expecting your call tomorrow morning. Good afternoon.' The voice hung up politely but abruptly.

'Good afternoon,' Charles said to a dead line. He replaced his own receiver thoughtfully. He couldn't rid himself of the feeling that for some reason it was very important that he hadn't had any genuine conversation with the red-headed

Amazon. Somewhere, he felt, there was a clue he was overlooking.

CHAPTER THREE

Wednesday morning found Charles wandering restlessly up and down Sloane Street, prowling through Harrods, browsing in Truslove and Hanson, anything to occupy him until his appointment with Fitzpatrick. Keyed up with anticipation, it had been hard enough for him to wait until nine before calling the Fitzpatrick office. The call then had been crisp and business-like. A well-organized Miss Barnes had told him that no, Mr Fitzpatrick had not yet arrived in the office, but that he had been shocked to hear of Charles' troubles with strange women, and would apologize in person when they met, at three at the Carlton Tower, where Mr Fitzpatrick had taken a suite for the day so that they could talk business in private and at length. Yes, Miss Barnes was aware of what Mr Fitzpatrick had in mind, but was unable to discuss it. She herself would be present to take notes, and would be grateful if Mr Hutchinson could bring with him all relevant tailor's measurements, including hat size, his passport and driving divence, and any medical records he possessed. No, she was not at liberty to explain why Mr Fitzpatrick required these, but she could assure him that it would save a great deal of time if he would do as he was asked. And good morning to you, Mr Hutchinson. Until three.

Having gone over and over the events of the day before, and tried to place them in the context of his knowledge of the Fitzpatrick enterprises, as he lay in bed, restlessly sleepless, Charles had finally shrugged mental shoulders and decided not to anticipate events. Just the same, he felt, this was certainly the most extraordinary interview for a job which had ever come his way. Best to leave it at that and wait and see.

After which laudable decision, he put on his best, indeed, his only remaining, decent suit – in a cream linen only barely suitable for spring-time London – and left his lodgings fully four hours before he needed, to wear out his shoe leather and worry at his problem, like a dog gnawing at an antique bone.

Accordingly, the Charles Hutchinson who presented himself at suite 387 of the Carlton Tower punctually at three o'clck was a leg-weary, irritable and confused young man, who had been unable to bring himself to eat, and whose ruffled spirits even vodka had been unable to soothe. By then he felt an indifference amounting to hostility towards the whole scheme, whatever it might turn out to be.

His host greeted him warmly.

'Hutchinson, my dear fellow. How nice to see you. Do sit down and have a drink. We've a long afternoon before us, and I hope that you'll stay for dinner – that is, supposing we come to agreement. No, no, no business before you've had a chance to relax. Jenny, my dear, come and be introduced to Charles Hutchinson – may I call you Charles? – and get the poor man a drink.'

Somewhat overwhelmed by this excess of affability, Charles found himself muttering confused platitudes to an unexpectedly gorgeous brunette in a red trouser suit and Pucci scarf who looked as unlike a confidential secretary as he could imagine, and whose warmly intimate smile and soft voice seemed a mile away from the cool-toned precision machine of her telephone persona.

'Sit down, sit down, Charles, Jenny knows what you drink. Have a cigarette? Or would you prefer a cigar?'

Charles found himself enveloped in a deep armchair with a fat Burmese cheroot in his hand, and used the ritual of inspecting and lighting the monster as an excuse to look round and get his bearings.

The sitting room was a full sixty feet long, with a giant sofa, four deep armchairs, a long table, covered with paper, a well-stocked bar, old prints of London on the walls and (what particularly impressed him) no less than two colour television sets in opposite corners. The long windows looked out over Cadogan Place, and the tips of the plane trees, just misting green, showed between great swags of brocade curtain.

He confirmed his first stunned impression of Jenny Barnes

as she came back towards him, his glass in her hand. Not an inch under five feet nine, he decided, with swinging dark hair, high cheek bones, a long straight nose, a generous mouth and deep blue, faintly slanted eyes under high-arched brows, she was indeed an impressive piece of femininity, with an opulent figure and a walk to match. She must, he knew, have a sharp intelligence, and the combination was undeniably striking.

'Vodka, with ice and a little tonic.' She smiled at him, showing even white teeth and an intriguing wrinkle across the bridge of her nose. 'How convenient that you share James's tastes so neatly. James told me you looked remarkably like him, but I must say I wasn't quite prepared for something so ludicrously exact. You know, James, it just might work.'

'Yes, well, enough of that now,' said Fitzpatrick hastily. 'There's quite a lot of groundwork to be got through before we can go into that.' He turned to the bemused Charles. 'You see, we have a job in mind for you which we think you will consider, but first of all, please bear with us. There are some questions, unavoidably intimate, I'm afraid, which we'd like you to answer first. If these details turn out to be satisfactory, then I promise you we won't leave you in any further suspense. Jenny, you have the file.'

Jenny Barnes sat down in a swivel chair by the long table, opened a fat buff folder, and handed a sheaf of foolscap to Fitzpatrick.

'Right,' he said. 'This,' he waved the sheaf,' is a dossier we have had prepared on you. It is fairly complete, but there are details that we'd like to check, and some matters that we were unable to discover in the time. I must tell you that so far it all checks out extremely well. Now I realize that you may be quite rightly indignant that we should have been beavering into your past without your consent, but I hope that you will forgive us when you have the full facts.

'We'll skip the educational details. There's no need to go into them at this stage. However, some of the Nigerian information is a little scanty. I take it you did not marry over there?'

'No indeed,' said Charles, surprised.

'But there was some trouble over a girl – Bisi was the name?

– wasn't there? Some question of a child?'

Charles flushed. 'She died,' he said shortly.

'And the child?'

'Look, I don't know how you found out about this, but I don't like it at all. For your information the child only lived three days, and I really don't see what business it is of yours.'

'Of course you don't, my dear chap. The point is, Bisi's relatives took rather against you, and I understand that you were pretty badly beaten up. Any permanent scars?'

'No. They broke some ribs, but that won't show except under X-ray. Look, what is all this?'

'All in good time, my boy, all in good time. Are you circumcised?'

'Good God. What on earth . . .'

'Please answer, it's important,' Jenny interrupted.

'Well, no, as it happens.'

'Good. Neither am I,' said Fitzpatrick with satisfaction. 'Warts? Moles? Birthmarks?'

'I really don't know.' Charles was as much intrigued as bewildered now.

'We must check,' Jenny said to Fitzpatrick.

'I agree. Charles, my boy, we must ask you to take off your clothes.'

'What?'

'Oh, don't be silly, Mr Hutchinson. I've seen naked men before.' Jenny sounded impatient.

'I'm sure you have, but I'm dashed if I see why you should see me!' Charles was emphatic.

'Charles, we must check. Otherwise the deal is off.' Fitzpatrick sounded almost pleading.

'What deal?'

'Later. But I promise you won't be disappointed. Jenny, the envelope.' Fitzpatrick took a fat buff envelope from his secretary and handed it to Charles. 'You'll find one thousand pounds in five-pound notes in there. Count them if you like. That is yours, whether we proceed further or not. Now will you undress?'

Charles accepted the envelope, and in a kind of dream found

himself taking off all his clothes, to stand awkwardly befor them. They examined him intently.

'Turn round slowly,' Fitzpatrick said.

'No appendix scar. That's awkward,' said Jenny.

'Can be fixed,' said Fitzpatrick shortly.

Charles felt like a side of beef. For some reason he found himself wriggling his toes in the thick pile of the carpet. Afterwards, whenever he thought back over that extraordinary scene, it was the sensuous feel of the pile under his feet that remained with him most vividly that and a stray patch of sunlight lighting up a print of early nineteenth century Regent Street.

'All right, you can dress again now,' said Fitzpatrick. Charles dressed in awkward silence, and sat down again. Jenny smiled at him shyly. There was a long pause.

Finally Fitzpatrick said, stroking his jaw thoughtfully, 'I think that's pretty satisfactory. It looks as though you'll do, at least physically. Jenny, get Charles another drink, and we'll tell him what we have in mind.'

As Jenny collected Charles' empty glass and headed towards the bar, Fitzpatrick got up and began to pace up and down between the windows.

'This is not easy,' he said. 'I must rely on your absolute discretion. What I am about to say must not go beyond these four walls. The job I am about to offer you is not easy. It will demand all your concentration and skill. The rewards, however, will be enormous, far greater than anything you have ever dreamed. And the conditions of work, if I can put it that way, will be comfortable to the point of luxurious. There are those who would say—' he smiled, and Jenny laughed from the bar – 'indecently so.'

'You can trust me to say nothing,' Charles said stiffly.

'Oh, I know I can, I know I can. What's more, I intend to make sure of it.' Fitzpatrick's smile was suddenly wolfish. The implied threat was unmistakeable.

The moment passed as Jenny laughed again, and walked across to hand Charles his drink. 'Oh, such hobs and goblins,' she said unexpectedly. 'Really, James, you'll frighten poor

Charles to death, and then what will you do?' She sat on the arm of Charles' chair, and Charles could feel the warm firmness of her hip against his shoulder. 'Why don't you just tell him and get it over with?'

Fitzpatrick, who had stopped his pacing to stare at Charles, relaxed and laughed in his turn.

'Sorry about that. I suppose I'm a bit keyed up. Excited, you might say. The fact is, Charles, I want you to take my place. I want you to become me.'

'What?' Charles sat bolt upright, nearly unseating Jenny. He could hardly believe his ears.

Fitzpatrick resumed his pacing. 'You heard me. I want you to take my place – at work, at home, at my clubs, with my wife, my children, my friends, even my girlfriends.' Jenny laughed, and Charles suddenly wondered about her relationship with her boss, and just what being a confidential secretary actually entailed.

'Bluntly, Hutchinson, I'm bored with the whole bloody business. I'd like to get away from the company and, to be frank, from my wife and family. Not necessarily for ever, but for at least a couple of years.

'That's a luxury not normally available to a man in my position. My departure would cause a crisis of confidence in the staff, our authors, everyone.

'I'm not really needed, but they don't believe that – and neither do the bankers. To leave my wife,' he smiled ruefully, 'would cost a fortune in reaching a settlement. And it would damage the children. Anyway, I've always wanted to study birds in East Africa, and that's what I'm going to do.'

'But it's impossible,' said Charles. 'You must be mad even to consider it. It's impossible in your business, and still more so in your marriage. This is either some kind of pipe dream or a joke.' Charles began to feel angry. After all this, to come to such a crazy anticlimax.

'Not at all,' said Fitzpatrick eagerly. 'Tell him, Jenny.' He went off towards the bar.

Jenny got up from the arm of Charles' chair and walked over to the table.

'You're quite right that it all started as a joke,' she said. 'About two years ago, James and I had dinner after the company's annual office party. James was bored, as he said, and we talked about ways he could get out of his life without stirring everything up.' She picked up two straining box files. We decided, just for fun, to work out in detail how it could be done. Here it is – a whole, carefully worked out scheme. All it needed was a double. Of course we never thought one would turn up, so the whole thing really was only a pipe dream. Until last week, when a friend of James's, who is a director of the Guildford and Godalming Life Assurance Company, told James at his club that his double had come in for a preliminary interview.'

Fitzpatrick laughed, and walked back to them, glass in hand. 'Old Stevens was quite indignant at first. Seemed to think I'd been playing some sort of practical joke on G&G.'

'Anyway,' Jenny went on, 'James got quite excited. He found out when your next interview was to take place, and followed you from the G&G office to the bar here. He had to meet you, you see, to find out whether it would work.'

'And it will,' said Fitzpatrick definitely. 'I'm sure of it. It'll take a few months to prepare you for your role, and to allow me to bow out without anyone noticing, and then, aside of course from Jenny, you'll be on your own. And I,' he said with relish, 'will be birdwatching in East Africa.' He drank with enjoyment.

'That's all very well, but what's in it for me?' Charles asked.

Jenny smiled at him lazily. 'Well . . .' she began. Fitzpatrick stopped her with an impatient gesture.

'£25,000 a year for two years, paid into any bank you like to name. In addition, you would draw my own salary and expenses, so that the £50,000 would be simply capital. At the end of two years, if the deception has worked, you will receive 25.1% of the shares in the company. Why the odd perecentage? It allows you the privileges of a major shareholder. You could, for instance, call an Extraordinary General Meeting if you thought your interests were being neglected.'

'That's remarkably generous,' said Charles, impressed. 'As a matter of interest, about how much would the shares be worth?'

'As of now, rather over half a million.' Fitzpatrick sounded justly proud.

'Goodness,' said Charles, inadequately.

'A lot to you, but a small part of my fortune,' Fitzpatrick explained.

'Well, what do you say?' He sounded as if he was trying hard not to sound over-eager.

'It's certainly an interesting propostion,' said Charles. 'But you'll have to convince me that it's possible. If you can, then I suppose I'd be a fool not to agree.'

'Good,' said Fitzpatrick. 'That's all I need to know for the moment. Jenny, let's have the briefing files. We might as well make a start, there's a lot to be got through.'

Jenny opened the big box files, and produced a small heap of folders. 'Business: past. Business: present. Business: future,' she said. 'Business associates. Business rivals. Business contacts. Personal holdings and affairs. That should do for a start. We'll run through a few of these today, and give Charles the digests.' She reached to the floor and produced an expensive looking tape machine and a large box full of labelled cassettes. 'These are tapes of meetings, of briefings, and of the voices of associates. You'll find a whole section here on the Fitzpatrick family, too. Play these over to yourself during the next week. I've arranged to test you on them at regular intervals, and as you absorb this lot, so we'll let you have some more.'

'You'll find minutes, balance sheets, cheque books, photographs, and samples of writing you ought to recognize.' Fitzpatrick was hunting through another pile of folders, and spoke without looking up. 'Here,' he said, picking out a thin green file, 'is my personal checking account, the one you will use at least, and some sample signatures. You'd better start practising my signature right away.'

Charles was still sitting silently trying to absorb the information they were throwing at him when Jenny handed him a large flat envelope.

'You'll find a cheque for five thousand pounds, a cheque book, and an account number for a bank in Burford, in Oxfordshire in here,' she said. 'You have a room booked there under your own name from tomorrow night.' She handed him another smaller package. 'Here are the keys to a Ford Cortina at present in the Carlton House garage. You'll drive that down to Burford tomorrow. We've booked you in to the Bay Tree for a month, under the name Fitzpatrick. We can't have you muddying the waters by appearing about town, can we? If you want cash, you'll have to learn to handle the signature as quickly as possible. Carrot and stick. It was James's idea.

'Didn't you take a lot for granted?' Charles was overwhelmed at the speed of the operation.

'Nonsense,' said Fitzpatrick. 'We've had all this planned for more than a year. It didn't take long to set it all in motion, you know. By the way, the car isn't registered in either of our names. Try not to bend it. It is insured, but the inquiries would be awkward if there was an accident. They might get traced back.'

'Did you bring your passport and the other details I asked for?' said Jenny.

Charles took them out of an inside pocket and handed them over. 'I can see that you'll have to get me a passport in my new name,' he said. 'But why the tailor's measurements?'

Fitzpatrick looked at him as if he was a fool. 'You can't arrive in my home in a whole lot of brand-new or unfamiliar garments,' he said severely. 'I need your measurements to get my clothes altered for you. Fortunately, I don't imagine there will be much difficulty. More a matter of tinkering, I think.'

'What about my own stuff?' Charles asked.

'Oh, we'll have that picked up and your bill paid tomorrow. We'll have to destroy your own clothes, of course. Good God, I never thought. You don't need glasses, do you?' Fitzpatrick seemed really upset at the thought that something had been left out of account.

'No.'

24

'Well, thank heaven. That would have presented difficulties. We will have to arrange for a thorough medical, of course, and that appendix will have to come out. You'll also have to see a dentist. I must say, I hope he'll have to work on you rather than on me. Don't much fancy a whole load of unnecessary fillings myself.'

'Why a dentist?' Charles asked.

'Because as far as possible, your chart and mine must be identical. My dentist's in that box file,' Fitzpatrick said, pointing to the second, and so-far unopened box. 'He happens to be a personal friend, and he'd know in a moment if the pattern looked wrong.'

Charles gulped. That thought hadn't even crossed his mind. 'But what about your wife and children?' he said. 'Surely she'll know at once.'

'Not a bit,' said Fitzpatrick cheerfully. 'We've lived pretty separate lives for years, now, you know.'

'And the two children?'

'Seen very little of them since they went to school,' said Fitzpatrick. 'No problem.' He paused, and then added with a metallic note, 'How did you know there are *two* of them? You seem surprisingly well informed.'

Charles wondered if he was simply imagining the note of menace. 'Felt I had to do some homework, you know,' he said awkwardly.

Fitzpatrick looked at him coldly for a moment. Jenny, too, paused in the process of riffling through the mass of files. Charles wondered just for a moment if there was something he was missing. There was simply no denying the tension.

Fitzpatrick seemed to make up his mind. Once more he was the genial conspirator. 'I like a man to be prepared.' If his chuckle seemed a little forced, Charles was not disposed to challenge it. 'You surprised me, that's all. Actually, if you've done a bit of sleuthing yourself, it should save us a good bit of time and energy. I take it you know the background of the business, then?'

Charles nodded. 'I've been through all the stuff on public record, of course. Pretty impressive, I thought. The only snag is that it's a business that I know nothing whatever about.'

'You will,' Jenny said. 'By the time we're ready to let you loose in the office, you'll know at least as much as we do ourselves.'

Fitzpatrick explained. 'You see, there isn't really that much for a chairman to do. I've been a figurehead for some time now. Of course that's the way I wanted it. All the same, it's convenient. The managing director handles all the routine business. A chap called Tom Irvine. You'll find a dossier on him in the file. Good man, very capable. You can have complete confidence in him.

'I don't see much of the staff, you know. And even if they did notice the chairman behaving oddly, they wouldn't dare say so. Besides which, they will be expecting to see me, and that's just what they'll see. It won't occur to anyone that a substitution is even a remote possibility.' The prospect of his staff's suspicion seemed to amuse him. 'In any case, you'll have Jenny to hold your hand.

'Now, I think we should order an early dinner here in our rooms,' said Fitzpatrick.

'Jenny, we might have some champagne, don't you think? To celebrate my impending relief from bondage.' He beamed at Charles. 'I can fill you in a little on Caroline and the family over food,' he said, 'I wouldn't care to do so on an empty stomach.' There was a flash of malice. Charles began to revise his opinion on Fitzpatrick's charm. It occurred to him that this wasn't really a nice man at all, though he couldn't quite pin down a reason for feeling so.

Jenny ordered dinner for three over the house phone, and Charles, at Fitzpatrick's urging, stayed in the bathroom while the waiters were organizing the meal. As Fitzpatrick said, jovially, there was no point in taking unnecessary chances. Afterwards Charles could never recall what they ate. He remembered that they drank a lot, though, two bottles of wine on top of the champagne, and a good half bottle of excellent brandy. It was over coffee and brandy, and another excellent Burmese cheroot that he recalled his encounter with the virago in Jermyn Street. Fitzpatrick laughed so hard he nearly fell off his chair, and even Jenny spluttered into her coffee cup with mirth.

'Helen,' Fitzpatrick cried. 'And how typical. That was Helen Wightman. She's in P.R. Very bright girl. You'll find her in the file. I visit her every Tuesday. She's been my mistress now for three years. Yes, every Tuesday, regular as clockwork. You'll like her Charles. She's temperamental, but marvellous in bed. Like's things a bit kinky. Goes in for games, blue movies, that sort of thing. Very imaginative. We quarrel a lot – she tends to get all possessive and nag, you know. Get enough of that at home. Without having it from my girlfriend. She'll come round, she always does. Buy her a flashy present. I always do. Works wonders.'

Charles couldn't help feeling that it wasn't going to be easy to fool a mistress of such long standing, but it seemed priggish and a bit windy to bring it up. Besides the insinuating fumes of a good deal of brandy were persuading him that it would all work out beautifully, and even if it didn't, he would receive handsome compensation.

At nine, the party broke up. Fitzpatrick rose and prepared to leave. Charles got to his feet too, and was astounded when Fitzpatrick waved him back into his seat.

'You're staying here tonight, Charles,' he said. 'Jenny's got a good deal of detail to go over with you before you can call it a day.' He winked. 'A lesson or two to give, I shouldn't wonder.

'Don't worry about the agreement. It's all drawn up, and the interim contract to cover the training period, as it were, will be ready for your signature before you leave for Burford in the morning. Jenny's organized you some clothes. Be sure to leave the things you're wearing with her tomorrow. Sooner they're destroyed the better.'

He collected a coat from the bedroom, kissed Jenny casually, said goodnight and left. As he went down the corridor to the lift, they could hear him whistling tunelessly through the closed door. Of one thing there was no doubt – James Fitzpatrick was more than pleased with the initial success of his outlandish scheme.

In the suite behind him there was constraint. Charles sat

swirling his brandy round the balloon glass, studying the random patterns it left. When he looked up, he found Jenny watching him, smiling.

'It's too late to do any work,' she announced firmly.

Charles was conscious of her intensely physical presence, and the rather heavy perfume she wore.

'You're staying the night here?' he asked.

'That's the plan.' She laughed happily. 'Somebody's got to show you how James makes love.'

'Are all Mr Fitzpatrick's ladies so forceful?' he enquired, a little nervously.

'I don't know about the others.' There was a touch of steel in her voice. 'But he's a powerful man. It's understandable that he likes dynamic ladies, I suppose.' Then the gaiety returned. 'Anyway, if I'm not complaining, why should you be?'

'I just feel embarrassed,' he said. 'I know it's not sophisticated, but this is pretty cold-blooded.'

'And you've had an awful lot to drink and don't know whether you can. I know.' Jenny sighed. 'I know quite a lot about men, you know. I find you very attractive. I'm likely to. You must have guessed that James and I are more than just business colleagues, and you and he are absurdly alike.'

'That's just the point,' Charles said, desperately. 'Can't you see?'

'Look, I'm not going to rape you.' Jenny got up from her chair and flounced glass in hand to the bar. 'I'm going to take another brandy to a nice hot bath, and then I'm going to bed. It's been a long day, and I'm tired. I don't give a damn if you sleep with me, or on the sofa, or on the floor if you prefer. That's entirely up to you. Don't bother to unzip me, and don't for heaven's sake get up to say good night.' She splashed brandy into her glass, slammed the bottle back onto the bar, and went through into the bedroom, banging the door behind her.

Charles looked at the closed door ruefully, and getting slowly to his feet, drifted in his turn towards the bar. Brandy bottle in hand, he paused, and contemplated the idea of another cheroot and a session with one of the files. He rejected the notion. Too late now, he'd drunk too much to concentrate properly. He shrugged, and poured himself another hefty tot, then swirled the golden fiery liquid round his glass with deft fingers.

He squared his shoulders and turned towards the bedroom. As an afterthought he picked up the brandy bottle in his spare hand, and was annoyed with himself when he had to put it on the floor to open the door. As he straightened up, bottle again in hand, he saw clouds of steam coming through the open bathroom door, and heard the sound of lusty splashing. He closed the bedroom door softly behind him and walked towards the sounds. As he entered the bathroom, Jenny looked up at him entirely unsurprised, from where she lay full-length in the bath. She smiled. He held up the bottle.

'Thought you might like a refill,' he said.

'How kind,' she said, twisting to reach for her glass on the ledge at her shoulder. The movement did marvellous flexing things for the full breasts. The nipples were taut and erect. She held out the glass to him. Then just as he was about to pour, she pulled it back to nestle it between her breasts.

'I think we'd better be closer acquainted,' she murmured. As he leant forward to fill the glass she wound a long wet arm round his neck and pulled his head down to hers. Their lips met. Hers were soft and open and deliciously brandy-flavoured. Her tongue was thick and wet and active. Charles closed his eyes and sank into a dark sensual velvet daze.

Suddenly she pushed him away. 'Hey, you're pouring brandy on me. Don't you think you should put the bottle down?'

Charles turned to get rid of the brandy bottle, and behind him Jenny surged upright to stand superb and dripping, hand outstretched for the towel.

'Take the drink and the glasses in to the bedroom. We've got a long night, and they'll come in useful.' She stretched suddenly, gloriously, catlike, and laughed again as she saw his expression.

Charles was sitting on the edge of the huge bed, pulling his shirt off over his head, when he felt her breasts on his back. 'Mmmmm,' she murmured, kissing the side of his neck. 'Nice.' A hand snaked round to flip his zipper open expertly, and delve inside. 'I've been thinking about this ever since you stood there this afternoon.'

In a confused and panting tangle they got Charles undressed. As he sank, too impatient to allow for subtlety, between her avid thighs, Charles reached for the bedside light.

'No,' she groaned against his mouth. 'I want . . .' Her nails dug into his back, and her hips began to move urgently. Lost in a sweet and sweaty turmoil Charles forgot everything but the urge to penetrate and conquer. Her anxious moans turned to long purring growls of satisfaction, and then upwards to a high wail of fulfilment. Charles, his face buried in the slippery tense angle of her neck and shoulder, almost blacked out as his own release swept over him.

'You are different, after all,' she murmured sleepily into his ear, nibbling gently on the lobe. 'James is a great man, and I'm devoted to him. But as a lover he's always a bit distracted, thinking of business.'

Charles groaned, and dragged his mind out of a warm haze of satisfaction. 'How the hell am I going to get past his wife, then? And what's her name?'

Jenny stirred, and began slowly to disentangle herself from the warm damp confusion of limbs.

'Don't worry,' she said. 'I'll teach you.' She leant up on one elbow, and looked down at him, her dark hair brushing his face. 'Anyway, he's going to pretend to have a nervous breakdown, which ought to explain any oddities. A psychiatrist friend's going to tell him how to fake it. It's all worked out.' She half sat up to drag her breast over his chest. 'And now, Charles, let's forget it. This is my night, and I don't intend to waste it. Anyone awake down there?' Her hand went exploring intimately. 'Oh, I see there is. Come, sir, we can't waste something like that. Let's see what we can do for your problem.' She flung a thigh across his stomach, and with a sigh of pure content sank down onto him. Charles' last thought was for James as her lips trailed wetly over the angle of his jaw, seeking his mouth. My God, he thought, I wonder if he knows what he's about to miss. His chuckle was cut off as Jenny's mouth closed over his, and her hips made urgent signals. It was indeed going to be a long night. Thank God.

CHAPTER FOUR

'Caroline will be here in fifteen minutes,' Miss Barnes said briskly. Charles wondered again how he had been persuaded into this bizarre impersonation of James Fitzpatrick. He was in the room of the elegant Surrey home where the Chairman had been comfortably ensconced for his simulated nervous breakdown.

Charles, suitably coached, was to take his place during visiting hours, so that he could make his first contact with James' wife Caroline under controlled circumstances. Charles' incredulity was put to rest by the information that James owned the home, through proxies, and that the whole encounter had been carefully planned. Jenny spent a weekend in Burford, rehearsing Charles for his scene until he was word perfect. His suggestion that Caroline might not know her lines was dismissed. According to Fitzpatrick, via Jenny, Caroline was a woman of habit, and all her previous visits to the home had been carefully analysed to work out exactly how she would behave. There would be no problems, provided that Charles didn't lose his head. Charles had a feeling that this was designed as a kind of field test for his whole impersonation, but Jenny would not confirm this.

All the same, it was a very nervous Charles who had been driven by Jenny into the wilds of Surrey to the elegant Edwardian house in which Fitzpatrick was enjoying ill health. When he was slipped through the back entrance into the pleasant sunlit room with its books and games, Charles found his heart pounding. Absurdly, he was taken aback that there was no James to meet him.

'Don't be stupid,' Jenny said impatiently. 'The less the staff see of two James Fitzpatricks at the same time the better. You won't see James again until you're ready to take his place.

31

And if you're as nervous as this now, that may be never.'

Charles tried to point out that even the best actors were entitled to stage-fright, but Jenny was obviously scornful of such amateurishness.

'Caroline will be here in fifteen minutes,' she repeated. 'James is reading this thriller' – she handed him a lurid paperback – 'which she brought over the last time she came. I suggest that you spend some time looking at it. She may want to ask you whether you liked it or not, and it wouldn't do for you not to have read it at all.'

She went out, closing the door sharply behind her. Charles sat uncomfortably in Fitzpatrick's big leather chair, and tried to concentrate on the book. He found it impossible. His ears were straining for every sound. The sound of heels clicking in the passage outside his room had him on his feet, and his knees almost gave way in relief when they tapped on by his door, and faded as the unseen walker – an attendant? Charles thought wildly, with visions of strapping brutal women with huge biceps – turned a corner, and went out of earshot.

So keyed up was he that he quickly fell into a kind of apprehensive exhaustion, and his reaction when a rap on his door was followed after a brief pause by its opening was appropriately offhand.

Caroline was tall and willowy, about five feet eight, with tow-blonde hair neatly tied in a knot. She was dressed in a sensible tweed skirt, with a fluffy pink twin-set and, Charles noticed irrelevantly, pearls. Her face was strong and slightly weatherbeaten, her complexion clear and girlish. She looked, with her almost ostentatious lack of make-up, like a typically English upper middle class country girl. Only her mouth, wide-lipped, sensual, almost too red, and her deep-set heavy-lidded eyes, so dark a blue as to be almost black, gave any indication of why the hedonist Fitzpatrick had come to marry her. Somewhere hidden there, thought Charles, is passion. And intelligence, he added to himself. Her photographs do her less than justice.

'Hello, James, darling,' she said, her voice low, clear and carrying. 'How are you today? The doctor says you're a lot better. I saw him on the way in, and he thinks you can come home in a week or two, and go back to work, so long as you take it fairly easily, in a month.'

Charles was a little startled that his timetable was so far advanced, and remembered only just in time that he was supposed to be gloomy and depressed.

'Hello, dear,' he said gruffly. 'That's not what he tells me. God knows what Irvine is doing to the business while I sit and rot here. Damn it,' he threw the paperback across the room, 'why can't I get out of here?'

Caroline was soothing. 'It's a good sign that you're impatient,' she said. 'A week or two ago you couldn't have cared less. You really are getting better, darling. And of course Tom Irvine will look after the business for you. Everything's going to be all right, you'll see, and you'll be all the better for a rest. The children send their love, and hope the doctor will let them come and see you next week. James is much happier about his exams now, and he's taken your advice.'

Charles had a moment of panic. Advice? What advice? He was aware that there was a problem about James junior's future, but his mind was a blank. He thought resentfully that Jenny had slipped up here. In all the dossiers and tapes he'd studied in the fastness of his Burford hotel there'd been no mention of this. For a moment he felt a sneaking twinge of satisfaction that the Fitzpatrick organization was not infallible.

'Advice? I'm sorry, love, I don't remember,' he said.

'To do maths, physics and chemistry, dear. Don't you remember? He wanted to do English, History and French, but you persuaded him that he wasn't any good at those, and ought to stick to the things he really could do. Well, he's decided to do just that. Aren't you pleased?'

'Oh. Yes. Splendid,' Charles said heartily, thinking grimly that he'd have a word to say to Jenny about this. He was more sure than ever that during her visits to test and question his absorption of all the data she'd given him no hint of all this.

'I knew you'd be pleased,' Caroline said happily. 'It's so right for him, you know. And Lucy is doing splendidly in the school play. She's so upset that you can't come to watch her.'

Charles remembered that one thing Jenny had emphasized was Fitzpatrick's very tepid interest in his children.

'Tell her how disappointed I am,' he said casually. A flicker crossed Caroline's face. She hadn't missed his offhand tone, Charles noticed. He watched with appreciation as she bit her lip to suppress an angry comment. He waited, poised, for her next gambit.

'Well, play or no play, I'll be glad to have you home,' she said. 'I'm sick of chauffeuring the children about. If it isn't to and from school, it's chess matches, hockey matches, ballet classes. And now it's discos in the evenings. Time you came back to do your turn.'

Charles picked up his cue.

'You should organize a rota with the other mothers,' he said, and watched her colour angrily. 'I've told you often enough. There's no need for you to do it all yourself, if you don't want to. I haven't time. And anyway, I'm not about to subsidize your inefficiency.' Charles was so pleased at producing what he felt was an authentic Fitzpatrickism that he almost spoiled the effect by smiling.

'You seem to be feeling better,' Caroline said tightly. 'Well, we mustn't quarrel, not yet, at any rate. But I give you fair warning, James, that from the moment you get back you are going to do your fair share, or the children can go without.'

With a visible effort, she changed the subject, and the rest of the visit passed uneventfully. As she picked up her handbag and bent over to kiss him a cool goodbye, Charles felt a sudden impulse to tell her the whole thing.

'Caroline,' he said before he could stop himself.

'Yes?' she said, eyebrows raised, hand on the door handle.

'Nothing,' he muttered. 'Drive carefully.'

She looked surprised for a moment, and then smiled.

'Thank you,' she said, and left.

Charles sighed with relief as the door shut behind her. That was a near thing, he thought. I wonder what came over me.

It was apparent that Jenny shared his surprise. 'What the hell were you up to?' she stormed, as she almost ran into the room. 'We thought for a moment you were going to give the whole game away.' She was clearly very angry. Reaction against shock, Charles thought, pleased that he seemed to be keeping his head better than she.

'I suddenly realized that all this is no joke. There's something rather grubby about it, don't you think?' he said.

'Don't be stupid. Think of the money. Besides, she's never been really happy with James. Maybe she'll come to like you better.' Something seemed to amuse her, and she laughed.

'Anyway, how did you know?' Charles asked suddenly. It occurred to him with something of a shock that she'd obviously overheard the whole interview.

'James and I were behind that one-way mirror.' She pointed out a large, oddly ornate fixture on the wall. 'The doctors use it to check on patients who really are crazy.'

Charles grimaced. For a moment he felt a rush of sympathy for Caroline, deceived and toyed with and forced to provide unwitting entertainment for a pair of conniving voyeurs. He felt obscurely ashamed.

'Anyway, James thinks you did very well on the whole. He's pleased.' Jenny looked at her watch. 'Come on. Time I took you back to Burford. I've some more tapes in the car. Concentrate on the Kurtz ones especially. We've fixed your appendix operation for next week, and James wants you to have Kurtz fixed in your mind before you go into the nursing home. By the way, he owns that one too, so don't be surprised at the VIP treatment you'll get.'

She ushered him out the back way and into the car. They were silent on the way back to the hotel, and Charles was abstracted as he said goodbye. He was wrestling with the fact that what had started out, if not as a game, as a challenge, now seemed not at all amusing.

The operation itself went without a hitch. Jenny came up to hold his hand, as she put it, and he was surprised to recognize her blue eyes over a surgical mask, just before he went unconscious. He was not reassured, however, when he came round to find her at his bedside. She'd been with him throughout, she revealed, to make sure that he didn't say anything embarrassing under the anaesthetic. Charles was feeling too sore, and too generally sick, to do more than grunt, but he found himself resenting, not for the first time, the thoroughness of the Fitzpatrick set-up. As he fell reluctantly asleep he remembered that he never had brought up the faulty briefing which had caused him such a frisson in the Caroline interview. His last thought was to challenge Jenny with it, but he was unconscious before he could force his unwilling tongue round the words he wanted to say, and when he woke she was gone.

The visit to the dentist was not so simple. His appendix scar was still tender when he sat down in the dentist's chair, resentful that this visit, when he could have done without a comforting hand to hold, he'd been forced to do on his own, following instructions issued crisply over the phone by Jenny, very much Miss Barnes. The dentist, a large, pale, smooth man who whistled Gilbert and Sullivan tunes slightly off-key in pepperminty breathiness as he stooped over Charles' tense but recumbent body, peering interminably around the interior of his mouth, congratulated him on the excellence of his teeth.

'Very good, very good, Mr Hutchinson,' he said. 'Fine teeth. Seems a pity to spoil them. I'm afraid you're going to need ten fillings and a bridge. Mr Fitzpatrick,' he was delighted, 'has not been so fortunate.' For a moment he frowned. 'I'm afraid Mr Fitzpatrick's dentist has made rather a mess of his teeth.' He sucked in his breath with professional disapproval of a colleague's remissness. 'Still, we'll do our best for you. You'll need another appointment, though. Be sure to remember to check with the nurse on your way out. Now . . .' He reached for the drill.

Charles was still so surprised at being addressed as Hutchinson for the first time in weeks that the first assault on his teeth had been made before he had time to react to the pain. But his writhings and inarticulate open-mouthed cries quickly left no doubt as to his reaction to treatment. The dentist paused and frowned.

'Surely you're not going to be difficult,' he said. 'It takes so much longer if you insist on injections.' Charles indicated vehemently that he didn't care how long it took so long as he didn't feel anything. The dentist sighed ostentatiously. 'Oh very well,' he said, and replaced his drill on its stand. The syringe he produced was a large one, and Charles looked at it doubtfully. 'Open wide,' the dentist said. 'We'll put a block in on both sides, top and bottom. Your mouth will feel swollen for some time, I'm afraid.' He jabbed the needle ruthlessly into Charles' jaw. Charles stiffened and twitched. A large deodorized finger rubbed fiercely on Charles' gums. 'We'll just give it a moment to take,' the dentist said. He turned to his drill again, and ran it experimentally. Charles sat numb and apprehensive. Then a large hand was on his forehead, and his mouth was full of drill and noise and the revolting smell of overheated tooth, and he sank into a haze of pain and endurance.

'That's it for now,' his tormentor said cheerfully. 'Rinse, please.' Charles leant weakly over the basin, and rinsed his mouth out with warm pinkish mouthwash. Dully he watched disgusting dark grey streaks swirl into the plug-hole, and congratulated himself on the fact that he was still alive.

'Remember to make another appointment,' the dentist said cheerfully. Charles groaned. That was something he'd conveniently forgotten.

But when the appointment came round, all was not well with Charles. Something, it seemed the injections, had seized up his jaw, and he could only with difficulty open his mouth. Jenny was worried about it, not, Charles realized resentfully, on his behalf, but because it looked like holding up the schedule. There was no question that the other fillings could be done. Charles was forced to chew on a sort of spring contraption designed to force open his mouth and strengthen his jaw muscles, and his bi-weekly report was made muffled and indistinct. Jenny cut it short with a frown, and hurried off, Charles felt sure, to Fitzpatrick's nursing home for further instructions.

At their next meeting it was clear that a lot of hard decisions had been made.

'James says we'll have to skip the dentist for the time being, and simply risk problems. The dentist says your jaw should be workable in a week, so we're to go on with the next stage.

You're to take over in the office in ten days' time.' Jenny frowned. 'I don't think you're ready, but James insists. He says you're to have a cold, which will allow for your voice being indistinct. He says the time-table has all to be moved up. Apparently there's new trouble with Kurtz in New York. James won't even tell me what it's all about, but it means that we have to hurry things a bit.' Jenny looked worried. 'It's unlike James to be so twitchy,' she said. 'I've never seen him so jumpy before. I'm sure there's something he's not telling me.'

Charles listened with interest. It was the first time since the Carlton Tower that Jenny had betrayed the least uneasiness over the progress of the scheme.

'What about the rest of the teeth?' he said.

'Oh, James says he'll arrange that we can fit that in the moment your jaw is OK,' Jenny said. 'The important thing is to get this office hurdle over first. If that comes off, we're in the clear.' There was a note of doubt in Jenny's voice. It was obvious that she had reservations. Charles waited to see if she would come out with any of them.

Finally, 'It's Tom Irvine,' she said, with a rush. 'There's something up with Tom Irvine. Even James doesn't seem quite to know what it is. He almost left the home yesterday and came into the office himself. We talked very seriously of dropping the whole thing.' She paused and looked blankly into space.

'Anyway, it's not your problem,' she continued. 'It just means moving rather quicker than we thought. Don't worry, everything is under control.'

But Charles found himself thinking that control seemed unaccountably to be slipping away. He didn't like it at all that Jenny, of all people, was out in the cold. Fitzpatrick seemed to have withdrawn his full confidence from her. And if Jenny's so worried, he thought, I should be scared rigid.

CHAPTER FIVE

'Welcome back to the office, James.' Jenny Barnes ushered Charles into Fitzpatrick's office, and went to make a cup of coffee, to be served in the Chairman's private white Rosenthal china. She was dressed for work in a plain white blouse and a simple white wrap-around skirt. She looked cool, neat, desirable, and admirably poker-faced.

Charles surveyed the office, recalling his meeting with Fitzpatrick the day before. It was a huge room, at least forty feet long, and some twenty feet wide with a high ceiling. A large desk of mahogany on glass legs supported a calculating machine, a clock radio, a push-button telephone, a wide intercom switchboard, and a dictating machine. Behind the desk was a revolving leather chair, black, with steel arms. Behind the chair, long curtained windows looked out over Soho Square. There was an enormous leather sofa; three matching chairs were scattered casually on the tan cord carpet. A huge wall unit stretched from floor to ceiling all along one wall, crammed with books, leaflets, and bundles of manuscript. One whole wall was covered with cork, on which were pinned quantities of flimsies, posters, schedules, photographs, all the paraphernalia of administration. On the third wall hung two handsome impressionist paintings: Charles had been surprised to learn that these were originals, a Monet and a Renoir, picked up by Fitzpatrick at auction for large sums of money, and listed as assets in the firm's books. In one corner, by the window, stood a depressed-looking rubber plant.

'Furnished to impress,' Fitzpatrick had said. 'Remember that a Chairman's office has to double as a temple, in which the Chairman plays God, and the directors priests. Psychologically speaking, I've always believed that my office should look functional, but throw-away grand, if you see what I mean.'

Charles sat down rather nervously in the big swivel chair

behind the desk, and noticed at once that it had been built up, so that a seated Fitzpatrick could dominate the room. He leant forward to play with the intercom switches. He was just about to press the toggle marked J.B. when Jenny came in with a tray on which was a cup of coffee and a plate of chocolate digestive biscuits. Charles looked at them with distaste.

'I hate those,' he said.

'Well, learn to like them,' Jenny retorted. 'James adores them, and won't have any others.' Charles noticed that her confidence seemed greatly restored since their last meeting.

'I have told everyone you will be busy catching up on your paperwork,' she said, putting the tray on the corner of his desk. 'The only meeting you have to have this morning is with Tom Irvine. He'll want to talk about New York. I'll bring in the latest file so you can brush up on Kurtz. Remember that James doesn't trust Woodward, Kurtz' assistant, and thinks Kurtz is a crazy egomaniac.'

'Look, Jenny, I know all that, remember? What else have I been learning for the last three months? And for all our sakes you'd better not mention James again, at least not in the office.' Charles felt a surge of irritation. All those weeks of preparation, and Jenny seemed to have forgotten it all in a morning.

She looked contrite. 'Won't do it again,' she said. Charles smiled at her, with a pleasant feeling of superiority.

'Well,' she said, 'we might as well get it over with. You'd better send for Tom Irvine to come right away. And, Jenny,' he added, as she prepared to leave the room, 'I think you'd better stay around. Maybe you could take notes, or something.'

'Very well, James.' Jenny was snapping back into character as the first strangeness wore off.

Charles leant back in his chair and thought back to his briefings on Tom Irvine. A Scot, a Puritan, a fanatical worker. Not much sense of humour, but great tenacity and drive. 'Rely on Irvine,' Fitzpatrick had said. 'He knows more about the business than I do. But don't imagine that he'll be any help with policy. That's your province. Jenny knows what I want, and she'll pass it on to you, at least until you've found your feet.'

40

A perfunctory knock on the door interrupted his musings, and a ruddy-faced man with steel-grey hair and bright, rather cold grey eyes came in at the brisk trot that was characteristic of Fitzpatrick's managing director. His suit was baggy and old-fashioned. His drab tie was only marginally clean.

'James,' he cried, advancing across the floor, his hand outstretched. 'Welcome back. It's good to see you looking so healthy and rested. We've all missed you a lot. I hope you're fully recovered?' He pumped Charles' hand with a firm grip.

Charles smiled at him. 'Apart from a foul cold, I'm just fine, thank you, Tom, and raring to go. What's been going on at the shop while I've been away?'

'I imagine Jenny's kept you pretty well in touch,' Irvine said. 'It's been fairly smooth and quiet here in London.' He frowned. 'But we're having a lot of trouble with New York.'

'I'm not surprised. Stan Kurtz getting paranoid again?' Charles slid neatly into his role.

Irving looked at him with a twinkle in his eyes. 'I can see you're back in form after your rest,' he said.

They plunged into a detailed discussion of the problem of the Kurtz affiliate, and Charles thanked his stars for the efficiency of Jenny and her briefing files. It was no problem to keep up his end, as Irvine outlined the many difficulties that had arisen between the two companies: the profits of the American firm were slipping fast, they needed more capital from the parent company, but treated every suggestion, let alone instruction, from London with suspicion and disdain. There seemed no reasoning with Kurtz, and Irvine brought up his doubts about Woodward, Kurtz' assistant.

'Woodward does his best to paper over the cracks,' he said, shaking his head, 'but I doubt he's really up to it.'

Charles remembered his lines. 'I just don't know how far I trust the man,' he said. 'Remember he's Kurtz' messenger boy, first and foremost.'

Irvine nodded agreement. 'So you've always said, James,' he said. 'I must say, you do stick to your assessments of people.' He sounded admiring. Charles wondered a little irritably if he thought that everyone else changed their minds every day and twice on Sundays. Then it occurred to him that this was part of the everyday flattery inescapable from chairmanship, and he chalked up a score to Fitzpatrick's shrewd assessment of industrial psychology.

'I think the immediate thing to do is for me to go over to New York right away,' said Irvine. 'Maybe something can be sorted out if I'm on the spot.'

Charles took time to look thoughtful, then gave his consent. He was delighted. A few extra days in the office without the managing director breathing down his neck: nothing could have been more fortunate.

'It is good to have you back,' Irvine said again. 'We need you at times like these.' As he got up to leave Charles wondered whether there had been any emphasis on his last words. Was there a hint that Irvine didn't feel Fitzpatrick was needed in the ordinary way?

Jenny stood up from her discreetly positioned chair as the door closed behind Irvine, and stretched luxuriously. 'Well done,' she said. 'That's far the biggest hurdle over.'

Charles spun round in his swivel chair, and got up to walk over to the window. He stared down at the row of cars parked round Soho Square with unseeing eyes.

'Don't you believe it,' he said. 'Caroline to come. And then, god help me, Helen!'

CHAPTER SIX

The Fitzpatrick dossier had contained a large number of photographs of River Lodge, Fitzpatrick's big comfortable Edwardian house on the Thames at Marlow, but nothing had prepared Charles for the sheer size of it. As the Scimitar swept up the short gravel drive, Charles was struck by the power of his alter ego's bank balance. In the evening light, with the sun casting long shadows over the immaculate lawn, the house looked huge, palatial, the sort of massive tribute to solid money that Charles remembered eyeing longingly from railway carriages when he was a boy. He'd weaved fantasies round houses like River Lodge, but he'd never expected to live in one, however false his pretences.

He left the car by the front door, and feeling oddly diffident, strolled round the side of the house towards the river. The sun was flashing from long windows overlooking a wide flagged terrace. In a neat rectangular pond surrounded by carefully landscaped rocks covered with heaths and ferns goldfish looped and turned. A young weeping willow hung in leggy adolescent vulnerability, dipping its long green leaves in the further end. Charles remembered that Caroline had planted it two years before, and that James had never liked it. The river gurgled gently past the stone facing of the embankment at the bottom of the close-cut gently sloping lawn. Tied along the far bank were neat white cruisers, each with its gay awning and complement of figures recumbent in deckchairs, drinks in hand. Tinny transistorized music tinkled faintly from upstream. Charles frowned. Dylan seemed out of place in a scene of such elegantly English complacency.

The sound of voices led him through a heavy-scented arch of roses into a neat and extensive vegetable garden. Charles paused to admire the rows of raspberry canes, the well-trained apple trees heavy with fruit, the colourful, carefully staked tomatoes, the phalanx of plump lettuces. Caroline and a pigtailed child, identified by the flashing band across her teeth as Lucy, were bent over a bed of strawberries. Charles had time to admire Caroline's trim outline in navy slacks before she turned and saw him.

She straightened with a smile. 'You *are* early, darling,' she said. 'How nice.' Charles felt a momentary awkwardness. He covered his confusion by making a big production of removing his tie and unbuttoning his shirt at the neck. Caroline strolled towards him, stripping off her sensible gardening gloves. She kissed his cheek casually.

'Nice to have you home again,' she said. 'Come inside and I'll pour you a drink. Lucy darling,' she called over her shoulder, 'bring that punnet into the kitchen, and we'll have them for supper.' She linked her arm in Charles' as they walked

43

back towards the house. 'Your favourite, darling, cold lobster. I know it costs a fortune, but it is your first night back.'

Lucy's stickily little hand clutched at his free one. 'Are you better, Daddy? The doctor wouldn't let James and me come to see you.'

Charles pressed her grubby fingers, feeling unexpectedly angry that James had sent an impostor to be greeted with this solicitude. 'Much better, darling,' he said.

He looked up to see Caroline regarding him oddly. 'Your rest seems to have improved your habits,' she said. For a moment Charles was sure he was going to blush. Desperately he willed Caroline to look away. Fortunately a withered bloom on a nearby rose bush caught his eye, and she reached out to remove it. Charles sighed inwardly with relief. A bad moment had passed. He wondered grimly how he was going to get through the others that were bound to come.

The three made a pleasant picture of domestic happiness as they strolled arm in arm up the steps of the terrace and through French windows into a big light sitting room, full of over-stuffed chintz-covered furniture. Charles felt more than ever a fraud.

'Lucy, get your cat out of Daddy's chair,' Caroline said, releasing his arm to walk over to a long chest on which was a silver tray with an assortment of bottles and an ice bucket.

Charles sank into a big armchair from which a fluffy black-and-white cat had been removed resentfully. He watched it struggling in Lucy's arms as she carried it out of the room, and thought, amused, that one member of the household was not deceived.

Caroline brought drinks over to his chair, and perched on the arm as she offered him a vodka and tonic. 'Cheers,' she said, sipping her sherry. 'You know, if the children are a nuisance you must let me know. The doctor said you weren't to be upset, and I know they get on your nerves sometimes.' Charles squirmed inwardly. He liked children himself, he always had. That was one thing he did not have in common with Fitzpatrick.

'I've thought a lot about what you said in the nursing home,' he said. 'I think I ought to make more effort with the children. At least I can try.' He took a long swig of his drink to avoid having to meet Caroline's eye.

'That will be nice, darling,' she said lightly. 'You won't mind if I believe it when I see it, will you? I must go and serve the lobster.' She rose and went out, pausing to look at the vodka bottle on the way. 'There's another bottle in the pantry, James, but I think there's enough in this one for one more drink before dinner.'

Charles got up to refill his glass, then strolled across to the mantelpiece to admire his reflection in the big mirror above it. He winked at himself, and raised his glass in a mocking salute. 'Cheers, you bastard,' he said aloud.

The door opened to reveal Lucy, carefully carrying a frosted wine bottle. 'Mummy says will you open this, and bring it in with you. Dinner's ready.' She produced a corkscrew from a pocket, entwined in a revolting handkerchief. Charles smiled and took the bottle from her.

'Won't be a moment,' he said, mentally checking to make sure he remembered where the dining room was. He'd memorized the lay-out of the house of course, but somehow the reality was hard to match to his mental image.

When he appeared at the table carrying the open bottle of Chablis, he found Caroline and both children waiting for him.

'Hello, Dad, glad you're better,' said James junior, tall, rangy, with a thatch of tow hair, and a slight nervous stutter.

'Thank you, James.' Charles took his place at the head of the table. 'I'm glad to be back. The nursing home was comfortable, of course, but home's best.' He smiled across at Caroline, and then mentally cursed. From the startled expression on all three faces around him, he'd said something wholly unexpected. 'You mustn't mind if I seem a bit odd,' he said hastily, hoping to retrieve himself, 'it takes awhile after a breakdown to get back to normal, you know.'

'Yes, of course,' said Caroline, after a pause. 'Now, children, you mustn't bother your father. Remember the doctor said he wasn't to be upset.'

Charles thankfully concentrated on his lobster, and thought

longingly of escaping back to the comparative safety of the office. 'Home' was all too clearly mined with explosive little pitfalls. He wondered if it was Fitzpatrick's vanity which had prevented him from being wholly candid about his home life. It suddenly struck him that Fitzpatrick had been so completely indifferent to his wife and children that he genuinely had no idea of how they thought of him, or of how he had behaved inside the family circle. He decided he'd have to concentrate all the time if he wasn't to make a serious mistake. There was only so much a breakdown would justify.

By the time the children had been excused, and he and Caroline were sharing coffee and an after-dinner brandy, Charles was grimly determined to introduce some changes in the Fitzpatrick persona. There was clearly no way he could maintain James' lofty arrogance without betraying himself daily. He wondered if Jenny would fake some kind of electro or chemo-therapy for him. Certainly a major personality shift was not just in order, but mandatory. He began to sweat lightly as he thought about the next hurdle, bed.

Caroline was talking of the immediate future. 'I realize that we've missed the chance of a holiday this summer, and that you won't be able to get away from the business for a skiing holiday,' she said with a trace of bitterness. 'Work must come first, of course. But do try not to work so hard. That breakdown was a warning. You must take a few days off from time to time. The children hardly know you. If you're serious about doing better with them, you'll have to begin by spending a little more time down here.'

Charles agreed, and exerted himself to get her to expand on the subject of the children. She showed no reluctance, but chattered on as the shadows lengthened in the long panelled dining room about James and his exams and cricket and tennis – 'You really should come and watch him play, you know' – and Lucy with her passion for horses. Caroline was planning to buy her one if she could show that she was responsible enough to look after it. Charles was reminded that money was no problem in the Fitzpatrick household.

At eleven o'clock she rose from the table to fetch Charles

another brandy. Charles wondered idly what Fitzpatrick's drink bills were like, and found he had a healthy respect for the man's obviously capacious liver. He tried to relax as he drank. But tension would not leave him. He wondered absurdly if he was expected to put out the cat.

At last Caroline rose. 'I feel very tired,' she announced, yawning delicately but without concealment. 'I know I should give you a big welcome back in bed. But quite honestly looking after the children on my own while you've been away has been a lot of extra strain. I should think you're a bit worn too, after your first day back to normal.' She looked at him meaningfully.

'Good heavens, yes,' Charles said, rather too heartily. 'I'll need a day or two to adjust, myself.' He stretched ostentatiously. 'Do you mind if I don't lock up tonight? I feel absolutely whacked all of a sudden.'

Caroline looked at him with slightly surprised relief. Obviously she hadn't imagined he'd take the hint, and was surprised and pleased that he had. 'Of course, darling,' she said. 'Your nightshirt is out, and there's a new toothbrush in the bathroom.' She went off to see to the final chores as Charles ambled slowly upstairs, thankful that he'd found a way to postpone for however short a time an encounter which gave him more qualms than all the Irvines and Kurtzs combined.

He was so wrapped up in his own thoughts that he barely noticed the elegance and femininity of the bedroom. He had time to appreciate the machismo luxury of the panelled dressing room behind whose flush doors yawned vast walk-in cupboards full, to Charles' startled eyes, of more clothes than any ordinary man could hope to wear. He goggled discreetly at the tiled, gadget-filled bathroom, but he was too anxious to be in bed and apparently asleep before Caroline appeared to do more than glance about him.

In the event, he needn't have worried. The nervous strain of a long testing day had tired him more than he had imagined. He was still worrying about feigning sleep when the real thing overtook him. When Caroline came softly into the room he was already deeply asleep, his head buried in the pillow, his arms flung wide. He never moved as she slipped into the other side of the vast bed, and he missed the rather puzzled look she bent on him before she turned out the light and fell asleep in her turn.

Sometime during the night he woke to find himself pressed close to her nylon-clad buttocks, and in process of erection. Impatiently he pulled himself away, and rolled onto his side so that they were back to back. Smiling, he remembered Jenny's words.

'James' love life at home is strictly regulated,' she had said. 'Never, never, wake Caroline up in the middle of the night. She'll either think you think she's Helen, or she'll smell a rat. Just lie back and think sad thoughts if the mood comes upon you.'

He chuckled to himself. Sad thoughts indeed. Smiling, he fell asleep again.

CHAPTER SEVEN

Charles quickly fell into Fitzpatrick's routine. Every morning he caught the 9.09 train from Maidenhead, acknowledging the stiff nods of his fellow-travellers in the first-class compartment, and thanking heaven that British reserve prevented the necessity of starting up a conversation so early in the morning. He was always behind his office desk by ten, with files of correspondence and internal memos ready for his attention. At ten thirty precisely Jenny Barnes would appear with coffee and her notebook ready for dictation. She would run quickly through his appointments, bringing to his notice any important details of the people he was going to meet, or the business he was about to discuss. At one he would leave for lunch, usually with an agent, an author, or a distributor. At three he would return to find his correspondence typed and awaiting his signature. At four, Jenny would bring him tea, and take any further dictation or instructions. At five-thirty he would say goodnight to Jenny, and leave to catch his evening train back to Maidenhead, where Caroline would be waiting with a drink and dinner.

The first weekend had been difficult, but with the help of fine weather, his boat, kept in a rose-covered boathouse at the bottom of the garden, and a fair quantity of vodka, he had got through it with no major solecisms. He had even managed to make rather dutiful love to Caroline, finding her robustly passionate in a matter-of-fact way which left little opening for imagination and seemed strangely out of keeping with what Charles was sure was a genuinely tempestuous personality, albeit kept under rigid control. He thought that life with Fitzpatrick had done much to suppress Caroline's real instincts, and he devoted considerable thought to plans for developing her potential for his physical profit without giving away his secret.

But on Monday something occurred which put all such notions out of his mind, at least for the time being. Jenny reminded him that on Tuesdays he always drove to work, and on his asking why, replied that Tuesday evenings were Helen's evenings, and that afterwards he invariably drove himself home. That evening he was too preoccupied with his own worries to appreciate the fact that Caroline apparently assumed, quite docilely, that this Tuesday would be the same as all the others.

Although his concentration was not what it should have been, somehow Charles managed to struggle through the long office day, including an interminable lunch with a loud and rather intoxicated American publisher. Five o'clock found him restlessly pacing up and down his office, however. Finally he came to a decision, rang for Jenny via the intercom, and went to Fitzpatrick's refrigerator and liquor store behind the rubber plant to mix himself a stiff drink. He didn't look up when Jenny entered the room, simply straightened, took a stiff swallow, and asked over his shoulder, 'Have a drink, Jenny.'

'You know I never drink with you during office hours, James,' she replied crisply.

He turned and glared at her in frustration. 'Oh, for God's sake, drop the perfect secretary number for a bit. I'm scared stiff, and you know it. What's more, you know why. Now have a drink before I do something I shall later regret, like throwing this damned rubber plant at you.'

'If you feel like that . . .' she said, smiling. Without asking, he poured her a vodka, drained his own and poured another for himself.

'Steady,' Jenny said. 'Helen won't appreciate a boozed James, particularly after such a long gap. I'm sure she'll have something special in mind, and she won't want vodka to spoil it.' There was a bitchy note in Jenny's voice which Charles hadn't heard before.

'Tell me again,' he said. 'When am I due?'

'At six thirty precisely,' Jenny began in a sing-song recital, 'you park your car outside her front door at 28 Connaught Mews. You let yourself in, using her key, which is on the same ring as your ignition key and the key to River Lodge. At ten thirty you leave, and you arrive home between eleven fifteen and eleven thirty. What you do in the interval is your problem. Yours and Helen's.' Jenny was talking in crisply normal tones now. 'I'm sure you'll have a perfectly delightful time. And since I'm breaking the rules anyway, I'll have another drink, please.'

Charles sat down behind his desk and stared at her thoughtfully.

'Our mutual friend was distinctly evasive about that interval,' he said slowly. 'I suppose you've no hints to pass on?'

Jenny perched herself half on the edge of his desk. 'As a matter of fact, I don't,' she said. 'James told me very little about Helen, aside from her existence, which he could hardly have hoped to conceal. I'm afraid you're on your own there. If it's any comfort I spoke to him last night, and he was most amused to think of this meeting. Sent you his best wishes.'

'Very helpful,' Charles said drily. 'I'm glad he's in such good form. I suppose there's no chance you would give me his number? I'm not sure that this part of the briefing was entirely adequate.'

'Not a chance, James, you know the rules,' Jenny said sharply. 'Only I make contact, and then only at special times.'

'I suppose you know when and where by watching the personal column in *The Times*,' Charles said with morose facetiousness.

'As a matter of fact, yes,' said Jenny calmly.

Charles looked startled. 'Goodness, isn't that all a bit thirties and E. Philips Oppenheim?'

'But effective,' said Jenny. 'And I shouldn't try and work out how it's done. You'll never guess.' She glanced at her watch. 'Time you left. Brush and comb your hormones.' She smiled, and stood up. 'Good luck. And remember that our mutual friend is a very dominating male in bed. There's a bunch of flowers on my desk. I got them while you were out at lunch. You'd better pick them up on your way down to the garage.'

'You think of everything,' Charles said, a little resentfully.

'Don't I, though?' Jenny said serenely. Then as he reached for his telephone she put her hand on his arm. 'You aren't going to call your wife, are you? I thought you were,' she said. 'Well, don't. She doesn't expect you, and she'll be very surprised if you call.'

Charles withdrew his hand guiltily.

'Just thought I'd remind her I'd be late,' he muttered.

'Don't be silly. She knows about Tuesday nights just as well as I do. Now off you go. Don't keep on trying to put it off.'

'Welcome back, my angel, my darling love.' Charles found himself caught up in a musky-scented tornado as soon as his key turned in the door. The softly female thing planting kisses all over his face was a far cry from the virago of Jermyn Street. All cunning pressure of braless breasts and firmly cushioned hips, silken auburn hair asway above the green jersey dress, arms locked round his neck, Helen was giving him a rousingly passionate welcome. 'Are these for me, my sweet? You are a poppet. And it should be me doing the apologizing. My darling. To hit you. And in the middle of Jermyn Street. And you not drunk, my poor love, but ill, really sick. Can you ever forgive?' Flowers snatched from his nerveless hand, Helen whirled away from him and swirled up

51

the steep flight of steps from the front door, talking continuously and laughing breathlessly.

Wary and tense, Charles followed her up into a handsome sitting room, beautiful but impersonal, as if copied from a photograph in a glossy magazine. This was obviously a bachelor girl's pad, a girl on the way up and moving fast. All chrome, suede and glass, with spotlights and 'focuses of interest'.

'You haven't changed your drinking habits while you've been in the nut-hatch?' Helen came bouncing back into the room from a tiny kitchenette, Jenny's flowers stuffed anyhow into a thin silver vase. She paused to put it on top of an opulent colour television set, and without waiting for a reply sloshed a huge quantity of vodka from an open bottle into a thick heavy crystal tumbler. With a flourish, she tipped in ice and tonic and handed it to him, all in a matter of seconds. Charles barely had time to wonder where she'd learnt to be so slick before he found himself raising his glass in salute.

'Let me look at you,' he said. 'It's been far too long.' Charles congratulated himself on a neat gambit.

Helen paused in the process of pouring herself a gin and Cinzano, and turned, giggling to pose theatrically, her right knee forward, left hand behind her head, lifting her hair. The green jersey material clung to every curve, outlining nipples stiff with arousal. She allowed her tongue to caress her lower lip, and with a sudden wanton gesture slid her right hand sensually up her thigh.

'Remember me?' she said, with deliberately artificial huskiness.

Charles felt suddenly aroused. It showed, he knew, because her eyes caressed him, and her smile deepened.

'I see you do,' she answered herself. She laughed and relaxed. Holding her drink, she walked over to flop into an enormous sofa, and curled her legs under her, exposing a good deal of delectable thigh. She patted the cushion beside her.

'Come and sit down,' she said. 'I've been thinking about the sort of therapy you need, and I've worked out a special game for tonight. You are to decide whether I'm wearing anything under this dress. If you win,' she smiled at him lazily, 'I will be your slave. But if I win, I shall be mistress of the revels.'

Charles stared at her, mesmerized.

'Now tell me, my poppet, all about your incarceration at the nursing home. Incidentally,' she added, 'I got all your messages and carried out all your instructions.'

Charles froze. What messages? Jenny had given no indication of any such thing. He wondered suddenly if Fitzpatrick was engaged in some kind of obscure double cross.

'Good for you,' he said heartily, hoping his confusion was not evident. He made a mental note that Jenny was going to have to contact Fitzpatrick right away.

'So tell me about the nut-hatch.'

'Nothing much to tell.'

Helen leapt to her feet, and began to stride restlessly about the room. 'Now tell me, sir, and tell me true, while you were away how many nurses had you?' She paused to watch him with dark cats' eyes.

'None,' Charles said, mentally crossing his fingers.

'Rubbish,' she said, tilting her glass upwards to drain the contents. She walked over to the bottles to make herself a refill. 'Three months without climbing into bed with anyone? Not you, James. And I bet all those randy nurses were starving for it.' She turned back to him. 'Tell me, James. You know it turns me on.' She sat down again next to him, put her arm round his neck and kissed him hungrily, her tongue hot and sharp and anxious. She pulled his free hand to her breast, and rubbed it over her stiffened nipple. Charles stirred restlessly. His arousal was painfully obvious. She left his hand on her breast to reach down and stroke him through his trousers.

'How many, darling?' she asked huskily.

'None.'

She jumped up again angrily.

'You bloody liar,' she shouted at him. She waved her arms and her drink spilled on the floor. 'I'm not your cold prissy bitch of a wife, you know. I'm Helen Wightman. Remember me? Now tell me, damn you.'

53

'None,' he repeated. Fitzpatrick, he thought was the type to screw every nurse within reach, but since he'd started out this way, he felt he couldn't go back.

Helen bent over him to stare him in the eye. There was a brief silence. Then she sat back down beside him with a sigh.

'My God, your cure has changed you,' she said. 'Before you'd have told me all about it, in graphic detail.'

Charles was worried. The dangers of making an error were too obvious. 'I really had a breakdown,' he said. 'Wasn't interested for the longest time.'

'Sure,' she said, cynically. 'Back to tonight.' She knelt up on the sofa beside him. 'Now tell me,' she said, 'am I wearing any underclothes? And not to touch,' she added, intercepting an exploring hand.

Charles leant back and appeared to concentrate.

'Nothing,' he said, remembering the welcome at the door, and the firm heavy feel of her smooth buttocks.

'Damn you. Your breakdown may have made you less boastful, but you can still read me like a book.' Helen was pouting. Incredibly, it seemed to matter to her that she had lost. She jumped up to walk to the tape deck by the television. 'I've a new tape,' she said. 'Very sexy. Get yourself another drink and see what you think.'

Charles went to the drinks tray, and was grateful that his back was to Helen when the tape began to play. It was blatantly pornographic tape of the sounds and words of passionate love making. As he walked back to the sofa he saw that Helen was sitting with her head flung back over the arm, her eyes closed. Her hand was moving rhythmically in her lap. In the charged room, her sighs and tiny moans kept pace with the incoherent gruntings of the tape. Suddenly her whole body stiffened, and a frown of ecstasy contorted her face. Her hand fell away from her lap, and she opened her eyes, relaxing. For a moment she looked at him vacantly. Then she smiled, and slowly lowered herself across his knees. She began to kiss him with languorous heat.

'Master,' she breathed between kisses, 'the slave requests one last favour.'

The requests on the tape became more and more explicit. Charles, drunk with lust, nodded against her mouth.

'The slave knows the master is a born gambler. Therefore the slave requests that her lord play his favourite game.'

Charles nodded again, helplessly. What on earth could Fitzpatrick's favourite game be?

'What does the slave have in mind?' he mumbled into Helen's ear.

'Strip matchsticks,' she replied, opening her eyes at him in surprise. 'And,' she kissed him enthusiastically 'winner takes all.'

'Suits me,' he said.

Helen uncurled from his knee and stretched across to a coffee table for a box of matches. She was a competitive lady, Charles decided: the thought of a contest roused her to enormous energy and concentration. His main concern, however, was that he had no idea of the rules, and realized that to admit ignorance would be disastrous. He cursed Fitzpatrick. There was no excuse for leaving him in this sort of fix.

Fortunately, Helen was too eager to notice his hesitation.

'I'll start,' she said, firmly. She took three matches in one hand, showed them to him, then put her hands behind her back. Then she brought her two clenched fists back in front of her and held them out to him.

'Where are the matches? In which hand?' she taunted.

With a sigh of inward relief, Charles recognized the game from his schooldays. With a mental prayer that Fitzpatrick hadn't seen fit to add any exotic variations to the rules, he reached out to touch first her left hand then her right.

'Two; one,' he declared.

She turned her hands over and opened them to show two matchsticks in the left hand and one in the right.

'Damn,' she said amiably. She unpinned a gold, diamond-studded brooch from above her breast. 'And you have more clothes than I have, too.'

But after his initial success, Charles' luck ran out. To Helen's increasing excitement he lost almost every subsequent contest. His jacket and tie were long gone. Then his shoes, his socks, his shirt. Finally, with Helen triumphant in her dress, Charles lost his underpants.

'I give in,' he said.

'Now I'm the boss,' she said, delighted.

She grasped him firmly by his penis, and drew him through to her bedroom and the vast kingsize bed. As he lay, almost light-headed with excitement, she abruptly pulled the jersey dress over her head, revealing a superb figure, the breasts taut with anticipation, the tight-curled auburn hair at her crotch dewy. She looked down at him with a throaty laugh.

'Wait a moment,' she said, 'I have a treat for you.' She fumbled with a switch. Charles had a breathtaking view of her breasts from below, the nipples taut and expectant. The lights dimmed, and a beam of brilliant illumination shone from above his head, focussed on the wall at the bed's foot.

'I picked up a blue movie in Soho this morning,' Helen said, joining him on the bed, and throwing a leg over his lap. 'Watch for a moment, lover, it may give you some ideas.'

On the wall, couples lurched and churned in athletic combination. Through the open door came the taped sounds of lust. In the sweaty tangle of the bed, Helen and Charles moved languidly, purposefully, then with frantic syncopated abandon.

She let him rest for a few minutes. 'Now,' she said sulkily, 'I am the master. You are the slave, lie on your back and keep still.'

She slipped a mask, taken from a bedside drawer, over his eyes. Charles felt her tying his wrists to two of the brass rails of the bedhead. He shivered with fearful anticipation.

She began to butterfly kiss his lips, then slowly moved down his body until she reached his crotch.

'O slave,' she murmured, 'you must rise to meet your mistress.'

Gently, expertly, she caressed his inert member with her hands, then as he began to grow firm, with her lips. When he was erect, she began to lick him as if he were an ice-cream, occasionally giving him tiny bites. His legs twisted and turned to gain further advantage of her mouth.

Just as he was about to explode into climax, she turned

away. Charles heard her light a cigarette. 'For Christ's sake, don't leave me now,' he begged.

'Then you must tell me,' she said calmly, expelling some smoke, 'how many nurses you seduced during your rest cure.'

His thoughts cascaded wildly.

'Fourteen,' he ventured.

'Fourteen,' she repeated. It was not an exclamation, more a sigh of satisfaction.

Slowly, she eased herself on top of him and rode him mercilessly until they both reached the winning post.

At ten thirty on the dot, Helen escorted him firmly to the door. Dressed again, her hair combed, smelling clean and fresh from her shower, she could have passed for a girl saying an early goodnight to a boyfriend who had called in for coffee.

'See you next Tuesday,' she said, rather as if confirming a hair appointment.

Charles kissed her chastely on the cheek, and climbed into the Scimitar a trifle stiffly. As he headed the car down the M4 to Marlow, he reflected that Helen was both physically and emotionally a challenge. He could understand why Fitzpatrick had kept so much concealed from Jenny. But he found it hard to believe that he had really found his life so repetitive and boring.

CHAPTER EIGHT

It was on the Friday, just after finishing his first reviving cup of coffee in the office, that Charles stumbled across some surprising facts.

It had already become clear that Fitzpatrick had an excellent system of keeping tabs on his companies without having to see anyone, or spend much time on them. The basis of this control lay in the correspondence system. Three copies were made of each letter written by any employee in the organization. The top copy was posted; the white copy was filed; and the pink copies circulated in a file for each division. It was a rule that every letter was put in the file, so that each file contained a great deal of no importance at all – sheafs of letters acknowledging the receipt of manuscripts, for instance. However, amongst all this dross were real nuggets of value. No director of a subsidiary could hope to conceal his errors – the evidence was freely available to the main board, and particularly to the Chairman, on file, in his own dictation. The file copies were covered in comments and suggestions from Charles' colleagues on the board, and of course Charles himself had a bird's eye view of the entire operation.

The more Charles delved into the files, the more impressed he was with the scope and efficiency of the Fitzpatrick organization. Letters to scientists of international fame, commissioning new works or asking them to check and authenticate other scientists' texts rubbed shoulders in the files with comforting letters to ladies who provided knitting patterns in large quantities for the consumer subdivisions. The sales and marketing efforts of all the divisions were abundantly evident; the company was well equipped to sell throughout the world in the English language everything from technical pamphlets translated from the Chinese – the foundation, and still clearly the base of the group's fortunes – to the large numbers of practical self-help books on knitting, crochet, flower-arranging, needlework, house-plants, cooking, dieting and child-care which the group churned out for the apparently inexhaustible feminine market the world over.

One aspect that surprised Charles was the number and variety of the titles taken by the Chinese, often in exchange for works on Communist theory, particularly those of Chairman Mao, currently enjoying a vast and profitable vogue in the West. He had never suspected that the People's Republic could absorb so many titles on woodworking, candle-making, renovating old furniture, growing tasty vegetables, and the many other occupations which he had always supposed to be the preserve of the British middle classes. But there it was. Through Hong Kong, and through the privileged channels in Peking originally negotiated by Fitzpatrick when the company was founded, vast numbers of titles like these flowed into China to the group's great profit.

Charles had been examining the accounts of the various companies within the Fitzpatrick group. Each group reported monthly, and the reports were consolidated into a total. As an accountant himself, Charles, while impressed by the form and structure of the accounts, which provided all the key information with which to judge the profitability of each publication, had been unable to resist the opportunity to do some cross-checking on his own account. He had spread the different sets of accounts across his desk, and was happily playing with his electronic calculator, when a number of oddities caught his trained eye.

The first anomalies turned up in the costs and revenues of the Fitzpatrick company's foreign sales. He had been impressed by the efforts made by the company to sell rights and co-editions of its products worldwide, beyond the traditional British market – the Commonwealth, as constituted in 1948. The concept of the traditional market was breaking down, largely under pressure from ambitious American companies with greedy eyes on the rich markets of Australia, South Africa and Nigeria. As a result, it was increasingly important for any British publisher to establish worldwide nets which allowed them to take a share from sales not only in America but also in France, Germany, Holland, Spain, Portugal, Scandinavia, even in quite small markets such as Turkey and Yugoslavia. At least twenty salesmen were employed by the various subsidiaries of the group to organize just this. They were well-paid, and received lavish expenses for a life-style that was elegant by any standard. Entertaining foreign buyers was not only allowable as an expense against tax, it was also extremely costly. The restaurants were of the best, and the hotels were always four star. They travelled first class, and they threw parties in princely style. But according to the figures, they made very little money. Indeed, although their turnover was high, their profit contribution to the group was pitifully small.

Charles frowned over his calculations, and checked them

again. When there could be no doubt as to the accuracy of his conclusions, he buzzed for Jenny Barnes.

Jenny looked at his figures with noncommittal self-possession. 'This is really Tom Irvine's affair,' she said. 'I should take it up with him when he gets back from New York.'

'Jenny, I can't sit behind this desk as a cipher. Our friend knew my background, and must have expected me to earn at least part of my keep. Get in touch with him. If he's not aware of this situation, he should be. And bring me the back files on the export figures, and also the correspondence on the foreign printing contracts. There seem to be some oddities there too. Is there no chance that I can speak to him myself? It would be much easier to explain at first hand.'

Jenny frowned. 'I can ask, but that was not the arrangement,' she said coolly. 'I still think you should wait till Irvine is back from New York, and take it up with him.'

'Jenny, has it occurred to you that some of this may be Irvine's fault? In any case, at this stage I need more facts, and I think James should be informed.' Charles was insistent.

'Oh, very well, I will see what I can do.' Jenny seemed reluctant. 'As for the other files you asked for, I can easily get you the back export figures. But you'll have to buzz Tom Irvine's secretary for the printing figures. That is strictly Irvine's business. I do urge you to wait. I don't think the Chairman would like you to dig too closely into what's not your business.' Charles noticed that she still talked of Fitzpatrick as the Chairman. Which I suppose he is, Charles thought.

'Jenny, if this arrangement is going to work long term, I must be allowed to pull my weight. If that wasn't in the original contract, then it should have been, and it's a bit late to go all broody and secretive now.' Charles pressed the buttons on his calculator at random while he tried to find an effective argument. 'Look, I've got problems enough as it is. How will it help to allow the Fitzpatrick group to go bankrupt?'

Jenny shrugged. 'I'll do my best,' she said, 'but it may take a while.'

'Never mind,' said Charles. 'That gives me a bit more time to organize my figures.'

Jenny left as Charles was trying to decide how best to approach the problem of the printing figures. He had noticed that there were wide variations in printing costs, and so in profit margins, here and there throughout the group, and there seemed no obvious explanation. But it was the managing director's bailiwick, and it wouldn't do to make it seem that there was an open breach between chairman and managing director.

He leant forward, and buzzed Jenny. 'Cancel my lunch appointment, would you,' he said. 'And tell me how I get to Irvine's office.' A personal visit to Irvine's secretary might be a lot more productive than a phone call, he decided.

Jenny's reply was cool, but Charles, feeling that he was hot upon some sort of scent, and not of red herrings, was too preoccupied to notice. As he swept down the corridor towards Irvine's office, he was quite unaware of the stir he caused among the smaller secretarial fry, many of whom had never actually seen the chairman in the flesh before. Irvine's secretary was flustered but cooperative. She hunted through the filing cabinets for all the correspondence she could find, and Charles bore off in triumph a massive armful of buff folders.

Back in his office, he found another sizeable array of files on his desk. Jenny had produced the export files, however reluctantly. He smiled to himself, and buzzed her yet again. 'Jenny, I'm not to be disturbed until further notice for any reason at all.'

'Yes, Mr Fitzpatrick.' Jenny's tone was arctic. Charles chuckled aloud as he turned to the mass of work on his desk.

Charles was quickly confirmed in his view that the affairs of the export sales department merited a close look. The back files showed that a marked deterioration in profit margins had taken place some four years before, and that apparently either this had not been spotted, or it had been overlooked. When he'd established the facts to his satisfaction, he leant forward to send for Jenny. With his finger on the switch he paused, thought for a moment, then slowly leant back without pressing it. He looked with distaste at the dictating machine, then reluctantly switched it on and picked up the microphone. Better to talk to the machine, however soulless, than to Jenny in her present mood. For ten minutes he recited facts and figures. Then he played back a sample, nodded to himself and took off the spool to replace it with a fresh one. There was no way, he thought, that Fitzpatrick could ignore this evidence. He slipped the used spool into a drawer of his desk.

The printing discrepancies proved a more elusive and complex problem. The Fitzpatrick group owned no printing companies of its own, but placed its work wherever it seemed best. Some of the books were produced in Britain, some in the United States, some in Europe, in Singapore, in Hong Kong, in Japan, some even behind the Iron Curtain. A lot of the business was in co-editions, where the same book would be printed for different publishers in several different languages. This demanded skilled administration, to get the translated texts from a variety of foreign companies in an organized schedule which allowed the printer to make his operation continuous, the basis for the sometimes massive savings in costs. It was clear that taking into account the various destinations of the finished products, the freight costs, the length of credit offered (often particularly generous behind the Iron Curtain, where nations were desperate for foreign exchange) and other factors, the Fitzpatrick companies had bought their printing at the cheapest possible price.

But there were five contracts on which the company had inexplicably placed work at fifteen to twenty-five per cent above competitive tenders, in spite of protests from within the group. Each of these had been personally negotiated by the managing director, according to the initials on the costing sheets, and each had been with the same printer in Hong Kong.

Charles puzzled over this for some time, reluctant to come to the obvious conclusion: that Irvine was taking some sort of kick-back and so defrauding the company he managed. Finally, he dictated a long account of his investigation, and headed back down the corridor to Irvine's office. It might be that there was some correspondence somewhere which would put a more innocent complexion on the affair. Irvine's secretary was again flustered but helpful. No correspondence showed up, however, and Charles felt handicapped because he was unwilling to reveal precisely what he wanted, and certainly not why. At last he brought up the name of the Hong Kong company. Irvine's secretary looked relieved.

'Oh,' she said. 'You should have said, Mr Fitzpatrick. That correspondence doesn't go into the regular files. Mr Irvine keeps that himself in his own office. But I'm afraid the filing cabinet's locked, and only Mr Irvine has the key.'

Increasingly suspicious, Charles returned to his office, added this last piece of information to his tape, and then rang for Jenny. There was no reply. Frowning, he glanced at the digital clock on his desk. It was only just after five. He rang again. Finally he got up to investigate. It was most unlike Jenny not be be on call. Her office, predictably, was empty. More to the point, her coat was gone, and the cover was over her typewriter. Clearly she'd left for the day, and without informing him. Puzzled and a little angry, Charles returned to his office, and began to stuff things into his own brief-case. There didn't seem a lot of point in lingering around. As an afterthought he took the second tape from his dictating machine, and went to put it in the drawer with the other. He paused with the drawer open before him, stunned. The first tape was gone.

CHAPTER NINE

That weekend Charles was a very preoccupied man. Caroline couldn't fail to notice his abstraction, and did her best to see to it that the children didn't distract him more than necessary. All Saturday he brooded in the Fitzpatrick library, surfacing only for meals and the odd drink. He was reduced to putting everything down on paper in his sprawling handwriting, reading it, grunting with dissatisfaction, and then destroying his handiwork – only to start the process all over again. The problem was quite simple, and virtually without solution: his status as Chairman de facto of the Fitzpatrick organization was such a shadowy one in practice, much less in law, that he had no real power to deal with Irvine and his peculations.

Undoubtedly, the right thing would be to consult Fitzpatrick. But not only did Jenny seem strangely reluctant to do so, but Charles was forced to recognize his own suspicion that she knew a lot more about the whole affair than she had been willing to admit, and he didn't fancy using her as an intermediary. It also occurred to him with increasing force that Fitzpatrick himself almost had to be involved, although in what capacity Charles found it impossible to judge. The Charles who eventually dragged himself to bed, morose, only to lie, hands clasped behind his head, staring into the darkness oblivious of certain gentle nudgings and hintings from Caroline was a far cry from the normally ebullient and generally bouncy creature she was becoming accustomed to as a post-breakdown James.

Sunday morning dawned fine, and promised a perfect day. With an effort, Charles thrust aside his problems, and took note of the fact that the sun shone, the temperature was set for the high seventies, a light breeze blew, and the river looked particularly inviting.

He smiled across the breakfast table at Caroline.

'Why don't we have a picnic today?' he suggested.

'Oh, yes, Daddy, yes,' Lucy cried, and James emerged from behind his portion of *The Sunday Times* to chime in with enthusiasm.

They set off at noon in their skiff. Charles took one pair of oars, James the other. Caroline sat on the cushions in the stern, steering with two blue ropes which controlled the rudder. She looked particularly fetching in a clinging pink tee-shirt, navy slacks, and a huge, incongruously elegant, straw hat with a wisp of pink tulle tied round the crown. Lucy sat in the bows, trailing her hand in the Thames and getting splashed whenever Charles or James caught a crab, which was frequently. Charles himself was clad only in a faded pair of bathing trunks, and he tugged at his oars in fierce concentration, as if every set of rings pushed down stream was a paralyzing memo designed to crush Irvine, and subdue Fitzpatrick.

After half an hour's hard pull, they paused for breath, and Caroline unpacked drinks – vodka for Charles, cider for Lucy,

James and herself – while they rested. A curious cow stretched down over them from the bank and snuffled sedately at a delighted Lucy. Once a big white cruiser roared past them as if on its way to a fire, the wash rocking the skiff till their drinks spilled, and Caroline was forced to stand up and brush cider off the lap of her slacks. They laughed a lot. It was a happy day.

They picknicked on an island, lighting a bonfire and roasting sausages on sticks, and baking potatoes wrapped in foil in the embers. Charles taught the children how to spear a sausage on a stick and balance it over a forked twig so that it would cook without burning, and without constant attention. He caught Caroline's eyes on him, but was too contented to care that he was stepping out of character.

Rowing back down stream as dusk was falling, Lucy sat in the stern with Caroline, and drifted off to sleep, relaxed against her shoulder, Charles and James tried a verse or two of the Eton Boating Song, but couldn't remember the words. Caroline laughed at them, and sang herself, snatches of Gilbert and Sullivan. Charles and James joined in the choruses, slightly off key. With boastful expertise they slipped the skiff into their boathouse. Tired, grubby, dishevelled, they stumbled happily up the lawn to the house, Charles with a sleeping Lucy in his arms. Caroline and he undressed her together, and tucked her into bed, unwashed and muttering querulously as she was half woken. She was leagues deep before they had closed the bedroom door behind them.

James yawned cavernously a time or two, and then, with sleepy goodnights all round, went off to bed himself. Caroline brought Charles a big snifter of brandy, and came to sit on the arm of his chair. She looked at him with surprise and affection.

'Thanks for a marvellous day, darling,' she said. 'The children had a super time. And so did I. You know, you really have changed. A few months ago, you'd have filled the house with your business cronies, and none of us would have seen anything of you except for meals. You never used to take the slightest interest in the children. Yet today you played with them all afternoon, and if you were bored you certainly didn't show it. You can say what you like, but I think it's a great improvement.' They sat together in comfortable silence, looking out over the river as the light finally faded, and warm little lights sprang up in the cruisers moored opposite. Then Caroline stood up and took his hand.

'Come on,' she said. 'Bed. You'll be back in the office tomorrow, and you need your sleep.'

She led him upstairs, and in the privacy of the big soft bed they made slow contented love.

'That was nice, darling,' she said affectionately when they had finished. 'You know, you've even changed in bed.' She sighed drowsily and turned to snuggle into his shoulder.

'How?' Charles asked cautiously.

'You're actually considerate.' She fell asleep.

Charles was still wondering about Fitzpatrick, and his lack of appreciation of the luck he had had in his family and wife, when he too drifted off.

Later that night, Charles woke struggling from a nightmare in which he was chasing Irvine down the endless mugger-infested canyons of New York, his feet apparently encased in treacle, to find Caroline bending over him in the darkness.

'Wake up, darling,' she was saying gently. 'It's all right. It's all right, I'm here.'

For a moment Charles forgot who and what he was and clutched at her for simple comfort. She yielded delightfully in his arms, comforting him with soothing hands and gentle kisses.

Then with sudden decision she pulled herself away, sat up and whipped her nightdress off over her head. He was about to protest when she smothered his incoherent words with a soft and hungry mouth.

'Don't talk, darling,' she sighed into his ear. 'Just take me.' With quick supple movements she adjusted herself above him, and urged him into a long, slow, deeply satisfying rhythm. As they surged to a climax she smothered a long cry in his shoulder, sharp little teeth biting down passionately.

Without a word they fell apart. As he drifted into a velvet

darkness, Charles remembered Jenny's voice: 'Think sad thoughts.' Much she knows, he thought with satisfaction, and fell asleep.

CHAPTER TEN

Monday found Charles submerged in instant crisis.

He came into the office determined to have it out with Jenny, to find her waiting for him, seated decorously in her hard secretarial chair beside his desk. She had his tape in her hand, and was bent over the dictating machine, about to insert it. At the sound of the opening door she looked up, not at all disconcerted.

'Good morning, James,' she said. 'I have a message for you.'

'You've seen our friend, then.' Charles turned to make sure the door was closed behind him.

'I've talked to the Chairman, yes,' she said. 'And he explained the matters you were worried about, and told me to wipe off this very indiscreet tape.' She looked at him indignantly.

Charles was taken aback. 'You mean you just took it, without so much as a by-your-leave?'

Jenny frowned. 'Remember who you work for,' she said crisply. 'The Chairman was most impressed that you'd picked up the point about the export profit margins. But he doesn't want you interfering. It happens that he sold the rights to all the company's foreign sales four years ago to a Swiss company for £20,000. The deal is that the Fitzpatrick company receives a royalty of five per cent on all such sales. The balance and all the profits on co-edition printing for different languages go to the Swiss company.'

'I can see that if the company was in a cash bind, £20,000 might be a godsend,' Charles said. 'But it wasn't. Surely he's simply giving the money away on today's turnover.'

Jenny smiled. 'The Swiss company is owned by James and Tom Irvine, eighty per cent and twenty per cent. It's a tax dodge, really. The Internal Revenue gets the tax on the five per cent royalties, but they get precious little, because the costs almost balance it out. All the real profits go to Switzerland. So no tax is paid, and the money is outside the sterling area, and beyond the control of the Bank of England.'

Very simple, Charles thought. And very clever.

'The Chairman added something else,' Jenny said. 'He said you mustn't interfere with Tom Irvine. He has the Chairman's complete confidence.'

'That's impossible,' Charles said flatly. He reached into his brief case and produced the second tape. 'If you'd waited on Friday night, you could have taken this tape with you. I've thought about it all weekend, and there's no doubt that it proves that Irvine is swindling the company, taking kickbacks from a printer in Hong Kong. I have a responsibility to look after the affairs of the Fitzpatrick group. I can't carry that out if I'm not allowed to question any action of the managing director's. Fitzpatrick can't have known about this fiddle. And he must. If Irvine hasn't a good explanation he'll have to go. There's no alternative.'

Jenny looked a little taken aback. 'You'd better give me that tape,' he said. 'I'll pass it on. But in the meantime you're to take no action at all on anything concerning Irvine.'

Charles handed her the tape reluctantly. 'You know, this is a ludicrous situation,' he added. He was very angry.

Jenny got up and walked past him to the door. With her hand on the handle, she turned to him.

'Maybe,' she said. 'But you're being very well paid to put up with it.'

Charles was still fuming when the next bombshell arrived, in the form of a cable from New York. It was wordily discreet, but in essence it was a long cry of 'Help!' from an obviously harassed Irvine. The Kurtz situation had got completely out of hand, and the Chairman's intervention was essential if the group wasn't to lose its entire investment in the Kurtz operation. Charles looked at it in dismay, and sent for Jenny.

He waved the flimsy at her. 'Now perhaps you'll understand the problem. What do you suggest I do about this, with no authority over Irvine, and no instructions from the boss?' He slapped the cable onto the desk in front of her.

She read it carefully twice, and looked at him. 'I can't reach the Chairman at the moment even if I wanted to,' she said. 'You'll just have to play this one by ear. I suggest you arrange to leave for the States tonight. I'll fix a plane ticket, and I'll warn Helen you won't be there tomorrow. Caroline I leave to you. But remember. No fighting with Tom Irvine. Whatever you suspect – and I can't believe that the Chairman doesn't know, or that it's dishonest – you'll have to declare a truce for the time being.' She smiled at him a little maliciously. 'Stan Kurtz is an ex-paratrooper. You'll need all the help you can get to handle him, without quarrelling with Tom on the side.'

Charles swivelled his chair round and looked out over Soho Square. He thought for a moment, and then said, his back to Jenny, 'The American company is into U.S. banks for four million dollars of unsecured loans. It's got a bad cash-flow problem, because supermarkets have too much clout to have to pay their bills on time, and they don't care much about books anyway, not even a fast-selling line like the encyclopedias we sell them. Advertising costs are going up all the time, and profit margins are chopped to the bone. From the figures – and remember, Jenny, I'm an accountant, and I know what I'm talking about – they need a sizeable injection of capital which they can only get from this country, or they'll be in danger of going under. Yes, I'll go over to the States. But this is one problem I'll handle myself, my way. The last time I saw Fitzpatrick he told me Irvine wasn't to be relied on for policy decisions, so you and your blasted Chairman will just have to leave this to me to sort out.' He spun round to face her, his expression grim. 'Any objections?'

'Of course not,' Jenny said coolly. 'Don't be so touchy. I'll get in touch with the Chairman as soon as possible, and if he's any comments to make I'll cable them to your hotel. I imagine you'll be staying at the Plaza? But I'm sure he'd tell me to leave it to you.' She smiled at him. 'Remember to read Kate Simon on New York while you're on the plane. The Chairman knows the city pretty well.'

A sense of rather childish satisfaction at being one up on both Jenny and Fitzpatrick carried him through a turbulent morning of frantic phone calls and altered arrangements. The most difficult, he found, was to soothe Caroline. She was uncomplaining, but sounded so obviously disappointed that he wouldn't be home that he felt a twinge of real conscience. As he put the phone down it occurred to him that it would be a complication, though a pleasant one, if she were to fall in love with him. For some reason the idea made him feel a surge of self-confidence. Nothing could prevent him from dealing satisfactorily with New York, and when he got back he'd fix Irvine – and Fitzpatrick too, for good measure.

That confidence was only a blurred memory as Charles sat, barely awake, in the Wall Street office of Wildenstein, Schranke and Svoboda, the company's attorneys, gazing down at the raucous traffic jam below him. Irvine had met him at Kennedy Airport as he stumbled off the plane, his whole metabolism sagging from jet-lag and a feeling of unreality. In the long drive into Manhattan in the hired Cadillac, Charles was briefed on the situation.

It transpired that the colourful President of the Fitzpatrick Corporation, New York, had been going to the dogs, or rather, too often to Las Vegas. He'd always been a gambler, and with the eighty thousand a year of his salary, with another fifty thousand commission on profits yearly, and his generous expense allowance, he could afford to be. But with the company grossly over-borrowed on the money market, the fact that Kurtz was rumoured to owe more than half a million in gaming debts, possibly to loan sharks, was a real disaster.

As Irvine pointed out, the banks only had to get a hint of the company President's irresponsibility, and they would withdraw their credit facilities at once. There was no alternative but to replace Kurtz immediately. With the vote of Bob Woodward, Kurtz' second-in-command, on their side, Charles and Irvine had the power to push Kurtz off the board and out of his job. Behind Charles in the office, Jim Stevenson, their lawyer, was going through the constitution of the company, and Kurtz' employment contract, clause by clause. A slip in the legality of Kurtz' dismissal could be very costly.

Charles listened to the murmur of worried conversation behind him without taking it in. Manhattan on a murky summer day was steamy and impossible. Even in the updraught of the air conditioning, Charles felt himself gasping for breath.

Stevenson had finished going through the legal papers, and was checking his notes. He looked up as Charles turned.

'I hope you appreciate, James, he said, 'that Kurtz won't go without a fight. He's a violent man and a highly intelligent one. Your board meeting tomorrow will be no pushover. You'd better get together with Woodward and Tom here over breakfast and rehearse what you're going to say. Of course we'll give you all the support we can, but I, naturally, have no vote, and with the best will in the world, Tom and Woodward can't do anything without you. So the confrontation will be up to you.'

Charles shrugged wearily. 'I know,' he said. 'There's no need to rub it in. I only hope I'll feel a bit livelier tomorrow. I couldn't face down a crippled Sunday-school teacher in my present state.'

Stevenson and Irvine looked at him sympathetically. 'Perhaps you'd better check in at the Plaza and get some sleep,' the latter said. 'Jim and I will sort out any details and report to you tomorrow morning.'

Charles nodded agreement, and bent to pick up his briefcase and over-night bag. A thought swam sluggishly up through his tired brain. 'Do you think we ought just to buy him out?' he said slowly. 'Wouldn't it be easier all round? I swear it'll come to that in the end anyway.'

Irvine and Stevenson looked shocked. 'But that may cost millions,' Stevenson said. 'No, no. He hasn't a leg to stand on. We'll get him out all right. Just don't hint that you ever even thought of a compromise. He's sharp. He'll take the company for all he can get if he thinks it'll work.'

Charles looked at them a little blearily. 'Oh well, I daresay you know best,' he said. 'One thing's for sure. I'm no good without some sleep. Can't think straight.' He yawned. 'Good night, or rather, good afternoon. I'm off.'

Kurtz was charm itself when Irvine and Charles entered his office the next morning. He was tall, well-built, with greying hair and the manner of an elder statesman, though Charles knew he was only forty nine. Behind his desk was a big grainy photograph of himself in action as a paratrooper. The years had not diluted the effect of uninhibited toughness.

'It sure is nice to see you, James,' he pumped Charles' hand. The empasis on the last word and the glance he shot at Irvine hinted that he had greater confidence in Fitzpatrick than he had in his subordinates.

He chatted amiably on as he distributed the copies of the latest financial statements, the agenda for the board meeting and other papers, asking after Caroline and the children, and recalling how much he had enjoyed staying at River Lodge. Charles was surprised. There had been no mention, in the dossiers, of Kurtz visiting London. He seemed a little put out at the presence of Stevenson, but there was no hint that he'd been alerted to his danger.

Kurtz called the meeting to order, and worked steadily through the agenda, lingering on the financial statements. He admitted that these were disappointing, but said that there was an upturn on the way, and that sales forecasts for the immediate future were good, with profit margins projected to rise sharply. By the time he reached any-other-business, his manner was expansive and he was exuding confidence. Clearly he considered that James was behind him. Charles was a little surprised that he didn't refer to the capital he was requesting from the parent company, but supposed that Kurtz was waiting to put some private pressure to bear, probably over a poker game.

Kurtz would have gone on without a pause to close the meeting, but he was interrupted by Stevenson.

'There is another matter,' Stevenson said. He spoke with an air of detachment.

'What's that?' Kurtz was eager to please.

'Your dismissal as Chairman and President of the Fitz-patrick Corporation.' Stevenson exaimined his steepled fingers with interest.

Kurtz went white. The shock stunned him into silence.

'I now call upon Mr Fitzpatrick,' the lawyer continued calmly.

Uncomfortably, Charles began to read out a long statement prepared the day before and checked off at the breakfast table. It listed a variety of offences Kurtz was alleged to have committed, many of them admittedly hearsay. Stevenson had pointed out that under U.S. law offences discovered after the dismissal of an employee can only be used to justify the firing if they've been listed before it, so it was customary to put into the original indictment every conceivable accusation, and to hunt round afterwards for justification. Charles hadn't liked the idea, but had been persuaded to accept it.

Kurtz barely listened to the catalogue. So stunned was he that he failed even to vote against his own dismissal and his replacement by Charles.

After the vote was taken and the result announced, there was a long embarrassed silence. Charles watched with alarm as Kurtz' face turned from ashen white to red, the veins beginning to stand out. His hands gripped the edge of the table with such force the fingers paled to the knuckle. Patches of purple began to spread above his cheekbones. Charles wondered if he was about to have a stroke.

With an obvious effort Kurtz stood up.

'This is a fix!' he roared. 'A fix! I've got no witnesses here, and I damn well should have my lawyer.'

He rounded on Woodward. 'You slimy sonofabitch,' he said with a careful restraint more ominous than his previous outburst. 'I've taught you everything you know about this business. And now you weasel behind my back for my job.' For a moment he glared at Woodward, eye to eye. Woodward quailed.

He turned slowly to Charles, and spoke with chilling emphasis. 'I would never have expected this of you, James Fitzpatrick. I thought you were my friend. More important, I thought you were straight, no backstabber.'

He swept up his papers, and strode to the door. It slammed behind him with a reverberating crash. The four men looked at each other askance and in silence. Finally Woodward stood up.

'Come into my office,' he said. His hands were shaking.

Sheepishly, they filed into the paper-filled cupboard Woodward claimed as his own. There were only just enough hard chairs to seat them all.

Woodward sat behind his desk, nervously fumbling with a letter-opener. 'What if he just walks back to his office and carries on as if he were still Chairman and President?' he said.

They sat glumly, considering this possibility.

'James had better move into Stan's office and sit at his desk. Then he *can't* sit there,' Irvine suggested lamely.

Stevenson looked at them with contempt. He produced a typed document from his briefcase.

'This is a letter forbidding Kurtz to enter his office,' he said. 'If he tries to ignore this, we can post marshalls to keep him out.'

Woodward was not reassured, and the four found themselves making stilted conversation as they waited for some signal that Kurtz had gone. When Charles found himself referring inanely to the weather, he began to wonder if all this was really happening.

At last a telephone rang. Woodward pulled the instrument out of the bottom right hand drawer of his desk, lifted the receiver and listened without a word. He replaced the receiver, and returned the phone to the drawer.

'It's over,' he said, clearly relieved. 'He's gone.' He noticed his visitors' surprise. 'Private line,' he explained apologetically. 'I kept it locked when I was out.' He indicated the two phones on his desk. 'Bugged,' he said. 'Stan used to keep tapes.'

Charles' eyebrows rose.

'Paranoid,' Woodward explained.

Irvine pointed to a handsome rawhide whip coiled on the desk next to the telephones. 'What's that for?' he asked.

Woodward's face lit up. 'Very useful,' he said. 'I've been practising with it for months. Want to see how it works?'

Irvine nodded, hypnotized.

Woodward pressed an intercom button. 'Mrs Goldberg, could you please come in, holding an envelope?'

The door opened and Woodward's grey-haired, middle-aged secretary came in, gingerly holding an envelope at arm's length. Woodward grabbed the whip with his right hand. The lash snaked out. There was a crack like a gun-shot as the broad tip slashed the envelope from the woman's hand. As it fluttered to the floor, Woodward expertly caught the returning thong, and began to recoil it. Mrs Goldberg smiled approvingly, and left.

'I've known for months that Stan would have to go,' Woodward said happily, replacing the whip by his phones. 'I've been practising with this whip so that if he comes through that door with a gun in his hand I can knock it straight to the floor.' He beamed at his visitors.

Charles and Irvine looked at the door with some apprehension.

'Wouldn't a gun be more useful?' Charles asked tentatively.

Woodward pulled open another drawer and produced a long thin stiletto 'paperweight'. 'And I've got this,' he said.

'Armed to the teeth,' murmured Irvine sarcastically.

'You seriously believe that Stan might try to kill you?' Charles asked curiously.

'You better believe it,' Woodward said. 'Not in front of witnesses, though.' The door opened, and Woodward grabbed for the whip. Mrs Goldberg came in with a tray of coffee. Woodward put the whip down and exploded: 'For God's sake use the intercom before you come in.' His secretary nodded, flustered and hastily put down the coffee, spilling it slightly, before hurrying out.

Charles and Irvine were glad to leave Woodward and his fears behind and seek some lunch. Stevenson took them to the Copenhagen on West 58th street for smorgasbord and aquavit. Over open sandwiches he amused them with tales of baling Kurtz out of his gambling problems. One weekend Kurtz had

75

lost sixty-five thousand dollars in six hours in a New York gambling joint. When the owner tackled him for the money, he had had the gall to tell the man that since the game was illegal under New York State law, he couldn't recover the money and to offer a mere twenty-one thousand in compensation. Stevenson said the deal was strictly above board, but the negotiations had been rough. Charles suddenly felt a certain sympathy for Woodward and his arsenal.

'By the way,' Stevenson said, 'are you listed at the Plaza?'

'What do you mean?' Charles asked.

'Some hotels are careless,' Stevenson explained. 'If someone calls you, and you aren't in, they will often give your room number so the caller can get straight through next time. So you can get unwelcome visitors.' He sipped his aquavit thoughtfully. 'Of course, if you're unlisted, they just say you aren't in the hotel unless the caller can give your correct room number.' He looked at Charles blandly. 'If you were to die, James, the Chairmanship and Presidency of the Fitzpatrick Corporation would automatically revert to Kurtz, under the company's constitution.'

'Scarcely a motive for murder,' Charles said with conscious bravado.

'Hit men don't cost a lot in New York,' Stevenson said calmly, 'and Stan owes one hell of a lot of money to some pretty tough and well-connected characters.'

Lunch over and pleasantries exchanged, Stevenson went back to his office, and Charles and Irvine returned to Charles' suite at the Plaza to discuss the financial implications of the morning's events. Despite themselves, they kept coming back to Stevenson's oblique warning. Finally they decided that people just didn't wander about killing other people in top-class hotels, even in violent New York.

All the same, Charles was not wholly reassured, and when, after a drink and some sandwiches, he and Irvine agreed to call it a day, he found himself checking his defences in an apprehensive way. His suite was on the eighteenth floor, with a view over Central Park. The rooms were furnished in a bastard Hepplewhite-Regency style. The sitting-room had an enormous semi-circular sofa, and two rather uncomfortable arm-chairs framed in wood painted in white and gold. Heavy yellow curtains framed the windows and muffled the sound of the air-conditioning. Off the sitting-room was a tiny kitchen/pantry, stocked with drink. As Charles prepared for bed, he went to fetch a stiff vodka from the bottles in the small but well-stocked refrigerator.

The bedroom contained two single beds, pushed together and backed with a high Regency headboard. Charles checked the fitted cupboards for intruders, and, feeling a trifle foolish, the curtains. Satisfied that he was alone, he undressed and got into bed. He put his unfinished drink on the bedside table and phoned the desk to arrange for a flight back to London the next day. Then he lay back and considered what he had learnt about Irvine, sipping his drink thoughtfully.

Almost in spite of himself, he found that he had an increased respect for the man, crook or no. There had been a quiet, un-fazed force about Irvine in the Kurtz deliberations which was in marked contrast to the witterings of Woodward, and even, thought Charles, to the flamboyant posturing of Fitzpatrick as he knew him. Charles decided that Irvine might make a good friend, but would certainly constitute a determined enemy. As he finished his drink and turned to switch off the light, he made a mental note to be wary of underestimating the man-aging director, who clearly had hidden depths.

Charles woke up with a start. It was still dark and only the diffuse orange light of the street lamps reflecting on the ceiling faintly illuminated the room. He fumbled for his watch, and succeeded in knocking over his forgotten glass, which thumped to the carpeted floor. It was three a.m. Charles frowned. Eight in the morning in London. Probably he was still adjusted to British time. His mouth was dry, and tasted stale. With a wide yawn, he slid his feet over the edge of the bed and began to pad towards the kitchen and a drink.

He was half way across the unlighted floor of the sitting-room when a voice stopped him in his tracks.

'Don't move,' it said.

Charles looked towards the window, and thought he could make out the dim outline of a man, and a hint of the metallic gleam of a gun-barrel in the raised hand. Instinctively he hurled himself toward the unseen feet in a rugger tackle. There was a soft coughing explosion above him, and a heavy grunt as his shoulder met a pair of hard shins and his attacker toppled to the floor. The two bodies twined and twisted on the floor, rolling to and fro. There was a crash as the gun left Charles' assailant's hand and smashed against the wall.

Under Charles' frantic hands a denim coat twisted, and buttons popped audibly. The struggling figure smelt sourly sweaty, and had a musky odour Charles recalled from Nigeria. Surely his attacker was black.

By now the struggle was centred on the gun. Charles was fully occupied in preventing his opponent from reaching the spot on the floor where it appeared to have thudded, his assailant in dragging himself to it. For a moment the black man tore himself free of Charles' grasp. Desperately Charles rolled towards him. There was a crash, startlingly loud, as a chair was knocked smashing against the wall. For a moment there was silence aside from the sound of laboured breathing. Then with a stifled moan, Charles' assailant plunged towards the door, wrenched it open, and stumbled out into the corridor. Charles saw a bulky outline against the lights, and as he regained his feet, heard the thud of footsteps, and then the heavy slam of the fire door at the end of the passage. By the time Charles had reached the door, the corridor was empty.

Charles switched on the sitting-room light and closed his door. For the moment all he could think of was a drink. He staggered wearily to the kitchen, drained by reaction, and poured himself a stiff vodka, neat. He swallowed it hastily, and poured himself another. The sharp bite of the liquor brought back his presence of mind. Glass in hand he went back to his bedroom to call the night desk.

A knock on the door heralded the house detective. The man wore a grubby raincoat over striped pyjamas, and had the tousled look of the newly awakened. Charles described the incident as coherently as possible, and showed the man the abandoned gun. The detective looked at it sullenly.

'Gloves?' he asked.

'I'm afraid so.' Charles shuddered as he remembered the sticky feel of rubber on his flesh.

'What makes you think he was black?'

'I smelled him. After years in Nigeria there's no mistaking that particular smell.'

'Wanna make a complaint?' The detective sounded discouraging.

'Should I?'

'Your privilege. But if you bring in the cops you'll be stuck here for days. And they'll never find anyone. This sort of thing happens all the time in this city. We do our best, but you can't stop the bastards. D'you chain your door?'

'Well, no. I didn't think of it.'

'There you are, you see. These guys all have pass keys. Can't stop 'em. Can't change the locks all the time. Always warn out-of-towners to chain their doors. They always forget.'

'Hadn't I better check to see if he's he's taken anything?'

'Sure. But if you saw him run off he can't have taken much, can he? Guess he didn't have time.'

'What about the bullet, though? Damn it, the guy might have killed me.'

'Never have touched you if you hadn't attacked him. 'Nother thing we tell out-of-towners.'

'All right, have it your way. We'll forget it, I suppose.'

'Sensible. Management'll forget your bill this trip, for the disturbed night. Next time you'll take precautions, eh?'

'Sure.' Charles was bitter. 'Any time you want an object lesson for your damned out-of-towners, don't hestitate to quote me.'

'Right.' The detective was owlish.

'Well, I'd better get back to bed. Thanks for your help.' Charles tried hard to let the irony show.

'No sweat.' He'd obviously failed.

The detective left without a farewell, and Charles carefully chained the door behind him.

*

Next morning, as Irvine took him by limousine to the airport, Charles recounted a watered-down version of the night's events. Irvine was shocked.

'You don't think it was Kurtz, do you?' he said.

'Don't know. Could have been, I suppose.' Charles wondered if Stevenson's warnings had been as casual as he'd assumed at the time.

'I'll get my room at the Algonquin changed right away.' Irvine sounded rattled. For a moment Charles was irritated. Then he remembered that he at least didn't have to stay behind in New York with a maddened and unpredictable Kurtz possibly on his tail. He looked at Irvine with the smug sympathy of the secure. Charles bit back soothing words. He didn't think they'd be appreciated.

Irvine's goodbyes were hasty and abstracted. The limousine was hurrying back to Manhattan almost before Charles had got his bags through the terminus door. As he searched the duty-free shop for scent for Caroline and cigarettes for Jenny, Charles found himself laughing aloud at the expression of affronted alarm he recalled from Irvine's face. He stopped guiltily as he saw other travellers staring at him, but he was still chuckling spasmodically when he accepted the first glass of champagne the stewardess handed him. Maybe he should think of giving Irvine a raise – danger money. Then he remembered Hong Kong, and decided against the idea.

CHAPTER ELEVEN

Punctually at 9.45 the next morning, Charles reached the office, and sank thankfully into his chair. A rapturous reunion with Caroline had done much to improve his morale, and he found that he was looking forward to describing his New York experiences to Jenny with keen anticipation.

Oddly, Caroline hadn't seemed greatly astonished at what he had had to tell her.

'I never could think why you backed that man,' she had

said. Charles had looked at her in surprise. It was the first time he had heard her refer to the business in anything but the most general terms. 'There's a kind of suppressed violence about him that's really frightening,' she went on. 'He's the kind of man who would beat his girl-friends.'

The attack in the hotel had upset her. Like Charles, she wasn't convinced it had anything to do with Kurtz, but not for the same reasons. Kurtz, she said, was far too efficient to have bungled the thing so badly on his home ground. She hadn't referred to it again, and Charles had been a little hurt that she took it so calmly. But during the night he had woken to find her weeping over him and stroking his hair. Their subsequent love-making had been particularly abandoned. Caroline, Charles was delighted to discover, had badly needed the reassurance.

Jenny, summoned early and regaled with the whole story, took much the same line. She didn't think it could have been anything to do with Kurtz, but she agreed that he was the sort of man to beat his girl-friends. She admitted that she'd seen quite a lot of him and had never understood why Fitzpatrick had given him so much leeway. Pressed, though, she'd clammed up, and refused to say how well she really knew Kurtz. Charles was sure that she was holding something back, but forebore to enquire further.

'Aside from that, did you enjoy Manhattan?' she asked.

'No.' Charles was very definite. 'It's all right in the winter, but in the summer it's unbearable.'

Jenny laughed. 'You're out of character,' she teased. 'You love New York, its pace, its zest, the aura of money. And its women.' She looked at him archly.

Charles grunted. 'No time.'

'James would have made time,' she murmured consipratorially.

'Good for him.' Charles was suddenly out of temper. 'Did you give him that tape?'

Jenny nodded.

'And what did he say?'

'Nothing,' Jenny said. 'He said he'd think about it, and

would arrange to see you himself. He said that in the meantime you should leave Tom Irvine alone. Oh, and he said he'd trust you to look after New York.'

'Nice of him,' Charles said drily.

'He seemed to think you'd handle Kurtz without trouble. "That's a tough bastard. Stan'll never put one over him." I quote.' Jenny smiled.

Charles fought to suppress a surge of satisfaction. He found it was nice to be appreciated. First Caroline, now apparently Fitzpatrick.

'By the way,' Jenny said, looking intently at the rubber plant, 'had you realized that tonight is the office party?'

Charles groaned. 'Oh God, do I have to be there?'

'Indeed you do. Essential for office morale that the minions should see the great man at play.' Jenny was flippant but determined.

'But what about Caroline?' Charles asked.

'She never comes,' Jenny said. 'And it breaks up awfully late, so you always stay in town. Don't worry,' she added, maliciously, 'I'll tell her for you. She won't hold it against you, I promise. Look,' she said more seriously, 'you aren't growing a bit too fond of Caroline, are you? There might be an awful lot of complications there, you know.'

Charles laughed a little guiltily. 'What with you on one side, Helen on another, and Fitzpatrick somewhere in the middle, I don't have much chance.'

Jenny considered him for a moment in silence. Charles suppressed a temptation to wriggle.

'Well, just be careful, that's all,' she said at last, and got up to leave.

'What time is this blasted party, and where do I stay afterwards,' Charles asked her retreating back.

'Seven o'clock, the basement of Wolsey's Wine Bar in Vine Street,' Jenny said. 'But don't worry, it's traditional for me to take you, and for you to give me a drink in the office first. You'd better have a nap this afternoon to recover from your trip. I'll keep the wolves at bay. And as for where you stay, that's traditional too. Wait and see.' She smiled at him and left.

Charles woke in the depths of his huge office sofa to find Jenny standing over him with a drink in her outstretched hand. For a moment he couldn't remember where he was, a confused dream of the towers of Manhattan and an ape-like Kurtz fogging his mind. He grasped the glass automatically, and emptied it in one long swallow. His eyes cleared, and he saw that Jenny was looking at him with amusement.

'Steady on,' she said, smiling. 'There's a longish night ahead.' She laughed at his lugubrious expression.

He scrubbed at his eyes, and stretched. 'Must I change, and if so, what into?' he said.

'You needn't, but I have to.' Jenny struck a pose. For a moment Charles was reminded of Helen. Then he noted, with a surge of interest, that Jenny was really a much more sensually attractive girl. Memories of that night in the Carlton Tower prodded at his libido. Something animal stirred deep in him and purred hungrily. This wasn't the trim Miss Barnes of the office routine. This was female on the prowl, in deep-slashed frilled white blouse, and full-length, clinging scarlet skirt, slit almost to the hip, and revealing a quantity of superbly fashioned leg. He noticed that she was wearing heavy eyeshadow, and a pale lipstick. There was an aura of expensive and opulently obvious scent. Deep in her cleavage, drawing extra attention to the smooth white slopes of her breasts, was a spectacular diamond brooch. Though she was wearing a bra – he could dimly make out the straps – it was a very thin one.

'I like your brooch,' he said, embarrassed that his reaction to her sexual challenge was so immediate.

'A discreet present,' she said, fingering it thoughtfully. The deep cleavage shifted slightly, revealing the shadowy underside of her left breast, and a hint of translucent bra cup. 'Nothing too extravagant, but just enough to make the other girls realize that I'm a little special.'

Charles felt a surge of raw jealousy. Damn Fitzpatrick, he thought, he's stamped his brand on the most attractive girls

83

I've met. He'd even given them the same jewellery. He held out his glass for a refill.

Jenny seemed to read his mind. 'No more now,' she twinkled at him. 'Time we were going.'

With an effort, Charles dragged his attention off her sensual charms, and helped her on with the raw-silk coat she held out to him. For a moment his hands brushed her shoulders, and he had to restrain an impulse to force her down onto the couch. With a sigh he released her, and accompanied her to the door. As he opened it for her, she looked up at him mischievously.

'Later,' she said. 'Don't be in such a hurry.' She walked out of his office and to the lift before he could react. When he caught up with her, she was openly laughing at him. He grinned reluctantly, and followed her into the cage.

To his surprise, Charles found that he enjoyed the party very much. The lighting, except above the improvised dance floor, was dim, the drink was good and lavish, the music was hot. There were excellent snacks, and after the first awkwardness, Charles found himself eating and drinking happily with employees he had never met before. Jenny kept fairly close to him at first, and was careful to steer the conversation into innocuous channels. But soon enough it was possible for both of them to relax and forget Charles' impersonation.

Charles was amused at the thoroughness of the Fitzpatrick staff dossiers. He had no difficulty in recognizing the male staff members from the photographs in their files. The women were more difficult, but he quickly found that this was a problem that he shared with the other men. The subdued business girls of the office had taken on a brilliant new plumage, and it wasn't at all easy to recognize a receptionist or a girl from the typing pool in a soignee and sexy creature, all see-through blouse and nudging hips. Charles found himself dancing with some of them. He was all right while he could use his Nigerian hi-life steps, and let them gyrate to their hearts' content in front of him. But he found that in the smoochier numbers they plastered themselves against him without inhibition. He was unexpectedly and rather obviously aroused by one particular pneumatic little creature, who turned out to be from the packing department, and who did the most imaginative things with her tongue as they swayed together. She noticed, too, and was elegantly bitchy when Jenny rescued him. Jenny insisted at once on dancing with him herself, and clung to him in a languorous embrace which made it impossible for him to leave the floor without embarrassment. Jenny's satisfaction at wiping out the memory of her immediate predecessor was smug, and gave Charles a twitch of inner hilarity which threatened for a moment to make him laugh aloud.

As the evening wore on, behaviour became less and less inhibited. In dark corners couples strained together. On the dance-floor, even directly beneath the strobe lights, hands slipped into blouses, and beneath waistbands. Once the sound of an audibly opened zip caused a ripple of breathy laughter. Jenny relaxed her guard on Charles to dance with a smoothly casual sales rep, and returned from the floor, her eyes huge, her lips damp and puffed, and her nipples starkly erect beneath her frilled blouse. In one corner, a group was furtively passing round a joint of marijuana from hand to hand. Charles found himself leaning, his back to the bar, clasping a glass of wine, and thinking sardonically that this was almost a caricature of an office party.

All too soon for some, the lights were switched up, and the party was over. The scent of sex was heavy under the low ceiling, but the smudged lipstick and puffy-eyed dishevelment of the tired and half-smashed individuals who staggered up to him to say their perfunctory thanks was pitilessly revealed under the dusty harshness of naked bulbs, and Charles was almost sorry for the grim disillusion of a late-night return to sanity.

When the last sodden lingerer had been dislodged from his hazy semiconsciousness and turfed out into the cool and sobering night air. Charles turned to find Jenny, combed and freshly made up, waiting for him by the door.

'Come on,' she said. 'Let's get out of here. There's nothing worse than instant replay of an office party.'

'Where to?' Charles asked. 'Night-club?'

'Not unless you'd rather,' Jenny said. 'I thought we might go back to the flat and try a little chambering and wantonness.' It was clear that Jenny wasn't entirely sober, but it was said with conspicuous lack of embarrassment.

Jenny smiled at his confusion. 'Where did you think you traditionally stayed after the office party, then? In the Savoy?' She mocked him gently. 'This is screw-the-secretary night, and this secretary has been going into training for it. You'd better not be drunk, you bastard. Your day's work's just beginning.'

In the taxi they stayed decorously apart. Charles knew that Jenny was teasing, but he'd drunk more than enough to let her have her way. They made polite and deliberately high-flown small-talk for the benefit of the taxi-driver. It took Charles a little time to catch on to the game – it was not until he found himself protesting quite seriously when accused by Jenny of not increasing her allowance to take account of inflation that he realized what was up. Encouraged by the gleam of mischief in her eyes, as seen in the passing street lights, he began to fantasise, and had achieved a considerable success with a withering denunciation of the squint possessed by Jenny's putative lover, when both realised that the taxi had stopped, and that a fascinated driver was reluctant to interrupt them. Giggling, they climbed out of the taxi, and as he paid the driver, Charles looked round and saw that they were in front of a big brick Victorian block in Pimlico, not far from Victoria station. He followed Jenny into the high lobby, wondering for the first time just how much she earned at Fitzpatrick. A ponderous lift took them to the fourth floor, and Jenny used two keys to unlock the heavy, dark-stained wooden door to her flat. She switched on the light, a chandelier of sparkling crystals, and preceded him, slipping her coat off her shoulders as she did so. Charles closed the front door behind them, and was surprised to notice that it was evidently metal-lined, in the New York fashion. His expression must have given him away, for Jenny told him that Fitzpatrick had suggested the precaution.

'I sometimes have to bring confidential documents home to

86

type,' she said, 'and they are often here for some days. James suggested that I have special security after there was a wave of burglaries in this block.'

She tossed her coat over a chair in the small hall, and led him into a big, high-ceilinged sitting-room. The furniture was old-fashioned, but comfortable, and the chintz coverings looked almost new. The walls were covered in cream paper, and there were two or three good watercolours, elegantly framed, hanging from the high picture rail. The curtains Jenny drew across the high windows were obviously heavy, and to Charles' untrained eye looked like plush. They were lined, thick, and chestnut brown. The carpet was Persian, and huge, though unfitted – the boards round the edges were painted cream to match the walls. Charles was admiring it when Jenny said, 'Another discreet present'. Charles looked up sharply to find her smiling at him. 'Yes, Mr Hutchinson,' she said, 'I do get very well paid. And as James' confidential secretary there are perks.'

Charles was startled. For a moment he had hardly recognized his real name. 'I'm sure you're more than worth it,' he said lamely, after a brief pause.

'And I am James' mistress,' Jenny said, 'if you're wondering. But James can manage three or four women at a time, bedwise, I mean, and I have just as much capacity as he has. So don't imagine you're poaching on private preserves. For tonight, you are Charles. I want you, and we're going to have a ball. Now, help yourself to a drink' – she indicated an elegant little Sheraton corner cable, on which was a silver tray with a bottle of Courvoisier and two big balloons – 'while I change. I hate bras, they do get in the way, and they're so awkward to get off. But at the office party I find one needs a little armour.'

Jenny's cool abandonment of the Miss Barnes persona left Charles stunned. He felt that he ought to have produced some witty rejoinder, but before he could think of anything to say, Jenny had left. Still taken aback, he wandered over to the brandy, and poured two sizeable shots. Over the table hung an intricately carved mirror. He was admiring it, and had decided that the hieroglyphic in the centre was a set of entwined initials, when warm fingers in the hair at the back of his neck told him that Jenny was back.

'Nice, isn't it?' she said, indicating the mirror. 'It was a wedding present to my grandmother, and she left it to me in her will.' She took the balloon from his hand, and spun away from him to the deep sofa. Charles watched her open-mouthed. Gone was the frilly, vee-necked blouse, gone the slashed long skirt. Now she was wearing a high-necked dress of some outrageously clinging material which outlined every curve and dimple of her superb body in a shimmer of midnight blue. What startled Charles was the fact that it appeared to have neither sleeves, nor sides, but swung quite free from the shoulders, exposing with every stride, and then artfully concealing, the fact that she wore nothing whatever beneath it. Jenny sank into the sofa, leaving her 'dress' carelessly arranged across her lap, one smooth hip exposed at the end of a long silken leg, and patted the cushion beside her.

'Join me,' she said.

In his haste to obey, Charles almost tripped over his own feet. Jenny had put her glass on the floor, and now began softly to undress him, taking off his tie, unbuttoning his shirt, pulling down his zip. All the while she was nibbling the side of his neck and tonguing his ear. Charles was almost unbearably aroused. The hand that held his brandy was shaking uncontrollably.

Jenny paused to retrieve her brandy, and sat next to him, drinking thoughtfully and exploring his body with light, skilled fingers. Charles took his cue from her, and began to explore on his own behalf. He hoped that he too was managing to maintain that aloof expression, marred in her case by the flaring of nostrils as she sucked in her breath in deep irregular gulps. He could feel himself sweating. The silence was thick with sexual tension, and Charles was frankly gasping now. He noticed a line of perspiration break out on her upper lip, and two patches of colour rise on her cheek bones. Trembling, he wondered how long she expected him to retain control.

Suddenly, she cracked. Her glass fell from her hand, and she hurled herself onto him, her mouth seeking his. Her lips ground against his. Somehow his clothes melted away. His shirt ripped audibly. One shoe stuck ludicrously until with a curse he disentangled himself to tear both shoe and sock off his foot and hurl it who knew where. They wrestled savagely, tearing at each other. Then they were on the floor, locked in a frenetic rhythm.

Somewhere in his frenzy Charles found Jenny's garment an impediment. 'Rip it off,' she gasped in his ear. 'Rip it. And rip me.'

Sometime in the course of the night, they ended up in bed. To Charles, the details of the whole episode were always hazy, but he recalled a paroxysm of breathless laughter as his outflung arm knocked aside a bedside table with a crash. But most of his memories were tangled up with Jenny's big urgent body, and his insatiable ambition to fill every part of it with his own.

They had little sleep. But as the pale light of a new dawn shone in the window whose curtains they had been to preoccupied to draw, they fell into an exhausted, intertwined doze – not so much asleep, more simply passed out.

A shrill alarm woke them. Groaning, Jenny disentangled herself from him to switch it off and stagger towards the bathroom and a shower. Charles lay naked face-down across the top of the bed until rudely wakened with a cold sponge in the small of his back. He rolled over with a curse to find Jenny smiling down at him, wrapped in a towel. 'Time to get up, James,' she said. He realised the night was over.

Except for the dark shadows under her eyes, and a faintly drawn look, Jenny showed little effect of the night before as she sat across the kitchen table eating bacon and eggs with him. The crisp blouse and neat skirt of the efficient Miss Barnes concealed some yellowing bruises, and a spectacular bite mark on the inside of a thigh.

Charles, however, felt like death, and looked pale and puffy. In the shower he had examined his own bruises, and had wondered ruefully how he was to account for them with Caroline. A moment's thought reassured him. She must be used to marks like these on James. A more urgent matter was his shirt, which, he recalled, would be very much the worse for wear. He was most surprised to find a new shirt, clean underwear and socks awaiting him when he emerged, towelling himself. But of course, he thought. Fitzpatrick must always leave some spare clothes here.

It was only on his second cup of coffee that he began to revive, just in time to take notice of what Jenny was saying.

'I'm leaving the company. As from this morning. Oh, do wake up and take some notice,' she said angrily. 'I'm leaving. Are you with me?'

Charles gulped in surprise. 'What?' he said.

'Ah. A reaction at last. I'm leaving. Today. I'm joining James, who wants me to handle his personal affairs. I've got you a replacement, and she's very good. Her name is Mary Peters, and she starts this morning.'

'I notice no one thought it necessary to consult me,' Charles said bitterly.

'Too bad,' Jenny said crisply. 'Remember who we both work for.' She got up to wash the dishes. 'I love James,' she said, her back to him. 'I always have. He's a great man. He can do anything. I've been waiting for this for three years.'

Charles stared at her busy figure. 'I suppose I should have guessed,' he said at last.

She turned to him. To his surprise, there were tears in her eyes. 'I'm sorry it has to end like this,' she said, shakily. 'Best you forget me. I have to go to him, I have to.'

Charles rose, and took her in his arms. 'Don't worry,' he said, 'I shall be all right. But how do I get in touch with you, and with Fitzpatrick?'

Jenny leant her head against his shoulder. 'He'll be in touch with you himself. I shan't. I think I'm getting to like you a bit too much.'

Charles smiled, and kissed her gently. 'Thank you for a marvellous night,' he said.

She smiled up at him gratefully. 'Thank you,' she said. 'If it's any help, you're much better in bed than James. I'm surprised Caroline hasn't noticed.'

I think she has, Charles thought, but was careful not to say so aloud. 'I'll miss you. We all will in the office.'

She kissed the angle of his jaw. 'Yes, well,' she said briskly, recovered, 'you won't know, will you, if you don't turn up there.'

Charles laughed, and they walked hand in hand to the door. Jenny stood waving to him as he stepped into the lift. As the doors closed between them Charles felt a wrench of regret, and an impulse to turn back. He fought it down. Don't be silly, he said to himself. Just remember that she has doublecrossed you, and Fitzpatrick, and everybody else without a qualm. She's altogether too tough for you, my lad. She and Fitzpatrick deserve each other.

It was mid-morning, and Charles was trying exasperatedly to explain to a willing but confused Mary Peters just how he liked his coffee, before he remembered that nothing had been decided about Tom Irvine.

CHAPTER TWELVE

For a month or two, life was peaceful enough at Fitzpatrick. Charles missed Jenny's experienced efficiency, and found himself often exasperated with Mary Peters, a thin, mousy, anxious little creature, whose shorthand and typing were superb, but whose initiative was nil. More to the point, he was increasingly frustrated by his inability to contact Fitzpatrick himself.

Sometimes he thought that Jenny and Fitzpatrick were enjoying a huge joke at his expense. But the companies were run efficiently by Tom Irvine, back from New York, and Charles had taken care to maintain a truce with his managing director. So far as he knew, Irvine was unaware that Charles knew anything about the Hong Kong arrangements. Charles was happy to keep it that way for the time being. In New York, there was no sign of Kurtz, who seemed to be lying low. Bob Woodward, in spite of his overkill defences against Kurtz' revenge, seemed to be doing a good job, and sales and profits in the States were up satisfactorily.

Caroline was extraordinarily nice to Charles. Their home-life was almost idyllic, and their encounters in bed increasingly satisfying and uninhibited. Charles found, too, that he was becoming very fond of the children, especially of Lucy, who had taken to following him about, when permitted, like a small and faithful hound.

Every Tuesday, Helen provided some sort of sensual surprise, sometimes welcome, occasionally frankly too much, as the evening when she introduced a third party, an elegant, crop-haired, ravaged-looking lady, and suggested a trio. She was disappointed but docile when Charles vetoed the idea, and didn't refer to it again. And every night she packed him off to Caroline at ten thirty.

All in all, Charles was congratulating himself on his good fortune and wondering why Fitzpatrick had abandoned it, when one Monday morning the whole thing began to fall part.

It all started with an unexpected phone call from Jenny, of whom Charles had heard nothing since the morning after the office party and their private celebration. She said that she had an urgent message from Fitzpatrick, and arranged for him to meet her at her flat the next day. On the Tuesday morning the blow fell. Charles received a call from a quavering old man who identified himself as Jenny's father.

'My name is Barnes,' the old man said. 'Jenny was to meet you this evening.'

'Oh, yes?' Charles murmured, wondering what this was all in aid of.

'Jenny's dead.' The old man coughed, and Charles heard him trumpet into a handkerchief.

'What?' Charles was thunderstruck.

'Her car crashed last night. She was driving up to London to see you, when it overturned just outside Horsham. The police told her mother and me at eleven o'clock last night.'

'I'm terribly sorry,' Charles said, groping for words. 'Can I do anything to help? I was very fond of her, you know.'

'Yes,' said the old man slowly. 'She talked of you a lot.'

There was a long silence.

Then, 'I wonder if we could impose on you?' the old man went on. 'It's hard for us to get up to London now. We've no car, you know, and we're not getting any younger. If I sent you the key, could you arrange to deal with her flat? Get in touch with the landlord, and so on? I don't know what you ought to do with her furniture and bits and pieces. We'd be grateful if you could check through her belongings and send down to us anything you think we ought to have. I'm afraid we can't really think what's best. She was our only child, you know, and so good to us.'

Charles felt a lump rise in his throat. The old man sounded so lost and bewildered.

'Of course,' he said.

'Thank you. We'd appreciate that. You know, Jenny was so excited. She was so much looking forward to going out to Africa for Fitzpatrick's. We knew we would miss her, but we would never have stood in her way. Thank you so much.' The old man rang off.

Charles stared at the receiver in his hand as if it had just bitten him. After the initial shock of the news, his mind was working overtime. Jenny had never told her parents that she had left the company, and she had been preparing to go out to Africa. To what, and to whom, Charles wondered. Fitzpatrick? He replaced the receiver thoughtfuly. She'd wanted to see him before she went, that was clear, and she'd been prepared to upset his Tuesday routine to do so. What could have been on her mind? Charles thought for a moment, and rang for Mary Peters.

He dictated a memo for the office notice board announcing the tragedy, and drafted a letter to Mr Barnes, expressing his sympathy, and enquiring about the funeral. Then he told Mary to look up Jenny's London address in the personal files, and to find and contact her landlord. As she hurried out to do his bidding, Charles picked up his phone and called the Horsham police. After some difficulty, he established his bona fides, and learnt that Jenny's little souped-up Mini had run out of road on a bend just outside Itchingfield. It was possible that her brakes had failed, but the car had turned over and burnt out. Jenny had been wearing a seat belt, and had been trapped in the burning car. What was left of her was not a pretty sight. Her father had fainted when called upon to identify her, and it was only that morning that the police had made a final identification, using her dental records. Charles shuddered, remembering his own torture at the hands of Fitzpatrick's dentist, and recollecting suddenly that the treatment had never been completed.

As he listened to the unemotional tones of the police sergeant reciting horrors as though reading a shopping list, Charles found a decision crystallizing in his mind. Somehow he had to trace Fitzpatrick, if only to tell him of Jenny's death. In any case, he felt, there was no useful purpose to be served in putting off a confrontation with Irvine indefinitely.

He said the appropriate things to the policeman, and rang off, his mind made up. It was with difficulty that he curbed an impulse to send a car down to Jenny's parents to rush the key of her flat up to London. Suddenly he was burning with impatience to search through it for clues as to Fitzpatrick's whereabouts.

That night, Charles had rather more to drink than he normally did, to help drown memories of Jenny which were altogether too vivid. At the same time, he was obsessed with the notion that there was some clue he was overlooking, something about Jenny and Fitzpatrick which he ought to remember, if only he could dredge it out of the recesses of his mind.

He stared out across the terrace of River Lodge, and answered Caroline's chatter in monosyllables. She had given him one quick glance as he came off the train at the station, and had been careful not to express surprise at his appearance on a Tuesday, and to send the children off out of the way. Now she sat at the other end of the sofa, swearing quietly over a cardigan she was knitting for a niece, from a Fitzpatrick pattern. It came to Charles that she was a very restful woman, and he was suddenly glad that he had had a good excuse to postpone another session with Helen.

'What's up?' he said.

'Well, it's a most attractive pattern, darling,' she said, peering closely at the page of incomprehensible instructions. 'But I don't seem able to follow it. I'm sure your people have got the stitches all wrong.'

'Quite likely,' Charles agreed, amused. Since he was completely ignorant of the matter, why argue? 'But frankly, my poppet, to judge by all the cursing and counting, it's equally possible that you just aren't a very good knitter.'

Caroline laughed, and leaned over to kiss his cheek, dropping another row of stitches as she did so.

'Damn and blast,' she said. 'Why do I bother to try to be a good housewife and mother when I'm so hopeless?'

'You're very good at it,' Charles disagreed.

'Well, even if I am,' she said, 'I'm fed up with it. I want to be a showgirl, and have lots of men drink champagne from my slipper.'

'Showgirls work long hours at hideously sweaty jobs for precious little money,' Charles objected. 'And champagne from a slipper must taste horrid. Think how sticky the slipper must be afterwards.'

Caroline laughed and went off to the kitchen to fetch a ham salad on a tray. She brought it to him in the snuggery, which opened out of the dining-room, and contained a sofa, two fireside chairs, and the family TV. She kissed him lightly as she handed him his meal. Charles felt a wave of affection for her. In the months since he had taken Fitzpatrick's place she had relaxed, and lost a great deal of her original formality and restraint. Charles realized that she not only needed to give love, she needed to be loved. With a stirring of excitement, he acknowledged that that was a role he could play without pretence.

'How was your day?' she ventured at last, glancing at him sideways over her knitting.

'Terrible.'

'Oh?'

'Jenny Barnes was killed in a car crash last night.'

'James!' Caroline was shocked and pale. 'How awful. What happened?'

Charles gave her the details, and told her of his conversation with Mr Barnes, carefully leaving out the detail about Africa.

'Oh those poor old people,' she said distressfully. 'Will they be all right? Did Jenny send them money, do you know?'

'I hadn't thought of that. I'd better inquire.' Charles sighed.

There was a long silence. Caroline continued knitting mechanically, staring in front of her, and apparently not noticing the stitches she was dropping. Charles was startled to see slow tears trickling down the side of her nose.

'Darling,' he said.

With an inarticulate wail, she dropped her knitting and hurled herself into his arms. 'But suppose it had been you?' she wailed. It was a long time before she would allow herself to be comforted.

That night, she made love to Charles very tenderly, for a long time. After they were finished, she lay half on top of him, her face buried in the hollow of his shoulder. Suddenly she was crying again.

'What's the matter, darling?' Charles said.

'I don't want you to die,' she said, her voice muffled against his flesh. 'I'm very happy with you – too happy.'

'But I'm not going to die,' he pointed out.

'One day you must.'

'Not for a long time though, darling.'

Caroline was silent for a long time. Then, when Charles thought she had dropped asleep, she murmured, 'She had the office party, though. That's something.' Charles said nothing. Caroline's breath deepened and slowed, and she fell asleep in a warm sprawl over him. Charles lay awake for a long time, holding her.

The next day, a registered envelope brought a key, sent first class from Horsham. Charles warned Mary Peters to put off any callers, and left the office for Jenny's flat, the key clutched in his hand. He felt oddly embarrassed as he let himself in. The air in the flat was stale, and the silence was a waiting one. Charles couldn't shake off the feeling that the flat was awaiting its mistress' return, and resented his interruption of its concen-

tration. He helped himself to the Courvoisier, and deter-
minedly shook off the mood of oppression which threatened to
overcome him. Presently he began to look round, notebook and
pencil in hand. With Jenny's parents in mind, he had decided
to take a rough inventory. There'd be time enough to dispose
of the fittings and furniture when it had been established what
was actually there.

In what was obviously intended as a spare bedroom Charles
found a neat office, complete with typewriter, dictaphone play-
back, and filing cabinet. In a folder on the desk were miscellaneous invitations, and bills clipped together and annotated as
paid and unpaid. Charles found in the drawers, among the
usual paraphernalia of paperclips, elastic bands, erasers, spare
typewriter ribbons, and odds and ends, an address book, a
diary, and a small bundle of letters tied with ribbon. He
slipped them into his briefcase, and turned his attention to the
filing cabinet. Fortunately, it was unlocked. But the cupboard
was bare. The files were neatly marked: Investments – U.K.;
Investments – U.S.; Investments – miscellaneous; Insurance;
Bank statements; Passport. But all were empty of papers.
Clearly these were the Chairman's personal files – there was
even an entry under Hutchinson – but there was no clue remaining.

Charles left the office and searched through the bedroom,
flipping through the clothes piled neatly on the shelves of a
walk-in cupboard, and riffling quickly through the drawers on
the bedside cabinets. He felt increasing distaste for the task,
but turned up more neat bundles of letters, which he pocketed,
and a package of photographs, which he riffled through, without recognizing a face, and discarded.

He forced himself to take comprehensive notes of the obviously personal belongings for Mr Barnes, but was aware of
an almost panicky impatience to be off. When finally he closed
the door behind him he was overwhelmed with a sense of relief
almost painful in its acuteness. Nothing, he knew, would drag
him back within those walls ever again.

Back at River Lodge that night, Charles locked himself into
his study on the pretext of urgent work, and examined his

trophies. The diary was cryptic. There were a lot of entries for dinner, concerts, dances, and so on, embellished with initials, among them S.K. Stan Kurtz, Charles wondered? He made a note of the dates and decided to check. The office party, he was amused to see, was circled in red and adorned with exclamation points. After a while, he noticed that a number of dates identified simply by J. stopped abruptly, just before the office party. Could it be that Fitzpatrick had left the country about then, and arranged for Jenny to follow him when some personal details had been settled? Charles filed the thought for later.

The address book was of no value at all. Charles waded carefully through it, but though there were a great many male names, none of them was Fitzpatrick or Kurtz. Charles made a note to send it down to her parents.

The first bundle of letters Charles quickly laid aside in embarrassment. They were love letters, stunningly specific in their imagery and forthright in their reminiscences and promises for the future. The other bundles seemed the same, and he laid them aside to be destroyed. But in the next to last bundle, the bundle he had taken from the desk, he came on treasure trove. He recognized the handwriting – it was Fitzpatrick's.

They dated back a long time. Some of the earliest, and most impersonal, were more than two years old. But the more recent one's were very different, and increasingly passionate. Charles found there references to Caroline which at first stunned him with their lack of sensitivity, then infuriated him with their casual callousness. So angry was he that he nearly missed the vital clue. A number of the later letters mentioned the fact that Jenny was to join him, and Charles had read no particular significance into this until his attention was attracted to the address at the head of one: P.O. Box 618, Nairobi. It wasn't the last in the series, but it was the only one that seemed to come from Africa. Coupled with the information Charles had gleaned from Jenny's father, he was convinced that this was the one to follow up. But a P.O. box number? True, he had perhaps pinned the target down to Kenya, but there was no clue as to the identity that Fitzpatrick was using, and Kenya was a sizeable haystack in which to look even for a white needle. Charles made a note of the box number, and locked the letters away to await destruction. He felt that he had only half the information he required.

And yet, as he lay awake that night, nagging away at the problem in his tired but restless mind, he felt sure that somewhere he knew, he *knew*, where Fitzpatrick was likely to be.

CHAPTER THIRTEEN

Oddly enough, it was Helen who finally fitted the pieces together.

Charles had been getting increasingly tired of Helen and had wondered how best to get rid of her. Their meetings had more and more developed a pattern – dinner in some public and trendy place, followed by strenuous but dispassionate sex. Helen, Charles knew, was using aids to passion now, pills and poppers of all descriptions. She'd also, he was almost sure, taken to whipping herself into a state of heat with the aid of a vibrator in preparation for him. Still, he found her inherently bitchy conversation amusing, and he liked her sufficiently well to be most reluctant to hurt her. He was wryly aware that in his position Fitzpatrick would have cut her off without a qualm. But that, he comforted himself, was Fitzpatrick. It was Charles not James that Caroline was falling in love with. The very thought made Charles swell internally with pride, like a turtle dove in the spring.

Helen had been shaken by Jenny's death, and quite subdued for some time. But nothing penetrated her armour of self absorption completely, and it wasn't long before she was speculating as to the why's and wherefore's in the most lurid imaginable way.

One night she was enjoying lobster mornay at the White Elephant in Curzon Street, tucking into her food with childish gusto, and spearing portions of mixed salad with a fork. It was just the kind of club she liked, filled with writers and artists, and it spurred her to reminiscence. She laughed with him about the time they met, on a plane to Paris, he to see a French publisher, she to take in the Spring collections.

'I met a super man on a plane this weekend,' she twinkled at him. 'He's a photographer, a damned good one, twenty-two and Greek. I'm taking him to Bradford on Thursday to shoot some of our new designs.'

Charles looked at her with detached affection. Her extravagant and theatrical manner concealed a generous if insecure personality. And her enthusiasm for life was pleasantly infectious.

'Staying overnight?' he quizzed her, teasing.

She laughed, and leant across the table to squeeze his hand. 'You know I don't pick people up for sex any more,' she said. 'You're quite enough to handle.' Charles didn't believe her, but it was pleasantly said.

'Don't worry,' she went on, 'he's like most of them, bent as a hairpin. But he's got talent. I'm sure he'll be famous one day.'

'What turns you on about a man, Helen?' Charles asked idly. 'Fame, money, or power?'

She giggled. 'All three, preferably. Like you.'

'What's your young man's name?' Charles asked.

'Peter Vlachos. He comes from Thessalonica. You should use him to take pictures for your company.'

'We probably couldn't afford him, now you're using him. Fashion photography pays five or six times as well as humble publishing.'

'How's the company doing?' Helen enquired idly, watching with interest while some new arrivals were shown to their table.

'Could be better, could be worse.'

'And the new secretary?'

'Oh, she's coming along.'

'You miss Jenny, don't you?'

'God, yes. I never appreciated her until she'd gone.' So far as he knew, Helen wasn't aware that Jenny had left the firm some time before she died. It had never been discussed.

'Stan Kurtz told me quite a lot about her,' she said idly. 'He was pretty impressed.'

'I didn't know you knew Stan Kurtz,' Charles said sharply, putting down his knife and fork in surprise.

'Oh yes, he took me out a time or two. Jenny too.' Helen was insouciant.

'Interesting. I thought Stan was supposed to prefer call-girls.'

'Are you suggesting I went to bed with him?' Helen bristled.

'Of course not, darling,' Charles said hastily.

'I should bloody well hope not,' she said. 'Of course, I can't answer for Jenny Barnes.'

'I wouldn't have thought she was the type,' Charles said thoughtfully.

'I expect he wanted to see what inside information he could pick up,' she suggested.

'She'd never have told him anything,' Charles said confidently. 'She was discretion itself.'

'I don't know, though,' she said thoughtfully. 'She told him about your passion for watching exotic birds. He went on about it for a long time. He was frightfully surprised. He didn't think it was your line at all.'

'I've never made any secret of it,' Charles said a little huffily, devoutly hoping she wouldn't follow up. He knew next to nothing about birds himself – the feathered variety, anyway.

But her mind was still in the past. 'She even told him where you'd always wanted to go,' she said. 'He noticed it particularly because he said she got all shiney with enthusiasm, and said she wanted to go there too.'

This wasn't at all Charles' vision of the sophisticated and sexy Jenny.

'Oh?' he said, carefully casual, all ears.

'Yes, some lake in Kenya or somewhere. Naivasha, is it? Come on James, 'fess up.' She looked at him, sparkling.

Naivasha, he thought, exultantly. Of course. He remembered the suite in the Carlton Tower, and Fitzpatrick explaining how he'd always wanted to write a book on African birds.

At last, the second part of the clue. He'd always known the answer was in his memory somewhere.

'You've found me out,' he said jovially, a little too hearty. 'Yes, I've always wanted to do a study of African birds.' He sighed, hoping she wouldn't notice the slight theatricality. 'But the business, you know . . .' He allowed his voice to trail artistically away.

But he needn't have worried. Helen had already lost interest, and was ordering strawberries and cream with a conscious charm which was bedazzling the waiter. They had coffee and brandy. Charles felt more relaxed and cheerful than he had since the news of Jenny's death. He mentally resolved to make this evening a stand-out in her sexual memoirs.

Later that night he checked Lake Naivasha in the big Times atlas in the River Lodge library. The next morning he called Caroline from the office, and warned her that he expected to leave for Nairobi – to sort out an important contract which was going wrong, he said – and instructed Mary Peters to get him a flight and to buy every available book on East African birds from Foyles. Within half an hour he was booked on a British Airways plane, and that evening he took off.

CHAPTER FOURTEEN

The change in the engine note as the 747 began its descent woke Charles from the deep sleep engendered by two large vodkas and two Mogadons. Wearily he struggled up from the sofa in the first-class lounge he had managed to grab in competition with a portly German, also experienced in the arts of long-distance air travel. His hair was tousled, and the B.A. 'Do Not Disturb' sign was still stuck to his forehead. For once, at least, it had done its job, and no stewardess with toothy smile had offered him plastic food in the middle of the night.

The plane was sweeping smoothly across a vast, dry, grassy plain. There was no sign of activity. They might have been landing on the moon. The plane levelled out and rumbled down the runway, braking steeply. Charles started to search around for his hand-luggage.

By 8.55 he was through immigration and in the eager arms of a taxi driver, who set off at high speed, weaving his way by some sort of telepathy through the goats that meandered to the danger of life and limb across their path.

'Your first time in Kenya?' the driver asked.

Charles grunted noncommittally.

'I think you are British, sir.'

'How did you know?'

The driver laughed with African satisfaction at his own cleverness. 'You are staying at the Norfolk Hotel, sir. All the British stay at the Norfolk.'

Charles thought gloomily that that wasn't any great recommendation, but half an hour later he had had time to revise his opinion. By then he had been established in a comfortable cottage, the receptionist, an exceptionally pretty girl, had greeted him efficiently, the manager had enquired after his health, the hall porter had delivered his luggage and reassured him that his tip to the taxi-driver had been adequate, and half a bottle of perfectly chilled champagne had been delivered to his door. The temperature was in the mid seventies, and the air was blessedly free of Western-style pollution. Charles began to revive like a fern in water.

He unpacked the pile of bird books that Mary Peters had bought for him and lay down on the bed to study them. In a moment he was yawning; in another he was asleep.

At 4.30 he awoke, refreshed. The worst of his jet-lag had gone, and he was able to concentrate on the bird guides. They listed a bewildering number of sanctuaries in Kenya, Uganda and Tanzania and Charles quickly decided that the first thing to do was to isolate the Kenyan sites. While it was possible that Fitzpatrick was using a Nairobi box number while living outside the country, it seemed unlikely. The snag was that even in Kenya there were a large number of possibilities. After thought, he isolated Lakes Naivasha, Nakuru, and Manyara, and decided that discreet enquiries there might flush out an Englishman recently from the home country and enthusiastically pursuing bird-life – of both kinds, Charles thought, remembering the Chairman's habits. He hauled a map out of his briefcase and ringed the lakes. Perhaps he should hire a car and explore them himself.

It was while he was delving into the case that he remembered a commission that Caroline had given him, and wondered if there was something to be gained from following it up. One of Fitzpatrick's more amiable characteristics had been his generous support of charities. Charles had always thought of this as some sort of insurance policy on Fitzpatrick's part, but for once it looked like coming in useful. For one of his favourite concerns was the Starehe Boys Centre in Nairobi, where he and Caroline maintained two orphan boys at the ridiculously low cost of £44 a year each. Charles was familiar with this sort of scheme from Nigeria, and had always thought them both necessary and effective. He had encouraged Caroline and the children to correspond and exchange photographs with their long-range foster children, and Caroline had reminded him to buy gifts for them. Guiltily he realized that in the rush of leaving he had forgotten to do so, but this could be remedied. Perhaps, he thought, the kids could help him by making enquiries at the post office. He was reluctant to do so himself, not only because he felt that a white face would stand little chance with a black bureaucrat, but also because he didn't want any comment on his resemblance to Fitzpatrick, in the event that he had been in the habit of collecting his mail himself. Thoughtfully, he reached for the phone, to call Starehe. He arranged to meet the boys the next morning, and made a mental note to leave enough time to buy them something on his way.

He was putting down the phone when another thought struck him. It was more than two months since Jenny had failed to join Fitzpatrick, and her parents had certainly not heard from him. Indeed there had been no reaction to her non-appearance at all. The more Charles thought about it the odder that seemed. Did Fitzpatrick know, somehow? If so, how had he found out? There had been no mention in the Press. And if he didn't know, why didn't he seem to care that she had been out of touch? Ruthless he might well be, but his last letters had given no hint that he was planning to ditch her. Charles filed the thought for later examination. There had to be an explanation, but he couldn't think of one. Unless there was something wrong with Fitzpatrick? The notion came unbidden, and Charles banished it uneasily. If Fitzpatrick was ill, or worse still, dead, the possible problems were overwhelming.

Reluctantly he abandoned his speculations, and began to think about dinner. After wallowing in a hot bath, enthusiastically scrubbing his back with a loofah, comforting relic of the colonial past, he changed into a cream-coloured suit, white shirt and dark tie, and strolled over to the main hotel building. A brief consultation with the hall porter decided him to try the supper club on the top floor of the Intercontinental Hotel, where the porter assured him, the food was good, the drinks generous, and the music compelling. It was only a short distance from his hotel, but the porter advised him to take a taxi. The streets of Nairobi after dark, he said, were unsafe, particularly for a solitary European. Charles took his advice. A mugging was just what he didn't need at the moment.

He saw her the moment he entered the room. She was blonde, tanned, and sexy in an off-white tunic dress which was military in style, and vaguely Chinese. Something about the way she moved, the way she smiled and talked to her companions, argued experience with a capital E. Charles wondered wistfully how Fitzpatrick would have gone about the business of picking her up and cutting her out from under the noses of her escorts, two clean-looking young men, fresh-faced, and dressed in the East African mode – neat white shirts and khaki shorts.

As he was escorted to his table, he thought about the problem, grinning to himself at the incongruity of two such different searches for contact in the same day. He studied the menu, and cast about for appropriate gambits. As he ordered papaya and a rare steak the perfect scheme occurred to him, flamboyant and pushy, but not calculated to invite a humiliating set-down. If you're going to be Fitzpatrick, you might as well behave like him, he thought to himself, and summoned his waiter.

'You see that blonde lady at the table over there?' The African nodded.

'I want you to take her a bottle of champagne, Moet et Chandon, properly chilled. Tell her it's from an anonymous admirer, who thinks she is the most beautiful woman in the room. On no account let her know it came from me. Do you understand?'

'Perfectly, sir,' the waiter grinned broadly. 'She is not to know you sent the champagne. Very clever, sir, if I may say so. Worthy of a Kikuyu.' He went off, chuckling.

The champagne was presented with ceremony, the head waiter bearing it over his arm, and an acolyte following with an ice bucket. Charles watched covertly as the woman smiled and asked an inaudible question. Her friends frowned, and she laughed at them. He looked down as he saw her turn in her chair to study her fellow diners. He wondered if her glance had lingered on him, but he was careful not to look up. When he raised his eyes again, she had obviously given up and was preparing to drink the wine. Charles saw the waiter twist the cork, heard the pop above the hum of conversation, and watched the wine foam into the woman's glass. Her companions had seemingly refused to join her. She held the glass to the light, and then made a toasting gesture, with a wide sweep of her arm which included the whole room. Charles felt acutely let down. He had counted on the girl twisting his waiter's arm. He shrugged to himself. Win a few, lose a few, he thought.

At midnight Charles finished his meal, paid his bill, adding an extra tip a little reluctantly, since the scheme seemed to have fizzled, and made for the lift. As he waited for one to reach the top floor, the head waiter hurried after him.

'I've been asked to give you this, sir,' he said, handing Charles a note.

Charles opened it. 'To the most interesting man in the room – 69048,' it said. He raised his eyebrows. 'A room number?' he asked, showing the note to the waiter.

'Oh, no sir, certainly not at this hotel. A phone number, perhaps.' The waiter pocketed the note Charles proffered him, impassively.

'Oh. Thank you. Good night.' Charles stepped into the lift, and pressed the button for the ground floor, his spirits rising as the lift descended. A phone number. Life was looking up.

Next morning, after a leisurely breakfast, he rang the number. A husky voice answered after a pause. 'Champagne,' Charles said briefly.

He enjoyed her laugh, low and rich. 'Ah. I hoped you'd call. It was a nice gesture.'

'I thought my ploy had failed,' Charles said.

'Never despair. Would you like to buy me a drink, round about five?'

'Where?'

'Where are you staying?'

'The Norfolk.'

'The Norfolk bar, then.'

'What about dinner afterwards?'

'I think we should see how we get on first, don't you? After all, for all I know you've got buck teeth and a squint, with a nice taste in champagne the only thing to recommend you.'

Charles laughed. 'OK,' he said. 'The Norfolk at five. You'll know me by the carnation held between my buck teeth.' He rang off, exhilarated.

He took a taxi to the Starehe, only fifteen minutes from the centre of the city, pausing on the way to buy a huge glass jar of sweets. The boys gave him a shy welcome, and greeted the sweets with rapture. They showed him round the classrooms, the dormitories, and wanted, bursting with pride, to show him the new dispensary. But the queue of patients, suffering from the very African complaint of 'general weakness', frustrated them. They were a charming pair, and on impulse Charles asked the director if he might take them back to his hotel for lunch. They were delighted, and later found the swimming pool a special treat. Over lunch and Tusker beer they confided their ambitions. The elder wanted to be an accountant, the other a motor mechanic. Charles, with a mental note to twist Fitzpatrick's arm, agreed to continue their sponsorship until they were qualified. They were touchingly grateful.

Finally Charles asked if they would do him a favour.

'Anything, sir,' they chorused with enthusiasm.

'I have a friend in Kenya I was hoping to see,' Charles explained. 'But I have no address for him except a PO box number, 618, in Nairobi. I am wondering how to get in touch with him.'

'That's easy,' said the younger boy, a round-faced jolly creature from Kisumu, on the Ugandan border. 'Just go to the post office and ask them for your friend's address.'

The older boy was shocked. 'It is siesta time for our sponsor,' he said severely. 'It is we who should go to the post office. It would not be dignified for our sponsor to suffer the noise and crowds of the General Post Office.' They rose and rushed off. Charles lay back to doze beside the pool.

When they returned they looked agitated.

'We cannot report success,' said the elder. 'At first the clerk told us that it was against the rules to give out the addresses of Post Box numbers.'

'We told him,' said his friend, 'that you were only here for a few days, all the way from London. And that you were a generous benefactor to two Kenyan orphans at Starehe. At last he gave in and agreed to help us.'

Charles congratulated himself on his foresight. Clearly it had required a good grasp of Swahili just to get this far, and Swahili was not a Nigerian language.

'Even so, the news is not good,' continued the elder. 'The man searched hard for us, but there is no other address for your friend but the box number. No letters have been collected for weeks, and it seems that your friend only collects his mail every month or two. The people at the post office think he must live some way from Nairobi. When he comes in he has thick dust on his clothes and shoes, as if he'd been on safari.'

'Whatever can I do, then?' Charles wondered aloud.

'Why don't you write him a note, telling him you are here,'

the younger suggested. 'Then if he comes to Nairobi he will get in touch with you.'

'We'll take it to the Post Office for you,' the elder offered. 'It's on our way back to the Centre.'

Charles thought for a moment, and then wrote a note on Norfolk Hotel stationery, saying briefly that he was in Nairobi, and needed to see Fitzpatrick urgently. He added a footnote to the effect that he had something important to say about Jenny Barnes. He felt that that ought to bring Fitzpatrick out of his lair.

He handed the note to the boys, together with a present of one hundred and twenty shillings apiece. They wished him well, and sent their regards to his wife and children. Charles watched them go, and was amused when the younger began to skip with excitement, and was called to order.

He was pleased with their help. They had not achieved a great deal, but at least they had avoided the major error, on his part, of going to the Post Office himself. It was clear that Fitzpatrick was not an unfamiliar figure to the employees there, and the appearance of a double would have been bound to cause comment. At least the fact that he had not picked up his letters for over a month helped to explain why Jenny's death had gone apparently unnoticed.

Charles remembered his date with the blonde, and found himself full of anticipation. She was obviously local. Perhaps she could tell him about bird sanctuaries. He headed back to his cabin, and was settling down to a further siesta when it occurred to him to wonder whether she had seen Fitzpatrick on one of his visits to Nairobi. The Chairman, he was sure, was not the man to have overlooked anything so immediately sensual.

At five o'clock precisely, Charles was strategically placed in the bar of the hotel's main building. On impulse, he had provided himself with a carnation, snatched furtively from a vase in the lobby. Corny, he thought, but it might break the ice. He watched her enter, with a feeling of enormous male satisfaction that this gorgeous creature was here solely at his behest. She paused in the doorway to look round. He had just time to grasp his carnation between his teeth before her glance reached him. She laughed aloud, and headed in his direction.

He rose from his chair, signalling for a waiter, as she reached him. They looked at each other critically. He saw an elegant blonde, with thick heavy hair, ice-blue eyes and a wide, heavily-lipsticked mouth. Her V-necked black blouse revealed the smooth brown slopes of her breasts, and was set off by a tan cotton skirt and white sandals. There were wrinkles round her eyes, effectively concealed by eye make-up. He decided that she couldn't be a day under thirty-five, and the better for it.

'No buck teeth, and not a hint of a squint,' she smiled at him. 'I like the carnation. Gives an authentic European touch.' Without an invitation she swung out a chair and sat down.

'What would you like to drink?' he asked, indicating the hovering waiter.

'Vodka and tonic,' she said. 'No ice.'

He felt absurdly pleased that vodka was her drink. It fitted his image of her so well. He gave the order and sat down, suddenly tongue-tied, fiddling with the carnation which seemed to him, all at once, part of a childish gesture.

She reached for his hand. 'May I have the flower?' she asked. 'It's the first time that anyone has ever met me with a carnation in his mouth.'

Charles smiled weakly. 'Sorry,' he said. 'It seemed like a good joke at the time. I've been wondering how to get rid of it.'

'Nonsense,' she said. 'I'm going to press it for my old age. I'll boast to my neighbours in the old folk's home that once a handsome stranger picked me up over dinner and met me in a bar, chewing a carnation.'

They both laughed, and the ice was broken. Charles introduced himself and learned that her name was Vanessa. By the time the drinks arrived, they were on good terms.

'How do you make your millions?' she asked, her eyes wide as she looked at him over the rim of her glass.

'I'm a publisher.'

'Pornography?'

'Afraid not.'

'Pity. It's impossible to get here. They're very straight-laced.'

'I'm afraid we're a terribly respectable company,' Charles said. 'Austere pamphlets on nuclear physics and research into flatworms. Cooking, breadmaking, gardening, that sort of thing. Very dull.'

'You work in London?'

'Basically. I travel around a lot.'

'Married?'

'Yes.'

'Children?'

'Two.'

'Good. I like to get the ground rules straight,' she said. 'Personally, I prefer married men. No hassle. They treat you well, and you both know it's just for fun. And if you get jealous, you've only yourself to blame.'

She sipped her drink in moody silence. Charles sat back in his cane chair and regarded her with satisfaction. She was well worth looking at, he decided.

'Anyway,' she went on, 'when you're thirty-two, like me, and you run into someone who sends you a bottle of champagne without being asked, and who stays in a luxury cottage at a top hotel, you can be bloody certain that someone has snapped him up.'

'What about you?' Charles asked, intrigued by her bluntness.

'Divorced,' she said, with an attempt at lightness. 'My husband ran off with my best friend. It's very common, you know. I had one child, but they look after her. They live in Malta. I just live for today.' She looked defiant. 'And I live very well.'

'Here's to us, then,' Charles said. He drained his glass, and ordered them both a refill.

Some time later, they agreed that it would be nice to have dinner in his cottage. Charles ordered, and laughing at nothing, they supported each other out of the bar and over to his den. She was openly impressed.

'Nice place,' she said, falling into a chair. Charles went to the refrigerator, and poured her another drink. He found her sprawling in front of the air-conditioner, her skirt hiked back to reveal her tights. 'Phew, it was hot in that bar,' she said. 'Must be another power cut. Happens all the time.'

Dinner arrived as he was admiring the view. They ate and drank, and laughed together. As they reached the brandy stage, Vanessa excused herself, and went off to the bathroom. When she came back, her crossed legs revealed that she had discarded the tights, and was wearing nothing at all beneath her skirt.

She intercepted his gaze. 'Admiring the merchandize?' she said provocatively. He stood over her speechlessly. She surged out of her chair, and took his hand. 'Come on,' she said. 'Food always make me horny.'

Later, she took him to Hisan's, a night-club in Government Road. They were the only white people there, and Charles felt uneasy.

'Don't worry,' Vanessa said, 'I know the owner. The people here are very nice.'

'It's just that they're looking at us a little strangely,' Charles explained.

'That's because we're on the wrong side of the tracks, and very few Europeans come here.'

The band played, rather well, a mixture of South American and West African tunes. Vanessa explained that Kenya had no music of its own and had to improvise from other people's. Charles felt a nostalgia for the forthright rhythms of the Paradise club.

Hisan's, too, it seemed, was basically a pick-up joint. The clientele was rather raffish, and the decor seedy. But the atmosphere was friendly, and Charles soon found himself dancing his hi-life steps with a series of elegant African ladies, while Vanessa gyrated before a succession of lithe African males.

Charles was not unaware of the invitations cast his way, but he was taken aback when Vanessa, on a brief refuelling trip to their table, hissed at him, 'Do you want some black velvet tonight? How about the tall girl in the miniskirt? I'm told by the owner that she's perfectly clean.'

'Not tonight, Josephine,' Charles replied. 'But I'd love to spend the night with you. It would be nice to wake up to your face on the pillow in the morning.'

Vanessa hugged him and kissed him with open sensuality, to the ironic applause of the onlookers. 'James,' she said, 'you're not just fun, you're a gentleman to boot.'

They returned to Charles' cottage at the Norfolk at three in the morning, tired, happy, and rather drunk. They wrestled together hilariously but inconclusively, and fell asleep. It had been a good evening.

CHAPTER FIFTEEN

The next day, Charles hired a Mercedes, and set out to visit his selected bird sanctuaries. He took Vanessa with him and turned the whole expedition into a holiday.

First they drove to Lake Nakuru to watch the flamingoes marching up and down in the mud, working their beaks like Hoovers. Then they swung north to Lake Naivasha, where they rowed about the lake until drenched by a sudden storm. Vanessa's opulent figure, revealed in explicit detail as the rain pastered her suddenly transparent clothes to her body, so turned Charles on that they stayed the night at the Lake Naivasha Country Club, making love with an abandon which caused the manager to phone through to their cottage in the middle of the night, asking them to make less noise, since there were complaints. Vanessa giggled, but Charles was hideously embarrassed, and hardly dared look at the manager the next day as he paid his bill. Next they made a longer expedition to Lake Manyara, and sat drinking sundowners, watching clouds of waterbirds wheeling in intricate patterns against the setting sun.

Everywhere, Charles brought the conversation round to the subject of bird-watchers, and their mad enthusiasms, trying to fish for information about Fitzpatrick. None was forthcoming. No-one, it seemed, had come across an enthusiastic Englishman intent on changing the textbooks and willing to wade thigh-deep in noisome mud to investigate the most commonplace bird.

Heading back to Nairobi on the fourth day, Charles was silent, lost in gloomy thought. It seemed that his clue was a false one. There was no sign of Fitzpatrick. He was thinking about extending the field of search, and trying to calculate his chances of being able to get into Uganda while Kenyatta and Amin swore at each other for the umpteenth time, when Vanessa, who had been strangely silent, interrupted his train of thought.

'Look, James, I wish you'd stop treating me like a fool. You're looking for somebody. Maybe I can help.' She was matter-of-fact.

Charles was just about to sidetrack her, when he thought again. This was a native, who spoke his language, and presumably Swahili as well. And she was gorgeous, in an overtly sexy way, which should help to open up any men they needed to question. Maybe it wasn't such a bad idea. The notion of taking her into his confidence grew on him moment by moment.

'You know,' he said slowly, 'that's not a bad idea. When we get back to Nairobi, I'll tell you what my problem is. Maybe you can help, at that.' He concentrated on guiding the Mercedes over the ruts and wash-outs of the road. The more he thought about Vanessa's involvement, the better he liked the idea.

The porter interrupted their pre-dinner drink by rushing into Charles' cottage with a cable.

KURTZ LAWYERS THREATENING WRONGFUL DISMISSAL SUIT FOR TWO MILLION DOLLARS STOP NET ASSET VALUE NEW YORK COMPANY 1,500,000 DOLLARS STOP SUGGEST OFFER 410,000 FOR HIS THIRTY PERCENT STOP IRVINE

Charles, who had thought that he had heard the last of

Kurtz, was startled by the size of the damages. Even though lawyers generally quadrupled the size of their original claim to allow for legal shrinkage, it was a sizeable sum. When the costs of fighting the claim were added – at least 100,000 dollars, even if the company won – the expense to the company was potentially staggering. Irvine was taking too short-term a view, he thought, mindful of Fitzpatrick's opinion of Irvine as a policy-maker. Kurtz' percentage was worth at least 450,000 dollars, even at the relatively low asset value of a million and a half.

While Vanessa looked on in impressed silence, and the porter shifted from foot to foot, he drafted a reply:

OFFER KURTZ HALF MILLION DOLLARS HIS SHARES AND AGREEMENT TAKE NO FURTHER ACTION AGAINST COMPANY STOP 24 HOURS ACCEPT REJECT STOP PAY IMMEDIATELY ON ACCEPTANCE STOP INFORM WE WILL FIGHT ALL WAY ON REFUSAL STOP FITZPATRICK.

He handed the form to the porter, and asked him to make sure that it went fast rate. As the man left, he leant back in his chair with a sigh and closed his eyes.

'Here you are, darling,' Vanessa put a new drink into his hand. 'You need it.'

'This is the last moment when I wanted a two million dollar law-suit,' Charles said bitterly.

'My God,' she said. 'No wonder you looked a bit tense.'

Charles sighed, and thought for a moment.

'Vanessa, my love, will you do me a favour?' he said.

'Anything,' she purred theatrically, sipping her drink.

'I've an old friend in Nairobi, and I only have a PO box number for him. I left a message a few days ago. Could you go down to the General Post Office and see if he's collected it? Just ask them if anyone has picked up the mail from PO Box 618 during the last week.'

'Of course, love, but wouldn't it be more sensible for you to talk to them yourself?'

'I must make a call to London right away,' Charles improvised.

She raised her eyes and whistled softly. 'Two million dollars. Of course. Anything to do with whoever it is you're trying to trace?'

He got up from his chair stiffly, and hauled Vanessa to her feet, slapping her bottom lightly.

'Go to the Post Office, darling, and I'll tell you all when you get back.'

She pouted, smiled, and went to do his errand.

'No joy, darling,' she said on her return. 'Your friend hasn't collected his mail for over a month and your message is still there.'

'It's vital that I see him. In fact, it's the main reason I'm here.' Charles frowned. 'But I can't stay forever.'

'All right, spill it,' she said tartly. 'You've been snooping around the last few days, asking artless questions which wouldn't deceive a maiden aunt, about an English bird-watcher. I began to get the feeling you were taking me around as some sort of local colour.'

'Well, as a matter of fact, I'm not too anxious to make a big parade of looking for him. He wouldn't like it.' Charles made a great effort to look open and forthcoming. 'But when you offered to help, I had an idea.'

'Why don't you tell me about him first? Maybe I've met him.' I'm surprised you haven't, Charles thought. 'What does he look like?'

'As a matter of fact, he looks rather like me.' Charles looked embarrassed.

'Oh. Then I haven't seen him. I'd have known at once. Darling.'

Charles smiled sheepishly.

'Why are you looking for him?' Vanessa went on.

'A business matter,' Charles said shortly.

'It must be one hell of a matter if it brings you all the way out to Nairobi for a matter of days,' Vanessa said thoughtfully. 'How much longer can you stay?'

'About a week.'

'All right then, why don't we take a safari round the other bird places, if you think he's watching birds? At least you could eliminate them and then go on to try somewhere else.'

'That's just what I was going to suggest. Can you spare the time, Vanessa? I really need someone who knows the country, and can help with maps and things, and tell me where best to stay.'

'On one condition.' She smiled teasingly. 'If you took two rooms for us it would cost 220 shillings a night each. One double room will cost you 330 shillings. I want the difference.'

'You can have as much as you like,' Charles said, puzzled by the modesty of her demand. 'You're not exactly going to save for your old age on five pounds a night.'

She took his hand and placed it at the top of her thigh. 'I thought,' she said, 'that you might like the idea of treating me as a tart. You'll have bought my services. You can do anything you like with me.' She moved his hand purposefully.

'That's not a bad idea,' Charles said, beginning to explore on his own account. 'Intriguing.'

'I thought you'd like it.' Vanessa leaned over to kiss the side of his neck. 'I'm not only the best lay in Nairobi, I'm also the cheapest.' She pulled his hand away for a moment, and then slipped it under her waistband, sucking in her breath. 'And now, darling, stop thinking about finding your friend, and concentrate on finding something else.'

For the next few days, Charles drove over more and worse roads than he had seen even in Nigeria. They crisscrossed the country, searching out all the places where a bird fancier might conceivably be expected to forage in search of his quarry. They saw great quantities of game – zebra, gazelle, wildebeeste. Once they watched, fascinated, as a wildebeeste gave birth, and was joined by four or five other females, who seemed to take up guard posts round the female in labour. They paused to watch baboons playing on a wooden bridge; gazed in awe at six hippopotami half submerged in a pond so small it would barely contain them; eavesdropped on lion and lioness mating while three other great shaggy-maned beasts lay nearby, looking bored. They met a number of rhino, to whom them were careful to give a wide berth.

Once they rounded a bend on a steep hill to find a huge elephant crossing the road in a leisurely way, fifty feet in front of them. Charles had never seen anything so impressive in his life before, and would have stopped to watch. But the elephant, resenting the interruption, advanced upon them, flapping its ears and trumpeting. Charles crashed his gears in his anxiety to reverse, and had a hair-raising slither backwards down-hill, as Vanessa prayed aloud that the elephant would lose interest.

Finally it turned away, and started to eat, slowly and thoughtfully, from the bushes at the side of the road. Charles stopped thankfully, and he and Vanessa sat in tense silence until the great beast lumbered off.

As its baggy hind quarters disappeared from view, Charles found that he was soaked in sweat, his hands slippery on the wheel. 'Was it dangerous?' he asked shakily.

'I don't expect so,' Vanessa said. 'But elephants don't like other animals close to them or crossing their path. They make a dummy charge to frighten them off – they'll even do it to rhinos. But once they've received an indication of proper respect they generally give up and rarely kill anybody.'

'Thank God for that. All the same, it felt a whole heap too close for comfort. What happens if Jumbo just decides to stand there?'

'You have to wait until he makes up his mind to move. Elephants have the right of way in East Africa.'

At Amboseli, the manager of the lodge insisted that they attend his lecture, which he gave nightly to newcomers. Mostly it consisted of warnings – about animals, about the roads, about the do's and don'ts of the motor safari. He emphasized that cars should always stick to the main roads unless there were at least two cars in the party. Side roads were liable to washouts, and to be turned, in a matter of minutes, into impassible quagmires, from which the passengers of mired cars had to walk out, sometimes trekking up to fifty or a hundred miles. Not all of them made it. 'There have been a number of sad cases, very sad,' the manager said thoughtfully. Of all the animals, Charles was surprised to discover that it was the hippo he was most concerned to warn against. 'Never get between a hippo and his water,' he emphasized. Charles noticed that his comments on the Kenyan administration were tactless, to put it mildly, and wondered how long he would keep his job. But by then Vanessa was stroking the inside of his leg, and his attention was wandering.

Next morning they were on their way to Nairobi when they stopped to watch a lioness ambling through the long grass while her cubs gambolled about, snarling and jumping around in play.

'Butter wouldn't melt, would it?' said Charles. 'But if we got out of the car, we'd be in dead trouble.'

'I don't know about the trouble, but dead, for sure,' Vanessa said.

Later that morning they stopped to watch a pair of cheetahs, probably mother and son, chase a baby zebra without success, and then, just as Charles and Vanessa were about to leave, start, and pull down, a Grant's gazelle, showing an astonishing turn of speed.

Enchanted by the sight, Charles turned to Vanessa. 'My God, that alone was worth the price of admission,' he said.

'Thanks very much,' she said, pouting. But she was not put out. She knew very well how much her services were appreciated.

Charles smiled at her. She had been suberb, able, inventive, and endlessly hungry for sensation. At first Charles had compared her to Helen, but he was forced to accept that Vanessa had a deep animal need that made Helen seem almost vapid in comparison. Sometimes there was about Vanessa a glazed insatiable relentless searching for the ultimate in fulfilment which was almost frightening. As a mistress she was a star. As a wife, Charles felt, she would be a quick ticket to an early and exhaustive grave.

Sexually, and scenically, the tour had been an unqualified success. But of Fitzpatrick there had been no sign. Both Vanessa and Charles had asked about Englishmen fresh out of England, madly pursuing birds, but although they had found themselves on the receiving end of countless anecdotes and complaints about tenderfeet photographic explorers risking their own lives and those of others through reckless inexperience, none of the people concerned sounded in the least like Fitzpatrick. Charles was beginning to think that he was on a wild-goose chase. The only thing to do, he decided, was to relax and enjoy Vanessa while he could, and arrange to get an early flight home.

Maddeningly, it was back in Nairobi, in the bar of the Norfolk Hotel, that the first concrete clue as to Fitzpatrick's whereabouts appeared. Charles and Vanessa were sitting at a table in the corner, arguing over a large-scale map of north-western Kenya, the only part of the country they had not covered, when a heavy hand fell on Charles' shoulder, and a deep, whisky-husky voice said, 'Well, if it isn't Charles Hutchinson.'

Charles froze. For a frantic second, he wondered whether to confirm or deny his identity. Was this a trap? Was it – God forbid – someone he'd known in Nigeria? He looked up with what he hoped was a look of casual enquiry.

'Must be three months since we met,' the voice boomed enthusiastically. 'Going to introduce me?'

Mechanically, Charles fumbled for a name for Vanessa. 'This is Miss Truelove,' he said at last, and writhed inwardly at the sheer banality of it. A tall lean, bespectacled man, with a weather-beaten, broken-veined face, shook her hand energetically.

'Jenkins,' he said. 'Extraordinary thing, meeting this bloke here in Nairobi. Thought he'd buried himself for good in that god-forsaken hole Olmesutye. Nothing but lions and birds there, you know. Primitive as hell, real Africa and all that. Used to know the old boy who put up the lodge there. Eccentric chap, Pauling, reckoned tourists would want to see the real thing. Wrong, of course, died broke. His son runs it now. This chap' – he indicated Charles – 'is the only man I know mad enough to stay there. Admire your taste in birds,' he said to Charles, leering at Vanessa, 'whole lot more interesting than the feathered variety.'

Vanessa was sparkling with malicious amusement as she

watched Charles floundering to recapture his poise. 'Do sit down and have a drink. Tell me more about Charles. He's a man of mystery, you know.'

Nothing lost, Jenkins settled down, accepted a large whisky and proceeded to regale a mirthful Vanessa with a highly-coloured account of Charles' eccentricities, while Charles himself, increasingly uncomfortable, ran a finger round his collar, and wished the man would go away. At last he had a real clue to Fitzpatrick's whereabouts, and this drunken old idiot was going to waste his time in futile blather.

Finally Vanessa indicated with delicate impropriety that time was getting on, and that she and Charles had more intimate things to discuss. After the appropriate spluttering exchange of goodfellowship, Jenkins lurched off into the night, leaving Charles staring at an amused Vanessa.

'Well, darling, a man of mystery indeed,' she said,' complete with a new name, to boot. So tell me, who is this Charles Hutchinson? Of course I guessed he was the man you've been looking for all this time. And you can congratulate me. I wrote down that place, while the old fool was ogling some poor woman who came in. Olmesutye. What's more, I've looked it up, and it's not far from Lake Magadi. Tomorrow, as ever is, darling. Tonight I want some food, and then a reward. So stay sober, my friend. Tonight you're going to work.'

Charles had told himself that he would have preferred to set out straight away. But in fact a night spent with the athletic Vanessa, and some deep and interrupted sleep, made him feel a great deal better the next day, as they set out for Olmesutye. He was almost bouncy when they reached a police barrier at Magadi. The initial euphoria soon wore off as he wrestled with the plethora of official paperwork which alone entitled him to go on.

When he had filled in all the masses of forms that were obligatory, the policeman looked at his destination and said, 'You are going to Olmesutye? What kind of transport do you have?'

'A Mercedes,' Charles said.

The policeman looked doubtful. 'When do you expect to return?' he said.

'In two days' time,' Charles said, a twinge of worry beginning to affect him.

'If you do not come back on the right day, we send out search parties,' the policeman said. 'A Mercedes is hardly the appropriate transport. It is very dangerous country.'

'Oh. Then you'd better make it three days, to be on the safe side,' Charles said, swallowing an impulse to call the whole thing off.

The policeman made a note in his book, and impassively handed Charles his documents.

'Good luck,' he said.

Even with all the windows opened, the car was quickly baking. It was an effort to breathe as they passed the soda extraction works. The two causeways before them faded into the shimmering heat-haze over the soda lakes. Charles chose the right fork at random. It was the wrong one, and twenty minutes later they were back where they had started. The left hand fork rapidly deteriorated. Soon they were forced to pull in to the side when they sighted a lorry on its way. And the hump in the middle of the road was grinding intermittently and ominously against the Mercedes' undercarriage. It was a relief to leave the lakes and the smell of rotten eggs. But their troubles were not yet over. Once again they lost their way. Some garbled Swahili, and a friendly Masai, finally put them back on the road, but it got worse and worse, and finally virtually petered out. Charles began to curse himself for trying this route in a saloon car. His hands began to shake with nerves, and he had to draw up.

They were sitting in the middle of nowhere, wondering what best to do, when a jeep came towards them. Charles flagged it down.

'How far is it to Olmesutye?' he asked the driver.

'About twenty eight miles,' came the reply. 'Are you thinking of trying it in that car?'

Charles nodded.

'About four miles from here you have to ford a stream.

Then you've got to get through two miles of sand drifts. And then you've got the escarpment.'

Charles gulped, and looked depressed.

'Got a gun?'

Charles shook his head.

'Water?'

Charles shook his head again.

'This is wild country.' The young man seemed irritated at having to spell out the facts of bush life to two city slickers. 'If you break down you can't get out. There are too many lions about. The last Mercedes that tried this road got stuck half way up the escarpment,' he said thoughtfully. 'It was three days before I happened to come by and managed to tow them out.'

Veronica looked distinctly frightened and Charles, with darkness fast approaching, lacked courage.

'I think we'll turn round and head back for Nairobi,' he said.

'You'd be wise,' agreed the young man. 'Get yourself a Land Rover and approach Olmesutye from the north, from Narok. That's not such a terrible road and you don't have to climb up the escarpment.'

Charles reversed the car cautiously. He felt frustrated: he had been buoyed up by the prospect of seeing Fitzpatrick. Somehow he felt that fate was against him. Maybe he was never going to find his benefactor.

Next day, however, he tried again. This time there was no nonsense about saloon cars. Charles had hired a sturdy Land-Rover, and was willing to fight all the way through whatever sand dunes, fords, washes, or just plain bad roads that fate could put up against him.

He and Vanessa bounced about in the cab as he fought the wheel. The truck turned out to be full of spikes and prominences against which they bounced and bashed, and not even the inadequate handholds saved them from bruises and abrasions of all kinds.

But at last they reached Olmesutye, and the decrepit lodge

that Jenkins had described. The lodge rather thrust itself upon them. The road simply ended in a clearing in the bush – and there was the lodge, stone built and straw-roofed.

Charles stepped down from the Land Rover. He shook his cramped legs, tired by incessant gear changes and non-stop action on brake or accelerator. He passed the back of his elbow over his sweaty and dust-drenched forehead. Within a few minutes he would be having a cooling beer with Fitzpatrick, who would no doubt congratulate him on his skill and perseverance in tracking him down.

Two Africans came to the steps to collect the luggage; then, as Charles took his elbow away from his face, they stopped, stared, and ran away round the back of the building.

Charles, puzzled, started towards the house, as a young white man, with a shock of frizzy brown hair, dressed in jungle-green shirt and shorts, came out of the doorway.

The young man, too, stopped and stared. Then he walked slowly towards Charles, his eyes on Charles' face. He stretched out of his hand.

'Who the devil are you?' he asked.

'I'm James Fitzpatrick.' Charles said, shaking the other's hand. 'This is Vanessa Truelove.' He thought it amusing to continue their private joke over her surname. Vanessa shook hands with the young man, who suddenly relaxed. Charles realized it must be a bit of a shock to find an apparent identical twin of one's guests arriving unannounced.

'Come in,' the young man said. 'I'm William Pauling. I expect you'd like a drink.'

He led them through to a large room, where a fire was laid in the grate.

'This place gets very cold at night,' he explained. 'It's 70 degrees at night. That's warm enough in England. But it's a drop of 30 degrees here – and that feels damn cold. I'll get the boys to attend to the rooms. Do you want one or two?'

'Have a guess,' Vanessa said, stroking Charles' arm.

Pauling laughed and went off to alert the servants and organize drinks. Vanessa, who had started to sparkle, as always, when introduced to a new and unknown male, decided to have a quick bath and brush up.

Pauling returned with a beer for Charles and a neat Scotch for himself.

'I need a stiff drink,' he explained. 'When I saw you standing beside the Land Rover I thought I'd seen a ghost.'

'I can imagine it was a bit of a shock,' Charles said. 'I understand you've had someone staying with you who's the spitting image of me.'

'Yes, we have.'

Charles wanted to enquire where the Chairman was, but decided to wait. Fitzpatrick had obviously gone to great lengths to preserve his anonymity, and Charles did not want to blow his cover. He was probably resting in his room before dinner. They could meet then, as strangers.

But the three of them dined alone. Vanessa, delighted that there was some competition to Charles even in the bundu, had put on a simple white dress with a scoop neck, which gave Pauling plenty of flashes of her breasts.

Charles feared that Fitzpatrick must have departed for one of his occasional trips to Nairobi. It would be just his luck to have covered vast areas of East Africa in his search, only to find that his quarry was at the very spot where the search had started.

After dinner they sat round the fire. Pauling explained that he had created his lodge for the small but wealthy band of tourists who wanted to see the real Africa.

'Take Amboseli,' Pauling remarked scornfully. 'At the new lodge they put cabbages out so that the elephants come regularly to feed. What a perversion of nature, to feed such majestic animals on cabbages!'

Vanessa agreed enthusiastically. Charles pointed out that she had not been averse to exclaiming over the rare rattels, or honey badgers, who had been lured into the floodlights on the lawn of the lodge at Amboseli by pieces of meat staked to the ground. Vanessa looked at him nastily and began to cross and uncross her legs, giving Pauling a tempting display of thigh as her dress rode higher and higher.

As Pauling poured a second round of brandy, Charles delicately began his questioning.

'We heard about my "double" in Nairobi,' he began, 'and someone said he was staying here. You know, I travel round the world a lot and I've kept on nearly bumping into him. So I thought it would be a good opportunity to finally come face to face with him and see some real wildlife at the same time.'

'Well,' Pauling said slowly, 'at least you will have the chance to see some animals. We'll get up early and take a Land Rover out. We should see something – but no promises. The animals aren't on parade here, you know, as they are in the parks.'

He embarked on another long tale of their remoteness and its hazards, with Vanessa as an enthusiastic audience.

Charles stood up and walked towards the window. 'Where is my double, then?' he enquired with apparent casualness.

'You've never met him?' Pauling asked.

'No,' Charles replied. 'I suppose it's just my luck that he's gone to Nairobi for a few days.'

Pauling stood up too, his back to the fire. 'Not to Nairobi,' he said slowly. 'No, I'm afraid he's almost certainly dead.'

'Dead?' Charles was shocked.

'I fear so,' Pauling said. 'You know, I always warn our guests that this area really is dangerous. But your double – Charles Hutchinson his name was – had been here for several months. He seemed to know how to look after himself. He was determined to produce the really definitive encyclopedia of East African birds. He brought a lot of very expensive photographic equipment up from Nairobi and used to go out every day, filming and taking notes. He always took a rifle with him and seemed safe enough.

'Ten days ago he went out, as usual, at about four o'clock, after a siesta. He never came back. We searched all night. Eventually we found the camera on its tripod. The rifle was about two hundred yards away – but there was no sign of Hutchinson.

'How can you be certain he's dead, if you didn't find the body?' Charles enquired.

'We can't be certain,' Pauling admitted. 'But otherwise why

wouldn't he come back here? There's no point in walking around in the bush at night and Hutchinson wasn't fool enough to leave his rifle behind.'

Charles sighed in depressed agreement, and they left to go to bed.

'Does it matter much?' Vanessa asked sympathetically.

'It sure as hell does.' Charles muttered gloomily. He had taken on Fitzpatrick's job, wife, family, mistress – everything. The only person who had known of the deception was Jenny. Now she was dead and Fitzpatrick too. It looked as if he, Charles, was stuck with the identity of James Fitzpatrick for life.

CHAPTER SIXTEEN

Charles was in no mood to think about game, or even about Vanessa, as they set off, next day, back to Nairobi. Vanessa was silent and resentful beside him. For the first time, his performance as a lover had been less than entirely adequate. What made it worse was that he couldn't even explain. Charles tried to adjust to the fact that he now *was* James Fitzpatrick, whether he liked it or not. Of course he'd always accepted that it was possible, even desirable that he'd be marooned in his role. Caroline, a flourishing business, more money than he could have hoped to see in a life-time, was now unassailably his. So why didn't he feel happy? Charles found, now that he had to abandon his own identity entirely, that up till now it had all been a sort of game. Suddenly he was faced with a lifetime of it – and it wasn't at all so amusing. In fact, Charles thought, as he wrestled the Land Rover through the ruts, it's not funny at all. And it's going to take a lot of adjusting to. He realized that he'd never really thought of it as permanent, never thought of the voluntary extinction of Charles Hutchinson as a fact. I *am* Fitzpatrick, now, he thought, starting to panic. There's no one left who knows any different. There's no one who even remembers that Charles Hutchinson exists.

Back at the hotel in Nairobi, Charles was still preoccupied. Vanessa, after a period of huff, had thought to tease him out of his mood, and was seriously worried when he failed entirely to react. He looked pale, and – yes – stricken, she thought. For the first time she wondered if the mysterious Hutchinson had been a brother, perhaps a twin. Alarmed, she set herself out to bring Charles back down to earth.

At first it was an impossible task. Charles was polite, but remote, and obviously unaware of anything but his thoughts. He allowed himself to be settled in a chair, and to have three gigantic vodkas poured down him before his stunned expression began to fade.

Finally he looked at Vanessa, really looked, for the first time that day. For a moment, she detected distaste. Her confidence already badly shaken, she burst into tears. Charles, who had been thinking longingly of Caroline, and who had been wondering what he had seen in this fading sexpot, snapped back to the present, and took her in his arms. She was so relieved, that their reconciliation was a dramatically passionate affair, and not soon over.

Later, sweat-soaked and contented, she broached the idea of going out to a movie. Charles was indifferent to the notion, but willing to please. They looked through an edition of the East African Standard, and settled on a lurid-looking American film at the Kenya cinema.

They parked in Government Road, leaving the Land Rover in the care of two small boys, who assured them that they would take the greatest care of it. Charles distributed the necessary largesse, and held Vanessa's hand as they walked over to the cinema. Possessively, she tucked their clasped hands high up under her breast. Charles felt the heavy weight of her flesh against his knuckles, and flashed her a smile of gratitude. She had, he thought, behaved rather well after the initial shock. A pity he couldn't tell her what the trouble really was.

The film was only just sufficiently interesting for Charles to keep awake. It concerned the complicated and unsavoury private lives of the citizens of a small American town. As they sat, surrounded by a largely African audience, watching a succession of seductions, rapes, abortions, divorces and suicides Charles wondered what image the denizens of Nairobi must take away of the U.S.A.

He and Vanessa were jostled in the crowd leaving the cinema and found themselves next to a prosperous-looking African. He had the smart suit, collar and tie, rounded stomach and self-important air of a Kenyan V.I.P. He was talking loudly to a party of five or six other Africans, who kept a foot or so away, protecting him from the throng.

The pressure of the crowd, as it pushed its way through the doors onto the pavement, forced Charles and Vanessa closer to this distinguished genial personage. He was joking with his attendants, who laughed in the sycophantic way that distinguishes the political hanger-on the world over.

Suddenly there was a sharp crack. The big black man fell to the pavement, his genial face a ruin. A high-calibre bullet had destroyed it. There was blood everywhere. Charles saw flecks of it on his suit. In the hushed vacuum of shock, Charles found himself kneeling over the man, feeling for his pulse. It was a purely automatic reaction, taken partly in protest against the fact that the big man's jackals had suddenly melted away into the crowd. Charles, blood on his suit, and now on his hands, spared a moment to think of them with searing contempt. The man was clearly dead. There was nothing for Charles to do.

Charles felt someone tugging at his collar. It was Vanessa.

'We must get away,' she said. 'God knows what will happen. If we get picked up by the police as witnesses we'll be here all night.'

Dazed, Charles looked up. The crowd round the fallen figure had moved well back. A ring of sweating black faces was looking with curiosity at the tableau he and Vanessa made. Reluctantly Charles conceded the force of her anxiety, and allowed himself to be dragged to his feet. The crowd parted for them, and then closed behind them. They hurried quickly along the dark pavement to where the Land Rover was parked. The two boys pocketed their reward, happily unaware of the tragedy which had taken place only yards away.

'Haven't we guarded it well?' they chorused. The tyres were still attached, and there was no wheel missing.

Vanessa hurried him into the truck and urged him to start it.

'Come on, come on,' she hissed, staring over her shoulder.

As they drove away, a cavalcade of police cars and ambulances tore by, sirens shrieking. Charles watched their lights flashing in his rear mirror for a long distance.

At the Norfolk, they slipped over to Charles's cottage, hoping that no one had seen them. Charles took off his jacket, and washed it, and his hands, as best he could. The water ran a macabre shade of pink as it swirled down the drain. Charles grimaced with disgust, and called over his shoulder, 'I wonder who he was?'

'Probably a politician of some kind,' Vanessa replied from the bar, where she was pouring both of them drinks.

She walked into the bathroom, carrying stiff vodkas for them both. 'They say,' she said, 'that when you squash a fly it has a climax in the split second before it dies. I find violence and death very stimulating.' She came towards him, glasses in hand, looking at the faint pink traces still staining the water as it sluiced through the linen of Charles' jacket. 'There's something about blood, when it's not mine,' she said thoughtfully. 'You know, I once had a huge orgasm at a bull fight in Mexico. I was frightfully embarrassed. I was just going to apologize to the man who took me when I realized that he'd had one too.'

She put down her drink and slowly drew his head down to hers. Her mouth was caressing on his, and then suddenly her teeth bit down on his lower lip. Charles had the metallic taste of blood in his mouth. 'Fuck me,' she said. 'Don't talk, don't think, just fuck me.'

It was 5.15 a.m. Charles was in a chair, in a pool of light. The man sitting behind a desk in the darkness kept on repeating the same questions. The police station in Harry Thika Road, a few hundred yards from the Norfolk hotel, was cool. Charles wished he had put on a jacket. 'What's the point of asking the same things time after time?' Charles began to lose his temper. 'I'm a perfectly innocent tourist, enjoying a peaceful safari. It's not my fault I'm next to a man when he's shot.'

The policeman stood up and came to the edge of the circle. He had a large round face, like the murdered man – probably of the same tribe, Charles thought.

'Don't start to shout at me,' the man said menacingly. 'Kenya is not a colony now. If I want to, I can keep you here as long as I like.'

Charles restrained himself. Losing one's temper never produced results with Africans – they just became increasingly mulish.

'Where's my girl friend?' he asked. He was not over-worried. Vanessa was tough enough to look after herself.

'The lady we found in your bed is being questioned elsewhere,' the policeman said. 'Do not worry. We are not savages, even if we have black skins.'

'I don't give a damn if you are black, brown, white or khaki.' Charles was stung by the implication that he was a racialist. 'I just object to people barging into my hotel room at four o'clock in the morning with guns in their hands.' Actually, of course he knew that police all over the world bring people in for questioning at 4 a.m., because that is the time they are at their lowest ebb.

'Don't you dare to complain about *our* behaviour.' The policeman came from behind the desk, and stood in front of Charles. He shook his finger in his wrath.

'One of Kenya's finest men is killed when you are right next to him. You run away. Don't you think that is suspicious?'

'I didn't know who he was,' Charles said. 'I just didn't want any trouble.'

'Now you are in big, big trouble, Mr Fitzpatrick. An innocent man does not run away and jump into bed with a white whore.'

Charles jumped up. 'She's not a whore,' he shouted.

'How would you know?' The policeman pushed him contemptuously back into the chair. He was very strong. 'Answer the question: why did you run away?'

'I was in a foreign country. I was afraid. I thought there might be a riot, or anything.'

The inspector leaned down, so that his face was only inches from Charles'.

'Nonsense, Mr Fitzpatrick.' The policeman stated. 'You ran away because you had killed Mr Mbangu. Now tell me who paid you to do it.'

Charles began to sweat with fright. He repeated his explanation that he had gone out for a perfectly normal visit to the cinema, witnessed the crime and hastened away to avoid any trouble.

'You are an educated man.' The policeman was sarcastic. 'Not a poor black primitive savage. You know that murder is a serious crime and any witness has an obligation to report anything he sees.'

He gripped Charles by the lapels of his shirt, pushing him against the back of the chair. 'I do not believe you. The people of this country will not believe you. The court will not believe you.'

Charles fought down panic. The man had a suppressed manic fury. 'But I have no reason to kill anyone. I have no gun, either.'

'Don't worry,' the African said, releasing his grip and smiling nastily. 'We will find the reason. And we will find the gun.'

'Where have you hidden the gun?' he suddenly bellowed.

'I have no gun,' Charles expostulated.

The policeman retreated into the darkness behind the desk. 'You think you are clever,' he said. 'But we will find the gun. If you are guilty and we do not find it, we will plant one on you. We will manufacture the reason. And if we do not think, even so, the case will stand up in court, we have simpler methods of disposing of murderers.' He drew his hand across his throat.

'This is ridiculous,' Charles said. 'I am not guilty. And there is no reason why you or anyone else should wish to convict an innocent man.'

'For Mr Mbangu's death, someone *has* to be convicted,' the African replied.

The two boy car-watchers, eyes round with alarm, were brought in to identify Charles. Then he was shown a series of photographs, all of Africans, and asked whether he recognized or knew them. Among the gallery were Jomo Kenyatta and his wife Mama Ngina. Charles became really alarmed: if the President or his family were remotely involved in this, then there was going to be big trouble. He asked why their photographs were included.

'Just to make sure you are not a complete liar,' the policeman explained rudely. 'If you had said you had not recognized them, it would have been quite remarkable.' The President's photograph, after all, was plastered all over every post office and shop in the country.

He came to stand behind Charles. In his voice was a silky menace.

'I hope you are not suggesting it is possible our President or Kenya's first lady could be involved in a case of – murder.' He spat out the last word.

Charles shook his head.

'I am glad. Otherwise I would not give that,' the man flicked his fingers, 'for your safety.'

At 6.30 Charles was left alone. At 7.30 he was put in a police car, which, siren wailing, took him to police headquarters on Jomo Kenyatta Avenue.

After a short wait in an ante-room, he was shown through a door marked 'Chief Superintendent J. K. Maina'. A tall African, with a thin, pointed face and spectacles, stood up from behind the desk. He read out a charge sheet. Charles gathered he was being arrested for obstruction of justice by failing to stay at the scene of the shooting.

'If you are arresting me,' Charles said, 'can I get in touch with the British consulate to send me a lawyer?'

'No,' the policeman said, 'you cannot. Sit down.' He offered Charles a cigarette and ordered some coffee. He was much more relaxed and sophisticated than the man at the Thika Road station. He went through the same questions, however, comparing them to some notes on the desk – notes either of his previous answers or of Vanessa's replies, Charles supposed.

133

'So, you have no explanation of why this gentleman was shot dead,' the Chief Superintendent concluded. 'You know nothing about it, you saw nothing, in sum you can give us no help.'

'I wish I could,' Charles replied with feeling.

A policeman entered, put down a tray with a silver coffee service and two cups. Maina poured the coffee carefully. 'Shall I be mother?' he asked with a little smile.

'How did you get hold of us so quickly?' Charles asked. 'I suppose the two little boys who were looking after the Land Rover remembered us.'

'Oh no,' Maina replied. 'They would be the last to volunteer information. They would be the last to want to see a policeman, in case they were sent to Starehe, away from their profitable little pitch.'

He thought for a few minutes, his fingers tapping gently on the desk top.

He stood up. 'I might as well tell you,' he decided. He picked up a copy of a newspaper from the desk and gave it to Charles.

MBANGU SLAIN, said the the headline on the *Daily Nation*'s front page. Underneath it was a photograph: the black politician was sprawled on the pavement; Charles was kneeling over him, Vanessa tugging at his collar to pull him away. The caption read: 'The murderer making sure his victim was dead? Police wish to interview the European pictured above.'

'My God,' Charles said. The picture did, at first sight, look very incriminating.

'It is fortunate, is it not, Mr Fitzpatrick,' the policeman commented calmly, 'that you do not carry a gun? Even as it is, I think you will be wise not to dispute your arrest. Mr Mbangu is, or rather was, one of our most popular M.P.s. If you were to venture on the streets of Nairobi right now, you would almost certainly be lynched.' Maina smiled.

'However, you can see that, with that photograph in my hands, I did not need to be Hercule Poirot' – Maina obviously enjoyed showing off his culture and command of English – 'to show it to the comparatively few hotels where a white man might be staying. It was, I must admit, time-saving to find you and the young lady in the picture sharing the same bed. Incidentally, I must compliment you on your taste.' He grinned to himself and poured some more coffee.

'The Kenya police are very reasonable,' Maina continued. 'We are also not fools.' A slight edge crept into his voice. 'Neither are you. You are the Chairman of a large and distinguished British publishing company. So I will ask you one question. But first some background.' He selected some papers from a pile before him, and examined them.

'The photograph was taken at the time of Mr Mbangu's death, 10.32 p.m. At 11.30 p.m. it was at the offices of the *Daily Nation*, just in time for the last edition. At 12.30 a.m., just too late to stop publication, the paper sent it to me.'

'The *Daily Nation* photographer must be blessing his luck to have been there at the time of the murder,' Charles observed.

'That's just the point.' Maina leant forward, watching Charles' eyes like a hawk. 'It wasn't taken by a *Daily Nation* staff photographer. It wasn't even taken by a freelance, who would have demanded a high price. It was delivered to the newspaper in a plain brown envelope, with no clue as to who had taken it.'

Maina leaned back in his chair. 'So now we come to the question: why should whoever planned this murder have arranged for a photograph to be taken of the event?'

'Why ask me?' Charles expostulated. 'It was just a coincidence that I was there.'

The chief superintendent shook his head slowly and sadly. 'We policemen do not believe in coincidence,' he pointed out. 'Someone wanted that picture published and the only point of publishing it was that *you* were in it.'

'To provide the evidence that Mbangu had been killed,' Charles suggested. 'Maybe he was a hired killer and had to have the evidence for his client.'

Maina nodded. 'Then why send it to the *Daily Nation*?'

'Because, by chance, it showed me. It offered a diversion – it threw suspicion on someone else.'

'Not good enough,' the policeman stated. 'Firstly, sending

the photograph in fact makes it very unlikely you were the murderer. Why incriminate yourself, unless you are trying a double bluff?' At this thought Maina's eyes suddenly became steel-alert. 'As to having evidence for your mysterious client,' he said sarcastically, 'Mbangu's death will be plastered all over the newspapers of Africa, let alone Europe.'

'There's nothing like a photograph,' Charles demurred.

'Ingenious, but not good enough.' Maina dismissed the idea. 'I have told you before, I do not believe in coincidence. Believe me, there is some key which links Mbangu, the murderer, the photograph and you.'

Charles was relieved that the police officer placed him separately from the murderer.

'That's impossible. No one knew I was going to the Kenya cinema last night, so nobody could possibly have planned to take that photograph. My presence was purely an accident.'

'It was Freud who pointed out that there is no such thing as an accident,' Maina riposted. 'I have been a detective for a very long time, and I warn you to believe me. There is a link.' He sighed, a man who only too frequently could not persuade lesser mortals to see obvious facts. 'Now to the routine.'

He went through Charles' visit to Kenya, his stay in Nairobi, his safari, finally his journey to Olmesutye.

Charles was amazed at this knowledge of his movements and the speed with which they had been obtained, within twelve hours of receiving the photograph.

'Like most tourists,' Maina suggested, 'I imagine you thought that filling in details of your car at the entrances and exits to our parks was a piece of typical African bureaucracy, eh? The natives exaggerating the red-tape of their former colonialist masters?' He laughed at Charles' discomfiture. 'Well, now you know that it makes it only too easy to check a suspect's movements. And believe you me, when one of our foremost politicians is killed, the radio-telephone can work even faster than the old bush telegraph.'

The questioning was routine, however. The only point which worried the chief superintendent was Charles' visit to Olmesutye. He seemed to find it hard to understand why he had wanted to go to such a remote spot in the first place; why he had persevered after the difficulties of the first approach via Lake Magadi; and why they left so quickly after taking so much trouble to get there.

Charles had decided not to tell the policeman about Fitzpatrick. The very fact that he had a double would only lead to even more extensive enquiries. He had a strong feeling he should protect his dead benefactor's privacy. He told Maina that he had wanted to see some really wild country, that his initial failure had only spurred him on the more, but that Olmesutye itself had proved a great disappointment.

The inspector was not satisfied and returned twice to the subject.

Finally, he rubbed his eyes as he finished his interrogation.

'You will remain under house arrest in your cottage at the Norfolk,' he pronounced. 'We have already impounded your passport. I still believe there is something you have not told me,' he continued, reprovingly. 'Something which links you to the murderer and the photograph.'

Charles shook his head.

'If you change your mind, or if you think of anything else, please let me know immediately.'

The telephone rang. Maina answered it and swivelled round, so that his back was to Charles. He spoke in Swahili, listening with deference and saying little. He replaced the receiver and stood up, looking Charles straight in the eyes.

'This is a very serious matter,' he said. 'Mr Mbangu was a popular politician. He won his popularity by attacking the Government, by accusing it of nepotism and of corruption. That is always the way of the demagogue, and it receives a ready response in a poor country like ours.'

He placed his hands, fingers outstretched, on top of the desk, his fingertips beginning to beat a soundless tattoo.

'Not long ago a similar demagogue, one Kariuki, was murdered. Your British newspaper, *The Sunday Times*, suggested the Chief of Police and even the beloved father of our country, Mzee Jomo Kenyatta, were involved.

'Yesterday was the anniversary of Kariuki's death. The students of the University held a little riot, and we had to beat up a few Marxist fanatics.'

Maina paused, to control his rising temper. Charles was astonished by the change from the placid, sophisticated person who had questioned him.

'We are surrounded, Mr Fitzpatrick,' said the chief superintendent, 'by Communists, envious of the peace and stability of our country. They have made Somalia, in the North, the best armed country in Africa; Tanzania, to the South, is putty in their hands, Uganda is stacked with Russian jet fighters.

'Already these infiltrators are spreading rumours around Nairobi that Mr Mbangu was killed by the old hawks of the government because he threatened to expose them. That is not true.' He was shouting.

He sat down, his hands shaking. 'I know you are not the murderer, Mr Fitzpatrick, because Mbangu was shot with a telescopic rifle from the first floor of an empty building on the other side of Government Road. We have found the murder weapon.

'But I think Mbangu was shot by Communists. This is a very serious matter,' he said. 'They chose the very day of Kariuki's anniversary, of the students' riot, when feelings would be highest. And now they are saying Mbangu was shot by a white mercenary, by you.'

'They plan to stir up a revolution against our President, Mzee Jomo Kenyatta, to inflame the people against him. If you know anything about it, Mr Fitzpatrick, you should throw yourself on our mercy. Those who attack our President threaten our freedom, our unity, our country.'

Maina walked round his desk and stood over Charles.

'If we find you are in any way involved, Mr Fitzpatrick, or if you have lied to us, then, with or without a trial, you will surely die.'

CHAPTER SEVENTEEN

The police escorted Charles back to the Norfolk in time for lunch. But food was a long way from his mind. He poured himself a long vodka, and tried to phone Vanessa. There was no reply. He wondered uneasily if she was still being interrogated by the police, and cringed in retrospect at the memory of their rude awakening, when naked and dishevelled, all too clearly ravaged, they had been snatched from their tumbled bed.

He thought for a while, sipping his drink slowly, trying to put himself in the place of an arrogantly successful man like Fitzpatrick. What would he have done? Charles found it hard to imagine. He had never felt more helpless.

Finally, he fetched the vodka bottle, and settled down by the telephone to try and get through to London. He had a confused feeling that Caroline might be able to help. But the hotel switchboard had had instructions to allow him no overseas calls, and no amount of argument would sway them. He realised apprehensively that his call to Vanessa, if it had been successful, would have been monitored. He felt suddenly naked and exposed, as if he had been flayed, and all his nerve ends left tingling.

At 8 p.m. his phone rang. It was Maina, who told him curtly that he was no longer under arrest, but his passport was still impounded and he was not to leave Kenya. Charles tried to ask what was happening about the murder, but Maina put the phone down before Charles had finished his sentence.

By now the level of the vodka bottle was low, and Charles was feeling slightly light-headed. A brisk shower did little to improve matters, and Charles realised that a day without food, spent largely brooding over a vodka bottle, had taken its toll. He dressed a little clumsily, and decided that he badly needed dinner.

On impulse, he tried Vanessa again just before he left the cottage. This time she was in.

'Darling,' she said, 'thank God you called, I've been frightfully worried about you. The police would tell me nothing, and I couldn't raise you on the phone – the hotel said you were allowed no incoming calls. Listen, I have an idea. A friend of mine is an important politician, close to the President. I've been in touch with him, and it's just possible that he may be able to pull strings to get you out of this mess. Come over to the Intercontinental as soon as you can, and make for room 543. I'll meet you there. And whatever you do, try not to be recognized. Everybody thinks you did it, and they may try to kill you.'

Charles gulped, and wondered how he was going to get through an angry city without being seen. 'Couldn't you come here?' he suggested.

'Don't be silly, love, it's not as bad as that. After all, it's dark. Just wear some sunglasses, or something. You'll be all right. And the Norfolk's out. Too British. I can't possibly meet you there. Now do hurry, there's a dear. I promise that I've got it all worked out.'

Charles remembered uneasily, as he turned the collar of his open-necked shirt up, brushed his hair forward over his forehead, and put on his dark glasses, that Vanessa was turned on by danger. Possibly she was enjoying the atmosphere of menace, and the real possibility that Charles might be brutally beaten, if not killed, on his way to meet her. He had a sudden vision of her in the arms of some man, perhaps her black politician, wildly stimulated by the knowledge that the body that had so lately loved hers was broken and bleeding. He shuddered, as he switched out the lights, and made a mental note never again to go to a bull fight. The thought of countless Vanessas enjoying the torment of the bull was frankly chilling.

The short drive in the Land Rover went without incident, though Charles was sure that every eye was on him, and found himself hunching over the wheel, willing the traffic lights to change and let him through. At the Intercontinental the askari on duty in the car park didn't even glance his way. Charles scuttled hastily past the deserted swimming pool, and in through the rear entrance without meeting a soul. It took a fair dose of courage to walk to the lift, and his finger was trembling as he pressed the button. He found himself nervously wiping the palms of his hands on his wilting handkerchief as he waited. Fortunately it came quickly, and was empty. Charles breathed a sigh of relief as he reached the fifth floor. He almost ran down the corridor until he reached 543, and he was panting with exertion and panic as he knocked sharply on the door.

It opened to reveal a tall, lithe black girl, who smiled at him gently and said, 'Hello, I'm Arabella. You must be James. Vanessa asked me to look after you. She says she may be some time, but you're not to worry, everything will be all right.' She glanced down the corridor, checking to see that he had not been seen, and drew him into the room. Her hand was velvety, and the long fingers seemed to linger in his palm. Charles wondered for a moment if he was drunker than he had thought, but a quick whiff of the smoke curling up from a thin cigarette on the edge of an ashtray on the coffee-table reassured him. If he was drunk, Arabella was high. The room reeked of marijuana.

Arabella brushed past him to the sofa, and picked up her joint. She took a deep drag, and handed it to him. 'We may as well enjoy ourselves,' she said. 'Vanessa's got work to do.' She smiled at him, and sank back into a corner of the deep couch.

Charles inhaled deeply, and felt his head begin to swirl in the familiar way. Suddenly he remembered the Paradise Club with a prick of nostalgia. Life had been so much simpler then. He thought wistfully of the companionship, so warm and uncomplicated, that he had enjoyed in Ibadan, and found himself looking at Arabella with speculation. Hastily he reminded himself of where he was and why.

Arabella was ordering food over the house phone, twisted in an elegant pose over the arm of the sofa. An intriguing length of smooth leg was revealed as her skirt rode up to her thigh. Charles watched it dreamily, and sucked again on his joint.

'Two lobster salads,' she was saying, 'and a bottle of champagne. And bring a bottle of brandy while you're at it. We won't want to be disturbed.' Arabella turned to wink at Charles. 'And four balloons. Yes, four. We're expecting guests.' She put down the phone, and smiled at him. 'Vanessa said you liked lobster,' she said, 'and I like champagne, so it's half and half. You'd better duck into the bathroom when the waiter comes. We don't want him to see you. You really are in danger in Nairobi, you know.'

'I know,' said Charles gloomily, watching the smoke from his joint curl blue and aromatic towards the ceiling. 'That damned picture.'

'Tell me about it. What did the police do to you?' Arabella was lighting a second joint.

Charles began to talk, reminiscently. Suddenly it all seemed comic and unimportant. They both giggled when he described how Vanessa had looked, tumbling nude and ungainly out of bed before the fascinated and lecherous eyes of two armed policemen. There were tears of mirth in Arabella's eyes when Charles repeated the disparaging comments one had made about his own shrunken equipment. It seemed natural and right that Charles' hand should be high on her thigh. As he began to recount the interrogation, Arabella's hips hunched forward, and Charles began slowly to caress her dampening mound through slick nylon panties which seemed to slide and dissolve under his fingers until his touch was full on her hot and slathered flesh. The air was full of musk and marijuana.

The waiter's knock disturbed them, and Charles hastily made for the bathroom. The mood was temporarily lightened, and they laughed and joked intimately over their lobster. Charles felt less light-headed after his meal, and just enough sanity returned to cause him to wonder if he was being a damned fool.

But brandy, and more marijuana, quickly undermined his good resolutions. This time there was no interruption. Arabella's coffee-coloured body was sleek and heavy-breasted, the nipples huge and dark. As her long legs wrapped themselves about his waist, she began to laugh and murmured in his ear, 'Vannessa knows that when I'm asked to look after someone, I look after them.' Charles slipped his hands under her supple buttocks, and forgot Vanessa, Mbangu, Maina. The world was reduced to this dark and moving flesh. He buried his mouth in the angle of her neck and shoulder, and began to move in slow, satisfying rhythm.

He was half asleep when she woke him.

'It's time to meet Vanessa,' she explained. 'She's waiting downstairs in the car park.'

'No brandy?'

'No time.'

The askari, his club dangling in his hand, opened the door of a large, black Mercedes by the hotel's back door. Arabella blew a kiss and turned back into the Intercontinental.

As the doorman slammed the door the car leapt into motion and Charles fell into the back seat. In the middle was Vanessa and one the other side a distinguished African dressed in shirt, tie and sober grey suit.

'Joseph Nkoli,' Vanessa introduced him. 'Minister of the Intreior. Known to his chums as Jo-Jo.' She laid a hand on the African's knee.

'Here is your passport,' the minister said, taking it from his breast pocket. 'We are putting you on the British Airways plane to London at half past midnight.'

'Why?' Charles enquired.

'You are an undesirable alien, Mr Fitzpatrick,' the minister explained smoothly. 'We are not going to deport you – just make sure you leave the country.'

'Oh, what a politician you are, Jo-Jo,' Vanessa exclaimed coquettishly. 'He's a real old smoothiechops,' she said to Charles. 'Actually he owes me a few favours,' she stroked the politician's thigh, 'so I asked him to get you out of this mess.' She whispered to Charles. 'Now I expect I'll have to give him a few more favours.'

'Vanessa sees everything in terms of sex,' Nkoli remarked. 'It's a pity life is not so simple.'

As they drove to Nairobi airport, the minister explained that they had discovered who the killer was: a white man who had shot Mbangu most professionally and then caught the midnight plane to London. The Kenya government could find no conceivable motive for the murder; the popular M.P. appeared to have no enemies, certainly not from abroad.

'Some mischievous agitators are suggesting he was killed on the government's instructions,' the minister said. 'I can assure you that is not the case – why, he was at school and at Oxford University with me.

'I am telling you this in confidence,' Nkoli continued, 'as you are a friend of Vanessa. We will put it around that the assassin was an agent of President Amin, who is claiming a vast part of Kenya for Uganda. It is not true, but it will divert the people from attacking us.'

They went into the departure building through a side entrance and up to the V.I.P. room, which was empty. The minister expertly opened a bottle of champagne.

A black ground hostess in British Airways uniform came into the room. 'The captain of the aircraft says he wants to leave,' she announced nervously. 'He's already half an hour late.'

'Tell the captain,' Nkoli said, sipping from his glass, 'that he is now in Kenya. And when he is in Kenya, he does what I say.'

The politician was wishing Charles bon voyage and Vanessa kissing him a champagne-tearful farewell when the door opened again. It revealed Chief Superintendent Maina.

'I thought Mr Fitzpatrick might be interested in the name of the murderer,' he ventured quietly. 'His name was Palmer and his passport number is UK 315945.'

He produced a grainy black and white photograph from behind his back. 'Interpol have wired us this picture of Palmer. Do you recognize him?'

Charles shook his head.

'Come, come, superintendent,' the minister reproved. 'The plane is already delayed. Why should Mr Fitzpatrick be interested in your long-overdue discoveries?'

'Because, minister,' Maina spoke with deference, 'the evidence suggests that Mr Palmer did not come here to kill

Mbangu.' He turned towards Charles. 'Mr Fitzpatrick, he missed his target. He was trying to kill you.'

CHAPTER EIGHTEEN

Flight BA 030 touched down at Heathrow at 6.30 a.m. Charles was in the deserted offices by 8.15, and telephoned Caroline at River Lodge. She was touchingly pleased to hear his voice.

'Darling,' she cried. 'Thank God you're back. When we didn't hear from you we were awfully worried. Lucy's been wandering round the house like a lost dog. How did it go? And did you get to Starehe?'

'Didn't you get my postcards?' Charles said.

'They arrived last Friday, but they weren't terribly inspired. I mean, they didn't really tell us much. Never mind, love, having you back is the real point.'

Charles thought guiltily about Vanessa and Arabella, and realised for the first time that one of the major problems of married life was that the experiences a man would most like to share, and chew over reminiscently, were precisely the ones he had most carefully to conceal.

'I did get to Starehe,' he said, 'but I had a perfectly terrible time. Got into a real mess. I'll tell you all about it later. Anything new?'

'Only an income tax demand. I sent it in to the office, you'll probably find it on your desk. Otherwise it's been very quiet. It'll be lovely to have you back.'

Charles felt a sudden urge to leave the office to look after itself for another day, and to go straight down to Marlow. But a glance at the fat folder on his desk changed his mind. He sighed. 'I'll be down as soon as I can,' he said. 'I'll try to get an early train. Kiss Lucy for me.'

He hung up, and opened the file on his desk. Even for the not particularly active Chairman of a big company, the detritus of essential trivia quickly piles up. He worked steadily through the file, making notes as he went, and by the time Mary Peters arrived he'd dealt with most of the urgent business, and had turned to the monthly accounts and company reports. He was immersed in these when the door opened to admit his secretary. She was gratifyingly glad to see him, and rushed off right away to make his coffee. He was sipping it, thinking that office routine had a lot to recommend it, when he came upon the Fitzpatrick Corporation file. Attached to it was his cable, with a note saying, 'Hold,' signed T.I. For a moment he looked at it unbelieving. Then with a roar of rage he shouted for Mary Peters.

'Get me Tom Irvine,' he shouted. 'I don't care where he is, or what he's doing. I want him now!'

After a startled pause, Mary Peters hurried out, and in a matter of minutes Irvine's face appeared round the door. He looked surprised and wary, but came forward with a smile of welcome. 'Good to have you back, James,' he said.

Charles looked at him coldly. He pushed the cable across the desk.

'What the hell's this?' he said, his voice deliberately soft.

Irvine looked at it for a moment, then looked up, puzzled. 'I don't understand,' he said.

Charles got out of his chair, and stood to look out of the window. To his surprise, he found himself literally shaking with anger.

'I thought,' he said to Soho Square, 'that my cable was quite explicit. I told you to offer Kurtz half a million for his shares, and to make the offer right away. Why do I come back to find a note saying 'Hold' on it?'

'The lawyers both agreed that it was too much,' Irvine said calmly. 'Kurtz will settle for less. It's all a bluff. His lawyers will never take us to court.'

Charles swung round slowly. 'Tom,' he said, 'I made a commercial decision. The company stands to lose altogether too much if by any chance the lawyers aren't bluffing. But that's beside the point at the moment. I made a decision, Tom. And I told you what to do. Why,' he said, with rigid care, 'didn't you do it?'

Irvine shifted uncomfortably. 'You weren't here,' he said,

'and I didn't think that I could spend half a million of the company's money without consulting Stevenson. He advised against.'

'Of course he did. How else could he get a fat fee? He wants us to go to court. It pays him to do so. Of course he thinks we'll win. And maybe we will. But it'll mean a cool hundred thousand to him, win or lose. Kurtz' lawyers are almost certain to be on a contingency basis, which means they'll split whatever they win with Kurtz fifty fifty. And they can't do that unless they go to court. If it comes to a trial, nobody wins except the lawyers, and in the meantime the Fitzpatrick Corporation is virtually out of business, and we've got a lot of money tied up in it. You know all this. Why didn't you do what you were told?'

Irvine flushed. 'I'm managing director, and in your absence it was up to me to make a decision, and I think I made the right one,' he said stiffly.

'*I* made a decision, in Nairobi,' Charles said, 'and my decision was to pay. Who is Chairman? You or me?'

'You are, of course,' Irvine said. 'But you didn't let us know where you were. And, 'he said with sudden malice, 'it's not that long since you had a breakdown.'

'Tom,' Charles said softly, 'if you ever countermand a direct instruction of mine again, you're fired. Now get out. And book a conference call with Stevenson for the earliest possible moment. I want Kurtz off our backs today, not tomorrow, and I don't care, within reason, what it costs.'

Irvine was very pale now. He opened his mouth to say something, and then obviously thought better of it. Charles stared at him implaccably. He hesitated, and then turned on his heel.

'And shut the door behind you,' Charles said. Irvine stiffened as if Charles had hit him. For a moment Charles thought the man was going to say something unforgiveable. He waited in anticipation. But the moment passed, and the door closed softly behind a truly shaken managing director. Charles relaxed, and sat down again. For the first time, the full impact of Fitzpatrick's death shruck him. I *can* fire him, he thought exultantly, and by God I will. He suddenly remembered Hong

Kong. He leant forward and wrote HONG KONG on his note pad in capital letters. This wasn't the moment, he told himself, but soon Irvine was going to have a lot of explaining to do.

The conference call took place that afternoon in Charles' office. By tacit agreement, neither Irvine nor Charles brought up their quarrel of the morning, though the atmosphere was strained, and Mary Peters was sufficiently affected by it that she dropped the loudspeaker on the floor, and thereafter it emitted a constant series of squeaks. Stevenson was distant and disapproving, but Charles was insistent.

'Do you think Kurtz is sane?' he said.

'Not entirely, no.'

'Then give him twenty-four hours to accept. The longer this drags out, the more difficult he's going to become. I want it settled. Quite apart from anything else, I value my life.'

The voice from New York was scornful. 'James, you're paranoid. Just because some sneak-thief panics, you think that Kurtz . . .'

'Someone tried to have me shot in Kenya,' Charles said. Irvine sat bolt upright in astonishment. 'Once is happenstance, twice is enemy action,' Charles went on. 'It's altogether too much of a coincidence that we quarrel with Kurtz, and all of a sudden I'm being shot at all over the world. I want that man off my back. And incidentally, I want him out of the Fitzpatrick Corporation's collective little mind. I want Woodward to concentrate on selling encyclopedias, not on practising with a whip.'

'Very well, James, I'll do as you say. I hope you won't regret it.'

'Settle with Kurtz, and none of us will regret it,' Charles said, and rang off.

'James, you didn't tell me you'd been shot at in Nairobi,' Irvine said.

'I didn't get round to it,' Charles said. 'According to the police, the man who shot Mbangu was aiming at me. You saw that he'd been killed?'

'The papers were full of it,' Irvine nodded.

'Well, I was arrested for his murder. When they let me go,

they told me that someone had tried to shoot me. A man called Palmer. They showed me an Interpol photograph of him. Thank God he couldn't shoot.'

Irvine looked stunned. 'Did you know him?' he asked.

'Never seen him before in my life,' Charles said, suddenly wondering if Fitzpatrick would have recognized the man.

Irvine looked worried. 'What if he tries again?' he said.

'Oh, I shouldn't think an unsuccessful hit man is given a second chance,' Charles said casually. Irvine looked relieved.

It wasn't until Irvine had gone, and Charles was alone, that it occurred to him that with a dark wig and a Che Guevara moustache, it might have been Tom Irvine who had sat for that grainy portrait he'd seen at the airport at Nairobi.

CHAPTER NINETEEN

It wasn't until he left the train at Maidenhead to find Caroline waiting for him in the Scimitar that it struck Charles that their relationship was quite different now that Fizpatrick was dead. As she kissed him rapturously, he was tempted, not for the first time, to tell her the truth. He suppressed the inclination, but with regret. Caroline was altogether too dear to him for Charles to feel comfortable to be living a lie.

He noticed that she was dressed to kill, her hair newly washed and bouncy, her dress a button-through black model of stark and expensive simplicity.

'I've got rid of the children for the night, darling,' she announced gaily, as the Scimitar swept out of the station yard. 'You're back, and I want to celebrate.'

'Goodness,' Charles said. 'Maybe I should go away more often.'

'Don't you dare,' Caroline said indignantly. 'Next time you can take me.' She was almost skittish with pleasure.

Charles sighed deeply with pure content. He hadn't realised how much he had missed her uncomplicated devotion. For a black moment he told himself that he'd never give her up now to Fitzpatrick. Then he recalled that he didn't have to, and settled back into the bucket seat with satisfaction.

'Tell me about Kenya. Did you meet any gorgeous red-heads?' Charles blushed, to his surprise, but Caroline was intent on wheeling the big car round a tight corner, and didn't notice.'

'No redheads,' he said. 'But I had some pretty hair-raising adventures.'

He was still telling Caroline a suitably expurgated story of his traumatic experiences with the Kenyan police when the Scimitar purred through the gate, and up the gravel drive to River Lodge. Caroline, who had been making suitably horrified comments as she drove, pulled the hand-brake on and the car skidded to a halt. She turned and hugged him convulsively.

'You've just got to be more careful,' she said. 'We can't spare you, you know.' There were tears in her eyes. Charles felt like a traitor.

With difficulty, he laughed. 'No problem now,' he said. 'I'm in the clear, and anyway I'm back.'

Caroline slipped out on the car, her skirt rucking intriguingly to the thigh. 'Just as well,' she said. 'Lucy would have gone into a decline.' She turned to lean on the bonnet, looking at him seriously. 'You know, that child adores you, James. This change of yours had better be permanent, or you'll break her heart. I felt dreadful when I sent her off to stay with a friend for the night. She cried. I nearly gave in. But wives must have some privileges.'

She turned and walked into the house. Charles watched her go with an odd feeling that all this was too good to last. As he fished his briefcase from the back seat he wondered how long he could live with the knowledge that he was deceiving her. More and more it mattered to him to be accepted by Caroline as Charles Hutchinson, not as a Fitzpatrick modified by a nervous breakdown.

Dinner was as usual superb. It was his favourite lobster salad, champagne 'to banish the memory of redheads,' Caroline teased him. Charles thought of Arabella, and grinned to himself. Afterwards, Caroline insisted that he sit in the drawing-room, and came, bearing brandy, to sit at his feet. They didn't bother to switch on the lights, but sat, watching the river, chatting with contented intimacy. She had been gay and provocative over dinner, but Charles felt that he preferred her as her grave, gentle self. With her weight warm against his knee, and her clear elegant voice crisp in his ears, he felt nerves disentangling he had not realised were taut. For the first time since Jenny's death he relaxed. In the midst of a story about Lucy and her schoolteacher, he fell asleep, his hand in Caroline's hair.

He woke to find her standing over him, a brandy in her hand, and fire in her eye.

'I didn't sent the children away for you to fall asleep,' she said, indignantly. 'I want some attention, Mr Fitzpatrick, and I want it now.'

He smiled up at her, and put his hand on her hip. Her eyes were suddenly smokey. Deliberately she began to undo the buttons of her dress, working from the bottom.

'Anything redheads can do . . .' she said. On the carpet, before the open terrace windows, she proved it.

It was with conscious complacency that Charles turned his key in the door of Helen's mews flat the next day. Back in Marlow was a gorgeous, increasingly passionate creature who loved him. Here in town was an equally gorgeous lady who might not love him, but who made the most strenuous efforts to keep him sexually contented.

'Hello, darling,' he cried. 'I'm back from darkest Africa.'

Without waiting for an answer he bounded up the stairs. If Fitzpatrick hadn't realised that life was good, he certainly did.

Standing on the hearth-rug in the chrome and leather sitting room was a large gentleman in a badly cut grey suit. Charles was so surprised that his jaw dropped, and he held onto the door handle, frozen in astonishment.

'Who the hell are you, and what are you doing here?' he said after a moment.

'I might ask you the same question sir. Mr Fitzpatrick?' Bushy grey eyebrows made it an accusation.

'Yes,' said Charles, taken aback.

'Good evening, sir.'

'Where's Helen?' Charles began to feel that he'd strayed into some sort of farce.

A voice from the bedroom door answered him. 'I'm afraid Miss Wightman's dead, sir,' it said.

Charles spun round to stare at the uniformed policeman who had just come from Helen's bedroom. 'Dead?' he said, stupidly.

'That's right, sir,' the plainclothes man said from the hearth. 'And you seem to be the last person to have seen her alive,' he added thoughtfully.

Charles gaped at him. 'But that's impossible,' he said after a pause. 'I've just got back from Kenya.'

'When precisely, sir?'

'Yesterday morning.'

There was a silence. The grey man with the eyebrows seemed to be thinking. Finally he said, 'Perhaps you'd care to identify the body, sir.'

As if in a dream, Charles walked forward to the bedroom. The uniformed policeman stood courteously aside. Helen lay on the kingsized bed, spreadeagled in ungainly death. She was wearing the same jersey he remembered from the time they had first met. Her hands were tied to the bedhead with two yellow scarves. Her face was contorted in an expression of ecstasy. She looked as if she'd died in orgasm. Charles turned away, nauseated.

The grey man had followed him into the room. 'Known Miss Wightman long, sir?' he asked.

Charles fought down the impulse to say 'about five months' and said instead 'About three years.'

'Obviously a close friend, sir.'

'She was my mistress, if that's what you mean.' Charles found himself longing for a drink.

'Imaginative girl, sir? Lively in bed?'

Charles was shocked. He nodded reluctantly.

'Fond of games, was she?'

'Well, yes, as a matter of fact. But what's all this got to do with her death?'

'Someone tied her up, someone she knew well,' the grey man explained, patiently. 'Almost certainly a lover.' He paused. 'And then he smothered her.' He made a macrabre complicated gesture with his hands. 'Used a damp pillow. Nasty sort of thing to do.' He watched Charles with beady eyes, like a bird contemplating an unsuspecting worm.

Charles walked over to the dressing table, and idly began to pick over the litter of objects on its surface. He looked unseeing at a film cartridge, labelled 'The Headmistress', and decorated with a picture of a busty lady with a whip confronting a cringing man. Both were naked. Irrelevantly, Charles thought of Woodward and his defences.

'Helen dead,' he said, almost to himself. 'It doesn't seem possible.' He dropped the cartridge and turned to the policemen. 'I'm going to pour myself a drink. Can I offer you one?'

To his surprise, the grey man accepted. 'That would be very kind, sir,' he said, primly.

Charles went across to the tray and helped himself to a vodka. He was oddly touched at the fact that the bottle sat there so very obviously waiting for him. He wondered if the film he'd toyed with had been part of some sort of welcome-back celebration Helen had planned.

A cough brought him back to the present. He turned to the grey man.

'What would you like,' he asked.

'A small whisky, if I may, sir.' The grey man was expansive suddenly, though his button eyes never left Charles' face. Charles wondered if at any moment he'd put his head on one side, thrush-like. 'This sort of case gets me down, if you know what I mean, sir.'

'I'm not surprised,' Charles said. He poured the drink, and handed it across.

'Cheers,' the grey man said, raised his glass in a deferential toast.

'Cheers,' Charles answered absently, his mind on the doll-like figure tied to the bed.

'You saw Miss Wightman often?' The grey man was almost genial.

'Every Tuesday. We had an arrangement.'

'Only on Tuesdays, sir? Isn't that a bit odd?'

'It's the way she liked it,' Charles said drearily. He wondered how he was going to tell Caroline.

'Then why did you call to see her yesterday evening?' The grey man pounced. Charles felt the sharp beak of his inquisition stab at his sensitivity.

'Yesterday?' he said, playing for time.

'Evidence of Mrs Farebrother, widow, seventy-two years old.' The uniformed officer was sepulchral. 'The lady lives opposite, and doesn't miss much, by all accounts.' He gestured to a lace-curtained window across the mews. 'Useful witness in this sort of affair.' He looked at Charles mournfully.

'Mrs Farebrother says she saw you enter the flat, using your own key, at 7.00 p.m.,' the grey man said. 'She says you left at 7.35. She knew your name and gave us a description.' A staggering thought crossed Charles' mind. Fitzpatrick! 'She confirmed the rest of your story,' the grey man went on. 'Says you've never been here before except on a Tuesday night.'

Both men looked at Charles expectantly.

'When was Miss Wightman killed?' Charles asked.

'We don't know yet, sir, we haven't had a lab report. But the old lady saw her at 8.00 p.m., letting out the cat. She called us this afternoon, because the cat hadn't been let out this morning. Regular as clockwork, letting out the cat, Mrs Farebrother said.'

'Did she ever ask you to tie her up and make believe that she was a slave?' The grey man was carefully casual.

'No.' Charles was firm.

'Tell us about her, sir.'

Charles did his best, realising as he did so how little he knew of Helen's life aside from her relationship with him.

The grey man sat staring out of the window at the flat across the mews, apparently paying little attention to Charles' recital.

'Where did you go when you left this flat last night, sir?' he said suddenly, interrupting Charles in full flow.

'What? Oh, home to my wife,' he said.

'Why didn't you admit it, sir?' The grey man was looking at him with his full attention.

Charles had a flash of inspiration. 'I didn't want my wife to know,' he said.

'We'll have to talk to Mrs Fitzpatrick.' It sounded almost like a threat.

Charles stood up and ran a hand through his hair. 'Ours is a very happy marriage,' he said. 'My wife will be very shocked to hear about Helen. Could you possibly give me a couple of days' grace, to tell her myself?'

The policemen exchanged glances. The grey man said reluctantly, 'In the circumstances, I think so, sir. But don't attempt to leave the neighbourhood. That would be most unwise, sir.' He smiled indulgently. Charles thought with a spasm of panic that all policemen were alike, from Neasden to Nairobi.

'Thank you,' he said with real gratitude.

Caroline was astonished when he walked into the house at 10 p.m. She was casual in a red housecoat, knitting from a Fitzpatrick pattern.

'Everything all right?' she asked anxiously.

Charles nodded, wondering how best to bring up the subject of Helen.

'You do know it's Tuesday?'

Charles nodded again.

'Do you remember what time I got home last night?' he said, abruptly.

'Eight o'clock,' she said. 'Why?'

Charles thought dismally that bang went his alibi. The police would latch onto the discrepancy in time like vultures. He wondered again about Fitzpatrick. 'Couldn't it have been nine?' he asked, without much hope.

'No, darling, it couldn't.' Caroline got up to get him a drink. 'Now sit down and tell me what the trouble is.'

'The police will be calling on you, and they'll want to know when I got home. Couldn't you say nine?' Charles began to feel desperate.

'The police?' Caroline began to laugh. 'Why, darling, what have you done?'

Charles took a sip of the drink she handed him and plunged desperately into his confession. 'A girl was killed on Monday night,' he began.

'A girlfriend of yours?' Caroline was concentrated on her knitting.

'Yes.' Charles gulped, and wished he was somewhere else.

'Which?' she asked, still watching her knitting. The needles seemed to hypnotise her.

'Helen Wightman.'

The knitting fell to the floor. Caroline looked at him with alarm. 'Helen?' she said.

Charles was diverted. 'You knew about Helen?' he said.

'Of course I did. You men are such fools.' Caroline picked up her knitting again, and the needles flashed. 'She called me when you had your breakdown. She was very worried about you. So was I.'

'Good God,' Charles said helplessly.

'We had lunch together several times. She depended a lot on you. We tried to work out ways to help you. I liked her, though I didn't think she was the right girlfriend for you.' Caroline was matter-of-fact. 'Too theatrical, too self-centred.' Caroline was absorbed in counting stitches. 'But then,' she said reflectively, 'I don't suppose it's likely that I'd be much good at picking your mistresses.'

Charles was speechless.

She looked up. 'The police don't suspect you, do they?'

He shook his head.

'Thank God. How did she die?'

Charles told her.

'How beastly.' She shivered. 'What kind of man would do a thing like that? First Jenny, now Helen. And someone's been trying to shoot you. I wonder when it'll be my turn.'

'Don't be silly,' Charles said sharply. 'Jenny died in a car crash, and Helen was obviously killed by a sex maniac. Why should anything happen to you?'

'Perhaps you're right.' Caroline was thoughtful. 'It couldn't be Stan Kurtz, could it?'

'Why?' he asked.

'Helen told me about him,' she said. 'He used to beat his women.'

She noticed his surprise. 'Oh, yes, Helen went to bed with him too. She was quite a tramp. If she was killed by one of her lovers, you may have to investigate half the men in London.'

Charles was hurt. He had supposed his and Helen's had been a rather special relationship. Perhaps Caroline was just being bitchy.

'We've settled with Kurtz,' he pointed out. 'We've paid him half a million dollars.'

'That would keep him happy,' she agreed. She moved along the sofa until she was next to him. She put her arms around the back of his neck and kissed him long and gently.

'You must track down Helen's murderer,' she said. 'Unless he's caught, I have this feeling that none of us are safe.'

She stood up. 'Anyway, poor Helen,' she said. 'She was almost one of the family.'

She took his hand, and pulled him from the chair. 'Come to bed,' she said, 'and comfort me. As I've said before, a wife has privileges.'

They had reached the foot of the stairs when the telephone rang. Charles swore.

'Who the hell can that be at this time of night?' he said. Reluctantly he released Caroline's hand and went to answer the phone.

A voice said without preamble: 'Eight thirty tomorrow morning, suite 837, Carlton Tower.'

The phone went dead, and then there was a dialling tone. Charles stood staring stupidly at the receiver. Fitzpatrick was very much alive.

CHAPTER TWENTY

'It's good of you to come so early.' The Chairman was expansive. Charles looked at him in amazement. If he hadn't known who his caller must have been he would not have recognized Fitzpatrick. Above the blue-and-white striped bathrobe, a brick-red tan reached half way up his forehead, ending in an incongruous milk-white strip which ran into the died hair, longer now by far than in the tycoon days, slightly wavy, and a dark brown with reddish glints. Round the once smoothly polished jawline ran a fringe of grizzled beard which effectively altered the outline of Fitzpatrick's face. The eyebrows had disappeared – shaved? Charles wondered – and the result had been to bring the eyes themselves forward, so that they looked almost popping. The eyes fascinated Charles. In place of the indeterminate hazel they were now a deep brown, almost black.

Fitzpatrick noticed Charles' interest, and chuckled proudly. 'Tinted contact lenses,' he said. 'Makes a big difference, doesn't it?' He helped himself to eggs, bacon and kidneys from under a splendid array of silver salvers, and waved the coffee-pot interrogatively at Charles. 'Coffee? Good. Couldn't have the hotel staff recognizing me, you know. And I didn't want any unfortunate incidents like your Jermyn Street encounter.' He laughed. 'I had lunch yesterday at L'Escargot, and there must have been a dozen publishers and agents there I used to know intimately. They didn't even glance my way.' He handed Charles a cup, and speared a kidney with relish.

Charles was struck once more by the aura of power and energy that surrounded the man. He seemed positively to buzz with internal dynamism. Charles thought of a bomb, the cartoon anarchist's kind, all dynamite and crackling fuse. And just as dangerous, he thought, looking at Fitzpatrick warily.

'I thought you were dead.' He spoke with careful indifference, holding his voice steady with an effort.

'Quite right, too. Cost me a good deal to set that up. I gather you got out to Olmesutye?' Charles nodded. 'Well, young Pauling's a nice enough sort of chap, but not uncommonly bright, and willing to believe anything of his beloved lions. I simply bought a second Land Rover, and arranged to be picked up in the middle of nowhere, abandoning the other one, along with my gun, and so on. Hey presto, Charles Hutchinson eaten by lions. Neat, don't you think?' Fitzpatrick began to sop up the yolk of an egg with buttered toast. Charles noticed that the smooth tycoon manners seemed to have disappeared with the appearance. Something of the man's basic coarse vitality had begun to emerge. It was not attractive.

'But why?' Charles asked.

'My dear fellow, that's why I've sent for you today. The fact is, I've been thinking, and I've come to the conclusion I like my new life too well to give it up. I gather you've been a great success as James Fitzpatrick. I suggest we make it permanent.' Fitzpatrick was genial and a little patronising.

Charles looked at him in surprise.' But what about Caroline and the children?' he asked.

'You're getting on all right with Caroline?' Fitzpatrick asked indifferently.

'Yes indeed.'

'I thought you might. She's not a bad old thing, you know, though not really my type. She's got money, of course. I needed that early on. But I can't see her birdwatching on the bundu, can you?'

Charles stared at him speechless.

'And as for the kids, I daresay you'll make them a better father than I ever would have. Never wanted them myself. They were Caroline's idea, and I thought they'd help to keep her happy.'

Charles remembered Caroline's mute acceptance of Fitzpatrick's infidelities, and suddenly felt an impulse to choke the man till his contact lenses popped out. A rage so murderous that it made his whole body tremble possessed him. This unspeakable bastard was discussing and dismissing the gentle, beautiful, and trancendently loyal Caroline as if she was a cart horse too young to send to the knackers and too old for useful work. Charles suddenly realized that before he allowed Fitzpatrick back into his family, before he permitted any further contact with Caroline, he would kill him. It was a novel emotion, and steadied him wonderfully after a moment. He hated the man with an intensity which was satisfying, like a hugh draught of raw oxygen.

Fitzpatrick seemed unaware of the effect of his words. 'I'm going to make you an offer you can't refuse,' he went on. 'In return for letting me continue my life undisturbed as Jeremy Fry – oh, yes, it's on my passport – I'll pay you £100,000 in cash, and give you the shares I promised immediately. My own shares will be transferred to Switzerland. Don't worry about that part of it.'

'And Caroline? And the children?' Charles was startled to hear his own voice so dispassionate.

'You think I should do something for them? Oh, well, perhaps you're right. 'I'll establish a bank account of £250,000 for them, and give you the account number. If you lodge it with a bank of your own choosing it'll take care of Caroline in the unlikely event that anything should happen to you.'

'Not so unlikely. I've been shot at twice,' Charles said baldly.

'Really?' Fitzpatrick was interested.

'Really. In New York and Nairobi. I wondered if it might be Stan Kurtz and his bully boys. In fact,' he looked at Fitzpatrick speculatively, 'it did cross my mind that you wanted out because Kurtz' heavy buddies had put out a contract on you, and you wanted them to find me.'

The Chairman roared with laughter. Spluttering crumbs and coffee he sat choking over his breakfast, tears of mirth running down his cheeks.

'Wish I'd thought of that,' he said at last, unsteadily, beginning to laugh all over again.

Charles looked at him coldly, and wondered just what was so very funny. He got the strong impression that Fitzpatrick knew something he didn't which made his idea so exquisitely humorous.

'Forget Stan. He'd never set the mob on you. It'd leave him with too many markers. But tell me about it.' Fitzpatrick listened with interest as Charles described the negotiations in New York and the attack in the hotel. Fizpatrick congratulated him on his handling of Kurtz, and agreed that his pay-off scheme was the only workable one.

'I shouldn't think too much of the attack,' he said thoughtfully. 'Probably just a burglar with a gun. I heard about the Kenya affair. In fact I saw your photograph in the *East African Standard*. But why should you think that had anything specific to do with you?'

Charles told him about Maina's warning, and about the photograph of Palmer he had been shown.

Fitzpatrick's face darkened with anger. Charles felt a wave of it cross the table. For some reason it seemed directed at him, though the Chairman's words gave no indication of it.

'The bastard,' he said. 'Jesus, the Kenya police could have locked you up and thrown away the key. It doesn't pay to get involved in black power struggles. They're always brutal, and generally bloody.'

There was a brief pause.

'I'm sorry about Jenny,' Charles said at last, looking at the floor.

Fitzpatrick sighed. 'Yes,' he said. 'I only found out yesterday. I had intended to take her back to Kenya with me. She was a good girl. There was a lot more to Jenny than you'd expect.' He sounded genuinely upset. Yet when Charles looked up again, Fitzpatrick's eyes, so dark and unexpectedly prominent, were fixed on him with hard intentness. Charles was puzzled, and looked it, for Fitzpatrick quickly changed the subject.

'And how is Helen?' He winked at Charles.

'Helen's dead.' Charles flung the remark at him brutally, hoping it would hurt. It certainly had some effect. The Chairmen went pale beneath his tan.

'Dead?' he said.

'Murdered.' Charles would volunteer no details.

'Good God. When?'

'Sometime between the time you saw her on Monday night, and the moment the police arrived on Tuesday afternoon.'

Fitzpatrick looked confused. 'I was going to tell you about that,' he said, almost apologetically. 'I had to recover some letters. We'd been exchanging notes by a kind of code based on Fitzpatrick books, you know. Childish, of course, but intriguing. Helen's idea. You know how she loved games. Some of them were dated after you had taken my place. I thought that was a detail to clear up.'

'You mean she knew?' Charles was astounded.

'Of course,' Fitzpatrick said impatiently. 'She had to. I needed someone to run errands, and keep an eye on things, and I didn't want any traceable connection with Jenny if it could be avoided, or at least, not outside the business.'

'All that time? All through the fake break-down?' Charles thought of Caroline swallowing her pride and making a friend of Fitzpatrick's mistress in order to help him. If Helen had known . . . The whole thing was suddenly disgusting.

'Of course,' Fitzpatrick said again. 'She helped to plan it all. Jenny didn't know that, mind you. Helen was a fascinating creature, but she treated all life as a game. Never really had a grasp of reality, you know, loved the intrigue of it all. Bit of a sexual troubador. She didn't mind our changing places at all. In fact she rather enjoyed it.'

It occurred to Charles that the Chairman was so pleased by his own cleverness that he had little time for regret over the death of his co-conspirator. He could almost smell the man's arrogance and self-satisfaction. He began to long to get away from the suite. The air seemed thick with Fitzpatrick's animal self-sufficiency.

'What about my offer?' Fitzpatrick asked after a pause.

'I'll take it,' Charles said.

'Good. I hoped you would. In fact I felt sure of it.' Fitzpatrick was all geniality again. He got up and went to the door. As he opened it, he held out his hand. With a distaste he hoped wasn't too evident, Charles grasped it. Fitzpatrick shook hands firmly, smiling.

'If it's necessary, you can get in touch with me at P.O. Box 618,' he said. 'Under my new name, Jeremy Fry, of course. But I hope it won't be necessary. Unless something very untoward happens, I don't think we'll meet again.'

Charles paused for a moment as he was leaving. 'What are you going to do with your life?' he asked with impulsive curiosity.

Fitzpatrick laughed. 'I'm going to write a definitive East African bird book. I've been collecting material already. Goodbye.'

Charles headed for the lift, thinking that that was one major lie Fitzpatrick had told. In all his enquiries at the bird sanctuaries in Kenya, there had been no hint of Hutchinson, or Fry. Fitzpatrick hadn't been there, not to any of them, Charles was certain. And if he'd been lying about that, what else had he lied about, Charles wondered as the lift took him down to ground level. He ran over their conversation, phrase by phrase, as he tooled the Scimitar through the elegant squares of Belgravia. Quite a bit, he decided, as he wound through Shepherd's Market on his way to Piccadilly. As he followed a taxi round the corner of the Regent Palace Hotel, it came to him that he didn't believe a single word Fitzpatrick had said, about anything. Not without outside confirmation, anyway. He wondered suddenly, feeling acutely exposed, just exactly what plans the Chairman had in store for his replacement.

CHAPTER TWENTY-ONE

By the time he had reached his office, Charles had decided that it could not be coincidence that Fitzpatrick's women were so accident prone. Somewhere, he felt, there had to be a clue to the whole mystery – and by now he was only too willing to include the very basic question of the impersonation at the heart of it all.

Sitting behind his desk, brooding over a cup of coffee in the Rosenthal cup, Charles decided that the first necessity was to investigate the death of Helen as thoroughly, and if necessary, as informally, as possible. It crossed his mind to offer a reward for information, but he quickly dismissed the notion. Not only would the police dislike the idea, he felt, but he couldn't see what was to be gained. All the same, he felt, he had no choice but to start with Helen herself. He had not forgotten how ignorant the police had made him feel about her private life. On an impulse he rang Helen's boss at the company where she had worked. He explained enough about his association with her to persuade the man to have lunch with him at the White Tower.

No sooner had he put the phone down, than it rang. The caller was his bank manager, confirming a draft of £100,000 received from Zurich. Fitzpatrick, he thought, was either very over-confident, or extremely fast on his feet.

He was about to telephone the police, to ask if there had been any further developments when the door of his office burst open without ceremony. It was Hugo Barnard, chief foreign rights salesman for the company.

'Mr Fitzpatrick,' he said. 'I must talk to you immediately.'

Hugo was six foot four, Norwegian by birth, but now more British than the British. He had brown hair which occasionally flopped into his eyes, a Roman nose, and was always dressed in Savile Row suits, the corner of a handkerchief poking out of his breast pocket. Although several of the salesmen he controlled were prima donnas, Charles had been struck by Barnard's own quiet efficiency. For him to burst into the Chairman's office in such an excited state meant that something serious had happened.

'If you don't stop that man, this business will be ruined!' the Norwegian exclaimed. Charles sat him down, got Mary Peters to bring a cup of strong coffee and persuaded the master salesman to calm himself.

Barnard's story was complex in detail but simple in essence. He arranged a great many co-production deals for the Fitzpatrick Company. This involved licensing publishers in European countries – France, Germany, Italy, Spain, Portugal and Scandinavia – to publish a book. The Fitzpatrick Company produced the pictures, text and design. The foreigners had to provide a translation in their own languages and send it to London. Barnard arranged for the printing of all the different language editions simultaneously. This saved a great deal of money, and enabled the book to be published in countries where the quantities would be too small for a separate printing.

He had arranged two big deals, at much expense of his own and his subordinates' time and at considerable cost to the company. Rarely had the champagne flowed and the caviar been consumed so lavishly in the capitals of Europe. Over £100,000 was involved in the creation of each book, and Tom Irvine himself had taken charge of their production. Imagine Barnard's consternation, then, to discover that the cost of printing would be fifty per cent higher than estimated, wiping out any possible profit.

'How can such a thing happen?' Charles asked, thinking uneasily about Hong Kong.

Quite easily, according to Hugo Barnard. Irvine insisted on using a particular Belgian printer whose rates were half as much again as his competitors.

Irvine insists that no one else can be trusted to produce top quality and organize it properly,' Barnard said. 'But that is poppycock! I know at least three other printers who are just as good.'

'Then what is the explanation?' Charles enquired.

Barnard got up, made sure the door was closed, and came to stand directly in front of the desk.

'I have worked for you for eight years, Mr Fitzpatrick,' he said quietly. 'You have always given me your confidence and your trust. So I have an obligation to say to you what I say now. There can only be one explanation: Tom Irvine is taking kick-backs from the printers. Either that – or Mr Irvine is going mad.'

After his meeting with Barnard, Charles barely had time to get the the White Tower for his 12.30 appointment. As he was leaving Mary gave him a message: a further £250,000 had been received by special deposit from Zurich. The Chairman was not being slow in implementing his side of the deal.

Helen's boss turned out to be an amiable Englishman in his fifties, with the sleek manner and polished humour of a top-class public relations man.

He was shocked by Helen's death, and readily answered Charles' questions. But he had little to contribute. Her work had involved getting new clothes designed, using the company's yarns. She would arrange for them to be photographed and try to get them published in newspapers and magazines. The public, if they liked the clothes and the models, would order the patterns and materials to make them. Or it would encourage the manufacturers to mass-produce those designs.

Helen had been good at her job. Her gregarious, fun-loving nature had helped her to influence her contacts in the fields of design, photography and journalism. There had been rumours that she had been a little too gregarious: that if certain photographers didn't give her favours after a session – and unless they performed properly – they didn't get many new assignments. Certainly, at trade fairs she had never taken long to find a partner for the evenings – usually a wealthy foreign industrialist. And somehow somebody always seemed to pay to upgrade her ticket home from tourist to first class.

But, the P.R. man pointed out, a girl's private life was her own. He believed Helen had a regular boy-friend who was very wealthy, which gave her some security. In any event, she worked hard and well.

The rich lover, Charles assumed, was himself. He asked if Helen's boss knew a photographer called Peter Vlachos, her latest discovery.

'We left all that to her,' was the reply. 'But I'll try and find his phone number for you, if you want.'

Charles walked back the quarter-mile to Soho Square, deep in slightly chagrined thought. No wonder, reflected, Helen had never complained at seeing him only on Tuesday nights. He had been lucky to be fitted into her calendar of lovers at all.

Back at the office he summoned Tom Irvine. The managing director pulled a chair up to the other side of the desk.

Charles showed him the papers left behind by Hugo Barnard: the specifications for the two co-edition books; the contract with the Belgian printer; and the quotations from three other reputable manufacturers at two-thirds of the price.

The Scot read them carefully, his ruddy countenance becoming slightly flushed.

'I don't have to explain my actions,' he said.

'On these figures you do.' Charles restrained his annoyance at the man's arrogance.

'Who gave them to you?' Irvine demanded. 'Hugo Barnard? If so I'll soon fix him.'

'No you won't. Not unless you have a satisfactory explanation of this incident. Barnard's under my protection.'

'Your protection?' Irvine laughed sarcastically. '*Your* protection.' He stood up and began to pace across the office. 'You sit here in this fancy room drinking coffee and playing with figures. It's Tom Irvine, good old reliable Irvine, who does all the bloody work around this place. And you encourage my senior executives to try and stab me in the back? Just who the hell do you think you are?'

'I'm James Fitzpatrick,' Charles said levelly. 'I'm Chairman of this company. And you still haven't given me an explanation.'

The Scot wagged his finger in rage. 'Don't cross-examine me as if I'm a criminal in the dock,' he shouted. 'Don't try and pretend you're the Father, Son and Holy Ghost rolled into one. Remember I know where the money from these foreign deals goes. Into our private Swiss bank account.' He thumped the desk. 'And wouldn't the Inland Revenue like to know about that?'

Charles stood up to face him. He had never been so angry in his life.

'Tell the Inland Revenue and they'll get you as well as me. And don't you dare blackmail me. Or I'll have you behind bars.'

Charles took several minutes to recover from the incident. Irvine's conversation was not just an admission of taking kick-backs; it was virtually a declaration of war. Why, Charles wondered, after fourteen years' loyal service to the Fitzpatrick Company, should the managing director step so far out of character? Most amazing of all, why had he tried to cream off the profits in such an obvious way?

He buzzed Mary Peters. 'Get me Scotland Yard,' he told her.

'An Inspector's outside, waiting to see you,' she replied.

It was the grey man from Helen's flat, still in grey suit, shirt and tie. His card, which he handed across Charles' desk, showed him to be Chief Inspector Pearson, of Scotland Yard.

His visit, he said, was to take a statement covering the points they had discussed in Helen's flat. With Fitzpatrick in mind, Charles was able to expand on the reason for his supposed visit; he explained about the letters, and added that they were mildly injudicious.

'Not injudicious enough to be a motive for murder?' the inspector asked.

'By no means,' Charles stated firmly.

'Anyway, it looks as if you're in the clear, sir. The old lady opposite saw Miss Wightman thirty minutes after you left. And the autopsy shows she was dead by 9.00 p.m. So she was murdered between 8 and 9. That let's you out – although we would still like to confirm your story with Mrs Fitzpatrick.'

'I've already told her about Miss Wightman,' Charles said.

The grey man managed to look both sympathetic and noncommital. Charles was forced to admire his professionalism.

Pearson took a packet of Wrigley's spearmint gum from his right-hand jacket pocket. He unwrapped it carefully and prowled round the office until he found the waste-paper basket, in which he deposited the wrapping.

He put a snapshot down on the desk. 'Recognize him, sir?' Charles shook his head.

'Name: Derek Palmer. Passport number: UK 315945.'

Charles sat up and paid attention: the assassin of the Kenya cinema.

'The Nairobi police asked us to make investigations, sir.'

'What have you discovered?'

'Not much, sir.' The Inspector seemed apologetic. 'Only the address Mr Palmer gave on his application.'

'Oh, yes?'

'Twenty-eight Connaught Mews.'

Charles was stunned. 'But nobody lived there except Miss Wightman.'

'Quite so, sir. Of course, it's a fake application in a false name. But it's odd that Mr Palmer, whoever he is, should have chosen that, of all addresses.'

'Very peculiar,' Charles conceded.

Inspector Pearson pulled a piece of paper from his breast pocket and read it. 'I've got a message for you from a Superintendent Maina of the Nairobi Police. We sent all the relevant information to Kenya, including the fact that Miss Wightman had been murdered at that address.'

'What was Superintendent Maina's message?' Charles enquired.

'I don't understand it myself, sir. The Superintendent says: "Do you still believe in coincidences?"'

When the inspector had gone, Charles sat back in his chair, and tried to think through his problems. Emphatically he no longer believed in coincidences, but where could he start? He decided that his original decision to follow up on the death of Helen was the right one. All the same, there was one lead which had to be either confirmed or denied.

He dialled Jim Stevenson at his Wall Street law office.

'How's the settlement with Stan Kurtz proceeding?' he asked.

'The papers are ready,' Stevenson replied in his usual slow tone. 'They're due to sign tomorrow.'

'I want them signed in London,' Charles instructed him. It was still only noon in New York, though 5 p.m. in London. 'Tell Kurtz if he wants his half a million dollars, he must catch a plane tonight to Heathrow. You can send the documents by courier. O.K.?'

'O.K.'

'And don't tell anyone else about it.'

CHAPTER TWENTY-TWO

The tall, lean American, his body still that of a sinewy ex-paratrooper, burst through the office door next morning.

'Good to see you again, James,' he said. His firm handshake made Charles wince.

'I'm surprised you're so friendly,' Charles said. 'I expected you to be pretty bitter after our last meeting.'

'These things happen in business,' the American said cheerfully. 'It's not the first time I've been fired. Anyway, I enjoy coming to London. You've got the best gambling clubs in the world.'

Kurtz inspected a hydroponic indoor garden on Charles' windowsill. Irvine had brought this peculiar construction back from New York: he had wondered whether the company should market it in Britain. It consisted of two plastic trays: the bottom contained water and a so-called 'miracle solution'; the top some polystyrene granules covered with gravel. A pump circulated a mixture of water and air through the materials in the top tray. It had to be switched on for half an hour three times a day. Charles had placed the seeds beneath the gravel with considerable doubt. But to his surprise some tomato plants had pushed their way up within a few days. Finally the American seated himself.

Charles had read through the papers brought by the courier with meticulous care. He signed them with a flourish.

Kurtz took out a handsome fountain pen – 'a present from General Eisenhower. I was one of his guard in Frankfurt after the war' – and added his signature. 'It's a princely pay-off. Worthy of you, James. You always were a big man.'

Mary Peters brought a cup of coffee and, for Kurtz, sanka coffee.

'Stan, where were you last Monday?'

'In Vegas, with my girlfriend. We spent a long weekend

there.' He was relentless in his visits to casinos. 'We flew back on Monday night.'

So he couldn't have been back in New York before midnight, or 5 a.m. Tuesday London time.

'Why?'

'Helen Wightman was killed on Monday evening,' Charles said.

Kurtz was unruffled. 'Helen who?'

He was an accomplished liar, Charles thought.

'Don't bull-shit me, Stan. You knew Helen Wightman. You knew her very well.'

The American spread his hands, conceding defeat. 'I admit it. I took Helen out a few times. I thought she was your girlfriend, that's why I kept quiet.'

'She was my girlfriend.' Charles was bitter.

'And that's why you asked me where I was last Monday?' Kurtz was indignant. 'You didn't think I was her murderer? You know me better than that.'

I hardly know you at all, Charles was about to say, then collected himself. As James Fitzpatrick, he had known Stan for three and a half years.

'I am determined to bring her killer to justice,' he said pompously. 'I have to check every possibility.'

'I couldn't agree more,' the American said. 'Look, I'll offer ten thousand dollars as a reward for any information right now. I'll make out the cheque and you can tell the cops.'

A fat lot Inspector Pearson and Sergeant Pyle would think of that. But Charles appreciated the gesture.

Kurtz racked his memory to see if he could recollect anything helpful from his meetings with Helen Wightman. Nothing emerged, but the affection with which he spoke of the girl and his indignation at her death seemed genuine.

Charles sent for Tom Irvine to witness his signature on the agreements. The managing director was amazed to see Stan Kurtz, who had meanwhile helped himself to a Bloody Mary. He explained it would be good for his jet-lag.

'What the hell are you doing here?' His Scottish accent was more pronounced than usual.

Kurtz laughed at his astonishment. 'Don't worry, Tom, we're all friends again. It's surprising what a cheque for half a million dollars can do.'

'I should say so.' Irvine was clearly wounded to the depths of his accountant's soul by the size of the settlement.

Just as Irvine was about to witness the documents, Charles interrupted.

'There's just one thing, Stan. You took a trip to London a while ago.' Charles was watching them both. Kurtz's face stiffened. But Tim Irvine's remained as unchanged as Edinburgh granite. 'We were surprised you didn't come to see us while you were here.'

The American turned round to the fridge to refill his glass and, doubtless, to give himself time to compose a reply.

'I came to meet some friends,' Kurtz said, sipping his drink. 'Just for a couple of days.'

'You saw my secretary, Jenny Barnes, while you were here.'

Kurtz lowered his eyelids, the sure sign of a man wondering whether to tell a lie. 'Yes, I did,' he admitted.

'You had dinner with her, two nights running,' Charles stated.

The American nodded.

'Why the hell,' Charles said, 'would you, a rich playboy, devote two consecutive nights to an ordinary secretary?'

Kurtz twisted the neck of the glass between his strong, stubby fingers. He rocked to and fro, like a gorilla in a cage.

'James,' he said slowly. 'I loved her.'

'You loved her!' Charles could not keep the disbelief from his voice.

Stan Kurtz put his left hand over his eyes, as if he was about to cry. He nodded, still rocking backwards and forwards.

'You know Jenny Barnes is dead.' There was ice in Charles' voice.

'Yes.' The American's voice was low and tortured.

'How do you know?'

'I tried to call her at home several times.' He spoke as if in a trance. 'I got no reply. So I telephoned the office. Mary Peters told me.'

Two women dead, Charles thought. Jenny Barnes and Helen Wightman. Kurtz had known them both, taken them both out to dinner. And, knowing the New Yorker, the price of the meal was a session in bed. But Charles did not want to pursue his cross-examination in front of Tom Irvine.

'I loved her,' Kurtz repeated quietly. He took his hand away from his forehead. New lines were on his now haggard face. He appeared to take a grip on himself. He took out a cheque book from his inside breast pocket, pulled his chair up to Charles' desk and began to write.

'For you, James, what I promised.' He pushed a cheque for $10,000 across the desk. If he was the murderer, Charles reflected, it was an easy way to divert suspicion. Kurtz drained his drink and left.

Charles looked coldly at Irvine. 'What,' he asked, 'do you think about Helen's death?'

'Helen? Helen who?'

'Helen Wightman. Didn't you know her?'

The managing director shook his head. 'Was she one of your girlfriends?'

'Yes.'

'You know I keep well clear of your private life.' There was a touch of Calvinism in his tone.

'She was a girl who had a wide acquaintance.' Charles tried to keep sarcasm out of his voice.

'I don't mix with girls of that set,' Irvine said.

'How do you know which set she belonged to?' Charles' voice was silky.

'All your girls are the same type. Fashion models, or ladies who work in advertising or public relations.' He was scornful. For someone who claimed to ignore his Chairman's private life, he was surprisingly knowledgeable.

'I wanted to bring up our discussion of yesterday,' Charles was menacing. He would make this graceless man sweat a bit.

'I lost my temper,' Irvine said reluctantly. 'I only wanted to ensure we get the best quality on these two books. Their success is critical for the future of our new list of titles. Once they've worked we can reduce the quality and make the profits.' He prepared to leave. 'However, you have my apologies.'

Charles came round his desk and put his hand round the managing director's slim shoulders. 'Good,' he said heartily. 'Just remember who's the boss. That's all.'

Irvine did not reply. But in his slate-grey eyes was a look of hatred.

CHAPTER TWENTY-THREE

That night he was sitting brooding in his chair, drink in hand, when Caroline interrupted him.

'James,' she said, 'you haven't said a word to me all evening, and you cut poor Lucy so short she didn't believe it. Don't tell me the bad old days are back with us again.' She was half laughing, but there was no doubting the genuineness of her worry.

With an effort, Charles threw off his absorbtion in his own problems, and prepared to concentrate on hers. 'Darling,' he said, on impulse, 'I've decided that there is altogether too much happening to me at the moment. Frankly, I don't think I'm a very good risk while people are taking pot shots at me all the time. I've eliminated Stan Kurtz, I think – did I tell you he was in love with Jenny? – but that simply opens the field. So I've arranged to set up a separate bank account for you and the children, just in case anything happens to me. I've put £250,000 in it to take care of their schooling and things,' he finished, lamely.

She looked at him in horror. 'You aren't thinking of leaving me?' she said, her voice beginning to break.

He laughed. 'You silly creature,' he said. 'Till death do us part, remember? No chance. No, this is just a precaution. Think me silly, if you like, but it makes me feel better to have you and the children provided with plenty of funds, just in case.'

She looked at him strangely. 'You've forgotten we were

married in a registry office,' she said. Charles couldn't imagine what she meant, and didn't bother to follow it up. Patiently he explained that the whole thing was to do with tax laws, but he didn't really believe his own words, and resorted to a hasty change of subject.

'What do you think of Tom Irvine?' he asked, abruptly.

'He was absolutely essential in the early days,' she said, thoughtfully, 'but I've often wondered if he was rather jealous of your success. Resented not being needed, you know?'

Charles thought about it. 'The sort of man who'd steal from the company, and clumsily at that?' he asked.

'Never,' she said firmly. 'And even if he did, it wouldn't be clumsy.'

Charles concentrated on Irvine. What did he really know about the man. Maybe there was a simple explanation for his actions. Suppose for a moment, he thought, that he too, like Helen, was in on the plot. Mightn't that explain a good deal? It did, he realized, it did indeed. He was elaborating on the idea when Caroline interrupted him again.

'Darling, you know there really are an awful lot of misprints in the Fitzpatrick books nowadays,' she said, puzzling over one of her interminable knitting patterns.

Glad to have some sort of distraction, he reached out lazily for her book. She handed it to him, and snuggled warmly against his shoulder. She was right, he realized, as she pointed them out. There were indeed a hell of a lot of misprints. He frowned. At least this was a concrete problem. He fetched some more Fitzpatrick titles off the shelves in the library, and began to study them, really for the first time. Oddly, in some books the couldn't find any misprints at all. While in others they occurred on every other page. Once again, it all seemed to come back to Irvine. Yet there was something else, some other factor gnawing at the edges of his mind. He struggled with it for a while, and then reluctantly gave up.

'I'll take it up with Tom Irvine,' he said. 'But for now, my love, bed. Helen's funeral tomorrow and that's going to be no picnic.'

*

The ceremony at the crematorium in Frome, Somerset, had an unreal quality. The words of the ceremony were moving, and Caroline wept behind her veil. But it seemed impossible that the vibrant, sexually athletic Helen could have suddenly been transported into an urn of ashes.

Her parents offered tea and biscuits at the vicarage in Chantry, a hamlet nearby. The mourners were few. Helen's boss was there – 'Ghastly things, funerals, aren't they?' he whispered to Charles – and a smattering of her girlfriends. Of all her alleged lovers, only Charles had turned up. Caroline explained to the bereaved parents that she had been one of Helen's closest friends.

Helen's mother was a powerful lady, tearful but showing all the control of a vicar's wife with a ceaseless round of Mothers' Union, Women's Institute, Young Wives, and other activities to organize. Her father was a scholarly, bespectacled man with food stains on his suit and dog collar and the odd burn mark where hot ash had fallen from his pipe.

Caroline put up a good performance. She was simultaneously depressed and aggrieved by Helen's death. 'After all, darling,' she'd said on the way down in the car, 'although I had nothing to thank her for she was good to you in her fashion. Something's got to be done about her murder.'

She told the parents that she had no confidence in the police finding their daughter's murderer; she thought her husband, a man of wealth and power, ought to pursue the matter separately.

Mr Wightman opposed this initiative. 'Leave it to the police,' the old man said. 'Death is not so terrible: Helen is with her Maker.' His faith was rock-like. Charles thought that the man of God might not have been so sanguine of the comforts of after-life had he known more of his daughter's life on earth.

Mrs Wightman, however, supported Caroline to the hilt. She too doubted that the constabulary would bring the monster who had murdered her daughter to book. She was all for private initiative. Inspector Pearson had visited them the day before; he had shown interest in only two of the dead girl's possessions: a bundle of letters and her address book, which he had photocopied in Frome. With compassion, he had spared the vicar and his wife both the manner of Helen's death and the style of her living.

Armed with the original letters and the book, Charles undertook the long drive back to Marlow. At last he had some evidence; he just hoped that, for the first time, it gave him a clue.

The letters were from James Fitzpatrick. As the Chairman had said, they were in code. The top letter was dated over fiftene months before, in September. 'The Fitzpatrick Encyclopedia of Carpentry,' it said.

page	2	line	4
page	108	line	22
page	219	line	35
page	8	line	29
page	18	line	14
page	181	line	5
page	150	line	42
page	8	line	34
page	91	line	3
page	154	line	40
page	9	line	3
page	230	line	22
page	85	line	17

It took Charles nearly two hours in the office to work out the message. He had to tear each of the relevant pages out of the book (one of the company's best sellers) and put them side by side. Then he had to look at the first word in each line to see if the combinations of the first word in each line made sense, then the second word, and so on. It was the ninth word which produced the message: 'Cannot come this week. Book flight to Frankfurt October five. Stay usual hotel.'

Charles checked back over Fitzpatrick's diary. The first week in October had been the Frankfurt Book Fair. Charles hadn't been to one himself, but from everything he'd heard, it was astonishing, and typical of the man, that he was able to deal with the hyperactive Helen while wheeling and dealing in the vast and airless halls of the Bookmesse. One publisher he knew had told him, 'The stories of sex life in Frankfurt are hopelessly exaggerated. If you do your job, you're either too tired or too drunk to make it. And anyway, ten to one at Frankfurt prices either you or the girl, or more probably both, are sharing a room. And it needs just the hint of a rumour in that vast Armenian rug-market, to have you married off to her, and she probably expecting her first child.'

He was puzzled that the Chairman should have been quite so concerned to recover relatively innocuous letters. But it was best to leave nothing to chance, and Fitzpatrick liked to clear up details.

He had neither the time nor inclination to decipher the other letters: it was unlikely that the clue to Helen's death lay in Fitzpatrick's carefully phrased and disguised communications.

The address book was far more interesting. There was one very odd aspect to it. It contained the normal plethora of girlfriends and, presumably, professional contacts. But there were also numerous men with foreign names.

Charles selected one at random: Benjamin Kimathu. He dialled the number and discovered he was talking to the Tanzanian Embassy. When he was through to Kimathu, he said: 'I understand you know Helen Wightman.' The line went dead as the Tanzanian replaced the receiver. Adamu Bitela of the Somalo Embassy and Mohammed Khan of the Bangladesh mission to London both denied any knowledge of the dead girl, although their names were in her book. Neither showed any eagerness to prolong the discussion.

Charles was on the point of phoning yet a fourth when his phone rang.

'Inspector Pearson here, sir. I understand you've collected some documents from Helen Wightman's parents.'

'Yes.' Charles decided to take the initiative. 'And a friend of their daughter's has offered ten thousand dollars as a reward for information.'

The Inspector let out a deep sigh, as if the strain of dealing with a simpleton was proving too much. 'It would be much better, sir, if you and your friends stopped meddling in this matter and left it to us professionals.'

'How much progress have you professionals made?' Charles asked tartly.

'The whole business is more complicated than might appear at first sight, sir.'

'So I should hope. It is the only thing which could explain why, after nearly a week, you have apparently got nowhere.'

The policeman took this attack with his usual phlegm. 'It is not only complicated, sir,' he continued, 'but it is dangerous. Miss Wightman was by no means what you may have thought. My job will not be assisted by the aid of bungling amateurs.'

Far from putting him off the scent, Pearson's remarks only encouraged Charles to pursue the chase.

CHAPTER TWENTY-FOUR

Jacques Livernoche was in his mid-fifties, tall with white hair, his shirt from Turnbull and Asser, and his suit from Savile Row. He shook Charles' hand softly, his hand limp; his voice was dove-like; his manner suave. But behind the clear blue eyes was a mind like a steel trap.

Livernoche published, under licence, the Fitzpatrick Company's scientific and technical publications on France. He paid over two hundred thousand pounds a year in royalties. Jacques was a fussy, difficult man who could tolerate nothing but the best. In Paris, for example, when he lunched at Maxim's, he had to have a table in the inside room; at dinner he insisted on a table in the outer room. So conscious was he of social niceties. He would deal with the Chairman of the Fitzpatrick company and no one else. He was in a strong position to obtain his demands.

Charles met him at the Etoile in Charlotte Street, knowing the Frenchman's love of the finer things in life. The waiters, in dinner jackets and bow ties and looking so old they appeared to have been fixtures at the restaurant since the end of the war, gathered round to discuss the menu. Jacques Livernoche took at least fifteen minutes to select his meal. The chef himself had to be called in from the kitchen for consultation. The choice of wines took as long again. Livernoche made a great ceremony of tasting it, taking a tiny sip, putting his head back and rolling the wine round his mouth until he deemd it satisfactory.

He was like many of the French publishers Charles had met since taking on the Chairman's job. They all had large offices in magnificent Paris houses, filled with plants and precious paintings and designed to look as much like a luxurious living room as possible. They published for glory not for profit.

It was over the selection of a cigar for himself that Charles made his mistake. He asked the waiter to pick out the best. The man himself was obviously scornful of this cavalier method, expecting Charles to investigate a variety before coming to a considered choice.

Livernoche was outraged at this departure from convention. 'My dear James,' he said softly but reproachfully, 'this is not like you at all. I have never been so impressed as that evening eighteen months ago during the Frankfurt Book Fair. You may recollect it, dear friend, because we had to wait two hours for dinner at the Frankfurterhof. I remember saying at the time: what is the point of a restaurant keeping live fish and shellfish in tanks of water so that one can choose which fish one desires, if it takes them two hours to cook it? But I stray from the point. When the meal was at last finished you and Monsieur Irvine decided to have cigars. Monsieur Irvine just took one from the box. But you got your girlfriend to roll some by her ear, to make sure they were properly put together, and then under her nose. Finally, she bit the end off the cigar she had approved for you.' The Frenchman paused to draw on his cigar.

'What a magnificent performance!' He put his hands palm upwards on the table as a gesture of astonishment. 'And now you ask the waiter to pick one for you! James, you must never treat important matters in life with such casualness.'

Charles felt uncomfortable. He had behaved out of character.

'What a beautiful young lady she was,' Livernoche added with nostalgia. 'The perfect companion for a man of your distinction. What was her name?'

Charles was even more uncomfortable. He had not the faintest idea.

'Ah, yes,' the Frenchman said happily. 'I remember her well. Her name was Helen Wightman.'

As he drove home, Charles was puzzled. Tom Irvine had denied any knowledge of Helen. Yet Livernoche remembered the four of them having dinner and spending the evening, and a long evening it sounded, together.

Tom Irvine's behaviour, and truthfulness, urgently needed investigation.

Irvine seemed genuinely baffled by Charles' questioning the next morning.

'I do vaguely remember having dinner with you and that puffed-up Frenchman at the Frankfurterhof,' he conceded. 'You brought along a very beautiful red-haired girl. A bit tarty, like so many of your women, but good-looking all right.' He crossed one leg on top of the other as he sat in the chair next to Charles' desk. 'What was her name?'

'Don't you remember?'

'Blowed if I can,' Irvine scratched the side of his head. 'I'm only interested in business. I leave the women to you.'

'She was called Helen Wightman.'

The Scot showed signs of interest. 'Helen Wightman? Isn't that the girl you mentioned the other day? The one who's been murdered?'

'Yes,' Charles said.

'So *that* was who she was. Poor girl. So young.' He got up to go.

'Tom,' Charles said, 'we've got some things to clear up.'

Irvine sat down again hastily.

'I've been checking over printing prices and production costs with Barnard, and on my own account. It won't do, you know.

And I don't buy your "quality" explanation any longer. Some of these invoices,' Charles patted a buff file, 'date back years. There's simply no doubt that Fitzpatrick have been using printers, quite deliberately, at up to fifteen per cent over the market price. Tom, I want to know what you've done with all that money.'

Irvine would not meet his gaze. 'I've got another meeting, James,' he said. 'We can talk about it later.'

Charles stared at him implacably. 'The fifteen per cent, Tom. Where is it?'

'That's no concern of yours.' Irvine's voice was gruff.

'It certainly is,' Charles spoke with some heat. 'It's the Company's money. Most of it should have gone to our joint account in Switzerland. You already have that stake in the profits. Why have you suddenly become greedy for more?'

'Greedy?' Irvine fastened on the word. 'You call it being greedy, wanting more than twenty per cent?' He ran his hand through his hair and made an effort to calm himself. Charles sat down on the sofa to hear his explanation.

'It was your nervous breakdown that did it.' His voice was flat and colourless. 'You went away for three months. I – and the company – didn't miss you at all. I suddenly realized that I had been taken for a ride. For fourteen years I'd worked my guts out for you, James. I'd slaved away for twelve hours a day, eating, breathing, living for the company. I was the one who woke up at four in the morning, worrying about the company's problems.

'And you – what did you do, James Fitzpatrick? You made sure you took all the credit and the glory. You had the beautiful house on the River Thames, the beautiful, well-educated wife, the young, frisky girlfriends.

'All I received was twenty per cent of the profits – a bone for the guard-dog. I felt I'd been cheated, James.'

'That's no good reason to cheat the company.' Or the Chairman, Charles thought.

'You dare to stand there and lecture me about cheating?' Irvine looked at Charles with astonishment. 'My God, you've changed since your breakdown. You've started to take an interest in the business again, you're calm, reasonable, unruffled . . . you're even being moralistic.' He looked keenly at Charles, who had reclaimed his swivel chair. 'It's as if you're a different man.' He paused.

'Maybe,' he said thoughtfully, 'you are a different man.'

Charles swivelled round to one side to avoid that calculating gaze. Irvine was getting too close to the truth. It was time to change the subject.

'Taking kick-backs is a criminal offence.' His voice was hard. 'You could go to jail.'

'Me? Go to jail? Are you mad?' The Scot was not tall, but he made an impressive figure as he leaned over the desk and wagged his finger. 'Don't you threaten me!'

'You have taken these bribes in a particularly obvious and stupid way.' Charles was unmoved. 'So obvious that Hugo Barnard spotted it.'

'Barnard!' Tom Irvine spat out his name with disgust. 'Who made that stuffed dummy what he is today? Me. That's who. And he has the nerve to bite the hand that feeds him.' He stood up, his face contorted with rage. 'Fire him!'

'Don't be stupid, Tom!' All the contempt he felt for corruption was in Charles' voice. His years in Nigeria preventing Africans putting their hands in the till came back to him. 'What do you think would happen if he went to the Unfair Dismissals Court and said he'd been sacked because he discovered his managing director taking kick-backs? It would cost us a fortune. And think of the scandal.'

The Scot was stopped in his tracks by the force of this argument. He thought for a moment and then a look of cunning crossed his face.

'Buy him off, James. You're very good at that.' He was sneering. 'You pay off your girlfriends when you're tired of them don't you? You keep Caroline sweet with fine clothes and all the glory of being a millionaire's wife. Well, pay off Barnard.'

His reference to Caroline particularly enraged Charles. He stood up to face the managing director.

'And why,' he enquired icily. ''should I involve myself in bribing Hugo Barnard just to save your rotten little skin?'

Irvine's face went puce, but his eyes remained as steely as ever. 'Because I can cause you a lot more trouble than a spell in jail.'

'Don't try to blackmail me,' Charles interrupted. 'We've had this dialogue before. That Swiss bank account is perfectly legal.' He realized he was skating on thin ice, but there was no alternative. 'If you tell the tax man he'll be on your tail as fast as he's on mine.'

'Swiss bank account?' Irvine said scornfully. 'Is that what you think I'm talking about?' He gave a derisive laugh. 'You're going to have to do a deal with me – one of your famous offers they can't refuse.'

He walked over to Charles and looked up at him. On his face was slyness, mixed almost with triumph. 'Shall I tell you why?' He left a theatrical pause. 'Because I know everything about you. Everything. If you are James Fitzpatrick, then you will realize what that means. And if you are not—' he paused, '—then, God help you.'

CHAPTER TWENTY-FIVE

The Tanzanian high commission is on the corner of the Strand and Trafalgar Square. The decor is nineteen-thirties Cunard. Fascinating though his quarrel with Irvine had been, and even more interesting the implications, Charles had decided his first priority was to continue his hunt for Helen Wightman's murderer. And the only way to do that was to discover more about her.

The receptionist, a pretty black girl with plaited and braided hair, was draped over the telephone, having a long and intimate conversation with a friend. 'Ehs' and 'ohs' and 'ahs' appeared to be her main contribution. After about ten minutes she replaced the receiver and deigned to take notice of Charles. He handed her one of his cards. On it he had written: 'I was a friend of Helen Wightman.' A surly messenger was summoned to take it to Mr Benjamin Kimathu.

Fifteen minutes later Charles was led down a corridor, past partitioned offices, until he reached a door marked: Mr B. Kimathu, Commercial Attache. The African who rose to greet him was tall, six foot four, with a black suit, white shirt with stiff collar, grey tie and perfectly manicured fingernails. He might have stepped straight out of the British Foreign Office.

The furniture was redolent of Whitehall, too. A solid oak desk was covered with neatly-piled stacks of paper; three round-backed chairs with faded leather seats; and in the corner a hat-stand bore a bowler hat and a neatly-furled umbrella. Whatever the British may not have bequeathed their colonies, they certainly created a carbon copy of the Civil Service.

'What can I do for you?' Kimathu was solicitous. He spoke with an Oxford accent.

'I wanted to talk about Helen Wightman. She has been murdered.'

'I know.' The African was grave. 'A most regrettable tragedy.'

'When I tried to talk to you,' Charles pointed out, 'you put the telephone down.'

Kimathu shrugged. 'A man in my position,' he said delicately. 'A diplomat. One has to be extremely careful what one says, and to whom.'

'What has made you change your mind?'

'I received a visit from,' he searched his memory, 'an Inspector Pearson. He told me of you. He said you were a responsible, indeed a distinguished person.'

The Tanzanian answered Charles' questions with courtesy and consideration. But he had little to contribute. He had met the dead girl two or three times, at diplomatic functions. He wasn't certain where, but he thought one might have been at the Ethiopian embassy, another at the Bangladesh High Commission.

She had been a lively, attractive lady, he recollected, who stood out in the dull round of the embassy circuit. She was interested in photographing some of her models in Dar-es-Salaam, to put a new angle on the clothes. He had found the idea worth pursuing, as it might help to publicize Tanzania and assist their tourist trade. He gave Charles a brief lecture in economics, explaining that tourism was one of the few industries which produced the foreign exchange they needed to import plant and machinery for their new industries. But, alas, Helen Wightman's death had occurred before any deal was consummated.

Charles was disappointed. He explained that he had been hoping to find, through her friendships, some clue as to her murder and its motivation.

'I am sorry I cannot be of more help,' Kimathu said smoothly. 'There was only one man whose name she mentioned – a Greek photographer of whom she thought highly. He was the one she had earmarked for Dar-es-Salaam.'

'Peter Vlachos?' Charles enquired. The rising star Helen had described as bent as a bedspring.

'That is the name,' the African nodded. He steered Charles towards the door.

'By the way,' he said, 'the Inspector asked me to give you a message.'

'Oh yes?'

The African smiled. 'Leave it to the Yard,' he said.

By the end of the afternoon, Charles was inclined to agree. He had phoned several of the foreign gentlemen in Helen's address book. All were embassies involved in trade or commerce; all tried to be helpful, but knew little; and all had been visited by Inspector Pearson. As he stepped into his cold Scimitar in Taplow station car park, Charles shivered. It had been a typical cold, grey day. The sun hadn't shone for over a week. He had to spray the windscreen to remove a film of ice and drove with care along the narrow twisting roads to Marlow.

Caroline had lit a log fire in the dining room, and the children were lying in front of it doing their homework. James was concentrating on physics, while Lucy became weepy over some simultaneous equations. She was not good at mathematics and dissolved into tears at the sniff of a problem. The two gave him affectionate hugs and kisses before they retired to bed.

Caroline had prepared baby chickens, with sprouts, picked

from the vegetable garden and potatoes stored from the previous autumn in the air raid shelter, a relic of World War Two.

The silver cutlery was laid out on the walnut dining table and she had produced their Waterford crystal glass. Caroline was wearing a flame-coloured kaftan, and its gold embroidered yoke sparkled in the candlelight.

She noticed Charles' surprise at the lavish setting. 'It's nice to see you on Tuesdays for a change.' She laughed. Then she realised she might have been a little tactless. 'How are you getting on with your detective work?'

Charles had to report his complete lack of progress. Caroline listened carefully as he recounted his unproductive round of calls.

'I still think it's a little odd,' she said. 'I can see that taking the occasional sequence of shots in sunny climates would be a good idea. But Helen seems to have had ambitions in every country in the third world. Her company could never have afforded to send photographers and models to all of them.'

'Well, you're wearing a kaftan,' Charles pointed out. 'Third world clothes are in fashion. Anyway I expect she counted on their tourist boards paying the bills.'

Caroline was not convinced, but could not come up with a logical objection. He told her of his unmasking of Tom Irvine and his kick-backs.

She was flabbergasted, and annoyed. 'After all you've done for that man,' she stated. 'I'd never have believed it.' It was a view in stark contrast, Charles noted, to Irvine's, namely that *he* had done everything.

'And, after fourteen years with you! What are you going to do, send the man to prison?' Caroline obviously would. An avenging angel, indeed.

'I don't know,' Charles replied.

'Darling, you're losing your grip,' she exclaimed. 'What's happened to the dynamic tycoon? I'd have the police around first thing tomorrow morning.'

'I'm not certain. I just wonder whether this Irvine business and Helen Wightman might not be connected in some way.'

Caroline was intrigued by this thought. She put her spoon

to rest in a plate of strawberries expensively imported from East Africa.

'I wonder if Jenny Barnes and Helen found out about his kick-backs and blackmailed him,' she said thoughtfully.

'Why do you mention Jenny?' he asked.

Caroline looked a little uncomfortable. 'It may sound silly, but it's my feminine instinct. I think Jenny's death is linked with Helen's. It's easy to fake a car accident, you know.'

It was a thought, Charles had to admit.

'But Helen didn't know Tom Irvine,' he objected. Then he remembered Livernoche's story of the dinner at the Frankfurterhof. He repeated it to Caroline, and told her of Irvine's faint recollection of the incident.

'Very suspicious, indeed,' she declared, pouring the coffee from a Georgian silver pot. 'Nobody could fail to notice a girl as sexy as Helen. Not even a dried-up old bachelor like Tom Irvine.'

She put down the coffee-pot with a thump. 'That's it!' she cried. '*Cherchez la femme.* I remember a local bank manager here was dismissed for embezzlement. He'd fallen for a blonde floozie and had to pay for her apartment. That would explain why your managing director has suddenly changed character, after fourteen blameless years. He's entranced by an expensive piece of fluff.'

Unlikely at first sight, but Charles had to concede there might be a germ of truth in it. In his experience in Nigeria principals who fiddled the funds rarely did it for themselves. Often it was to acquire the bride-price for a new, young, comely girl.

He returned to Caroline's first theory. 'Even if he was being blackmailed,' he pointed out, 'it's scacely a sufficient motive for murder.'

But Caroline was not to be put off her second suggestion. She had convinced herself that the granite-faced Scot had acquired a mistress. She instructed Charles to follow him one evening to catch him out.

Her excitement at her imagined cleverness, however, persisted until they were in bed. She kissed Charles passionately.

Moving over to her side, he felt a hard lump under her pillow.

'What's that?' he asked.

'Just a book.' She laughed nervously and pulled it out to place it on the bedside table.

Charles took it from her. It was a Japanese pillow-book, tastefully illustrated with erotica.

'Well,' she said, 'now you're at home on Tuesdays, I must find out what Helen was so good at. And they say there's nothing like a good book.'

'True, true,' Charles murmured.

'So, darling. I'm your slave. Whatever you want me to do, tell me.'

Charles accepted the invitation with delight. Afterwards, she was glowing. 'Dear me,' she said. 'I've never been so ravaged. I feel as if I've wasted fourteen years of marriage.' She laughed happily.

Charles was satiated. But as he drifted into sleep, one worry niggled at the back of his mind. What was the dynamite Tom Irvine was so confident he could place under the Chairman?

CHAPTER TWENTY-SIX

Helen had been as inaccurate in her description of Peter Vlachos as in her assurances of her fidelity. The young Greek was not homosexual, as she had claimed. On the contrary, he was plainly a ladies' man.

His studio was on the fifth floor of an apartment building in Broadwick Street in Soho, ten minutes' walk from Charles' office. It was an old, nineteenth century building with a rickety flight of stairs. Sloping windows on one side of the room gave plenty of light. It was filled with cameras on tripods, reference books on shelves. Cushions and sag-bags littered the floor. A dense-looking model, with the fine face bones but vacant look so beloved by photographers, poured red wine for them from a well-stocked sideboard. It was obviously the Greek's studio, living room and bedroom rolled into one.

A delivery-boy from a nearby delicatessen came in with American-style open sandwiches – lashings of ham and piles of lettuce and tomato on a thick slice of wholemeal bread. The photographer lounged on a floor-sofa composed of multi-coloured patchwork cushions, his loins encased in denim jeans which emphasized his physical attributes, his chest rippling in a white T-shirt emblazed with the legend: Mandarin Hotel, Hong Kong. The studio had the studiedly casual atmosphere created by a professional salesman.

'Helen Wightman,' Vlachos said thoughtfully. His long black locks cascaded around a thin, sensitive face. His lips were wide and sensual. 'You want to know about Helen.' The model, un-bidden and silent, topped up their glasses. Charles was sitting on a sag-bag, working his bottom into the canvas-covered poly-styrene granules to obtain a secure base for himself.

'You went to bed with her?' Vlachos enquired.

'Yes.'

'So did I,' the photographer said unemotionally. 'So I guess did a lot of men. In the fashion business, it's almost obligatory to go to bed with the client. Usually they are older and less attractive women than Helen. But if you want the work, you pay the price.'

He talked about Helen, the sessions of photographs they had taken together. She had promised him a lot of work and men-tioned that she was trying to arrange a number of overseas loca-tions for her clothes. They had coupled several times. Usually the models had been dismissed by Helen and she had taken her toll of the photographer on his patchwork cushions. Twice they had gone back to her flat, but only in the afternoons.

'She kept the evenings free for her regulars,' he explained. 'I gather she kept Mondays for one man, Tuesdays for the next, and so on. They were her bread and butter – the afternoons for Helen were an extra bit on the side.

'Christ, I'm tired,' he said unexpectedly. The model brought over a yellow plastic bucket and sponged his face with cold water. 'I've got to photograph this stupid bitch all afternoon.' The model was unperturbed by the appellation and refilled

Vlachos' glass for the third or fourth time. 'These broads are so dim it takes you two hours to get any poses from them that aren't straight out of the textbook.'

The telephone rang. The girl unplugged it from the wall next to the drinks cabinet and pushed the lead into a plug next to Vlachos' sofa.

'It's for you,' he said. Charles was startled. So far as he recollected, nobody knew he was having an informal lunch with the photographer.

'James Fitzpatrick?' The voice was soft and lush. It poured out of the telephone like treacle. 'My name's Anne Lesley. I understand you are looking into the death of Helen Wightman.'

'Correct,' Charles said. 'How do you know?'

'You've telephoned a number of her friends. They have telephoned me. I suggest we meet for dinner tonight. I may be able to help you.'

'That sounded like Legs Lesley,' Vlachos said, when Charles had replaced the receiver.

'She said her name was Anne Lesley.'

'That's Legs, all right. She's called that for obvious reasons. Her legs are fantastic.'

'And you've seen all of them?' Charles enquired mischievously.

'No,' Vlachos said casually. 'Very few have. She's a powerful lady. A friend of Helen's.' He rolled onto his side. 'Now if you'll excuse me, I'm going to have thirty minutes shuteye before I get down to work.'

As Charles reached the door, the photographer sat up, cross-legged, attempting to look like a twentieth-century Buddha.

'Try this idea on for size,' Vlachos said. 'Both times I went back to Helen's flat, a hatchet-faced old biddy was watching from a room on the opposite side of the road. Until Helen pulled down the blinds in the bedroom I felt I was being spied on by a Medusa. If you want to find out who knew Helen Wightman, try the old lady opposite.'

Mrs Farebrother, Charles thought. He'd overlooked her. But first the powerful Legs Lesley. He left the flat and hurried off to find a telephone. He'd get Mary Peters to call Caroline. It would sound better coming from his secretary.

There were flurries of snowflakes as Charles walked down Dean Street to Gennaro's restaurant. If the snow settled, it would be the first of the winter, a welcome change from cold and rain.

He had no difficulty recognizing Miss Lesley. It was 7 p.m. and she was the only girl in the semi-circular cocktail lounge, with its leather seating running round the wall. She stood up to greet him. She was five foot ten, nearly as tall as he was, in her mid-thirties. Her blonde hair fell below her shoulders, and framed a long intelligent face, with sparkling blue eyes and over-wide lips. She unclipped a black cloak and handed it to an apologetic Italian waiter. The staff were taken unawares by diners arriving so early.

She was wearing a black sweater, tan skirt and black leather calf-length boots. Her necklace was of twisted thick gold chains, and a locket bobbed between her breasts as she moved. She had the English country look of a girl accustomed to sit astride a horse. Her handshake was feminine but firm.

Her manners were good, Charles thought, as he sat on a chair on the other side of a small black drinks table with a gold rim. More than could be said of the man next to her, who had remained seated, huddling inside a clerical grey suit and tan raincoat.

'What are you doing here?' Charles asked the graceless male. It was Inspector Pearson.

'He's a colleague of mine, in a funny sort of way.' The girl gave a wry smile, as if recognizing the incongruity of the association between a dynamic young lady and a plodding policeman. Her voice was soft, and intimate, so that Charles had to bend forward slightly to hear her. The locket again drew his eyes to her ample bosom.

'Don't worry,' Pearson said dourly. 'I'm not staying for dinner.'

Charles ordered his customary vodka and tonic. Anne Lesley

requested a Bloody Mary and the Inspector elected for a pint of beer.

'Why are you so interested in Helen Wightman's murderer?' the blonde asked, after the waiter had laid out their drinks on little cotton mats. She lit a cigarette, a John Player Special, and fitted it into a black holder.

'She was my girlfriend.' Charles' explanation was simple.

'She was the girlfriend of an awful lot of people.' There was a bitchy note in Anne Lesley's laconic tone. 'Thank God the rest of them aren't as concerned as you.'

'Why?' Charles asked.

'Helen worked with me,' she said. 'I'm officially with the Department of Trade. In fact my job is counter-espionage.' She was very matter-of-fact about it. Charles looked at her, astonished.

'There you are,' Pearson said morosely, 'now you can understand why I've tried to stop you meddling in this case.'

'I'm damned if I do.' Charles was angry. 'Why the hell should the fact that Helen was involved in counter-espionage protect her murderer?'

'You're getting it all wrong,' Miss Lesley interposed smoothly. 'Of course Helen's killer must be brought to book. But her involvement with us makes the whole matter a little delicate.'

'Delicacy be stuffed! What I want to see are results.' Charles realised he was beginning to sound more and more like the real James Fitzpatrick. A case of environment moulding the man, he thought, irrelevantly.

Anne Lesley put her hand over his wrist for a second. Touching is the first move to defuse opposition, Charles reflected. 'I can quite understand a businessman like yourself,' she said conciliatorily, 'becoming impatient. All we are saying is that the investigation into Helen's death is not as easy as it might seem.'

The Inspector wagged his head in doleful endorsement.

'How far have you got?' Charles asked the policeman nastily.

'We have not got very far,' the blonde said. She drained her glass and ordered a refill. The Inspector turned down the offer of a second pint. 'Let me reverse the question. You know that Inspector Pearson has talked to all the people you have talked to – and a great many more. How much have you discovered, Mr Fitzpatrick?'

'Not a great deal,' Charles conceded.

'All wind and no whistle,' Inspector Pearson commented sagely. 'All criticism and no performance.'

'You know that Tom Irvine, your managing director, was one of Helen's lovers?' Anne said.

Charles could only goggle at her. Was *Helen* the femme he should be checking? No wonder he was making hints about Fitzpatrick.

'Monday nights,' Pearson said gloomily. 'But he wasn't there on the night concerned. We checked with the Farebrother woman.'

'Dear Helen,' Anne Lesley said. 'So clever, so thoughtful. Always backing both ends against the middle. If anything happened to the chairman she had a fall-back position with the managing director.'

'Not fall-back,' the policeman corrected her. 'Lay-back.'

Charles was still stunned by the news about Irvine. Just how long had he been sharing his mistress with his managing director?

'Anyway,' Pearson continued, 'I've had a long talk with your managing director. He's clean – like you. He was just a friend of the dead girl, not involved in her espionage activities.'

'That doesn't mean he mightn't have killed her,' Charles objected.

'Not entirely, I agree. But, believe me, sir, Miss Wightman was killed because of her work for Miss Lesley here. That is why the investigation has to be handled with considerable diplomacy.'

He rose to his feet. 'I see it's snowing,' he said gloomily. 'I'll leave you to your dinner. I just came along to tell you two things. Firstly, Miss Lesley is very high-up in Intelligence. Secondly, stop muddying the pond and let the professionals do their job.'

'You have a nice line in mixed metaphors,' Charles was acid. 'I suppose, as this is involved with espionage, you must be part of Special Branch?'

The Inspector nodded.

'Then God save us if you are all that stands between us and the Communist menace.'

The Inspector did not rise to the bait, but made his departure in dignified silence.

'You're too harsh about Inspector Pearson.' Anne had just finished their first course of avocado pear with shrimps. They were dining in the quiet back room of the restaurant, next to a log fire. 'He's not as stupid as he appears.'

'I should hope not,' Charles said.

The waiter served two portions of Fegato alla Veneta.

'Let me tell you about Helen,' Anne Lesley said. Her narrative was well-ordered and dispassionate. Helen Wightman had worked by day for her multi-national yarn company. But at night, other than on Mondays (reserved for Tom Irvine) and on Tuesdays (reserved for himself) she had worked for British Intelligence. She had specialized in entertaining diplomats from Third World countries – 'some of my girls won't consort with black or brown men,' the blonde explained seriously. 'Helen didn't mind what colour they were. As long as they were men.'

'How did you get to know her?' Charles asked.

'We were at school together.' The blonde laughed. 'A lot of our best girls were educated at convents.'

Helen Wightman had been a natural for the work. She was high-spirited and enjoyed parties. And she was virtually a nymphomaniac.

'I gather she was good at her job,' the blonde said. 'She was meant to be terrific in bed. All her reports were alpha plus.' She looked mischievously at Charles. 'But you'd know more about that than I would.'

'I couldn't say anything against Helen.' Charles was serious. 'But where did you get the reports of her sexual prowess?'

Anne Lesley explained that the world of espionage was labyrinthine. Most of the men with whom Helen consorted were people from whom the British wanted information. But occasionally, without realising it, she looked after men from her own side. They monitored her performance and reported to H.Q.

Charles was surprised that Britain still employed the technique of offering available girls. It sounded a bit like Mata Hari and the First World War. Miss Lesley laughed gaily at his ignorance.

'There's nothing to beat a pretty face and a good pair of legs,' she said. 'You men are all alike. If you sniff a conquest, you start to boast about how important you are. Part of that is how important your work is. Men like to impress girls by telling them how many secrets they know. A clever lady plays the coquette and flutters her eyelashes. And unlocks a great deal of information from the simple male.'

Anne obviously had a low opinion of men. In fact it almost sounded as if she despised them. She was a tough, cynical lady. And that, to Charles, made her rather attractive.

The girls could sometimes, she explained, be used for blackmail. But in the modern free-loving world, that was proving less and less useful. For African politicians in particular the revelation of a torrid affaire with a beautiful white girl would not harm their standing at home. In fact it would probably improve it.

But what secrets, Charles enquired, could a man like Kimathu, working in the Trade division of the Tanzanian High Commission, have that were of interest in Britain?

Anne Lesley warmed to an explanation of her work. Top level technological information, like nuclear secrets, was becoming less and less important. In the new era of détente, the super powers exchanged a great deal of information anyway. Satellites could monitor the build-up of arms, and their types, far more easily than a network of spies.

The greatest danger to the West, according to Anne, lay not in the threat of military attack. No country could afford the devastation of a nuclear war. The threat now was of a massive rise in the prices of commodities, and particularly of oil, minerals and food, from the Third World.

'Macmillan bowed to the winds of change and gave away an Empire,' she said. It had all seemed too much of a burden for the white man. And everyone had assumed the ignorant natives would continue to supply oil, copper, cocoa, aluminium and iron at rates which just enabled them to subsist.

For the West, already crippled by a fourfold rise in the price of oil, the prospect of similar price hikes in other essential commodities was horrendous. British industry, for instance, almost entirely depended on imported raw materials.

For the poor countries of Africa and Asia, a massive rise in revenues was not merely the only way to increase prosperity; for some it was essential to survive the rise in the cost of their imports from the West. And they had learned the lesson of OPEC, the oil-producers' cartel: if all the suppliers of one commodity banded together they could reverse the long process of political and economic colonialism imposed by the great powers. It would be the emergent countries which would divide and rule.

Meanwhile, Miss Lesley pointed out, the Russians and Chinese were stepping up their penetration of Africa and Asia. The Chinese were already entrenched in Tanzania, having built the great Tanzam railway from Dar-es-Salaam to copper-rich but landlocked Zambia. The Russians and their satellites had almost encircled South Africa, that treasure-store of gold, diamonds, platinum and other precious metals, with the collapse of Angola and Mozambique. The fall of Vietnam and Cambodia endangered the whole of South-east Asia.

'I can't imagine poor, pretty Helen being very good at economic espionage,' Charles observed.

'She didn't have to be. She just had to get the information and give it to us. She only had to be good in bed.'

'She certainly was that.'

A look of feline pride crossed the blonde's fine-boned face. 'All my girls are,' she said with satisfaction.

Anne accepted a vintage port, while Charles nursed a brandy. Anne Lesley, he thought, took her job seriously. Her summary of international politics had been brief and to the point. She was indeed a powerful lady.

She leaned over the oak table so that he could light her

cigarette. As she did so the locket swayed forwards and then back to the cleavage between her breasts.

'There's just one thing I want to ask you, Mr Fitzpatrick.' She blew a puff of smoke from her holder.

'Call me James.' He had nearly said 'Call me Charles,' but collected himself in time.

'There's still just one thing, James. Why are you so interested in Helen Wightman's death?'

'I've already told you.'

'I don't believe it.' She was quite dispassionate. 'You're obviously a man who has slept with plenty of girls. You've no problem in finding a replacement for Helen.'

'Helen was special to me.' That was true, he thought. But Anne Lesley's question still worried him. Clearly, Helen Wightman had been a high-class tart, laying down her all for Britain only too often and too eagerly. Why then was he so concerned to discover her murderer?

'Has anyone tried to kill you?' The girl was even cleverer than she looked, Charles thought.

'No,' he lied easily. And yet, it was odd. It was because of Caroline that he was pursuing his search for Helen's killer. And Caroline had known of Helen's open-bodiedness, indeed had commented on it. 'Helen was very special in bed,' he continued doggedly. It sounded thin, even to him.

Anne Lesley put her hand over his and squeezed it gently. 'I've got plenty of girls who are more special than Helen.' Her voice was so soft he had to move forward until she was almost whispering in his ear. 'What do you like, James? Blue movies, two girls at once ... You name it and I'll arrange it.'

'Now why would you do that for me?' he mused. 'The colour of my eyes, my debonair manner ... or maybe if I give up investigating Helen's death.'

She laughed with genuine amusement. 'I like you,' she said. 'And after all, millionaire publishers aren't two a penny. I dare say my young ladies wouldn't object to meeting one.'

She took a sip of port, and leaned back, her eyes sparkling with the excitement of negotiation, her lips slightly apart. 'But you're right. All these telephone calls are upsetting our customers. It's bad enough Inspector Pearson questioning them, without you barging in as well.'

She leaned forward enticingly. 'Now don't be shy,' she admonished. 'You can't shock me. There's nothing I don't know about men and sex. It's my job. Do you like English upper-middle-class girls like Helen, or Jamaican ladies, or Brazilian or Kenyan . . .?'

It was as if he was choosing coffee, Charles thought and abruptly remembered Arabella. 'I'd like you,' he said bluntly.

The colour left her cheeks. She was shocked. 'I'm not for sale,' she said slowly. She began to finger her necklace. For the first time she had been put off her stroke. 'I'm the one who runs the operation. I have to be purer than the driven snow.'

She accepted a second glass of port. She still seemed a little shell-shocked by his request. It was time to get down to business, Charles decided.

'Tell me about Tom Irvine,' he said.

'Tom who?' She recovered fast. 'Oh, Tom Irvine, your managing director.' She took a sip from her glass. 'Forget about him. He's nothing to do with us.'

'It seems he's something to do with Helen,' Charles continued firmly.

'Irvine's in the clear,' she said.

'I wonder, Charles thought. He didn't trust the dangerous and attractive Miss Lesley.

'What about Stan Kurtz?' he asked.

She took a puff at her cigarette to gain time. 'The man who's offered a ten thousand dollar reward?' You're slipping, my dear, Charles thought. Only Inspector Pearson knew about that. On the other hand, the two were clearly working hand in glove.

She bit her lip. 'It's a little suspicious, isn't it. He only went to bed with Helen a few times, and yet springs ten thousand dollars for information leading to the arrest of her murderer.'

'I suppose Kurtz works for the CIA on the side.' Charles meant to be sarcastic. But she took it seriously.

'No,' she said. 'We've checked him out, and he's not working for any of the American intelligence agencies. As far as we can tell he's not working for anybody.'

'He's not even working for my company any more.' Charles essayed a joke.

'But it's still worrying.' She ignored his attempt at humour. 'I know you paid him off handsomely' – Charles was shaken that she had this piece of information – 'but ten thousand dollars is a lot of money to put to the memory of a round-heeled girl like Helen.'

'Round-heeled?' Charles was puzzled.

'Push them over and they fall flat on their backs,' she explained with masculine directness.

Outside the restaurant, it was still snowing. Taxis would be as rare as hen's teeth. He offered her a lift home in his Scimitar, and they trudged along Dean Street, heads down into the driving snowflakes, to Soho Square.

Once the heater had warmed the car, she removed her cloak. Charles noticed the gold locket glinting in the light of the street lamps.

'What have you got in your locket?' he asked.

She laughed. She had relaxed since leaving the formality of the dinner table. 'A photograph of my target.'

'Someone you're going to kill?'

'No,' she said with over-played solemnity. 'The Mr Big I'm going to expose.'

'I don't believe you.'

'You're quite right.' She was all mock apology. 'You're too clever for me. I'll tell you the truth.'

'I don't believe that either.' He spoke lightly.

'Well, you're wrong.' She slurred her w's. Perhaps the port had affected her more than she recognized. 'It's a picture of my one and only lover.'

'I don't believe a girl as beautiful as you has only had one lover.'

'You flatter me, sir. It's amazing what a strict upbringing can do. I was twenty-six before I succumbed to the temptations of the flesh. When I fell, I fell hard.' She seemed good-humoured enough at the recollection. It might almost, Charles thought, be true.

'He was a remarkable man. He initiated me into sex, and he initiated me into British Intelligence.'

'What happened then?'

'After a few years he got tired of me. He decided he needed younger women.' She laughed.

'I still don't believe you,' Charles said. Yet there was an air of authenticity about her story.

'Well,' she said, 'you pay your money and you take your choice.'

She lived in a modern block of flats in Notting Hill. The snow had stopped, leaving two or three inches on the ground. It was bitterly cold.

'Can I offer you a nightcap?' she asked. They walked up two flights to her front door. Although the living room was quite warm she switched on a fan heater and put a Diana Ross record on the turntable. She flung her cloak over the corner of a sofa. Behind it was an Impressionist print of a naked lady, bottom uppermost. Three deep armchairs and a long low glass-topped table completed the sparse decor.

Anne Lesley went next door into the bedroom and Charles heard her unzipping her calf-length boots. She returned with a glass of brandy and handed it to him.

He looked at her with open admiration. 'I can see why you're called "Legs" Lesley,' he said.

'I'm very proud of them,' she confessed. With a sudden movement she undid a button at her side and twirled away her tan, wrap-around skirt. She was wearing purple pants with matching suspenders.

'Magnificent,' Charles breathed. And indeed her legs, slim and long as a chorus-girl's, were superb.

She pulled her black sweater over her head and shook her long blonde locks until they fell into place around her shoulders. Her bra was purple too, low-cut and displaying the pear-like slope of two handsome breasts.

Her cheeks were flushed. Her irises dilated as she viewed his enjoyment of her figure. She came to sit on his lap.

'Now, James,' she said, kissing him with moist lips, 'tell me what you like.'

'Do you have any blue movies?' Despite his excitement, he was still searching for a clue to Helen's murder. He couldn't remove from his mind the movie projector and the film in the dead girl's bedroom.

'If that's your fancy,' she said, kissing him again, 'I must send you Charmaine.'

'I don't want Charmaine.' He was firm. 'I want you. Just you. Plain and simple, with no trimmings.' He put one hand over her breast.

She stood up and took his hand. She led him towards the bedrom. 'What a treat,' she observed. 'I never expected to meet an Englishman who was normal and straightforward.'

'When shall I see you again?' He was at the front door. Anne, clad only in her cloak, was giving him a goodnight peck.

'Never,' she said. 'Forget me. And forget Helen Wightman.'

It was not until he reached Chiswick and the Scimitar was purring peacefully along the Motorway that Charles realised the obvious. Anne Lesley had not taken him to bed because she was slightly drunk, or nymphomaniac, or smitten with his charms. She was a powerful, dangerous lady. And she had wanted to divert him.

And that meant Miss Lesley, headmistress of a school of available ladies, had something important to hide.

He made a mental note to attack another formidable lady at the first possible opportunity. Mrs Farebrother, he thought grimly, you are going to tell me a lot about Tom Irvine, or I'll know the reason why.

CHAPTER TWENTY-SEVEN

The next morning, a Thursday, Charles found trying. Even the coffee failed to revive his spirits. Exhausted by his encounter with Miss Lesley, it was all he could do to cope with the flood of letters, cables and telexes which were contained in a neat file on his desk.

It was lunch-time before he could get to Mrs Farebrother's mews flat. He found he simply couldn't look at Helen's front door.

Initially, the old lady looked suspicious. She opened the door only a few inches. Her wrinkled face, peered out at Charles under unkempt, flowing grey hair, as if he might be the rent collector. She was all prepared to slam the door on an unwanted visitor.

However, a slight flicker of welcome crossed her features as she saw Charles.

'I'm sorry to disturb you,' he said. 'I wanted to ask a few questions about the death of the girl opposite. Miss Wightman.'

She bowed her head and opened the door. She hobbled down a dark passage and up the stairs until they reached her sitting room. It was a late nineteenth-century artist's studio, with large windows of leaded glass. Looking across the street, Charles could see straight into Helen Wightman's flat. What, he wondered, had the old lady thought as she watched the procession of lovers visiting the young and vibrant girl opposite? What memories had been stirred, what hostility aroused?

'Would you like a cup of tea?' she croaked. Without waiting for a reply she manipulated her wizened frame out of the room, presumably to the kitchen.

The room was well furnished. A settee and two chairs were covered in chintz, a variety of small tables and the mantelpiece were covered in bric a brac. A coal fire burned in the grate and the room was tolerably warm. To Charles' surprise, the television set was a colour model. Unlike most old ladies still living in London, even paying low rent and rates on an aged building, Mrs Farebrother looked to be living well above the poverty line.

She staggered in carrying a wooden tray with teapot, milk-jug, sugar-bowl and cups of a pattern frequently advertised in the colour supplements at bargain rates. Charles made haste to remove from her the burden of the tray and placed it on a side-table.

'I've told the police everything I knew,' she said, after pouring out the tea. 'I told them about your visit to that girl, the night she was murdered.'

Charles nodded. 'You did quite right.' His tone was designed to soothe. He sat down on the settee. It was an old sofa with a tilt towards the floor. It was a struggle to stay on it.

She looked up from her armchair with a quick, birdlike movement of her head.

'I told them that I saw her alive after you left.' She was defensive.

'I know,' Charles said. 'It's as well you are so observant. Otherwise I might be a suspect.'

She warmed to his commendation. 'Mind you, it's unusual for you to come on a Monday,' she observed. 'You were the Tuesday boy.' She reflected on this odd alteration to a regular itinerary.

'It was the cat that made me suspicious,' she confided, leaning forwards. Her s's hissed from her almost toothless mouth. 'Whatever people may say of that girl, she was very good to her cat.' She wagged her head sagely. 'When she didn't let the pussy-cat out on Tuesday, I knew something must be wrong.'

Charles tried hard to remember a cat in Helen's flat. He couldn't recollect seeing it at all. But after all, he reflected, my time was 6.30 to 10.30, Tuesday evenings. Maybe it wasn't in then. Yet it seemed unlike his Helen to keep a cat.

'You were very wise to inform the police,' Charles commended her. 'You saw me visit Miss Wightman on Tuesdays. Tell me who else she used to see.'

'Men.' The old lady spat out the word. 'Nothing but men.' She considered her statement. 'She liked the men,' she concluded. There was envy as well as hostility in her voice.

'Tell me about them.' Charles' voice was inviting.

She hesitated. 'There were a lot of black men.'

Charles drew in his breath in disapproval – a response he hoped would encourage Mrs Farebrother to unburden herself.

'She would come back about midnight, often with a black man.' She paused, then gained confidence. 'The sitting room light would go on for a few minutes. Then it would go off, and the bedroom light came on.'

She pursed her lips. 'Then that light would go off. The men would leave at about two o'clock in the morning.'

She poured herself another cup of tea, with an arthritic hand. 'I'm sorry to have had to tell you this,' she said, 'you being a good friend to her. Mind you,' she added judicially, 'one thing I'll say for her. She was always very good to her cat.' This appeared in her view to redeem some small part of Helen's rackety life.

Charles felt he was getting nothing, other than confirmation of Helen's catholic taste in the male sex. But what was wrong with that, he wondered. She had always been very good to him.

'Did any of these black men come back fairly regularly?' he asked.

Mrs Farebrother shrugged her shoulder. 'They all look alike to me,' she said.

'But she entertained white men too,' he suggested.

'Oh yes,' she replied.

He described, as best he could, Stan Kurtz. The old lady nodded eagerly.

'He came round three or four times,' she said. 'He was a real gentleman. He always used to bring her a bunch of flowers.'

Typical of that two-faced American, Charles thought. He took from his inside pocket a photograph of Tom Irvine, culled from the album Jenny Barnes had prepared of the company's staff.

Mrs Farebrother pulled a pair of pince-nez from inside the top of her dress. They were held by a chain around her neck. She scrutinized the photograph.

'That's the man who came on Mondays,' she said.

'The man who came on Mondays,' he repeated. 'Every Monday?'

'For the last four or five months,' the old lady said. 'Didn't you know about it?'

Charles did not reply. 'Did they go out for dinner on most evenings?'

'No.' She looked interested. 'You're right. That was very unusual. He used to arrive around seven-thirty, and he'd leave at eleven.'

'And did the bedroom light go on?' Charles put an almost salacious note into the question.

'Oh yes.' She smiled at him as if they were conspirators.

He pointed to the face in the photograph. 'And did he visit her on the Monday night she died?' He looked Mrs Farebrother straight in the eyes.

'Yes,' she replied. Then her gaze faltered, and she put her hand to her mouth. 'What have I said?' There was panic in her voice. 'I never told the police,' she mumbled. Charles felt suddenly excited. This at least was something he'd found out for himself.

'I'm not the police,' he said. 'I won't tell them.'

'I don't want to get anyone into trouble.' She looked anxious and scared.

Charles knew he was on the edge of a breakthrough. He remained solid and comforting.

'Don't worry,' he said again. 'I won't tell the police.'

'I don't like the police.' Her voice was quavering. 'They might come and put me away in a home.'

'Don't worry,' he repeated. 'I'm nothing to do with them. I won't tell anybody.'

She pulled a faded linen handkerchief from her sleeve and dabbed her eyes.

'What time did he come on that Monday?' he asked.

She searched her memory before she replied. 'He came at nine-thirty. He used his key to get into the house. He only stayed for about ten minutes.'

She looked at the photograph, almost with horror, as if she

was viewing a picture of Jack the Ripper. 'Did he kill that young girl, then?'

'No,' Charles replied. He was disappointed. 'She was dead before he arrived.'

When he got to the front door, he pulled out his wallet and handed her ten pounds.

'Thank you,' he said. 'You've been a great deal of help. There's just one thing.'

Mrs Farebrother looked up alertly.

'Don't mention my visit to the police,' he said.

He picked up a taxi and returned to the office. Another piece had been added to the jigsaw. But he was still no nearer fitting the pieces together.

It was nearly four before Charles got back to his office.

At half past five, having dealt with innumerable queries and minutiae, Charles visited the men's room. He found Tom Irvine grimacing at the mirror, inspecting his gritted and newly-cleaned teeth. He was dressed in a dinner-jacket and his hair was carefully combed.

'Going out on the town?' Charles enquired breezily.

'A wee dinner party with one of our printers,' the Scot replied.

Charles forebore to ask whether they would hand over the bribes before or after the meal. But in the peace of his office, sipping a reflective vodka-and-tonic, he decided to take Caroline's advice and follow Tom Irvine. He phoned her at Marlow and outlined his plan.

'I'm glad you're doing *something*,' she said, a little ungraciously, he thought.

He watched Soho Square from his window, looking over the flourishing tomato plants in his hydroponic 'miracle' garden. At six-thirty sharp, the bow-tied Scot bowled out of the building, clearly looking for a taxi.

Charles bolted downstairs. Fortunately London was, as always, bereft of cabs. He held the front door a few inches ajar and kept the managing director in his sights. Eventually, a taxi hove to, and Irvine climbed in.

At this point, Charles recognized his lack of training as a sleuth. There was his quarry, climbing into a cab and departing for some unknown destination. And there was he, Charles Hutchinson, without a taxi and without any way of pursuing him.

By extraordinary good fortune, however, a second cab, its sign lit to attract intending passengers, came into the square from Oxford Street.

'Follow that cab!' Charles cried, feeling somewhat foolish. The driver, a gnarled old man bent over his wheel, found nothing unusual in this instruction.

Irvine's taxi turned left out of Curzon Street and pulled into the entrance of the Hilton Hotel. Charles stopped his cab in Park Lane. Pulling the collar of his winter coat up around the bottom half of his face, he passed through the revolving door of the hotel.

A large lobby, like a miniature station concourse, met his gaze. To the left were shops selling watches, jewellery and expensive clothing. To his right was a long and busy reception desk. In the centre were ranks of leather sofas, filled with the flotsam and jetsam of international travel. Tom Irvine was nowhere to be seen.

To his right was a door marked St George's Bar. He sidled through the entrance, to find a dimly-lit bar, of the American type, where darkness is regarded as essential to cloak the depravity of drinking. It took his eyes a few seconds to adjust to the lack of light, and he felt conspicuous. Nobody, however, paid him the slightest attention. Finally he located his managing director. He was seated at a table towards the far end of the bar, pouring peanuts from a bowl in front of him, down his upturned mouth. On one side a blonde, a fur wrap around her shoulders, was patting her hair with the aid of a hand mirror. On the other a brunette wearing an unseasonably low-cut dress was watching, with apparent approval, Irvine's uncouth performance with the peanuts.

Printers, Charles thought sarcastically, were either changing their sex or going up in the world in the services they provided for their customers. A waiter brought drinks to the trio and a clinking of glasses took place, accompanied by some simpering from the young ladies.

Charles retired to the sofas in the lounge, choosing the one furthest from the entrance and closest to the lifts to the hotel bedrooms. He bought an *Evening Standard* partly to read and partly as a possible shield for his face.

It was half an hour before his patience was rewarded. Benjamin Kimathu, the tall Tanzanian, strode out of the revolving doors, a carnation in the buttonhole of his dinner-jacket, and headed with jaunty step towards the bar. It was another thirty minutes before the party of four left the hotel.

They walked into the chill wind blowing down Park Lane, the girls holding their hair, their coats flapping. Charles saw them turn into Curzon Street. Following discreetly at a distance, he observed them enter the White Elephant Club, some two hundred yards down the road. He was reminded of his last dinner there with Helen Wightman, when she had so much enjoyed being surrounded by celebrities.

By the time he passed through the entrance of the eighteenth-century building, Irvine, Kimathu and the two young ladies were engaged in excited conversation at a table some way down the long dining room.

Charles lurked at the bar and had a steak au poivre brought to him. He asked the genial barman whether Tom Irvine was a frequent visitor. To his surprise he discovered that the craggy Scot was well-known at the club. The ill-dressed man of few words when in the office transformed himself in the evenings into a suave, dapper boulevardier. According to the barman he was always accompanied by young ladies of undoubted glamour.

Charles enquired how long Irvine had been a regular diner. Only for the last six months or so, the barman opined. In fact, Charles thought, since he had taken over from James Fitzpatrick.

The four revellers at the far-away table continued to drink brandy and port until well after eleven o'clock. The Tanzanian became particularly jovial as he was plied with liquor and was encouraged by the two girls, who every now and then patted and stroked his shoulder, his cheek or his hands. Whatever business Tom Irvine was doing, it certainly wasn't on behalf of the Fitzpatrick company.

Charles nipped out of the club just before the quartet left and stood in a doorway some twenty yards away. The uniformed and bemedalled doorman hailed a taxi. Kimathu and the two girls climbed in, the Tanzanian giggling with delight at the prospect ahead. Irvine, his work as introducer and procurer completed, got into a second taxi. Charles was about to leave when he noticed a black Rover 2000 move away from the kerb almost opposite him and follow Irvine's cab. It passed under a streetlight. In the passenger seat was a familiar face: Inspector Pearson.

Charles returned to the White Elephant for a thoughtful night-cap. The Inspector had told him Irvine was in the clear regarding Helen's murderer. Why then was he following him? The old lady had said Irvine had visited Helen's flat at 9.30 p.m., half an hour after she had died, according to the police. But could the forensic scientists time a death by suffocation to within one hour, when it had been nearly a day before the body had been discovered?

Three things were clear. There was a great deal more to Tom Irvine than met the eye. There was more to Inspector Pearson than that apparently stolid individual let on. And the one person who might have a clue as to what was happening was Anne Lesley.

He found the scrap of paper on which he had jotted down her telephone number the night before. She was drowsy when she answered the call. She was already in bed, she explained, and half-asleep. But she would expect Charles and leave her door on the latch. For him, she said, she would do anything.

The door of Anne Lesley's flat opened to his touch. A sidelight gave faint illumination to the living room. Charles walked through to the bedroom. Anne had returned to sleep. She lay on her back, her face as smooth and innocent as a baby's, framed by a wickerwork Italian bedhead. Not much security for a girl high-up in British Intelligence, Charles thought. But again, who would want to kill her, and what would it gain?

The same, however, could be said of Helen Wightman, a much smaller cog in the wheel. But she had been killed, cold-bloodedly and sadistically, after the murderer had taken his pleasure of her. Frustration and wrath at the web of deceit in which he was entangled welled up inside him. But he recognized that to get any information from Anne Lesley, he would have to be cunning.

'Wake up, Anne.' He sat on the bed and stroked her forehead.

For a few seconds her eyes were quite blank, then a look of alarm as she gained consciousness was replaced by a warm smile as her brain recognized him. She sat up. She was sleeping in the raw and his eyes fastened on her luscious breasts.

The locket swung between them on its chain.

'Darling,' she said, kissing him tenderly. 'I didn't expect you to come back to me so quickly.' Her eyes were soft. She had the look of a woman about to fall in love. 'I'm most flattered.'

'I've come to talk business,' Charles said.

'Oh.' She sounded disappointed. 'Well, we might as well enjoy it.' She got up and opened the door of a wall cupboard. She poured him a Heine brandy and added some ginger ale to her own. A revolting mixture, Charles thought, much loved by Englishwomen.

As she handed him his glass, Charles could not but relish her slim, trim figure and long, willowy legs.

She sat down next to him and he told her of his evening, following Tom Irvine. Finally, he revealed that he had spotted Inspector Pearson.

'What's he doing, following Irvine?' he asked angrily. 'You both told me Tom Irvine was in the clear.'

'Last night you were complaining that Pearson was incompetent,' she pointed out quietly. 'Now you're objecting because he's following up every lead.'

She asked for a description of the two girls and looked decidedly thoughtful.

'Are they two of yours?' Charles enquired.

She stroked his cheek with the back of her hand. 'You wouldn't expect me to say, darling, would you?'

'All right,' he conceded. 'But I'd like to find out why Inspector Pearson was tailing my managing director.' He rather liked this proprietorial note.

'I'll find out,' Anne was brisk, 'and let you know. Of course,' she added thoughtfully, 'it may not have been Irvine he was following. It may have been you.'

This had occurred to Charles. He was impressed that she came out quite openly with the suggestion. Unless she was double-bluffing, it implied she was on his side.

She refilled their glasses. Instead of handing him his brandy, however, she dipped her finger in her balloon glass and smeared the spirit on her left breast. She leaned forward, keeping her shapely legs together, until his mouth closed round her nipple. It swelled as his tongue searched for the brandy.

She undressed him, kissing each part of his body as she removed his clothes. She looked at him admiringly. 'I'm glad to see you're ready for me,' she said.

Charles was perfectly happy to postpone his interrogation.

'Darling,' Anne said, climbing onto the bed, 'there's just one favour you could do me.'

'Anything,' Charles said. He meant it.

She took the chain from around her neck and handed it to him, smiling shyly. 'Beat me gently with this.' She turned over onto her stomach.

'Alright,' he said. He was breathing fast. Softly he applied the thick twisted gold chains to her backside, almost stroking her with them. Anne began to roll softly from side to side, her breasts hardening, her legs moving slightly apart.

'Tell me the truth about Tom Irvine,' he said.

'Not now, darling. Later.' Her whole body was quivering. She had difficulty in speaking.

'Tell me about Tom Irvine,' he repeated. He took a leather belt from her bedside table.

'I'm not certain,' she breathed.

He applied the belt.

212

'Harder.'

'Tom Irvine and Stan Kurtz are in league, aren't they?'

Her bottom rose with the sting.

'I'll tell you later,' she said.

'Now.'

Her body writhed with pleasure.

'Tom Irvine and Stan Kurtz,' he repeated slowly. 'They're up to something, aren't they?'

'Harder still,' she said. Then, 'yes.'

'What are they up to?'

'I don't know.'

Her whole frame shuddered.

'I'll tell you later.' Then, 'oh darling.' It was a low moan of satisfaction. 'I promise I'll tell you later. Now, for God's sake, take me.'

Anne lay, her eyes closed, at peace with the world. Charles refurled the belt and placed it on the bedside table. He picked up the gold necklace by the locket to put it there too. His hand must have brushed a hidden spring. The locket swung open.

Charles was transfixed. Inside the thin gold casket was a photograph. It was of himself.

She sat back in one of the black leather chairs. 'I'll be perfectly honest with you,' she said, putting her arms towards him.

'That will be a pleasant change.' He trusted her about as far as he could throw a ten-ton truck.

'Darling, I can only tell you what we know.' She waved her arms despairingly. 'About eight months ago, you had a nervous breakdown.'

Charles nodded.

'The day after you went into hospital, Tom Irvine began to take an interest in Helen.' She had put on her tan wrap-around skirt and nothing else. She shivered and turned on the fan heater. 'We monitor all our girls, as you know,' she added.

'Irvine spent a lot of money on her, sent her flowers, chocolates, expensive presents. Well,' she shrugged, 'you know Helen. It wasn't long before she succumbed to that sort of treatment.'

She shivered again, and pulled the electric fire closer. 'Then, five months ago, just after you got out of hospital, Irvine introduced Helen to Stan Kurtz.'

'*Irvine* introduced her?' Charles was incredulous.

'Not only that,' Anne continued firmly. 'Irvine took them both out to dinner two or three times. Each time he let Stan Kurtz take Helen home. You know what that implies.'

'He was letting Kurtz have a slice of his bacon.'

'Precisely. We became very interested. It's unusual, to say the least, for a businessman to shower a young lady with presents and then hand her over to somebody else.'

'So, all the time Irvine and Kurtz were apparently fighting each other within the company, they were meeting on the side.' Charles was thoughtful.

'But you see, darling,' Anne said, 'although it looked odd, we couldn't establish any reason, any other link. We checked Irvine and Kurtz thoroughly. There's nothing on the record against either of them. It seemed that maybe it was just one randy middle-aged businessman helping out another.'

'There's more to it than that,' Charles asserted.

'Obviously.' Anne laughed wryly. 'From your story of Irvine's activities tonight it appears he's trying to infiltrate my network. But for whom, and for what reason, we haven't got a clue.'

Charles stood up.

'Sit down.' Anne was brisk. 'There's just one more thing you should know. Stan Kurtz took a great interest in your secretary, Jenny Barnes. Three months ago he flew to London specifically to take her out to dinner on two consecutive evenings.' She took a final sip of her brandy and ginger ale. 'Two months ago,' – she spoke solemnly – 'Jenny Barnes died.'

'I know.' The memory was still painful.

'All I will say,' Anne continued, 'is this. In your preoccupation with Helen, don't forget Jenny.'

She followed him to the door. 'When shall I see you again?' she asked. She sounded quite concerned.

'I'll call you,' Charles replied. 'Just one thing, Anne. The man whose picture is in your locket. Is he your first lover or your prey?'

She laughed. 'Darling, you performed beautifully tonight. But one swallow doesn't make a summer.' She tossed her head and her naked breasts bobbed in time. 'Maybe the two are one and the same.'

By the time he reached Marlow, Charles thought he had a good idea of the identity of Helen Wightman's murderer. Anne had given him sufficient clues. But how to prove it? And how to work out how all the double-dealers by whom he was surrounded fitted into the jig-saw puzzle? That, he decided, would take him a few days. At least.

CHAPTER TWENTY-EIGHT

Friday was a busy day at the office, packed with meetings. Tom Irvine attended a few of them, and was his normal self, saying little but picking up any inaccuracy and clobbering any foolish remarks. In his baggy grey suit, he bore no resemblance to the gay clubman of the previous evening.

Charles forebore to challenge him. He had decided to give himself the week-end to think over his plan of campaign. He was now suspicious of everyone. And he wanted to talk to Caroline.

She had arranged a dinner party at River Lodge for the Friday evening and very entertaining it was. It was not until Saturday, when the children were tucked up in bed, that he was able to talk seriously to her.

This time, however, she took the initiative.

'I detect that you've discovered a new Miss Tuesday night.' Her voice was frosty and wounded. 'Only she appears to be Miss Wednesday and Miss Thursday. I've been wondering whether to talk to you about it all day.' She sounded almost ready to burst into tears.

'What are you talking about?' Charles said guiltily.

'You didn't get home until 1 a.m. on Thursday morning and 4 a.m. on Friday,' she said tartly.

'I thought you were asleep.'

'I was, until you drove your noisy great Scimitar up to the front door, slammed the car door and bumped into the bed on your way to the bathroom.'

'I'm sorry,' he said placatingly.

'So I should hope.'

'You've got the whole thing wrong,' he said hastily. He pointed out that it was she who had told him to investigate Helen's death. That was exactly what he had been doing.

The prospect of hearing about his detective work made her less glacial, and he gave an edited account of his evening with Inspector Pearson and Anne Lesley. The fact that Miss Lesley had been a friend of Helen's re-aroused Caroline's suspicions. So he tactfully implied that the Inspector had stayed with them throughout dinner.

The revelation that Helen had been involved in espionage completely diverted her, however. She became extremely thoughtful. As Tom Irvine turned out to have been one of Miss Wightman's many bedmates, she suggested that he too might be working for Intelligence.

Charles' account of his observation of the managing director at the Hilton Hotel and White Elephant Club so confirmed her theory that she was delighted by her own perspicacity.

'I told you so,' she said. 'If only you'd listen to me a bit more.'

'You also told me that there was a connection between the deaths of Jenny Barnes and Helen Wightman and the attempts on my life.'

She nodded.

'And I believe,' he said, 'that is true too.'

'There you are. I'm right again.'

'I think it's odd,' Charles said quietly.

'What's odd about it? It takes your plodding, logical masculine brain ten hours to arrive at what a clever woman can work out in twenty minutes.'

'It didn't take me ten hours,' he objected. 'I just didn't have the information until Thursday night.' He looked Caroline straight in the eyes. 'You came to the same conclusion without knowing anything. Apparently.'

Her eyes dropped. 'What do you mean?' she asked.

'I'm just wondering.'

'Can you believe,' she looked straight at him, 'that if I discovered anything that could help you – or protect your life – I wouldn't tell you?'

'I hardly trust anybody,' he explained.

'Darling!' She was shocked. 'You must trust me.' She put her hand on his.

'Then do you solemnly promise that there is nothing you know about me or these deaths which you haven't told me?'

She stood up to get their nightcaps.

'Yes,' she said, as she walked away.

Charles did not believe her.

When Charles reached the office the next morning, after a sleepless night, he found Mary Peters almost in tears. 'Don't go into your office,' she pleaded. 'It's in chaos. There's been a burglary.'

Charles swore. Their offices, being in Soho, were particularly subject to intruders. Usually they were not harassed by professionals. But on Saturday nights, particularly after things like the Cup Final, bands of marauders would break in to spend the night. And like all other Soho offices, they were plagued with drug-addicts looking for a quiet place to shoot up. These intruders rarely stole, but the damage they did was extensive and often costly. Charles had experimented with bars over the windows, but the resulting prison-like atmosphere was so depressing that he had had them taken off again.

Mary had called the police, but Charles didn't wait for them. They always came, and would fingerprint everything, but never caught anybody.

His office was a blizzard of papers. His drinks cabinet had been broken into, and an empty bottle lay on the floor, surrounded by a litter of broken glasses. Someone had pulled almost all the books out of the bookcase, and had scattered them around the floor. His desk had been broken into, and to his annoyance he found that his passport had been taken, though not his unused travellers' cheques. How typical, he thought. What possible good could his passport do anyone.

Idly he picked up a battered book from the floor, in a vague attempt to help Mary, who was fluttering about, madly picking up papers, and dropping them again in her haste and upset. He glanced at it, and recognized the knitting book Caroline had shown him a few evenings before. A familiar page caught his eye. Of course, the misprints. He had meant to have that little matter out with Irvine, but events had rather overtaken it. As he glanced round his office, a surge of fury overcame him. Now, he thought, is the time, and I'm going to get that bastard to rights.

'Leave all that,' he told Mary Peters curtly. 'I want you to do something for me. Go down to the production department, and bring up all the sets of manuscripts and proofs you can find or carry from the back file. You and I have some checking to do.'

'Yes, Mr Fitzpatrick,' she said apprehensively, and hurried out to do his bidding, leaving a paper trail of scattered documents behind her.

Charles collected a pile of books from the floor at random and started to check through them for misprints. He quickly found and noted a large number, and was ringing them with a blue pencil when Mary came in, staggering under a pile of manuscripts and proofs.

'These were all I could carry, sir,' she said anxiously, puffing slightly.

'That's fine,' Charles said. 'Now from that pile sort out the homecraft titles, and arrange them so that the manuscript and the proof are side by side. I want to check back from the finished copy, through the proofs to the manuscript. Somewhere along the line, far too many misprints are slipping through. I want to find out why and where.'

It took some time, but finally they had collated three titles, and began the tedious task of checking the corrections against the misprints in the finished editions. Most printing errors arise from the original setting of the manuscript, often because the compositor makes an error in setting up the type, but quite often because the original manuscript is faulty. The galleys, long thin strips of type, are then cut up into page lengths by designers, and sent back to the printers after correction.

Sometimes new errors creep in when the actual physical job of translating the cut and pasted paper into print is carried out. Usually these corrections are made on the page proofs. Red ink is used for errors the printers make themselves, and for the correction of which they must pay. Blue is used for corrections for which the publishers admit responsibility. Green marks the queries which the printers' own readers have made. It is rare for more than a handful of printer's errors to carry over from galleys to page poofs, if they have been spotted.

What soon became clear, as they worked through the proofs, was that new errors did seem to be amazingly common, new errors altogether. And this should be virtually impossible. Charles puzzled for a while. Suddenly to his surprise he realized that someone, in blue ink, was actually introducing misprints into the page proofs. He collected a number of samples, and then told Mary to call the production department. He wanted to know who passed page proofs for the printer. The answer was immediate, but puzzling: Tom Irvine. It appeared that he had made a house rule that all page proofs were to be checked by him personally, on the grounds that editors, with their tendency never to leave well enough alone, would make further expensive and unnecessary corrections at that stage. At approximately 75p per correction, the sums involved could mount up.

'So whose writing is this?' Charles said to himself in surprise.'

'Oh,' Mary said proudly, 'that's Mr Irvine's. I recognize it. Before Miss Barnes died, I used to work in the production department.'

'Then whose is this?' Charles pointed out a second hand which had been used to make what were certainly deliberate errors on a set of pages.

'Why, Mr Fitzpatrick,' Mary said reproachfully. 'That's your writing.'

Charles gaped at her. He had had nothing whatever to do with the actual production of the books since he had taken over from the Chairman. But why on earth should the Chairman, not to mention the managing director, have been deliberately putting errors into Fitzpatrick books? For some reason his mind flashed back to the game that Helen and Fitzpatrick had evolved. A code? But why? And for whom?

On a sudden impulse, Charles called the production department. He read off the three titles over the phone, and asked where they had been printed. There was a short delay, and then the answer came back – Hong Kong.

Charles sat back in his chair, and tried to collate the information he'd received. First of all, both Fitzpatrick and Irvine had been involved in setting up deliberate errors. Secondly, the books he had checked had been printed in Hong Kong. And Irvine's favourite kick-back printer was in Hong Kong. It all looked like some kind of highly confidential affair, in which Fitzpatrick had been deeply involved. No wonder Charles had been warned off when he threatened to expose Irvine. And no wonder, now he came to think of it, that Irvine had been so surprised and threatening when challenged. Charles sat up abruptly. Irvine must have guessed, indeed he must *know*, that Charles was not Fitzpatrick. Had he known all the time? Charles remembered Jenny and Helen, and Fitzpatrick's penchant for never using one string when two or more would do, and decided that he had not, at least to start with. He wondered suddenly where Irvine had been the night Jenny died.

A new and startling thought came into his mind. What if the Chairman was involved in something really big? And it was going wrong? And he had the opportunity to put someone else in his place, someone who by the very nature of the original bargain, wouldn't be in any position to ask too many questions? A cat's paw, in effect? Or an Aunt Sally? No, a cat's paw. Charles was supposed to be clever enough to eliminate a lot of Fitzpatrick's problems by himself – Kurtz, for instance. And then? Charles shivered.

'Why, Mr Fitzpatrick,' Mary Peters broke into his thoughts.

'You've not watered your garden.' She was reproachful. She'd taken a proprietary interest in the toy and its burgeoning tomato plants ever since Irvine had brought it back from New York. She bent to fiddle with the pump. There was an enormous bang and a flash. The plug seemed to explode from the wall in a cloud of acrid smoke. The power point had virtually disintegrated. Mary Peter's crumpled body had smashed against the desk. She lay in a graceless huddle on the floor, a look of fatuous surprise frozen onto her small undistinguished face. The hydroponics garden was on the floor beside her. With macabre irony, a tomato plant, green and fragrant, lay between her clasped hands. She was clearly dead.

Charles sat frozen in his chair, staring at the wrecked garden, the smoking hole in the wall, and the crumpled corpse of his secretary. Almost certainly, that corpse would have been his own, if he'd noticed that the little garden had lacked water. Slowly, stiffly, moving like an old man, he rose, and was trying to straighten out Mary Peter's twisted limbs, when the door of his office burst open, and people hurried in, attracted by the explosion. He took no more notice of them than of the water soaking through the knees of his trousers as he knelt beside the body. With shaking hands he tried to order her hair. It seemed obscene for others to see her so dishevelled in death. If Fitzpatrick or Irvine had anything to do with this, he vowed silently, I'll see them dead.

A voice from among the babbling crowd behind his desk caught his attention. It was Inspector Pearson, trying to force his way through the crowd. A uniformed sergeant was pushing the curious physically apart, and urging them to clear the room. Charles tried desperately to pull himself together and to get to his feet. The Inspector took his place by the body, and with brisk efficiency confirmed that Mary was dead. A brief word had the sergeant phoning for an ambulance and reinforcements.

Charles was still standing aimlessly by his desk when the inspector went over to the plug, lying charred on the carpet. He pulled from his pocket one of the Swiss army's useful all-purpose pocket knives, and using the screwdriver prodded among the ruined and odorous plastic. He examined the wrecked interior for what seemed a long time. Then he turned slowly to Charles.

'Who usually used this thing?' he asked.

'I did,' Charles said huskily.

'Then you're a very lucky man, Mr Fitzpatrick.' He held out the plug, and Charles saw, in the remnants of fused wire, that the earth wire had been disconnected, and instead of the fuse, a twisted skein of heavy-duty wire cable had been inserted.

'Someone wants you dead,' the Inspector went on. I told you before that you should leave all this sort of thing to the professionals.'

'How did you get here so quickly?' Charles asked.

'We came to investigate your burglary,' the policeman replied.

'You?' Charles was incredulous. 'I didn't know Chief Inspectors of Special Branch were sent round to investigate common or garden break-ins.'

'Nothing's common or garden about you,' came the reply. 'Any incident involving you has to be reported by the uniformed branch to me. Too many people close to you have been killed.'

'You're a lot cleverer than you like to appear, Inspector,' Charles said.

'I should hope so.' The Inspector smiled. 'Otherwise I'd be a bit of a fool, wouldn't I?'

'Mind you,' the Inspector added, 'you've got a pretty good head on your shoulders yourself, according to Miss Lesley.' He paused. 'She seems to have taken quite a shine to you, sir.' He was choosing his words carefully. 'I hope she didn't tell you too much.'

'She said what she intended, I'm sure.' He was, too.

The Inspector nodded thoughtfully. 'Let's get back to the main question: who is trying to murder you?'

'Me?'

'Yes you. According to your statement, it was an accident that Miss Peters switched on your hydroponic garden. Normally you switch it on and off yourself.'

Charles nodded agreement. 'What about the burglary? Can that be connected with it?'

'I don't see how.' The Inspector pondered. 'Maybe it was a coincidence.'

'I thought policemen didn't believe in coincidences.' Charles remembered Superintendent Maina's message to that effect.

The inspector leafed through his notes. 'Somebody got into your office over the weekend and altered the wiring in the plug so that it was a death trap.' He looked at Charles. 'Maybe that was the real purpose of the burglary. But whoever set up the murder attempt must have known about the garden, and that you, sir, normally switched it on.' He stroked his chin. 'That,' he concluded, 'tells me its an inside job. In which case why should the killer set up a fake burglary?'

'To divert our suspicions,' Charles suggested.

The Inspector was doubtful but decided to get on with the job. Charles listed the staff who knew about his hydroponic toy: apart from Mary Peters, only five or six of the company's senior people visited his office.

Charles was allowed to stay in the boardroom while the police questioned them. Inspector Pearson thought he might spot any inconsistent behaviour. But all the executives assumed that it had been an accident; all were deeply shocked; and it had occurred to none that Charles might have been the target.

Both the Inspector and Charles were convinced of the innocence of all those they had interviewed. Only one person remained from Charles' list: Tom Irvine.

'What's going on around here?' the Scot asked aggressively. He banged the table. 'Why are you wasting everyone's time investigating an accident?'

Inspector Pearson had been doodling on a pad in front of him, his head down.

He looked up. 'It wasn't an accident,' he said quietly. 'It was attempted murder.'

'Don't talk nonsense' – Irvine imagined he was talking to the normal, rather unintelligent man from West End Central, their local police station.

'We will show you the evidence,' the Inspector said. He nodded to the sergeant, who handed Irvine the plug.

Charles' office had been cleared and tidied. Mary Peter's body had been taken to the mortuary. Only the broken window testified to the burglary.

'My God!' Irvine said. 'His jaw fell open. 'I apologize,' he muttered. 'I hadn't realized.' He sat down on the settee. 'Who on earth would have wanted to kill Mary?'

'They didn't want to kill Mary,' Charles said. He was sitting on the front of his desk, an officer on each side. 'They wanted to kill me.'

The inspector broke in to read the part of Charles' statement in which he affirmed that he normally dealt with the 'miracle' garden.

'Why on earth would anyone want to kill you?' the managing director asked Charles. He appeared genuinely bewildered.

'That is what we would like to know,' Pearson spoke with gravity. 'I suppose you wouldn't have a reason, Mr Irvine?'

'Me?' He was outraged. 'James and I have worked together for fifteen years. We started the company together, we're almost blood brothers.' A remarkable change of tune since their last, fiery discussion about kick-backs, Charles thought.

'Do you have a key to the office?' Pearson asked.

Irvine produced a ring of keys.

'Do you carry them with you, always?'

Irvine said he did. And confirmed that all the executives they had interviewed had keys to the offices.

'You'll keep this information to yourself,' the Inspector requested.

'Aye,' he said. 'I'm very good at keeping secrets.' He looked at Charles, and in that look was a warning if not a menace.

Charles glared at him. 'I'm amazed to hear you tell the Inspector we were like blood brothers,' he remarked, 'in view of the rows we've had over the last few weeks.'

Irvine looked as embarrassed as can a man whose face is an expressionless mask. 'Quarrels among old friends, James,' he said dismissively. 'They can't break a partnership that's lasted for fifteen years.'

Charles ignored this reply. 'Just before Mary died,' he proceeded, 'she and I made an important discovery. We discovered that the misprints I've been complaining about in our books are not accidental. They are deliberate.'

Irvine's bottom shifted slightly on the chair. But his face remained impassive. 'Nonsense. A misprint is a mistake. By definition. So it can't be deliberate.' He was scornful.

'I wouldn't be so superior about the matter if I were you. I believe they are by no means accidental.' Charles tried to sound as Chairmanly as possible. 'And I am sure they are connected with you and your young ladies.'

'My young ladies?' Irvine appeared astonished. 'My dear James, you're the specialist in that department.'

'You're a liar, Tom Irvine.' Charles was quite unemotional.

Two red spots appeared in the middle of the Scot's cheeks. 'Don't you dare talk to me like that.'

Pearson, who had sat watching this scene unmoved, shifted in his chair.

'May I ask, Mr Irvine, where you were on the night Miss Barnes died?'

Charles and Irvine looked at him in amazement.

Irvine said contemptuously. 'I was in Wales with a printer. Call him. You can't seriously be making anything of poor Jenny's car crash?'

The inspector looked at him solemnly. 'We're inclined to believe,' he said, deadpan, 'that there is a connection between the death of Miss Barnes and that of Miss Wightman. Miss Peters is the third connection of Mr Fitzpatrick's here, to die in very strange circumstances. Too much for coincidence, wouldn't you agree?' He seemed to be waiting for an answer.

Irvine said nothing. The inspector took a photograph from his pocket, and held it out to Irvine. 'Do you recognize this man?' he asked almost casually.

'Never seen him before in my life,' Irvine said, barely glancing at the picture before handing it back.

The inspector looked at it ruminatively and then replaced it in his pocket. 'The resemblance to yourself,' he said pedantically, 'is truly remarkable. His name, by the way, is Palmer.'

'It's amazing how many people have almost identical doubles,' Irvine said. He shot Charles an unreadable glance. 'There's nothing in that.'

'True,' the inspector said thoughtfully. He smiled at Irvine. Charles wondered when he was going to ask for an alibi for the Kenya trip, but for the moment at least the inspector seemed to want to drop the matter.

There was a pause, then Charles broke out. 'Helen Wightman.' Charles' voice was icy. 'You told me you didn't know her.'

'So what?' The Scot was belligerent.

'You've been sleeping with her for the last six months. Every Monday night.'

Irvine spread his hands, palms upwards. 'All right, I admit I lied to you about Helen. I thought you'd be annoyed if you discovered I was double-dating your girl friend.'

Charles continued his interrogation. 'How did you meet her?'

'She telephoned me while you were taking your rest-cure. She wanted to know how you were. I suppose, in your usual arrogant fashion, you didn't bother to keep in touch with her. Anyway, I took her out to lunch to console her.'

'And then you decided it would be even better,' Charles said, 'if you consoled her in bed.'

Irvine nodded calmly. 'It made a change from working for you sixteen hours a day.'

'You saw Helen on Monday nights?'

'Aye. Monday was the night she kept for me.'

'So you saw her on the evening she was murdered?'

'No.' He paused for thought. 'I had to fly up to Edinburgh late on Monday evening. I'd told Helen I couldn't see her.'

Charles leaned back in his chair. 'You are a liar,' he said again.

Irvine, having been caught once, was less aggressive this time. 'What do you mean?'

The inspector held up a hand to stop Charles. He looked at Irvine benignly. 'You were seen visiting Miss Wightman's flat on the evening of her murder,' he said.

The Scot covered his eyes with a hand for a few seconds. 'The old lady in the flat opposite,' he said suddenly, with venom.

The inspector nodded. Charles picked up his letter-opener and tapped the glass top of his desk.

'I didn't get there until 9.30,' Irvine claimed. 'I'd been working late, getting the papers ready for the visit to Wales.'

'Any witnesses?' the inspector asked.

Irvine shook his head. 'I had a key to Helen's flat. I let myself in and went up to the sitting room. She wasn't there. I waited for ten minutes. I thought she'd probably gone out in a temper because I was late. She was like that, you know.'

'Frankly your story is a little improbable,' Charles said. 'You only saw her on Mondays. I'd have thought you'd have been too impatient for your weekly ration to stay late at the office.'

Irvine turned to him and smiled grimly. 'I've always been a stickler for work. You, of all people, know that.'

'Are you sure you didn't see Helen earlier that evening?'

'Positive.'

'And you didn't go upstairs to the bedroom?'

'No.'

'Why were you interested in Helen Wightman?' Pearson asked.

The managing director began to pace back and forth across the office. 'That's a bit embarrassing.' He was wringing his hands behind his back. 'I've always been a staunch Presbyterian. I've never looked at woman, particularly not of Helen's type. But when I met her, I found her quite fascinating. She was such a pretty gay little thing. I asked her out to dinner and then . . . well, it just seemed perfectly natural to go to bed with her.' He sought for words to explain his kicking over the traces. 'It was as if God had made her for it.' He sat down and buried his face in his hands.

'That is the third lie you've told,' Charles said. 'Your real

227

interest in Helen Wightman was because she worked in British Intelligence.'

'In Intelligence? Helen? Don't talk nonsense.' Irvine raised his voice. 'I didn't know anything about that. What do you take me for?'

'A liar and a knave,' Charles replied coolly. He told Tom Irvine of the evening only five nights before, when he had followed him from the Hilton Hotel to the White Elephant. Pearson looked annoyed, but did not interrupt.

'That's a hell of a trick to play on a partner.' Irvine's response to being caught out was to become aggressive. He claimed that he had met Ben Kimathu through Helen; the Tanzanian had kept in touch and invited him out for an evening with two young ladies.

It was a quick and clever cover-up, Charles thought. But his own hands were tied: he couldn't reveal his acquaintance with Anne Lesley and the information she had given. 'Why did you introduce Stan Kurtz to Helen?' he enquired, changing tack.

The mention of the ex-paratrooper slightly unsettled Tom Irvine. He ran his hand through his hair and his answer was unconvincing. The American, he said, had wanted to find a girl in London. So he had introduced Kurtz to Helen, in the hope that she would lay on a friend for him.

Charles found it hard to believe, and was about to burst into speech when the inspector held up a restraining hand.

'In the matter of Derek Palmer,' he said, absently doodling on his note-pad. 'Are you sure you've never come across him?'

Irvine looked at him, surprised and disconcerted. 'Certainly,' he said.

'Palmer was the man who tried to kill Mr Fitzpatrick, here, in Nairobi. I wonder,' he said casually, intent on his doodles, 'where you were at the time?'

'In the office, I should think,' Irvine said contemptuously. 'Why don't you check?'

The inspector looked up sharply. 'We will,' he said mildly, 'we will.'

Charles left his chair, and began to walk restlessly about the office. There was a silence.

'Can I go now?' Irvine said insolently. 'I have work to do, unlike some others.'

Charles swung on him. 'I believe you're the person who's trying to kill me,' he shouted, losing control for a moment.

'You're mad.' Irvine appeared incredulous. 'Why on earth should I want to do that?'

'That's exactly what I would like to know.' Charles' tone was silky. 'But I'll tell you one thing. You made one mistake, Tom Irvine. You thought a false beard and moustache would prevent Derek Palmer being identified as you. But when you filled out your passport application for Palmer, you made one slip: you used Helen's address.' A sudden thought struck him. 'I suppose she kept the passport for you, when it arrived. Perhaps that's why she had to be killed.'

Pearson and Irvine were on their feet simultaneously. 'Who the hell are you to reveal that information?' the former shouted. 'Sit down, Fitzpatrick. And don't open your mouth again until I say you can.' He was livid.

The twin spots of wrath had reappeared on Irvine's cheeks. 'You're insane,' he shouted. 'You should be certified.' He came towards Charles as if to strike him.

'It's not me who's going to be locked up, Tom Irvine.' Charles gripped his shoulder and shook the man. He fought back a primeval urge to throttle him. 'It's you. You're not just a liar and a thief—' he lowered his voice to a snarl— 'but a cold-blooded killer. And I'm going to prove it.'

Pearson got between them and held them apart.

The small, slightly-built Scot shook himself free. His eyes were cold as marble, his lips twisted in a sneer. 'All I can say to that,' he said with quiet menace, 'is that if you're right and I am the murderer: if you've still got to find the proof, you had better be quick.' He turned on his heel and left the office. The door slammed behind him.

Pearson was still very angry. 'God damn it,' he said, abandoning for good his policeman's discretion. 'I encouraged you because I thought you might needle him into revealing more than he meant to. But I didn't expect you to blurt out all the information I should never have given you.' Still fuming, he brushed past Charles and went back to his seat. He sat there, stabbing at his notebook with his pencil.

'But what about the misprints?' Charles said.

Pearson looked at him. 'We knew about those,' he said crisply. 'And I wasn't too anxious for Irvine to find out we knew. Evidently Miss Lesley should have told you more, or nothing.' He glared at Charles.

'But don't you think it's significant?' Charles stared at Pearson, baffled. 'It has to be a code of some kind, it has to be.'

'Of course it is. Do you think we're fools?' Pearson was impatient. 'If only you would leave these things alone. We'd do much better without amateur help.'

Charles shrugged angrily. 'Very well,' he said. 'All the same, I'm going back to Kenya. The key is there, I'm sure of it.'

Pearson looked at him shrewdly. 'So are we, sir,' he said, getting up. 'I'd hoped you were thinking of going back. It might be that we'd have something to ask you to do. In the meantime,' he said, heading for the door, 'I'm sure you'll want us to replace your passport.'

He'd actually left before Charles realized that he hadn't told Pearson about the loss of his passport, and no one else knew.

CHAPTER TWENTY-NINE

Caroline took the news badly. Her egg-spoon dropped onto the saucer.

'Why on earth are you going back to Nairobi?' she enquired in some agitation.

'I think I'm close to finding Helen's killer,' he explained. 'But I can't get anywhere without a bit more evidence. And what I need can only be found in Kenya.'

She shrugged ill-temperedly. She was never exactly jovial in the early morning.

With an ill grace Caroline hurled his clothes into a suitcase.

'I'm not going to see a leggy redhead,' he joked, hoping to disarm her suspicions.

'It's not that.' She said no more.

On the doorstep, she suddenly changed. When she kissed him, he noticed that she was crying.

'I won't be away for long,' he comforted her.

'It's not that.'

'What is it then?'

'Nothing,' she said. Then she held him very close.

'For God's sake be careful. And come back in one piece.'

By some miracle Charles got through by telephone to Nairobi. Although the line crackled and burbled and strange singing noises interrupted the conversation he was able to explain the reasons for his visit to Superintendent Maina. The Kenyan policeman volunteered to telex within an hour whether Charles would be allowed entry. First he had to consult the Minister, Mr Nkoli.

Not only did an affirmative message come within the hour; Inspector Pearson managed to have a new passport issued by lunch-time.

Charles told no one at the office about his impending departure. In an awkward way, he felt that it was somehow propitious to keep this visit quite apart from his business. He had a superstitious feeling that he was about to face the Minotaur, in the person of the Chairman, and he didn't want to clutter his rear. He thought rather wistfully of how much he had enjoyed his ill-gotten publishing career. I could have been a fair publisher, he thought, if I'd had the chance. He shook off his gloomy reflections and relegated them to the limbo in which he had placed Caroline; packages marked 'Not To Be Opened On Voyage'.

On his way to the airport he stopped at Connaught Mews. It didn't take long to extract the truth from Mrs Farebrother. Her breakdown under questioning was aided by her bewilderment. 'But it was *you*, Mr Fitzpatrick,' she protested, 'who ordered me to tell the police you left the lady's flat at 7.30.

Why, you gave me a thousand pounds to forget you were really there from eight to eight forty-five.' She began to cry in confusion.

'Then why, when I was last here did you give me all that nonsense about the sweet little pussy-cat?' Charles asked.

'I thought you were testing me, Mr Fitzpatrick, to see if I'd told the police the right story.' She dabbed her eyes with a small lace handkerchief. Her voice quavered. 'I haven't done anything wrong, have I? You've always paid me well to keep watch on Miss Wightman and report to you.'

Charles felt sick. 'No,' he said, to calm her. 'You've done what you were told.'

But as he pointed the Scimitar down the motorway his disgust at Fitzpatrick's duplicity changed to an anger of chilled, tempered steel.

British Airway's first-class lounge is a pleasant spot to await a departure. Deep comfortable chairs and sofas are arranged round a bar, where the parched or nervous traveller can help himself to drinks.

That evening the lounge sported an additional attraction, a tall blonde, wearing a square-cut dress which revealed the slopes of her breasts and emphasized the length of her legs. Her locket was still suspended from a gold necklace, and nestled intriguingly in its warm and perfumed hollow.

'What on earth are you doing here?' Charles asked.

'I came to see you,' she said, 'and we haven't much time. What I am about to do, with the assistance of Inspector Pearson,' she frowned, 'who, I notice, is not yet here, is most irregular. But I have clearance from the very highest channels, so I suppose it'll be all right.' She descended from the Olympian to the merely ordinary with a bump.

'I'm authorized to make a deal,' she went on. Then she paused, obviously trying to think of the right words.

'Have a drink?' the totally befogged Charles suggested.

'Thanks.' She smiled dazzlingly. 'A vodka, please, Charles.'

Charles turned to the barman and had actually given the order before her words sank in. He turned slowly to her.

'Oh, your secret is safe with the Special Branch,' she said. 'But surely you didn't expect Fitzpatrick to keep the secret indefinitely? Anyway, we've had you followed for some time, ever since your trip to Nairobi. And we were there when you met the mysterious Mr Fry at the Carlton Tower. Incidentally, did you know that Mr Fry flew from Kenya to London two days before Jenny Barnes was killed, and out again that night? We may never prove he killed her, but it won't be for want of suspicion.'

Charles looked at her in amazement. 'But how did you find out about me?' he said. There didn't seem a lot of point in arguing.

'We checked,' she said, 'as soon as we began to think that Fitzpatrick didn't seem Fitzpatrick any more. And we found that a certain Charles Hutchinson, looking remarkably like Fitzpatrick, had been rushing round London looking for a job, and had then abruptly disappeared. Did you know that your luggage was never picked up from that seedy hotel you were in when you became involved in all this? A bad mistake on our James' part. In any case, Helen told us everything, as she was supposed to do. Of course we knew. But I admit that proving it would not be easy. You are remarkably alike, you know.'

'Indeed you are,' said a voice behind them. It was the inspector, bearing with him a package which Charles took to be his passport. 'As a matter of interest, can *you* prove that you're not Fitzpatrick?'

Charles thought for a moment. 'I can,' he said. 'I was supposed to get my teeth fixed so that our dental charts would be identical, but there was a hitch, and since I hate dentists, I never had the thing completed.'

'Good,' said Pearson. 'When you come back from Kenya, we'll check that. If you really have got different charts, then you'll be off the hook.'

'But what about Caroline? And anyway, what's Fitzpatrick done?'

'We've no interest in the Fitzpatrick family,' the inspector said robustly.

'As far as we're concerned, you can go on living as Fitzpatrick,' said Anne. 'That's what I came to tell you. We have a deal to make. As far as we know, James Fitzpatrick has been supplying classified information to the Chinese for the past fourteen years. At first we think it was pretty straightforward. It was only later that he started getting complicated. We think he quarrelled with Peking, and that's why he set you up. But we can't be sure. We are pretty certain though, that he caused the death of Jenny Barnes, that he may have murdered Helen Wightman.'

Charles kept his conversation with Mrs Farebrother to himself. He was already the cat's paw of the Chairman; until he was certain what they were up to, he wasn't also going to be used as a decoy by Special Branch.

There was no one he could trust but himself.

'He's also been trying to kill you,' Pearson said. 'We want you to turn the tables. We'd like you to have a crack at him. If you succeed, then as far as we are concerned, you can live as Fitzpatrick for the rest of your life.'

'Of course, you'll have to submit to a dental test when you return to this country,' Pearson added. 'And then we'll help you to take the rest of the treatment. Can't have any doubts, can we?' He smiled at Charles benevolently.

'But what about the Chinese?' Charles asked.

'Oh, don't worry, we'll find a way to let them know. You won't be troubled,' Pearson said breezily. He glanced round the lounge, then handed Charles a heavy package, which was clearly *not* his passport.

'Insurance,' he said. 'I'm sure that with your initiative – what we used to call good officer material – you could find a way to get rid of Fitzpatrick without our help. But just in case, you'll find a gun in there and some spare rounds. Get rid of it when you've used it. We don't want it back.'

Charles found it hard to comprehend what he had just learned. But the gun was, to put it mildly, a more than welcome present. The final call came through for his flight. 'Good God,' he said, 'I'll have to go.'

Anne kissed him, pressing her breasts aggressively against his chest. 'Don't forget to call me,' she said, 'when you get back.'

Pearson tugged at an inside pocket and produced a small package. 'Your passport,' he said. 'The airline and the Kenyan authorities have been alerted, there'll be no trouble about the gun.'

Charles began to move towards the embarkation gate. Suddenly he turned. 'What about Irvine,' he cried. 'He knows, he has to.'

'Don't worry about Mr Irvine,' Pearson smiled wintrily. 'We'll take care of him.'

Charles' flight, BA 031, took off at 8 p.m. Precisely two hours later Kenya Airlines flight 615 followed it towards Nairobi. Among the passengers, wearing dark glasses and headscarf as a primitive disguise, was Mrs Caroline Fitzpatrick.

CHAPTER THIRTY

Superintendent Maina met Charles at the airport and steered him speedily through immigration and customs.

'It's worth being picked up by the police,' Charles joked. 'You get through airports even quicker than VIP's.'

The Kenyan was not amused. 'We've had a communication from London about you,' he said. 'It seems that you will be able to solve the murder of Mr Mbangu.' He looked at Charles with restrained hostility. 'It also seems that you may hold the key to the increasing Chinese-inspired opposition to our President.' Charles thought that the Special Branch were still playing their cards awfully close to the chest.

Maina ushered him into an official limousine, and the driver set off at a sedate pace towards Nairobi. The rains had come, and the dry grey grass of Charles' previous visit had been miraculously converted to a flourishing green.

'We've been unable to pin down the elusive Mr Palmer,' Maina said. 'Interpol is searching for him now. But there is no clue aside from the passport address, which apparently is that of a Miss Helen Wightman, who is in some way connected

235

with your Special Branch.' He looked at Charles coldly. 'That is not an encouragng sign for relations between our countries,' he said.

'I don't think that the Special Branch had anything to do with it,' Charles said. 'I think it was by what one might call an unhappy chance.'

Maina looked unconvinced. 'Let us hope so,' he said. 'This country is beset by enemies as it is. Uganda threatens us. Libya threatens us, we have trouble with the Ethiopian and Somali rebels. And the Chinese are concerning themselves overmuch in our affairs. We do not need the enmity of your Special Branch. I am forced to trust you, Mr Fitzpatrick, but I tell you freely that it is against my inclinations.'

Charles said placatingly, 'I'm here to trace a Jeremy Fry. He may not have killed Mr Mbangu, but we're convinced that he ordered the assassination, even if it was meant for me.'

'So I am told. I hope it is true. In the meantime, you may rest assured of my reluctant but total co-operation.' Maina took off his spectacles and polished them. 'We had no instructions, but we have booked you temporarily into the Norfolk. The cottage you occupied before. I hope it will not have too many unfortunate associations.' He smiled wintrily.

Decorating the verandah of cottage number five was Vanessa. She was drinking champagne and raised her glass in a toast.

'Welcome, oh distinguished visitor,' she said lightly. She was wearing a white shirt and pleated skirt.

'How did you know I was coming?' Charles asked warily.

'Jo-Jo, the minister, told me.' She laughed gaily. 'He's a regular visitor to the Intercontinental these days. I'm not certain who he prefers most – me or Arabella.'

She poured him a glass of champagne and volunteered to unpack his suitcase. On the verandah of the next-door cottage two black men were engaged in earnest discussion. Visiting politicians, Charles supposed, to be staying in such luxurious accommodation.

Vanessa returned and poured out the last of the champagne.

'You must be tired, after your flight,' she said. She walked over to him and stroked the back of his head, pulling his face into her bosom, so that he could feel the firm breasts, bra-less beneath her cotton shirt. She led him to the bedroom. She removed his shoes, his socks, then his trousers and unbuttoned his shirt.

'As the air hostesses say,' she remarked, playing with the few hairs on his chest, 'it's coffee, tea, or me.'

'Or, if you're busy,' Charles said, 'Arabella?'

She shook her finger mischievously at him. 'No more Arabella for you,' she said. 'You're too sexy to share.' She kissed him.

Suddenly all the jet-lag, all his worries, rolled away. People go to East Africa, Charles decided, to see wild animals. And what better animal to start with than Vanessa?

They were having lunch by the pool: curried chicken, with all the trimmings of tomato, peppers, pineapples, coconut, cucumber, bananas, papaya, lettuce and sliced onions. Her costume, a blue bikini dotted with white stars, was minute. The band of airline crews and armaments salesmen who were idling around the bar eyed her with lustful appreciation.

'I've got a message for you,' she said, enjoying the stir she was creating. 'A man called Jeremy Fry telephoned me this morning. He wants you to meet him at Kilaguni Lodge to-morrow for lunch. That's about two hundred and eighty kilo-metres from Nairobi, in Tsavo National Park.'

'Did he leave a telephone number?'

She chewed a piece of chicken. 'He wouldn't give me his number. The line was very faint – it sounded as if he was calling from up-country.'

Charles looked at her, all his senses on the alert. He'd been sure that something was phoney since the moment he had seen her on his verandah. It had all been too pat. And how had Fry/Fitzpatrick known where to find him? Suddenly he re-membered his earlier suspicions that Fitzpatrick could never have been in Nairobi for long without coming across the gor-geous Vanessa. He was sure, all at once, that it was a trap, delightfully baited. Vanessa was sure to have an extra special orgasm at the thought that she was betraying him to his death. He looked at her dispassionately, searching for the tell-tale clues to corruption. She smiled at him, unaware. He decided coldly that one more night couldn't do him any harm. And he'd heard that sex was good for the nerves.

With Vanessa sweaty and snoring slightly beside him, Charles lay awake, planning how to deal with her the next day. Not for the first time he reflected that he was growing as ruthless in his way as Fitzpatrick. The job moulds the man, he thought. He smiled into the darkness. Whatever happened, he thought, Caroline would be spared the bastard for good. At the thought he edged further across the bed. Contact with Vanessa seemed intolerable.

They set off at 8 a.m. in a hired black Mercedes. The bougainvillaea along the middle and the sides of the Uhuru highway – Nairobi's floral mile – almost sparkled in the cool morning air. They passed the turn-off to Machakos. Little boys jumped up and down on the side of the road, beseeching them to stop and buy oranges, apples and tomatoes. Three dusty chickens were also on offer, their survival for another day dependent on a motorist's whim.

The park was dusty, red-earthed, a bleak landscape littered with the dead withered trees pushed over by the elephants in their remorseless quest for food. Charles waited until they had driven a few miles into the park. Then he stopped the car.

Vanessa, who had been looking eagerly over the dusty plain, hoping to find game (preferably killing each other, Charles had thought bleakly), turned to him.

'What's the problem?' she said.

'You are,' he said. 'Out.'

'What do you mean?' Vanessa was pale beneath her honey blonde.

'Out,' Charles repeated.

'You're joking.'

'Try me.'

'But why?'

'You and Fry must think I'm a bloody idiot,' he said. 'I don't know how long you've had me set up, or if all my enquiries were useless last time because you were in his pay, but I'd have been mad not to realize that I'd been had this time. Out,' he repeated.

'Darling . . .'

'Don't call me darling,' he gritted.

'James . . .'

'And I don't like James much, either.'

'Charles, then,' she said defiantly. 'You can't leave me out here. You need my help. All right, I admit I was paid to set you up, and you were right about Fry. But he threatened to have me deported, and he could have, too.' Vanessa shuddered. 'I didn't mean you any harm. And I'll help you if I can. He's waiting for you in room 35. And he means to buy you off, not to kill you. Let me help, darling, it'll be worth it.'

Charles smiled at her. 'Darling,' he said, 'I never really believed it.'

He took her in his arms. Their kiss was torrid.

'God, you bastard,' she murmured huskily in his ear, 'for a moment I thought you meant it. And you're much better in bed than he is.'

Charles kissed the side of her neck, his free hand groping for the handle to the Mercedes' door. He found it and pulled, at the same time pushing hard against Vanessa's chest. Her breast gave deliciously under his hand.

'Don't be so rough . . .' she was trying to say as she catapulted out of the car, and sat down hard on the dirt of the roadside.

'You bugger,' she shouted, as he pulled the door shut behind her. 'You fucking swine.' Her face was distorted with fear and hate. 'I hope he kills you. Slowly.' Her voice rose over the revs as Charles accelerated away.

She was still shouting abuse when a Land Rover drew up out of the dust-cloud of his departure. A large black policeman jumped out of the back and picked her up bodily.

The Land Rover turned, creating a dust cloud, back towards

Nairobi. As the policemen in the back began their interrogation, Vanessa began to scream.

Charles drew the Mercedes to a stop, and laid his head on his hands on the wheel. He was trembling. It was the first time he had ever condemned another human being to almost certain death and reaction had hit him. At first he had thought merely that the road was becoming an ever fainter track, almost impossible to follow. Then he had realised that he was crying, and had pulled up, no longer able to see. He sat there in the hot leather seat, tears trickling onto his clasped fingers. He could not decide whether he was crying for Vanessa or for his own lost innocence. With an effort he dismissed Vanessa from his mind, and sat up. The Chairman was to come, and it was no use facing him in an emotional tangle. That was precisely the leverage Fitzpatrick had had on his previous victims, Charles decided. It would never do to provide him with another.

He pulled himself together, deliberately allowing his attention to wander, staring round him at the bleak dusty landscape. Under a twisted thorn tree to his left a bundle of tawny fur shifted and sighed audibly in the still air. A tangled heap of lions was attempting to sleep through the stupefying mid-morning heat. The tree itself was gnarled and distorted by the pressures of survival in a hostile environment. On a broad low limb, its head comfortably pillowed on a surreal convolution, a lioness sprawled luxuriously, its heavy paws dangling, an expression of feline bliss clear over the two hundred yards or so between it and Charles. Charles smiled. After the twisted depravities and corruptions of sophisticated menace with which he had been surrounded for so long it was a pleasure to see simple-hearted savagery taking its ease.

He twisted to take his briefcase from the back seat. He had no doubt that Vanessa had searched it, but thought it unlikely that she would have risked a phone call to Fitzpatrick to betray its contents while Charles was treading so blindly to his fate. Indeed, he thought, as he pulled out the gun and checked the instructions with it to see how it loaded, her specialized libido might well have been tickled by the thought that Fitzpatrick himself was approaching the hunter's bullet all unknowing. The pistol was a well-used, short-barrelled Browning. To Charles the bullets looked alarmingly large-calibre, and he sat, after he had fumblingly loaded the monster, slipping the safety catch on and off and wondering whether he could risk firing off a shot at some target to see how he got on. He had a nervous and well-founded belief that he'd find it hard to hit anything.

He wound down the window, closed against the dust, and held the gun out uncertainly. It felt immensely heavy in his outstretched hand. He slipped off the safety catch, and took the first pressure on the trigger, aiming at a boulder some ten yards from the side of the road. He took a deep breath and began to squeeze. A comfortable moan from his left distracted him. A lion had turned in its sleep. With some relief Charles brought the gun back into the car. It would be a shame to disturb them simply for target practice, he told himself. Besides, with a bullet that big anywhere would do if he hit Fitzpatrick, and he could surely make sure he was so close that a miss was impossible.

Anxiously checking the safety catch, he pushed the weapon into his waistband and buttoned his light linen jacket over the bulge. Huge sweat patches were spreading under his armpits. He wiped his face with his handkerchief, and reached forward to turn the ignition key. A sharp pain in his abdomen caused him to wonder how fictional heroes found it so easy to wander about with guns disposed about their persons in this way. He thought of putting it into his pocket, but decided against. The weight would pull his light jacket hopelessly awry. Better to put up with the discomfort than give away his only advantage. As he put the car into gear, he noted with detached appreciation that his hands were no longer trembling.

The Chairman was expecting him. The door of the room swung open before he had time to knock, and the over-powering presence of Fitzpatrick in person had its usual slightly disorienting effect.

'My dear Charles.' Fitzpatrick seized his reluctant hand and pumped it. 'How nice to see you. Have a drink, and tell me why you came all the way out to Kenya, unannounced and unbidden, as it were. Our mutual friend Vanessa – where is she, by the way? – told me you were here, and naturally I made arrangements to see you as soon as possible. Have a drink, and tell me how it is that you seem to be on such good terms with the Administration.'

Charles entered, startled and wary. He had not expected such instant bluntness.

'I didn't think we needed company, so I gave Vanessa the slip,' he said cautiously.

The Chairman frowned for a moment, then smiled widely. 'Good thinking,' he said. 'Always do your hard bargaining alone and in person. You're growing with the job. I congratulate you.' He handed Charles a drink and waved him to a hide chair, settling in another across from him.

On the verandah cold lunch was laid out.

Zebra and impala, impervious to the harsh sun, circled the pools in front of the lodge nervously before they drank, posting guards against any lurking predators. In the background were the Chyulu hills, covered with green rain-forest. Behind them towered the snow-cap of Kilimanjaro.

'I've done a lot of investigating over the last few days,' Charles said carefully, 'and I came here because I found a lot of questions to which only you could have the answers.'

The Chairman waved an expansive paw. 'Glad to oblige,' he said happily. 'I gather you have rumbled Irvine, and presumably you've come to all sorts of facile conclusions.' He drew on his drink and smacked his lips with studied uncouthness. 'Ask away. I don't promise to give you all the answers, but I think I can promise you a deal you won't be able to refuse.'

'The misprints,' Charles said. 'I assume they were a code?' Fitzpatrick nodded, beaming.

'But who for?' Charles asked. 'I thought the Chinese, but I couldn't see why.'

'For some years,' the Chairman explained, 'the Chinese gave me their publications, the bedrock of the company.

'They told me I could only keep exclusive rights to their material if I gave them secrets from the West.'

'How were you supposed to do that?' Charles asked.

The Chinese had been cunning. They suggested that Fitzpatrick expand his business by publishing original scientific and technical works commissioned in the West. These were sent to British Intelligence to delete classified information. But Fitzpatrick knew what the deletions were – he was to pass it on to Peking.

Fitzpatrick had devised a method to tell the Chinese how the information was being sent. He put deliberate misprints into his company's 'normal' books on cooking and such-like. From these the Chinese worked out the system by which the information was being transmitted.

'Did Tom Irvine know about this?' Charles enquired.

'He had to.' The Chairman mopped his brow. Kilaguni was like a furnace in the mid-afternoon heat. 'He would never have allowed misprints in our books unless he knew the reason.' Fitzpatrick laughed. 'Tom didn't mind. Don't forget he was receiving 20% of the profits, through our Swiss company.'

'Then you were both working for the Chinese,' Charles said.

'Oh, no.' The Chairman beamed. 'We were working for British intelligence. The information we gave the Chinese was just a little inaccurate.' He laughed.

Charles felt as if he had been punched in the solar plexus. For a moment the room reeled before his eyes. Then he remembered Anne Lesley, and a new thought struck him.

'At first, yes,' he said. 'Then you found you could make more money playing both sides against the middle.'

The Chairman's smile had not wavered, but the eyes were hard. 'Clever,' he said. 'Yes, something like that. It was the bloody Trident deal that let us down. The Chinese found out, when they received their Tridents that there'd been a few deliberate omissions in the jet technology I'd slipped them. They put quite a lot of pressure to bear on us. But it was profitable, all the same.' He smiled. 'I was sorry to leave it, really,' he said, 'but the whole thing was getting out of hand.'

'Because of Kurtz?' Charles asked.

There was no smile on Fitzpatrick's face now. 'How did you guess that?' he asked.

Charles smiled. For the first time he felt that he had a slim edge over the dangerous animal he was confronting.

'I guessed that you could never resist the sort of money that Kurtz' Mafia contacts had available. And so much of that New York office was phony. Woodward and his whip. And I couldn't understand at first why Irvine was so reluctant to pay Kurtz off, or indeed why you'd gone into partnership with a maniac. Then it occurred to me that the Kurtz business was really a legitimate shell, and that made a lot of things fall into place. I suppose you pulled a fast one on them, and they are dodgy people to cheat.'

A spasm of real anger twisted the Chairman's face. 'That idiot Kurtz,' he said. 'He borrowed money from loan sharks to finance his gambling debts, and the mob started to check up on the information we were peddling to them. And of course a lot of it was phony. It's not hard to cheat places like Albania, but it is hard to keep the supply moving when ignorant peasants who barely speak English want higher turnover. Sicilian scum. They're hardly out of the Stone Age.'

Charles looked at him thoughtfully. It occurred to him that Fitzpatrick was pretty Stone Age himself.

'So that's why you killed Helen Wightman. Kurtz told her too much, and she had to go.'

With a snarl, Fitzpatrick lunged out of his chair. For a moment Charles thought the man had gone berserk. But with an effort Fitzpatrick reasserted control. He lumbered heavily across to the bar and splashed vodka into a glass with a liberal hand. With his back to Charles he said, 'Drink?'

'Thank you, no,' Charles said.

The caution in his voice restored Fitzpatrick to good humour. 'Don't worry, I'm not about to slip you a Mickey Finn,' he said. 'Useless thing to do, and not my style.' Smiling he returned to his chair. Charles had an uneasy feeling that the confrontation had staggered out of his control again.

'What makes you think I killed Helen?' Fitzpatrick said.

'Because the way she died was so much your style,' Charles

said. He had to protect Mrs Farebrother, in case the Chairman survived his mission to Kenya.

Fitzpatrick laughed. 'You know I made love to her first? I enjoyed that.' He laughed again. 'That's all she was good for, really. But you'll never prove it you know.'

'What about Jenny?' Charles asked.

'Ah, Jenny,' said Fitzpatrick thoughtfully. 'Now she was a disappointment. I was fond of her, you know. She was a passionate creature, with damned little in the way of scruples. Rather like Vanessa, but with brains. Then she got squeamish for some reason. I think she was getting too fond of you. While the cat's away and the mice are having a ball, they sometimes transfer allegiance, you know. Anyway she was determined to warn you. I couldn't have that, it would have spoiled everything. So I hired a car and forced her off the road.'

For a moment Charles couldn't trust himself to speak. The urge to put down this . . . animal . . . was almost overpowering. When his mind cleared, he found Fitzpatrick smiling at him.

'What *did* you do with Vanessa?' he said.

'Turned her out of the car and told her to walk home,' Charles said curtly.

Fitzpatrick laughed. 'Neat and economical,' he said. 'You're learning fast.'

'And what's going to happen to Irvine?'

Fitzpatrick's face darkened. 'He's bungled,' he said shortly. 'I was to look after the girls. His job was to take care of you. He missed you in Nairobi, and that hydroponics caper was too clever by half.' The Chairman shifted heavily in his chair. 'The trouble with Tom is that his Presbyterian principles are always getting in the way of his love of money. And vice versa. Very unstable combination, religion and crime. Besides, he might talk.' He pondered. 'It looks as if he'll have to go.' He was clearly capable of anything.

'What about Caroline?' Charles asked.

The Chairman paused to consider. 'I've been wondering about her. She's a stupid bitch, of course, but I'm beginning to think we may have to get rid of her. She talked to Helen, you know. I don't know what was said, because I hadn't time to find out. But it's not a risk we can afford to take.'

'We?' Charles was so surprised that for a moment his burning anger at this dismissal of Caroline was supplanted by curiosity.

'My dear fellow, you don't think I want to kill you now? Why you're so much more intelligent than I had thought. I think we'd make a good partnership, don't you?' Fitzpatrick levered himself out of his chair and beckoned to Charles. 'Come, my boy, I think the charms of nature might help us to work out a useful contact, don't you?' he said with ponderous and unlikely skittishness.

Mesmerised, Charles found himself following Fitzpatrick out to the Mercedes. In a daze he drove off, following the Chairman's instructions. The interview had taken such a wholly unexpected turn that he didn't know what to think.

Mzima Springs, some thirteen kilometres from the lodge, was a cool oasis in the parched land. Large numbers of hippos and crocodiles dozed in the afternoon sun, only their snouts exposed above the crystal water. Charles remembered the manager at Amboseli. He glanced at Fitzpatrick, who seemed to be thinking of nothing but the peacefulness of the scene. If that man had known Fitzpatrick, he thought, he wouldn't have said that the hippo is the most dangerous of animals. Safer by far to get between a hippo and his water, than between Fitzpatrick and his ambition. He took comfort from the weight of the gun at his waist, and gratefully breathed in the clear air. A closed car was no place to be with Fitzpatrick in his present state.

'Now,' said Fitzpatrick, 'let's talk about our future relationship. I think, under the circumstances, fifty fifty would be fair, don't you? Of course, you'll have to get rid of Caroline.' He paused. 'I suggest drowning,' he said thoughtfully. 'She doesn't swim very well, you know. She never wanted to live on the river. I sometimes wonder if I bought River Lodge with her disposal in mind. The subconscious works in the most remarkable way.'

Charles looked at him coldly. 'Fitzpatrick,' he said, 'partnership or no partnership, Caroline stays alive and well.'

Fitzpatrick raised his shaven eyebrows. 'If you feel so strongly, of course,' he said soothingly. 'But she remains a threat, you know. More to you than to me, however. It's your risk.'

Charles clasped his hands together to conceal their shaking. 'Those are my terms,' he said.

'Oh, very well. Now, about the financial arrangements . . .' Fitzpatrick went into great detail about shares, the Zurich account, various properties, salary and accounting arrangements. Feeling as though he was trapped in some nightmare fantasy, Charles found himself discussing the arrangements, and even disputing points with some heat. We're *both* insane, he thought, arguing about the valuation of Caroline's jewellery, this conversation can't be happening.

Finally they thrashed out their macabre compact, and the Chairman stretched luxuriously. 'I knew you'd be sensible. You drive a hard bargain, too. I like a man who can do that. You'll find the Chinese are hard, but fair.' He looked round with satisfaction. 'I think we should go back another way,' he said. 'You might as well see the sights while you're here.'

Charles nodded agreement, and started the car. At a sign saying 'Shetani Rocks' the road began to twist through outcrops of volcanic rock. Charles slowed to a crawl, nervous of meeting a bull elephant round one of the hairpin bends.

Fitzpatrick misconstrued his nervousness. 'Don't worry,' he said. 'No one's likely to be coming in the other direction. This road's not on the tourist maps. You might as well be on the moon here. But it's impressive in its way, don't you think?' he gestured at the lava with almost proprietary pride. Charles made no reply. A particularly hair-raising bend was coming up, and he needed all his concentration to ease the big car round it.

He was creeping cautiously forward in bottom gear when something hard was smashed into his side. He gasped and winced and the car slid sideways, to crunch heavily into a tall lava rock.

'Good,' Fitzpatrick said. 'I wanted you to stop, and very nicely you've done it. Couldn't be better.'

Charles looked at him. There was no geniality in Fitzpatrick now. The dark contact lenses concealed little of the malice and contempt in the Chairman's regard. The gun in his hand was unwavering. Automatically Charles rubbed at the place high on his ribs the muzzle had bruised. He felt the suddenly reassuring bulge of his own gun beneath his wrist.

'Now,' Fitzpatrick said quietly, 'get out. Slowly.'

Charles stared at him helplessly for a moment, and then turned to the door. He tugged on the handle, but nothing happened. A hurried glance at Fitzpatrick's expression caused him to attack the door ferociously. It refused to budge. He recalled the crunch and heavy scraping of the collision. The car had slid clear of the rock, but the door panel had been bashed in far enough to jam it solid. He told Fitzpatrick so, and was annoyed to hear his voice trembling.

Cautiously, Fitzpatrick felt behind him for his own door handle, and pulled on it. His door opened, and he eased himself out. 'Now,' he said, 'you follow me. Carefully. I don't want to kill you in the car, but if I must, I must.'

Charles began awkwardly to slide himself across beneath the wheel, and out over the passenger seat. Out of one corner of his eye he saw Fitzpatrick standing in the track, watching him impatiently. Suddenly he swore. 'Come on,' he said, 'we haven't got all day.' Automatically, he glanced at his watch.

Desperately Charles tore at his jacket and hauled the gun from his belt. Fumblingly he pushed at the safety catch and hauled on the trigger. Nothing happened. Fitzpatrick was staring at him in panicked surprise. It hadn't occurred to him that Charles could be armed. As he belatedly started to raise his own gun, Charles at last pushed off the safety catch and fired. There was an enormous bang, deafening inside the car. Charles' wrist was wrenched upwards. For a moment he thought it was broken.

He looked at where Fitzpatrick had been, but there was no sign of him. I've shot him, he thought, exultantly. Then a bullet smashed past his head, and he dived to the floor. The bruise in his ribs was agonizing for a moment. In the brief silence that followed, he thought that he might have known that he'd miss.

As he lay half on and half off the passenger seat, he say a gaping hole in the roof above him. So that's where my bullet went, he thought in self-contempt. Might just as easily have shot myself.

'Come on out,' Fitzpatrick shouted from somewhere near at hand. 'You might as well. Otherwise I'll come and get you.'

Charles lay where he was, wondering desperately what he was to do. Sweat dripped off the end of his nose. The scuffed carpet by his face smelt musty.

A shot smashed into the back of the car. He could feel the car rock to the impact. Shuddering, he thought of the bullet smashing into his flesh. He cringed.

'Come out.' Fitzpatrick's voice rose to a shriek.

Charles fumbled his gun off the floor and wondered where to aim it.

Then a second shot was followed by an enormous, whomping explosion. The whole car lifted on its springs, and seemed to twist in the air. Gigantic flames were everywhere. The instant heat was intolerable. Without thinking, Charles was out of the car, and running desperately into the lava field. As he flung himself behind a rock, panting, he realised that the petrol tank had exploded. Above his rock a greasy coil of black smoke rose lazily into the air. There was no sound but the crackle of flames. Charles' hip ached abominably from the contact it had made with the car door as he had scrambled out.

He lay and sweated behind his rock, and wondered whether to give in. He was conscious of a suicidal urge to call Fitzpatrick to come and get him. He felt intolerably hot and tired. He tried to brush the hair out of his eyes. It came away in his hand, he stared at it stupidly. He had no recollection of it, but somehow he had been badly singed as he fell out of the car.

A long silence fell. The car crackled and smouldered. The smoke thinned and vanished in a shimmer of heat. Charles clung, sweating, to his friendly rock, and watched a column of busy-looking ants going about their inscrutable business, inches from his nose. One or two came towards him, antennae waving. He blew them away, furtively, feeling like some crippled Gulliver. The scorched skin of his face stiffened in the stifling heat.

Aeons later, as he lay in a kind of stupour behind his rock, resigned to extinction, he heard the crunch of booted feet cautiously approaching. With a convulsive effort, he raised his gun and fired blindly. The report was oddly flat, but the wrench on his aching wrist was agonizingly familiar.

The crunching stopped.

'Charles,' Fitzpatrick said, 'this is silly. You can't win. Why make it uncomfortable for yourself?'

With a convulsive heave, Charles twisted behind his rock and fired blindly at the sound. In reply, a bullet ricocheted smartly off the face of his rock and whined into oblivion. Charles froze.

'Charles,' said Fitzpatrick gently, 'do stop being stubborn. I have it all worked out and there's no way you can win. Die by a bullet, or die of thirst and exposure. The first would be quick and relatively painless. Try it.'

'Fuck off,' Charles shouted, amazed at how weak his voice now sounded. Painfully he scrabbled behind his rock, the lava dust grinding into his chest, tearing his shirt to ribbons. Small rivulets of blood began to flow in the dust. More and more of the ants began to turn aside, intrigued. Charles shivered.

'You don't seriously think I ever intended you to live?' Fitzpatrick's voice was odiously reasonable. 'You were always intended to die, and you knew it. You have to die. I set you up to die. You have been a cat's paw from the first. Why go on?'

Charles said nothing. A dim vision of rowing gently up river, watching Caroline laughing at him from the stern of the skiff began to obsess him. He almost called out to her.

'Of course, I can't let Caroline live,' Fitzpatrick said quietly. 'She almost certainly knows too much.'

Charles, with one last convulsive effort, drew himself to his feet, and fired blindly in the direction of the reasonable voice. To his amazement he saw Fitzpatrick, seated on a nearby rock, tumble out of sight, in an untidy, sprawling way that told Charles, unbelieving, that at last he had scored a hit.

Gun hanging loosely in his hand he swayed across towards the place where he had last dimly seen Fitzpatrick. He saw the tumbled figure dimly, sweat blurring his vision. As he approached, the figure stirred and sat up. In desperate slow motion Charles tried to move. But the gun flamed, and bammed in his ear. He felt himself smashed aside. He thought incredulously that he'd been hit, but he couldn't think where. He fell bonelessly, consciousness fading.

He lay watching the earth without interest. There was no gun in his hand and no hope in his heart. Now, he thought, Now.

A dark shadow fell across his face. He turned painfully, and found Fitzpatrick staring down at him, his face twisted.

'You bloody idiot,' he was whispering. 'Did you really think you'd fooled me? You were never more than bait. Now it's your turn to die. And you can take to hell with you the knowledge that I, James Fitzpatrick, will be better off for your death. That's what you are worth. All you are worth.'

With agonising slowness the gun settled on him. Charles watched as the finger tightened on the trigger. There was a click. Nothing happened. All round there was silence. Charles fancied he could hear his ants rustling in search of their blood. Then the gun clicked again. And again and again in a frenzy.

'Christ,' Fitzpatrick screamed, and threw the empty weapon at Charles' prostrate body. It bounced in front of Charles' face, and smashed into his teeth. He tasted the metallic taint of blood as he spat out two teeth. Fitzpatrick hurled himself on him, punching and gouging insanely. Charles lay there under the assault. Suddenly he felt teeth on the back of his neck. Outraged, he uttered a yell of indignation, and sat up. He was crushed back into the dust, as Fitzpatrick landed on him once more, and hands fastened round his neck. His face distorted, Fitzpatrick began to strangle him slowly. The edges of his vision were blurred with red, and closing in. In a gesture of instinctive survival, Charles groped for a weapon. A rock fitted itself into his hand. With a last desperate effort he smashed it into Fitzpatrick's face.

A hundred feet away, tucked into the grass on top of a hill Caroline gripped the rifle Superintendent Maina had handed her. He lay next to her a yard to the right and a foot behind was a crack marksman from Kenyatta's personal bodyguard.

They had lost the Mercedes after Mzima Springs. Only the smoke from the burning car had alerted Maina. The climb up the lava rocks to the top of the hill had been painful.

In her telescopic sights Caroline could see two men. Lying unconscious on the ground, in shirt and slacks was the man she had followed from Heathrow. In front of him the Chairman, in denim shirt and shorts, was slowly raising his gun.

'You're sure you know how to shoot?' Maina whispered.

She nodded. The tip of the foresight was just above the shoulder of the rearsight, the trigger eased towards her.

'Shoot now,' said Maina. In the noise and recoil of the shot Caroline didn't notice that the Kenyan marksman to her right had obeyed the same instruction. She saw the Chairman crumple and fall. She lay on the hard rocks, drained of energy and emotion.

It was good, Maina reflected, that she believed she had killed him. She would never talk.

'Let's collect your husband,' he said calmly. 'The other one we can leave to the lions.'

Later that night, in London, Tom Irvine stepped, a little wobbly with liquor, out of the White Elephant club. The doorman was nowhere to be seen. The two handsome Africans, with the two frisky white girls, waited on the pavement as Irvine stepped into Curzon Street to stop an approaching taxi.

The cab accelerated. Irvine's body was thrown off the wing, his skull smashed into the trunk of a white Rolls-Royce at the kerb. The taxi didn't stop.

In his office Inspector Pearson took the news calmly. He picked up the phone and called West End Central. It wouldn't do for the uniformed branch to waste too much time investigating such an accident.

Charles woke in softness and darkness, dreaming of Caroline, and unable to imagine where he was. He made a great effort, and focused his eyes. Surely he was back in his cottage at the Norfolk? It looked familiar. He was unwilling to make the effort to identify it. With a sigh he leant back, conscious that there was a bandage round his head, and others on his chest and arms. There was an elusive scent in the air. Caroline he thought woozily.

Someone was leaning over him, tears dripping steadily onto his face and chest. He protested feebly.

'Darling, thank God you've come round. You've been unconscious for two days. I thought you'd die.' Warm soft arms closed round his neck, and lips caressed his bruised mouth.

'Caroline?' he mumbled. 'Caroline?'

'Who else, you fool,' she said fondly.

'Caroline,' he said again weakly, 'I'm not James, you know.'

'Of course you aren't. You gave yourself away a dozen times. Do you remember that business of "Till death do us part"? If I hadn't known long before I'd have guessed then.'

'What are you doing here in Nairobi?' Charles was beginning to feel better.

'Something told me you were going to be in great danger.'

'Something,' Charles said, 'or somebody.'

She stiffened. 'Helen told me enough to make me think you'd have to come here to solve everything. And that you'd be in danger. She stroked his cheek. 'But what does all that matter now? He's dead.'

'Don't you mind?'

She had stopped crying. 'I hated him. I hated his arrogance, his egotism, his cruelty.'

'But you lived with him for fifteen years,' he reminded her.

'Not *lived*. Not like it's been with you. I knew he would kill you if you got in his way. So he had to die.'

As always, he thought, Caroline made complex issues simple.

She sat up and smoothed the pillows around his head. 'Now you must rest. When you wake up you can tell me about everything.'

She laughed. 'In fact you can tell me who you are. Not that that matters.'

She kissed him and lay down.

He was half way to sleep when she whispered, 'Are you still awake?'

He nodded lazily.

'I know you're battered and bruised,' she said. 'But I suddenly feel very sexy.' She kissed his earlobe.

Charles began to feel much better.

'I feel much better,' he said.

Gently she stroked him until he was ready, then lowered herself onto him, rocking backwards and forwards. He opened his eyes. She was looking not at him but at her reflection in the large mirror behind the bed. She had certainly changed a great deal since the day he had first met her.

'Caroline,' he said, 'you're a changed woman.'

She laughed happily. 'I need to be,' she said. She increased the pace of her movements. 'From now on,' she bore down on him harder and harder, 'there are going to be no more Helens. Only me. Do you promise?'

'Oh Caroline,' he breathed, as she brought him to his climax, 'Yes.'

J. BARNICOAT
CASH SALES DEPT
P.O. BOX 11
FALMOUTH
CORNWALL TR10 9EN

Please send me the following titles

Quantity	SBN	Title	Amount
————			————
————			————
————			————
————			————
————			————
		TOTAL	————

Please enclose a cheque or postal order made out to FUTURA
PUBLICATIONS LIMITED for the amount due, including 10p
per book to allow for postage and packing. Orders will take
about three weeks to reach you and we cannot accept responsibility for orders containing cash.

PLEASE PRINT CLEARLY

NAME...

ADDRESS..

....